Charmless

SUSAN CARROLL

OLIVERHEBERBOOKS

One

The crowd of curious neighbors lingered after Florian had departed. When some of them started through the gate to congratulate me, I bolted for the house, nearly knocking Em over in the process. I dragged my stepmother inside with me. Slamming our front door closed, I leaned up against it. Em regarded me with confusion.

"Ella, what are you doing? It is only natural that our friends would wish to rejoice with you."

"What friends? We barely know those people. They are nodding acquaintances at best."

"That is all about to change when you become their princess."

"Em, I am not—" I tried to protest, but Imelda tugged me away from the door, nudging me in the direction of the stairs.

"You need to run up to your bedchamber and make yourself look more presentable while I invite everyone into the parlor and put the kettle on for tea."

"Tea! We have not even had breakfast yet and you cannot be serving refreshments to half the neighborhood. I have carefully allotted our supplies to last until the end of the month."

"Oh, pooh, you silly child. When you marry the prince, do you not realize what that will mean? We will never have to worry about such horrid things as budgets or taxes and running out of tea or having fried eels for supper ever again."

"Em…"

"We will live in grand apartments in the royal palace, and we will have ever so many servants. I am sure you have worked very hard looking after us, my darling girl, but you need never lift another finger."

"Em!" I nearly had to shout to stem her enthusiastic gush. Moderating my voice, I said, "I already told you. I will never marry Prince Florian."

"Surely you cannot still mean that. Not after the way you kissed him. And in front of the entire neighborhood."

"I did not kiss him. He kissed me. That is a very different thing."

"But what a kiss it was!" Em sighed. "So passionate! Enough to make any girl swoon." She frowned. "I am glad you did not because there is that dreadful law about fainting in the presence of royalty. But surely it will not apply to you once you are a princess."

"It doesn't matter. The only way I will ever pass out in Florian's presence is if he suffocates me with his mouth."

My stepmother had been raised with all these romantic notions about charming princes who swept maidens off their feet with the tenderness of a kiss. If I was ever going to disillusion her about Florian, I was going to have to be brutally frank.

"I don't want to shock you, Em, but apparently Prince Florian has spent much time on this island called Lothmara." I hesitated.

Mal had told me all about this place, but I didn't want Em to know that. She already deplored my friendship with Mal and her low opinion of his character would not be improved if she realized he had been discussing such a salacious subject with me.

I continued, "Someone informed me that this island is populated by these seductive women who school men in the arts of passion. Most particularly a kind of kissing that involves much use of... well, tongues."

I waited for Em's gasp of horror, but she nodded, "The siren's kiss."

"You know about that?"

"Oh, yes. The siren's kiss can be quite enervating when done properly."

Now I was the one who was shocked. "But surely my father never..."

"Of course not, my dear. Your papa always treated me with great propriety," Em said ruefully. "My first husband was not all that ardent either. But when I was a girl, I did have this one beau. We used to steal away together and well!" A secretive smile played about the corners of Em's mouth. "Charles Redmond certainly knew a thing or two about siren kissing," she murmured.

"Lord Redmond! You mean Chuffy? That gallant elderly gentleman you introduced me to at the ball?"

"I would hardly call him elderly. Chuffy is only a few years older than me. Believe it or not, my dear, we were young once and oh, those blissful moments we spent in my Papa's summerhouse."

The memory sent a rush of heat into Em's cheeks, and she fanned herself with one hand. When she realized I was gawking at her, she lowered her hand and said primly, "However, this is not a proper conversation to be having with my daughter."

It certainly wasn't. It threatened to fill my head with the kind of images one does not care to entertain about a stepmother or any parent for that matter. But I could not help asking her, "If you and Lord Redmond were so enamored of each other, why did you never marry?"

"There is more to a good marriage than thrilling kisses or so my Papa told me. Chuffy had a reputation for being a bit of a rake and my father did not approve of him. Papa convinced me that

Albert Wendover would make me a far better husband, such a sensible, practical man. But we know how that all ended." Em gave a sad sigh.

My stepmother seldom mentioned her first husband, the Honorable Albert Wendover who had turned out not to be so honorable after all. Caught out in a scheme to defraud the king, Wendover had been arrested and sentenced to be executed at the hands of the Royal Garrotter. Strangulation was the preferred method of execution in Arcady, our king having an aversion to bloodshed.

Em brightened as she went on, "After that I was fortunate enough to meet your father, the true love of my life."

I winced when my stepmother made remarks like that. Em tended to romanticize everything. She regarded my father as a knight in shining armor who had rescued her and her two young daughters from poverty and disgrace. To hear her tell it, my father had swept her up in his arms and carried her off to live happily ever after.

Nothing could be further from the truth. My father had never loved any woman except for Cecily, my mother. When Mama had died, I had lost my father as well. Overwhelmed by his grief, he had become something of a recluse, even though I was only six years old at the time and desperately needed him. I believe he had only married my stepmother to provide someone to look after me so he could remain shut away in his library with his books. Em tended to gloss over how unhappy my father's indifference and neglect had made her.

Before she could indulge in any further reminiscences about the love between her and my father that had never existed, I changed the subject back to Lord Redmond.

"What about Chuffy? Did he ever marry?"

"No, he did not." Em smiled. "Last night, he whispered in my ear that he was never able to love anyone else but me. All nonsense, of course, but I must admit that seeing him made me feel as joyously giddy as a young girl again. Which I am not."

My stepmother sobered. "I am a widow with three grown daughters to look after, but now one of you could have the most dazzlingly brilliant marriage if you do not foolishly throw away such an opportunity. I am sorry that you did not find the prince's kiss satisfactory. Perhaps Florian could be persuaded to return to Lothmara for a few more lessons."

"That man is so arrogant and thick I doubt that he could ever learn anything." I was interrupted by a knock at the door.

I had hoped when I flounced back into the house and slammed the door it would have been enough to discourage the neighbors from rushing to congratulate me. Apparently not.

"Don't answer that," I said. "In fact, I do not think we should ever answer our front door again."

"Don't be silly, dear. We mustn't be rude. Run along up to your room and at least brush your hair. We can finish our discussion about the prince later."

As far as I was concerned, it was finished. As Em moved toward the door, I beat a swift retreat. By the time I reached the upper landing, I could hear the front hall echoing with a hubbub of excited voices. As I headed for the security of my room, I was not unaware of the irony of my actions.

How often I had criticized my father for doing just this thing, barricading himself away to avoid dealing with any unpleasant situation. If I had any gumption at all, I would go back downstairs and put an end to this nonsense. Just announce in a very loud and determined voice that I had no intention of marrying their idiot prince.

But I held back for two reasons. First, it would have completely humiliated my stepmother.

Secondly, there was only one person whose opinion I cared about and that was Horatio. I was hurt that he could think that I was the kind of woman to callously spurn his love the moment a prince beckoned. I thought Horatio knew me better than that by now, that I had assured him...

Of what exactly?

When Horatio had asked me if there was a chance that I could learn to return his regard, I had answered, *yes, I believe that I could.* And I kissed him very enthusiastically. Why had I not told him what he obviously wanted to hear? *Yes, Horatio, I love you, too.*

Because after the heartbreak I had suffered in my youth, those words no longer tripped lightly off my tongue. I had learned to play it safe and not be so impulsive about revealing my emotions. And to be completely fair to my forthright commander, Florian had put on a very convincing display. Horatio was a modest man, self-conscious about his own humble origins as a foundling.

There is no greater stigma in our kingdom than being born not knowing who your parents were. It was a commonly held belief that only monsters would abandon their babe and therefore that child must carry the taint of its parents' evil blood. I never credited such nonsense, but most people in Arcady did. Foundlings were raised in an asylum deep in the northern mountains far away from all civilized society. Most of them ended up working in the silver mines or laboring in the fields.

Horatio had been one of the rare fortunate ones, adopted by a young lieutenant and his wife who had lost their own son. When Horatio confessed the truth to me about his birth, I thought I had convinced him that it didn't matter to me.

When I recalled his devastated expression as he had ridden away, all I wanted to do was take him in my arms and reassure him again and clear up this foolish misunderstanding about the prince.

I darted into my room and changed my old worn frock for one of my few respectable gowns. Flinching, I managed to work my sore feet into soft woolen stockings and sturdy, but comfortable walking boots. I spent a few anxious minutes in front of the mirror as I brushed my hair and tried to decide. Should I tie it back with a ribbon or simply let it fall loose about my shoulders. I had almost opted for the ribbon when I recalled something Horatio had said to me.

I prefer you with your hair down. It makes you look softer, approachable.

I smiled at the memory as I ran the brush through my hair until it was soft and shining. It had been a long time since I had taken such pains with my appearance, my heart quickening with anticipation of meeting a lover. Not since those days, seven summers ago, when I had stolen away to meet Harper, the handsome itinerant musician who had broken my heart.

Except that his name had not been Harper, nor had he been a traveling minstrel. My fingers tightened on the brush, my smile vanishing as I relived that dreadful moment at the ball when I had discovered the truth. The lad with the golden voice I had known as Harper was Prince Ryland, one of Florian's younger brothers.

A prince in disguise wooing a lovely young maiden. What could be more romantic than that? Most girls would sigh. Except that it wasn't, not when the prince left you waiting all night for an elopement that never happened, vanishing from your life without a word of explanation. The worst part of encountering Harper again— or I should say, Ryland— was that he still professed his love for me.

"There has never been anyone but you. I have not even touched my lute since I last saw you. When I had to leave you, all the music died."

He had looked so sad and sincere, I had even been enticed into kissing him again. It made me angry to recall my own weakness and that I had been willing to listen to his explanation of why he had abandoned me. Ryland had insisted he had done it for my sake. When word of his secret trysts with me had reached the palace, he had been warned to stay away from me.

Warned by the same king who now seemed ready to accept a Midtown girl instead of a wealthy princess as his daughter-in-law? Was Florian merely bolder when it came to defying his father or had Ryland not loved me enough to do so? Either way, it no longer mattered because my heart now belonged to a very different sort of man, one who was honest and true.

As I swirled my shawl about my shoulders, I vowed that nothing was going to threaten my happiness with Horatio, neither the arrogant determination of Florian to wed me, nor any lingering painful memories about his brother. But first I needed to avoid my stepmother and all our newly found dearest friends. Cracking open my bedchamber door, I crept into the upper hall and tiptoed down the stairs.

I need not have worried about being so cautious. My quiet steps could not have been heard above the loud hum of conversation and laughter emanating from the parlor. It sounded as though Em had most of the neighborhood in there, no doubt swilling our tea and gobbling up the last of our jam and muffins. The thought caused my stomach to emit an angry growl. I sought to ignore it as I contemplated my next course of action.

I didn't dare risk going out the front door for fear of encountering even more well-wishers coming up the walk. My best avenue of escape was through the library. I darted inside and headed for one of the windows.

Knotting my shawl about my shoulders so that it didn't slip off, I flung up the sash and climbed out, lowering myself to the ground. I crouched behind an overgrown lilac bush, realizing I couldn't just slink across our rear gardens. Anyone who chanced to glance out the parlor windows would easily spot me. My safest route lay in cutting through my neighbor's gardens.

A low wooden fence separated our property from Mrs. Biddlestone's. I have had no trouble scaling it ever since I was a child. But my skirts had been shorter then, and I had been much more agile. As I vaulted over the top, my toes caught in my petticoat and I fell, landing with a jarring thud in Mrs. B's delphiniums. My arm banged against one of those colorful rocks she used to line her garden bed.

"Ow," I whimpered, struggling to sit upright. My elbow was throbbing, and I was going to end up with a spectacular bruise. But it could have been worse. I could have landed in the rose bushes. Or on Mrs. Biddlesworth.

I should have paused before scaling her fence, to make sure my neighbor was not in her back garden. But there she was, her bead-like eyes glaring at me from beneath the brim of a straw hat. I scrambled to my feet and babbled, "Hallo, Mrs. B. I know this must look a trifle odd, but I can explain and I am so sorry about your flowers. But look, I am sure I can fix them."

I bent down and attempted to resurrect one of the delphiniums I had flattened. Its head flopped over as though I had broken its neck. In my efforts to fix it, I decapitated it entirely.

"Sorry," I said weakly, holding out the handful of broken petals like a guilty peace offering. Mrs. Biddlesworth sucked in her breath with a furious hiss.

Despite our less than amicable relationship, I have never thought of Mrs. Biddlesworth as particularly menacing. She barely stood five feet tall, a round dumpling of a woman. But even dumplings can appear dangerous when they advance upon you, glowering and brandishing a pair of pruning shears.

I backed away from her. "Please, Mrs. B. I am sure we can work something out. I will buy you some new bulbs and replant that entire bed."

My words trailed off as her face contorted in a most violent and peculiar fashion. Oh, frap, I thought. I had finally done it, aggravated the poor woman to the point of having an apoplectic fit.

"Mrs. Biddlesworth, perhaps you had better sit down."

Her lips twisted and stretched wide at the corners, exposing her teeth. "Pray accept my sincerest felicitations, my dear."

Was it possible that Mrs. Biddlesworth was smiling at me? Or trying to do so. I have seen pleasanter expressions on the faces of stone gargoyles.

"Felicitations? For what?" I asked.

"Why for landing the prince, you silly goose."

"Oh. *That.*"

"When will His Highness be sweeping you off to his castle far, far, far away?"

"You do realize that his palace is only a few miles from here, just up the hill, but—"

"Oh, that will be quite far enough." She chortled, clicking her shears. "When is the wedding to take place? Name the day when I shall— I mean— you shall become the happiest woman in Arcady."

"Unfortunately, I cannot do that."

"What!" Her mouth collapsed into its usual surly expression. "Why not?"

I edged further away from her, nervously eying those shears. "Well, because— because—"

"Listen, you idiotic girl. Instead of climbing fences and running about like some half-mad hoyden, you need to go grab that man and get him to the altar before the spell wears off."

"Spell? What spell?"

"Whatever enchantment you put on Prince Florian to make him fall in love with you."

"I assure you I did nothing to bewitch the prince. Quite the contrary. I am sorry if I have teased you in the past, but truly, I am not a witch."

"Ha! Of course, you are not." She snorted. "And I should truly regret having to imply otherwise to the royal authorities."

"Are you threatening me, Mrs. Biddlesworth?"

"Not at all, my dear." She forced her lips back into that hideous grin. "Merely offering you the wisdom of my council."

"Uh... thank you. I shall certainly take all that you have said under advisement." I replied, moving toward the path that would lead me to her front gate. "Now you must excuse me. I really need to be going."

"You do that. Go find your prince and set a date."

As I darted around the side of her house, she shouted after me, "And you better start acting more like a princess. I'll be watching you."

"What else is new," I muttered as I crouched down, slinking toward her gate. I managed to make it across the street unseen and ducked into the bushes of the house opposite, pausing to catch my breath. With Florian vowing to pursue me, half of the neighborhood crowding into my house to congratulate me and Horatio believing I had thrown him over for the prince, I had not seen how this situation could get any worse.

But now I had Mrs. Biddlesworth hinting that she would denounce me as a witch. She had often threatened to do so before. This time she might be provoked into doing it if I disappointed her by not marrying the prince and moving far, far away.

Being a witch or a wizard in our kingdom was not illegal if one had the proper permit. These were quite costly and very difficult to obtain. Practicing magic without a license carried heavy penalties and lengthy confinement in King's Royal Prison, a grim fortress, more commonly known as the Dismal Dungeon.

I shoved all worries about Mrs. Biddlesworth aside for the moment. My immediate concern was getting to town without being accosted by any more of my neighbors, well-wishing or otherwise.

At least the house whose bushes sheltered me was quiet, the windows still shuttered, although for a sad reason. The entire Hanson family along with several other Midtown citizens had been arrested at the ball last night. Myrtle Hanson had faked a swoon to attract the attention of the prince. The poor girl had been unaware that our king had recently enacted another of his petty decrees. This absurd law had made fainting in the presence of royalty a serious crime. When Myrtle had been seized by the palace guards, her brothers had tried to rescue her, starting with a bout of fisticuffs which degenerated into an all-out brawl between

Midtown boys and some of the young aristocrats from the Heights.

It had been fortunate for me because it had supplied the distraction I needed to sneak into the king's treasure room and steal the orb. But not so fortunate for the Midtown folk who ended up incarcerated in the Dismal Dungeons. But Horatio had intervened successfully on their behalf, appealing for mercy from the second most powerful man in the kingdom, His Majesty's Chief Wizard, the Great Mercato. Horatio had secured a promise from Mercato that the Hansons would be released soon.

I continued to skulk in the Hanson shrubbery until I was convinced it was safe to emerge. The excitement occasioned by Prince Florian's eruption into our neighborhood appeared to have dissipated. The lane was empty except for a farmer's wagon trundling past, followed by one of those oversized pumpkin shaped carriages that were the current rage among the aristocrats in the Heights.

As I passed by the main street where most of the shops were located, I pulled my shawl up over my head like a hood to avoid being recognized. It turned out to be an unnecessary precaution. In the days preceding the ball, the shops had been crammed with rabid women shoving and poking each other to get first pick of the finest silks and furbelows.

Today the town was devoid of clamoring customers, so I ventured to come out from beneath my shawl. Almost faint from hunger, I was overwhelmed by the scent of fresh baked honey rolls emanating from Crumpet's Bakery and Tea Shop. I seldom indulged myself, but when my stomach emitted a loud growl, the temptation was too great to resist.

I cracked open the door, taking a cautious peek inside. Ordinarily at this time of day, all the linen-covered tables and chairs would be occupied by ladies sipping tea, buttering scones, and gossiping. After Florian's performance at my house this morning, I feared much of that gossip would involve me.

But perhaps most of the bakery's usual customers were still abed, nursing sore feet from dancing at the ball. Much to my relief, the shop was empty except for a young man standing at the counter. Despite the obvious quality of his clothes, he appeared rather disheveled, his fine lawn shirt untucked and hanging over his breeches. Besides lacking a frock coat, he was also shoeless, his white hose stained with mud and grass. Something about him struck me as disturbingly familiar, but I could not see his face because he had his back to me.

Unlike the sort of plump, jolly woman one might expect a baker to be, Mrs. Crumpet was tall and angular. A widow with far too many children, she frequently appeared harassed and impatient, but I had never known her to be downright hostile to a customer.

Moving a tier of honey rolls out of the young man's reach, she was red-faced and all but shouting at him. "You better pay for all those rolls you took."

"Pay? But you urged me to try them, so I thought they were free," he faltered.

"Free! I should think not! How do you expect me to support six children by giving my wares away?"

"I don't know," he squeaked. "Six children? Oh my!"

"By my count, you scarfed down three of those rolls, so you owe me three coppers."

"But I don't have any money." As the young man shifted to turn his breeches pockets inside out, I caught a glimpse of his profile.

I blinked in surprise. I recognized the king's second eldest son, Prince Kendrick, just as Mrs. Crumpet whipped around the counter, brandishing a rolling pin.

"Thief!" she cried. "I'll send for a Scutcheon officer and have you clapped in irons."

Kendrick shrank back and he appeared ready to bolt for the door. Mrs. Crumpet seized him by the front of his shirt. The woman looked so angry, I feared she was about to whack the prince with her rolling pin. Recovering from my astonishment, I hastened to intervene.

"Mrs. Crumpet! Stop!"

Keeping a firm grip on the prince, the baker turned her head to glare at me. "You stay out of this, Ella Upton. Just look at him! He is clearly one of those feckless idle lads from the Heights. I am sick to death of them thinking they can prance into my shop and help themselves to whatever they please just because they are sons of aristocrats."

"But he is not a feckless, idle— " I hesitated. From what I knew of Kendrick, he likely was feckless and idle. But he was feckless, idle *royalty.*

"This is His Royal Highness, Prince Kendrick," I said.

Mrs. Crumpet snorted. "He doesn't look like any prince I have ever seen."

"And exactly how many would that be? I danced with His Highness last night at the ball and I assure you this is indeed Prince Kendrick."

Mrs. Crumpet paused, looking uncertainly from me to the prince who bobbed his head up and down to assure her of his identity. When it dawned upon Mrs. Crumpet how close she had come to assaulting royalty, she dropped the rolling pin, her face draining of color.

She sank to her knees. "Oh! Please, forgive me, Your Highness. I didn't know who you were, or I would never have— "

Her voice broke into a sob. "I have nine children so please, please don't send me to the Dismal Dungeons or have me executed."

"No, I would never do a thing like that. Um— *nine*, you say?" The prince's brow furrowed in confusion.

I had noticed that Mrs. Crumpet tended to exaggerate the number of her offspring when she was stressed. Or perhaps the poor woman really did have so many children, it was difficult to keep an accurate count.

By this time Mrs. Crumpet was weeping too hard to speak. Kendrick looked far more discomfited by her sobs than when she had threatened him. His eyes turned to me in mute appeal.

Placing my hands on her shoulders, I managed to coax the baker to her feet. "Pray, calm yourself, Mrs. Crumpet. I am sure His Highness realizes this was all just a huge misunderstanding. He has taken no offense."

"No, indeed I have not," Kendrick put in eagerly. "And I will happily pay you although my father never trusts me with money. But I could give you my shirt."

He examined the frills adorning the lawn fabric and frowned. "I appear to have spilled some wine on it. But what about the silver buttons on my breeches? I am sure they must be worth something."

"No!" Mrs. Crumpet and I gasped in unison as the prince lifted his shirt and appeared ready to start undoing his breeches' flap.

Mrs. Crumpet recovered herself enough to stammer. "No payment necessary. It's my honor to - to serve Your Highness." She mopped her eyes. "Would you like another roll or perhaps a scone or I have some bread fresh from the oven?"

Kendrick left off undoing his buttons and lowered his shirt. "Well, I do rather like bread, but—"

"Good. I shall fetch Your Highness some at once." Mrs. Crumpet retrieved her rolling pin and backed away, curtsying until she turned and fled through the door that led to her kitchen.

"What a nice woman," Kendrick said. "Although I have never been menaced with a rolling pin before. Still all good fun and a bit of an adventure, eh?"

The prince beamed at me, and I remembered that I ought to be curtsying as well. Before I could do so, Kendrick grabbed my hand. After what I had endured with his brother, I braced myself to fend off another wet, sloppy kiss.

Instead, Kendrick shook my hand with such fervor my elbow ached from the bruise I had sustained in Mrs. Biddlesworth's garden.

"Thank you, Miss Upton for recognizing me. That was quite amazing!"

"Was it?" I asked as I tried to pry free of his grasp. His enthusiastic handshake caused my shawl to slip from my shoulders. Mercifully he released me as he bent to retrieve the garment.

"Oh, yes," he said. "I am always so delighted when anyone remembers me. Most people don't, not even the king. My father usually just refers to me as the spare or the idiot. But with great affection, of course."

"Of course," I murmured. As he handed my shawl back to me, I had to swallow my true opinion. Far from being affectionate, the king struck me as monstrously cruel, even to his own son.

Although he was never seen outside the royal palace, Kendrick had somehow acquired the reputation for being the amiable, cheerful prince. He was handsome in a bland sort of way, but his features were undistinguished. He was also shorter than his tall, strapping brothers. I could see how Kendrick might feel overlooked, so I reassured him.

"Certainly, I remember you, Your Highness," I said. "You favored me with a dance last night. I am only astonished you remember me."

"Oh, I could never forget *you*, Miss Upton. You are so beautiful."

I shook my head, demurring. "I am sure you must have danced with many lovely ladies at the ball."

"I suppose I did, and they were all lovely and polite and flattering. But I could tell that they would have much preferred to be dancing with Florian. Most of them kept sneaking glances, looking to see where he was. But you were different. You gave me your complete attention. I was enjoying our dance until I ruined everything by speaking of my brother Ryland and how he could no longer play his lute and lost his joy in music. Then I started crying."

Kendrick blinked hard and I tensed, fearing he was about to repeat his disconcerting performance at the ball when he had wept uncontrollably in the middle of our promenade. But the prince swallowed and managed to contain himself this time.

"You were so wonderful, Miss Upton." He smiled mistily at me. "So kind and sympathetic."

The prince was giving me far too much credit. I had been utterly mortified when Kendrick burst into tears in the middle of our dance. But I had tried to soothe him so everyone would stop staring at us.

But the prince seemed excessively grateful for the smallest scrap of sympathy or kindness. It spoke volumes about how bleak his life must be beyond those palace walls.

"You must have thought me a perfect fool." He sighed.

"No, you just seemed very tender-hearted."

"That is what Ryland tells me. He says I feel things too deeply."

"What is wrong with that?" It was certainly not a quality any of his brothers appeared to possess.

Kendrick smiled ruefully. "It is wrong because I don't feel the things that a prince should. Confidence, boldness, bravery. This is the first time I have ever dared to venture into Midtown although I am not quite sure how I got here. Probably another prank by my two youngest brothers. Dahl and Dashiel are quite mischievous."

The prince's cheeks reddened as he said, "I am ashamed to confess that sometimes I have sampled pixie dust. I know I shouldn't because it leaves me in such a befuddled state I don't know where I am. The twins find it amusing to lead me far away from the palace and leave me. One time they abandoned me at a

17

poultry farm. I woke up very surprised to find myself sleeping in a chicken coop. Although not as surprised as those chickens."

The prince gave a light chuckle, but I was appalled.

"That's horrible."

"No, no, it just the twins' idea of a harmless jest. Someone at the palace eventually notices I am missing, and the guards are dispatched to find me. Look, here they are now."

Kendrick gestured toward the bakery's bow-front window. In the street beyond, I could see two mounted palace guards leading a riderless horse. They were moving at a slow pace, the better to scan the area for any sign of their missing prince.

"I had best be on my way, Miss Upton, but it was delightful seeing you again." He bowed and smiled, then darted out of the shop, waving his arms, and hallooing to attract the guards' attention.

Prince Kendrick was certainly none of my responsibility, but the man possessed an almost boyish innocence. I found myself watching until I saw him safely claimed just as I would have done any lost child.

At that moment, Mrs. Crumpet returned, straining under the weight of basket she had heaped with baked goods. Peering at me over the top of large crusty loaf of bread, she demanded, "Where is the prince?"

"He has left, returned to the palace."

"Oh! Thank the fairies." She blew out a deep breath and plunked the basket on top of the counter. The poor woman was so grateful to me for preventing her from attacking a prince, she wanted to give me all the pastries she had gathered to appease Kendrick.

I politely refused and insisted upon paying for my one honey roll.

"After all, you have your nine children to think of."

Mrs. Crumpet smiled sheepishly. "I only have six, but my youngest, Jacko is such a little demon, I tend to count him thrice."

Munching the roll and savoring its sweetness, I continued toward the Midtown garrison. My encounter with Prince Kendrick had not been as unsettling as the one with Florian. But I longed for my world to return to some semblance of normalcy. Alas, that was not to be. As soon as I set foot in the town square, I knew that something was terribly wrong.

Two

The Towers Quadrant for The Administration of Midtown Order and Justice was intended to be an imposing structure with solid gray stone walls and four conical towers. Instead, it looked as though some mischievous fairy had decided to drop a small castle in the middle of our town square near our work-a-day world of shops, markets, and modest homes. If one were going to have a castle, it would seem appropriate to also have a moat. But some whimsical (or perhaps drunken) architect had decided it would be nicer to have a fountain in front of the castle instead. This fountain with its burbling waters might still have managed to appear charming if it had not been dwarfed by an enormous statue of Prince Florian, depicting his muscular frame and flowing locks as he held aloft a sword.

Most Midtown folk simply referred to this absurd building as Quad Hall. Besides the Midtown garrison, the structure also housed the magistrate's court, the offices of the Exchequer, Registry and Licensing, and the tower containing the mysterious Aura Chamber. Unless it was tax gathering time or some unfortunate prisoner was being paraded out for punishment in the Yoke of

Shame, Quad Hall was a quiet place with citizens coming and going to conduct their business in orderly fashion.

This morning, however, the Hall resembled a castle under siege with Scutcheons everywhere. The garrison soldiers in their navy and dun-colored uniforms and floppy black berets guarded the main archway, while some marched along the parapets. More Scutcheons wielding halberds blocked the tower entrances, all tensed and ready to repel an imminent attack.

But the only invading army I could see was a crowd of some half-dozen very angry young women. The fashionable design of their frocks and bonnets marked them as being ladies from the Heights.

As furious as these girls were, I could not imagine the entire garrison had been called out merely to repel this petticoat onslaught. I crept closer, trying to get within earshot, yet remain as inconspicuous as possible. The girls directed their wrath at a strapping young officer who would have appeared formidable except for the boyish smattering of freckles across his nose.

The officer flung up his hands in a gesture of strained patience. "Ladies, please. For the third time, you cannot see Commander Crushington. He is unavailable."

"He had best make himself available!" A thin girl with a pinched nose, who appeared to be the leader of the group, shook her finger at him. "Do you have any idea who I am?"

"No, miss."

"I am the Honorable Miss Ardelia Vanderwix and I demand to see your commander at once."

"And I am the slightly honorable Major Thackery Frackles and I am telling you that you can't. Quad Hall is closed until further notice. If you have some complaint, you should take it to the Commander of the Heights and Palace Guard. His office is located at---"

"I know where his office is," Miss Vanderwix snapped. "Commander Berryhill is a fat lazy lout, too preoccupied with his breakfast to be bothered. He said that because we all bought that Elixir of Love— ”

“An *Elixir of Love?*” Frackles could not quite suppress his smirk.

Miss Vanderwix pinned him with her steely gaze. “As I was *saying,* we bought that false elixir from a peddler here in Midtown so that places the matter within Crushington's jurisdiction.”

The major vented a wearied sigh. “What was this peddler's name, miss?”

“How should I know some peasant's name! That is the Commander's job to discover.”

My breath caught in my throat. Ardelia Vanderwix had no notion about the identity of that peddler, but regrettably, I did. Blast you, Malcolm Hawkridge, I thought. I had warned my friend not to sell that stupid elixir. There was no such thing as a genuine love potion and even if there had been, Mal would not have been able to brew it. His magical efforts never succeeded. Magic, I might add, that he should not even have tried because he had no license. But did he ever listen to me? No!

I shuffled from foot to foot, torn between the urge to rush to Misty Bottoms and alert Mal that trouble was heading his way and my equally strong need to see need Horatio. Not only to reassure him that I had no intention of marrying the prince, but also to try to defuse this situation. I felt sick at the thought of a confrontation between my closest friend and the man I cared for so deeply. If only I could get to Horatio first before these women had a chance to file their complaint.

But as I edged closer, it was obvious that none of us were getting past Frackles. Locking his arms across his broad chest, he said, “Ladies, I shall forward your complaint to the Commander. When he has time, he will investigate it.”

“That is not good enough, Major Freckles,” Ardelia cried.

"The name is Frackles, miss and I strongly suggest— "

"Stuff your suggestions." She stomped her foot. "I want Crushington to hunt that bald-headed rogue down and arrest him this instant."

The other girls chorused their agreement.

"That's right!"

"Chain him up in the town square."

"Horsewhip him."

"But that peddler was so handsome, and he had such a seductive smile." A bubbly little blonde chimed in. When her friends glared at her, she amended, "I mean, yes, get that rogue. Tar and feather him."

"If you will all just be patient—" Frackles began, but Ardelia cut him off again.

"I am done talking to you. Come on, ladies." Miss Vanderwix beckoned to her friends to follow her beneath the arch, but when she attempted to sweep past the major, he moved to block her path.

"Get out of my way," Ardelia snarled.

"Sorry, miss, but I have my orders. No one is to— ow!" Frackles yelped as Ardelia delivered a hard kick to his shins. As he hopped about, Ardelia led the surge forward, but the major was quickly reinforced by several other Scutcheons.

I could tell at once the poor soldiers were in something of a quandary. These were girls from the Heights, the daughters of aristocrats. Even lawfully restraining them, the Scutcheons were obliged to proceed gently. The ladies suffered from no such compunction, shrieking, slapping, and kicking.

I must admit I was impressed. Who would ever have thought those prissy girls from the Heights had it in them? I lagged, keeping clear of the guards, looking for an opening to dart beneath the arch. I finally saw my chance and rushed forward only to halt when someone boomed out, "What is going on here?"

The voice belonged to a man who caused us all to freeze. Long, silver-streaked black hair flowed over his shoulders, his gaunt frame garbed in a flowing dark blue robe spangled with strange symbols. It was as though he had sprung out of nowhere in a puff of smoke and perhaps, he had, for this was the king's chief wizard, the Great Mercato.

He was seldom seen outside the palace and never far from the king's side. I and the other women gaped at him with shock. Frackles looked uneasy as the wizard advanced upon us, brandishing his golden staff.

"Major, what is the meaning of this?"

"I am sorry, sir," Frackles stammered. He was still clutching Ardelia's arm, a red imprint upon his cheek where she had slapped him. He released the girl and snapped to attention as he continued, "These ladies are trying to get into the Hall. They want— "

"It is of no consequence what they want. I thought I made my orders quite clear. No one is to be admitted."

Ardelia had been as cowed as the rest of us by Mercato's sudden appearance. She recovered her voice although she did not sound quite as strident as before.

"Sir, apparently, you do not know who I am."

"I don't care. Be gone!"

"But I am—"

"I said, be gone!" Mercato struck his staff against the ground, sparks shooting out of the tip.

Shrieking, the girls fled from beneath the arch, nearly knocking me over in the process. They took shelter behind the fountain as though that statue of Florian could protect them.

I found myself alone, staring into the cold, narrowed eyes of the most powerful wizard in the kingdom. But I held my ground. I was not afraid of this man, although perhaps I should have been. The Great Mercato was reputed to be a master of all magical arts, the designer of the infamous Aura Chamber and he held great sway over our irascible king.

Consequently, Mercato was pompous and arrogant to the point of absurdity. With his flowing beard and glittering robes, he seemed more like a strolling player performing the role of a terrifying wizard. Besides, I knew his secret. Mercato's real name was Sidney Greenleaf. Was it truly possible to be that frightened of a man named Sidney?

When I did not flee as the other girls had done, Mercato glared at me. "Are you hard of hearing, young woman? I said go! "

"I heard you well enough, sir. But I need to see Commander Crushington."

"You and every other idiotic wench in the kingdom. I should not be in such a hurry to bring myself to the commander's notice if I were you. I believe that purchasing fake elixirs is as much against the law as selling them."

"Really? So now being foolish and gullible is also a crime?"

"If it is not, it should be."

I started to retort and instead took a deep breath. I would gain nothing by antagonizing this man.

"I am not here to complain about that potion," I said. "I have other more urgent business with the commander and I'm sure he will want to see me. My name is Ella Upton and—"

"Ah! Yes. The lucky young woman the prince has chosen for his bride." Mercato stroked his beard and subjected me to an assessment, his eyes filled with scorn he took no pains to hide.

I was far more distressed by the resentful look I received from Major Frackles. He and most of the garrison were aware of their commander's tender feelings toward me. The major's expression made it clear that he thought I was a heartless jade.

Addressing myself more to him than Mercato, I said, "No matter what you might have heard, I have no intention of marrying the prince. I did not go to the ball with any desire to attract His Highness's attention."

The Major's expression lightened, but Mercato sneered. "Perhaps in the future, you should be more careful where you leave your shoe."

With a swish of his robes, he turned to head back into Quad Hall, but I grabbed hold of his sleeve. "Please sir, wait."

Mercato spun around, glaring at my hand so fiercely, I was surprised it didn't turn into a withered stump. I hastily released him. Forcing a smile to my lips, I tried to flatter him although the effort was enough to make me gag.

"Oh, Great Wizard, I know Commander Crushington holds you in the highest esteem as do I. He told me how kind and beneficent you are, persuading the king to release the Hanson family and—"

"I don't have the least idea what you are talking about," he interrupted me. "That Hanson girl had the temerity to pull my beard. Why would I want any of those wretches released?"

"But Horatio— that is, Commander Crushington assured me that—"

"You likely misunderstood him."

"No, I certainly did not. If I could just see the commander—"

"There is no use importuning me any further. You cannot see the commander for the simple reason he is not here." Mercato puffed out his chest. "I have sent him off on a mission, a very important and dangerous one."

"Dangerous?" I faltered.

But Mercato was already striding away, rapping out a command to the major.

"Freckles, I want no more such disturbances. Lower the portcullis and lock this place down completely."

"Aye, sir." The major snapped off a half-hearted salute, muttering under his breath. "But the name is Frackles."

Momentarily stunned by what Mercato had said, I stood frozen. But as the wizard vanished inside the tower door that led up to the Aura Chamber, I started after him, only to be intercepted by Major Frackles.

The contempt I had glimpsed earlier in his eyes was gone. His voice was kind, but firm as he said, "Please, Miss Upton. You must go."

"But is it true what Mercato said? Is the commander in danger?"

"I am sure not, miss. You must not worry. The commander is well able to look after himself. "

"But what is going on here? Why is Quad Hall being locked and guarded?"

"I'm sorry. I cannot tell you. Your best course is to return home, and I will let the commander know you were looking for him. Now please, step back."

Frackles called up to a Scutcheon private on the wall above, ordering him to lower the portcullis. I had never even realized that Quad Hall had such a thing, despite the building being fashioned like a miniature castle.

As far back as I could remember, the gate had never been lowered. The device was so ancient, it creaked and groaned. It appeared as if it might get stuck half-way, but with a mighty shudder, the rusty portcullis clanked to the ground.

Major Frackles gave me a sympathetic smile before disappearing inside the towers. I pressed my face against the iron bars of the gate and watched him go, my mind reeling with questions and new worries.

The Major's kind words had done little to reassure me about Horatio's safety. Where had Horatio been sent and what kind of mission had he been given? Did it have anything to do with the reason Quad Hall was locked down? And why had Mercato denied all knowledge of his promise to Horatio that he would release the Hansons and the other Midtown citizens?

If it had been any other man besides Horatio, I might have suspected he had been boasting when he claimed to have influence with the king's chief wizard. I knew my honest commander better than that. Horatio, unlike Mercato, was not the sort of man to try to puff up his own importance.

It was obvious I would learn nothing more, lingering by the gate and fretting. My best course was to head to Misty Bottoms and seek out Mal. I needed to warn him there was a mob of angry women out for his blood. Mal also might have some insight into this strange business at Quad Hall. My friend had an uncanny way of knowing when anything untoward or mysterious occurred in our kingdom.

As I turned away from the gate, I was surprised to see Ardelia Vanderwix and her friends lingering in the square. I would have thought they would have run shrieking all the way back to the Heights by now.

They were talking among themselves and stealing glances toward the lowered portcullis. I became uncomfortably aware that it was me and not Quad Hall that had become the focus of their interest. Snippets of their conversation carried to my ears.

"Is that really her? The girl the prince wants to marry?"

"Impossible!"

"You heard what the wizard said. And Mama heard a rumor this morning that the prince had lost his head over some mysterious Midtown beauty."

"But she looks like a beggar woman!"

I didn't wait to overhear anymore, heading determinedly across the square in the opposite direction. The rustle of skirts warned me the girls were coming after me.

"You, there! Wait," Ardelia commanded.

I grimaced and thought of making a bolt for it, certain that I could easily outdistance these ladies in their dainty heels. But I was a Midtown girl and something inside me revolted at the idea of running from a pack of snobbish chits from the Heights.

I halted and came about, waiting for them with my arms locked across my chest. The girls approached me warily, except for the bubbly blonde who bounced up and down and squealed, "Yes! It must be her. I recognize her from the ball last night."

She was cut off by Miss Vanderwix. Thrusting the little blonde aside, Ardelia studied me skeptically.

"What is your name?"

"Who wants to know?" I demanded.

Ardelia's eyebrows rose haughtily. "I am the Honorable Miss Ardelia Vanderwix. And this foolish creature is my sister, Priscilla." She waved a languid hand toward the bubbly blonde.

"Halloo." Priscilla waggled her fingers and beamed at me. "I have seen you about town before, haven't I? We have never formally been introduced."

"Happily, no. I mean unfortunately not."

"But you are Miss Ella Upton, aren't you? The girl Prince Florian is going to marry?"

I admitted reluctantly, "Well, yes, my name is Ella Upton, but—"

I got no further because Priscilla launched herself at me with an ear-splitting shriek.

"Congratulations!" She enveloped me in a constricting hug. "I am so happy for you, Miss Upton. Or should I say, Princess Ella?"

"No, please don't say that." I gasped for air. For such a little thing, she had an astonishing grip.

I had no sooner managed to pry her away when I was swarmed by the other young women. I had never been subjected to so much hugging and giggling in my life, not even by my own stepsisters. The Honorable Miss Ardelia Vanderwix deigned to offer me a few air-kisses.

All the girls pasted on fake smiles as though they were delighted to congratulate me on my good fortune. All except for one chit with strawberry-colored hair who sobbed on my shoulder.

"I sh-shall try to be happy for you, P-princess Ella. Even though my own heart is breaking."

"Don't be ridiculous, Lucy," Ardelia snapped. "As if you would have ever had a chance of winning the prince."

The younger Miss Vanderwix was kinder. Priscilla said soothingly, "Indeed you must not take it so hard, Lucy. Remember the prince still has four younger brothers that are unattached."

"That is right," the other girls seconded in eager agreement except for Ardelia who said, "None of them can compare to Florian. He is the handsomest and the heir to the throne."

Lucy emitted another mighty sob. I patted her back awkwardly. "There, there. No need for all this fuss. I don't want the prince. You may have him."

Lucy drew away from me, leaving a damp patch on my shoulder. She regarded me through shocked, tear-drenched eyes. The other girls gaped at me until Priscilla tittered.

"Not want the prince? Oh, what a jokester! How amusing!"

The rest burst into laughter as though I just made the best jest they had ever heard. Lucy even managed a weak smile.

"I was being quite serious," I said, but none of them paid the least attention.

"Is that how you charmed the prince?" Lucy asked. "By being witty and clever?"

One of the other girls chimed in, "Oh, yes Miss Upton, please, you must tell us your secret. We are dying to know how you won the heart of the prince."

"Yes, we would all dearly love to know *that,*" Ardelia said. Her gaze swept over my old frock and disheveled hair, and she sniffed. She had the haughtiest nose I have ever seen. I wondered if she had to sleep with a clothespin on her nose at night to achieve that snobbish tilt.

Before I could come up with any sort of an answer, Priscilla gushed, "Miss Upton's secret is obvious. She is the most beautiful creature. At least, she was last night when she was wearing that fabulous gown."

"Indeed! That gorgeous river silk, all silvery and gold."

"Those darling puffed sleeves."

"And the perfect way it tapered at the waistline."

I could only stare at these young women in amazement as they went into raptures over my gown. I could not have told you what any of them had worn to the ball. I would have been hard pressed to have described my own gown in such detail.

"Where did *you* get such a gown?" Ardelia demanded.

I hesitated. I could hardly tell them that my gown had been a gift from Malcolm Hawkridge, the same man who had sold them the fake elixir. The incredible gown had been designed by a woman who adored Mal as much as she despised me.

"Who is your seamstress?" Ardelia persisted.

"Um— Delphine."

"I have never heard of anyone in Midtown by that name."

"She lives in Misty Bottoms."

"Misty Bottoms!" Ardelia's lip curled in disgust. "You shop in *that* part of the kingdom?"

"I would go there for such a gown." Her younger sister sighed. "Where exactly can we find this Delphine?"

"Yes, please tell us," Lucy begged.

"Oh, no, no!" I said, fighting to conceal my alarm. "I would not advise you to seek out Delphine because... because she has been forced out of her dress designing business. The woman was too unpleasant to her customers. To be honest, she was a bit of a witch."

Actually, Delphine *was* a witch, possessing among other things the ability to transform herself into a black cat. I feared what she might do if any of these foolish ladies turned up on her doorstep, demanding gowns from her. I might find these Heights girls a trifle annoying, but I had no wish to see any of them cursed with boils or turned into toads.

"Truly, I was only jesting about this Delphine," I lied. "I fashioned the gown myself."

"You *sew* your own garments?" Ardelia said in same tone she might have accused me of picking my nose.

I was sure she had maids for that. The sewing, not the nose picking although perhaps she had a servant for that as well.

"Look, it has been really interesting meeting all of you, but I must be going."

I tried to edge away, but Priscilla caught hold of both of my hands, protesting, "You still have not told us all the romantic details about you and the prince. Can you not give us one small hint about what you did to make him fall in love with you?"

The girls all leaned forward eagerly, even Ardelia, as though they expected me to impart some astonishing secret.

I pulled my hands away from Priscilla. "Truly, I don't know how it happened. I danced with Prince Florian once and later I bumped into him in the royal garden. His Highness had obviously been—" I paused, realizing that I could hardly accuse the heir to the throne of snorting pixie dust.

"He had been freely enjoying the wine, so he got a little too amorous and I ran off and I lost my shoe."

"Was it a magic shoe?" Lucy asked.

"No, I keep those locked away in my closet."

Assuming that I was jesting, the girls burst into giggles again.

Ardelia frowned and admonished me. "Do be serious, Miss Upton."

"I am! It was just an ordinary old dancing slipper I lost. But the prince was able to use one of those ugly aura cats to hunt me down and then he proposed."

"How romantic." Priscilla interrupted me with a sigh that was echoed by the other girls.

"No, it really wasn't," I said. "It was more embarrassing than anything else. If you want my advice, you all make a great mistake by trying so hard to pursue Prince Florian. He is rather like a hunting spaniel. He loves to be the one doing the chasing."

"Do you think his brothers are the same?" Priscilla asked.

"Very likely."

"Let me get this straight," Ardelia said, knitting her brows. "When a prince approaches one of us, you are recommending that we just run away?"

"That's right. Flee in the opposite direction as fast as you can."

"But ladies are not permitted to run," Lucy wailed. "I am not even sure I would know how."

"It's easy. Just pick up your feet like this." Lifting the hem of my skirts, I tore off running from the square, leaving all the Heights girls gawking after me.

Three

I was sweating and panting by the time I reached the outskirts of Misty Bottoms, but I grinned, remembering the shocked expressions of Ardelia and her friends. No doubt they were still exclaiming over my unseemly behavior and condemning it. Those Heights girls had no idea what pleasure they were missing. There was nothing like a good run to give you a giddy feeling of freedom, tossing aside all cares and leaving your troubles far behind you.

My worries caught up with me all too soon as I entered the poorest section of our kingdom. There was a saying in Arcady. *The sun never shines in Misty Bottoms.* Of course, it did, the same as anywhere else. But here in the Bottoms, that warm gentle light became a harsh glare, exposing the extreme poverty of the region, dilapidated cottages, boarded over windows and tumbledown fences. An unpleasant scent hung in the air, difficult to describe. If hopelessness and misery had an odor, it would probably smell like Misty Bottoms.

I could feel my tension mounting as I wended my way down a weed-choked lane, heading for the street closest to the river. I had not been to Misty Bottoms since that day I had come here to sell my mother's earrings to obtain money for tickets to the ball. That dreadful afternoon I had gotten lost in the heavy fog drifting in from the Conger River and I had been set upon by an ugly thug named Iggy Burt, determined to relieve me of my purse. I could have been killed if not for the timely intervention of Horatio.

I drew some comfort from the memory, recalling how Horatio had bested that giant brute. The commander was a fierce and skilled fighter when the occasion called for it. I should not worry about him and yet I did.

If only I knew where he was and what danger he might be facing on this mysterious mission of Mercato's. What if I never saw Horatio again and he died, believing I had forsaken him for the prince?

"Stop it, Ella," I scolded myself. I had never been the sort to give way to melodramatic imaginings.

"Don't go borrowing trouble, child," Mal's wise old grandmother had told me, a maxim that I have tried to adopt as one of the guiding principles of my life. My formidable commander was able to protect himself well. I would see Horatio again soon and clear up this misunderstanding between us. He would take me into his arms, and everything would be fine.

I focused on my goal, to find Mal and warn him there could be trouble heading his way because of that stupid elixir. As I hurried down Rock Gunnel Street, I kept my wits about me. Even on a sunny day, the Bottoms could be plagued by unscrupulous characters, thieves, rogues, and thugs like Iggy Burt.

Mal had vowed to hunt the villain down, much to my alarm. I worried how far Mal might go to avenge the attack on me. I much preferred the idea of Horatio bringing Iggy to justice. But the wily cutpurse had managed to elude both men, presumably by fleeing the kingdom.

I have often wished my friend would have located his apothecary shop, The Hawk's Nest, in a more respectable part of the kingdom. But considering that Mal engaged in the practice of illegal magic and other dubious occupations such as smuggling, the more distance between him and the Midtown garrison, the better.

When I arrived at Mal's shop, I dreaded finding the Hawk's Nest already under siege by angry women clamoring for his head. The ladies from the Heights might not have a clue to his identity. But my roguish friend was better known among the girls from Midtown and some of those women would have had no qualms about hunting him down.

To my relief, all seemed quiet and normal at Mal's apothecary. There was a notice on the front door proclaiming the shop to be closed. That did not necessarily mean that Mal was not inside. He often closed the Hawk's Nest when he was busy concocting some special potion, especially if he was dabbling in forbidden magic. If I knocked loud enough, I could usually get Mal to admit me.

But beneath the closed sign, there was another notice.

Apothecary away on holiday.

Below that was another sign;

Shop closed until further notice.

And finally, another in huge black letters.

I REALLY MEAN IT. GO AWAY!!!

Judging from those signs, Mal was aware that his *Elixir of Love* had resulted in some fiercely dissatisfied customers. I pressed my face to the window and squinted inside the dim interior. The shop's main room was empty, but I was unconvinced that Mal was not skulking somewhere inside the building. He was eager to figure out how to use his grandfather's orb that I had recovered for him. I did not think Mal would have strayed far from his books and magical apparatus. But if he was avoiding enraged patrons, he was unlikely to answer, no matter how hard I knocked. Fortunately, I knew where he hid the key to his back door.

I circled around his shop, creeping past Delphine's house which was right next door. If the witch had disliked me before, she must truly hate me now that I had stumbled upon her secret and told Mal. I stole a nervous glance toward her side window, but the lace curtain did not twitch. No Delphine glaring balefully at me either as herself or in her guise as Ebony, the cat. I shivered and hurried along the path until I reached Mal's backyard.

He had left some laundry hanging out to dry, several shirts and pairs of stockings, a sign that I was right about him being home. His garden was as well-tended as always, neat squares of herbs and medicinal plants. Mal's house might be a total disaster, but he kept those herb beds weeded and trimmed since they were his stock in trade.

The area beyond the garden was less tidy. Mal's property sloped down toward the river. The muddy ground was thick with reeds and there was a small wooden dock where Mal's boat was kept, but the skiff was gone.

I crept closer just to be sure. The thick rope that usually held the *Ella Marie* tethered to shore was looped around the dock post. Shielding my eyes from the sunlight sparkling on the water, I squinted across the river. I saw a few of the flat-bottomed boats used by the snigglers casting their nets for eels. The Conger River had an ample supply. But there was no sign of Mal's small skiff.

"Oh, frap, Hawkridge!" I muttered. "What a time for you to take off to consort with your smuggler and pirate friends."

The depth of my disappointment astonished me. I felt almost hollowed out by it. After the wretched morning I had had, I needed Mal. My friend could always make me laugh with his wicked sense of humor and put my troubles into perspective.

When Mal took off on one of his trips downriver, there was no telling how long he would be away. Perhaps not long this time if he had left his wash on the line, but I could not afford to wait for his return. Em would realize I had slipped out of house by now. Although I was not eager to return home to her scolding and pleading, I did not want her worried about me either.

I started back up the embankment when I noticed something rustling through the reeds. Misty Bottoms was plagued with a large nasty species of river rat. I tried to skitter out of the way to avoid it. The creature slunk out into the open, revealing itself to be a sleek black cat.

I would have much preferred a river rat. Ebony, or should I say Delphine, hissed at me, her lip curling back to reveal her small, pointed teeth. My heart flipped over and I looked wildly about for some sort of weapon or help.

There were only the snigglers out on the river, hauling their net onto their barge. Still, they were a deterrent of sorts. Other than scratching or biting, I did not see what harm Delphine could do to me in her guise as a cat and she did not dare to transform. Not without appearing stark naked in front of those men.

Delphine slunk closer, crouching as though she was getting ready to pounce. I snatched off my shawl, flapping it at her to fend off her attack.

"Shoo! Scat!"

"R-r-r-eow!" She growled at me arching her back higher and higher.

To my horror, I watched her fur start to molt away, revealing patches of pink skin. Her body elongated and stretched upward, fur and whiskers slowly disappearing until Delphine loomed before me in all her naked glory. Her black hair curling wildly about her pale, angry face, the witch pointed at me, her long finger trembling with rage.

"You! You are a treacherous little minx."

I shrank away from her, stammering, "And you are quite naked. There are men out there on the river, staring."

"Oh?" Delphine's attention swiveled in that direction. I

expected her to shriek with embarrassment and try to cover herself. But she strolled boldly closer to the shore's edge.

The witch's hair had a strange property of changing color according to her moods. Her tangled tresses ebbed from jet black to a bright orange as she beamed and waved both arms at the men in such a way as to fully reveal her small, firm breasts. Mal had often referred to Delphine as being a fine old girl. But I judged her to be not more than thirty. Aside from the fact of her strange hair, she was not an unattractive woman.

The snigglers apparently thought so too. They waved back enthusiastically. One man, craning for a better look, fell overboard with a loud splash.

Delphine chortled with delight. "Oh, the poor dear. But occasionally, I do love to give the lads a little thrill. Fishing for eels must be such a boring occupation, don't you think?"

"I wouldn't know. I have never given the matter much thought." I should have kept my mouth shut. I should have taken advantage of her distraction to escape, not stood gaping at her brazen performance.

She whipped around, glaring at me, the tips of her orange hair curling back to black like wood shavings scorched by a fire. "I doubt you ever give anything much thought because you are a brainless twit. Nonetheless I need to have a word with you."

"About what?" I asked, although I had a pretty good idea about the cause of her grievance. As she stalked up the bank toward me, I averted my eyes. It was disconcerting enough having a conversation with an angry witch, let alone an angry naked one. I wanted to fling my shawl over her, but I was afraid to get that close.

Delphine snorted. "Well, if you aren't the dainty little modest wench. Fine! I will spare your virginal blushes."

Crossing over to Mal's wash line, she snatched up one of his shirts and tugged it over her head. The well-worn fabric did not cover much because it was still damp and much too large for her. It hung loose on her frame, skimming the top of her thighs, but it was better than nothing.

"There!" Delphine stomped back toward me. "Now what was I saying? Oh, yes. You brainless twit. You little sneak! You betrayed me. You told Mal I can transform into a cat."

"I am sorry, Delphine, but you were deceiving him. Sneaking into his house disguised as Ebony, rubbing up against him, snuggling beside him in his bed, spying on him when he was getting dressed—"

"That was always my favorite part of the day," Delphine interrupted with a sigh. "Licking my paws, grooming myself while Mal bathed that magnificent body of his. I hated it when the time came for him to towel dry and don clothing. Did you know that the rogue doesn't wear drawers beneath his breeches?"

"Er-no." I had no desire for such information about my closest friend, although knowing Mal as well as I did, it didn't surprise me. "The point is, Delphine, what you were doing wasn't right. It was kind of creepy and you ought to be ashamed."

"Oh, please!" Delphine rolled her eyes. "Every woman needs to be a little sneaky to get closer to the man she loves. I daresay you've got a few tricks of your own. But now that Mal knows the truth, he wants nothing to do with me."

Delphine's lip quivered. "Mal ordered me to stay away from him and after all I have done for the ungrateful wretch, helping him to master his magic. When he was trying to develop his hair potion, I even let him test the first batch on me and look what happened." Delphine held up one of her tresses as it faded from black to a deep shade of blue. She sniffed. "I ended up with hair that turns every color of the rainbow."

"Mal did that? I thought that was caused by your own magic."

"Why would I do such a thing to myself?" Delphine demanded indignantly. "A woman likes to have a bit of mystery about her, not hair that alerts the world to her every mood. But I forgave Mal for his little accident because I adore him that much and now, I have lost him forever."

Delphine hung her head, her hair turning completely blue. Despite my disapproval of the deceit she had practiced upon Mal, the witch looked so forlorn, I could not help but pity her.

"I am sorry if you and Mal have quarreled." I said. "As Mal's friend, I had no choice but to tell him the truth."

Delphine's head jerked up, resentment filling her eyes. "His *friend?* Don't even try that one on me, missy. I know your schemes, always running to Mal with your problems, batting your pretty blue eyes at him, making him pine after you. You wanted Mal for yourself or at least you did. Now I hear you're all set to marry the prince and break my poor boy's heart."

"None of that is true," I protested. "I am not marrying any prince and Mal and I will always be close friends, nothing more."

"Ha! Try telling him that."

"I have! Many times."

"You should have tried harder! You could have convinced him if you had really wanted to. I certainly know how to discourage a man's unwanted attentions."

"You do?" I asked. I could not keep the hopeful note out of my voice, even though it was unlikely Delphine would do anything to help me solve my problem with Florian.

She pursed her lips for a moment before saying grudgingly, "Pizzle Powder."

"Pizzle what?"

"Pizzle Powder. It is my own special concoction. Whenever I have some overly persistent suitor panting after me, which happens to me all the time, I might add." She glowered, as though daring me to contradict her.

"Yes, I am sure it does," I said. "Because you are so - so uniquely attractive."

"Humph!" The witch shot me one final glare before continuing, "When a man gets too lusty with me, I just give him a sweet come-hither look. When he starts undoing his breeches, I dump my powder all over his pizzle. Gives him a horrible blistering rash and he never bothers me again."

"I should imagine not," I murmured, my flicker of hope dying. Even if I could have persuaded Delphine to give me some of her powder, I could not have used it on Florian for several reasons. One, I would be executed for mounting such an attack on the heir to the throne. Two, I don't think I possess a sweet come-hither look. And three, mainly three, I never wanted to get that close to Florian's breeches or his pizzle.

Delphine regarded me through narrowed eyes and smiled at me. It was not a particularly pleasant smile. "What I do to my unwanted suitors pales in comparison to the things I have done to other women who have vexed me."

I inched away from her. All this talk about Pizzle Powder had lulled me into forgetting I was alone with a dangerous witch who detested me.

Delphine prowled after me, purring. "I have given considerable thought to exactly what I would like to do to you. How about a nice ugly wart on the tip of your nose that oozes pus every time you sneeze?"

I clapped my hand over my nose. "No, Delphine, please."

"Or perhaps a few wiry hairs that will sprout from your chin and grow thicker when you try to cut them."

"Delphine, I *said* I was sorry." I backed further away but she just kept coming, that dreadful smirk on her face.

"Or maybe I should pop those blue eyes out of your head and turn them into marbles. Which curse do you prefer? Your choice."

I tried to flee, but I didn't get far. I tripped over a root and sprawled backward into Mal's tansy bed. Delphine paced toward me, her hair turning deepest black. She flexed her fingers as preparing to hurl one of her curses at me.

Could she do any of the things she had threatened? Was she

really that powerful? Why was I foolish enough to even question that? The woman could turn herself into a cat, for frap's sake.

I flung my shawl over my head, curled up into a ball and waited. For a sudden clap of thunder, a crackle of lightning, I scarce knew what. I had no idea how curses were enacted.

The moments seemed to stretch into hours as I waited and waited, heart pounding. The scarf muffled my hearing, but I thought I detected the snap of a twig underfoot.

This was it, I thought, closing my eyes tight and bracing myself. More seconds passed and nothing happened. I finally heard a deep familiar voice call my name.

"Ella?"

I summoned up the courage to shift my shawl. Peeking over the edge of it, I gazed up to find Horatio bending over me, his gray eyes filled with concern.

"Ella? What's wrong? Are you all right?"

I sat up with a gasp, grabbing Horatio's arm. "No! Be careful. Look out!"

Horatio spun about, clapping one hand to the hilt of the sword, tensed, and prepared to protect me from any threat. Mal's shirt lay discarded upon the grass, the fabric rippling as Delphine in her cat form, slunk out from beneath it.

Horatio's brow furrowed with confusion. "Look out for what, Ella?"

"For the cat," I said weakly.

Delphine hissed, giving me a baleful look before scampering off. With a flick of her black tail, she vanished into the shrubbery that separated her property from Mal's.

Horatio relaxed his protective stance and extended his hand down to me. I was still trembling as he helped me to my feet. He regarded me with surprise.

"I had no idea you were so afraid of cats."

"I am not!" My cheeks warmed with embarrassment. "Just that one. You see she is really—" I hesitated. Horatio obviously had not seen Delphine pull off her transformation. If I tried to tell him about her strange ability, he would think me mad or worse still if he believed me, he might feel duty bound to arrest Delphine.

I wasn't sure if there was a law in our kingdom against turning oneself into a cat but considering that our king wanted to control all magic, there likely was such an ordinance. If Horatio tried to arrest Delphine, the blessed fairies alone knew what she might do to him. I didn't want my commander afflicted with warts or worse still, a blistered pizzle.

Realizing that Horatio was waiting for me to finish my sentence, I concluded, "She is really fierce, that black cat. She might look quite small and harmless. But she has a nasty bite and very sharp claws. Grr!" I demonstrated by cupping my hands and displaying my fingernails.

Another man might have laughed at a woman for expressing such a nonsensical fear. Mal would likely have teased me about it. But Horatio touched my cheek and said gently, "Never mind. There is nothing for you to be afraid of. The cat is gone, and I am here now."

Yes, he was, although I had no idea how or why when I had imagined him to be carrying out some dangerous mission far away. Horatio Crushington seemed to possess an almost magical ability to appear when I needed him, just as he had done when I had been attacked by Iggy Burt weeks ago.

I gazed upward, drinking in the sight of him. After our sunrise tryst in my garden, Horatio probably had not had the luxury of snatching a few hours' sleep like I had. His eyes were rimmed with exhaustion and a hint of beard shadowed his jaw. But never had any man looked so wonderful to me.

I cast myself against his chest and his arms tightened around me, holding me close and suddenly everything in my world felt right again. For so many years, I had to be the strong one, looking out for my stepmother and sisters. I had forgotten what it was like to feel protected. As I nestled in Horatio's arms, I emitted a tiny sigh, thinking I could get used to this.

Unfortunately, he eased me away from him, his eyes filled with longing and regret.

"I am sorry. I should not have. Not after you and the prince... " He faltered and then drew himself upright, adopting a more formal tone. "May I offer you my sincerest congratulations."

"Don't you dare, Horatio Crushington," I said fiercely. "I swear I will box the ears of the next person foolish enough to congratulate me."

"You do realize it is against the law to strike a Scutcheon commander."

"Then you will have to arrest me." I extended my hands, wrists held together. "Please. Lock me up in your deepest dungeon where no one can find me but you."

"I don't have a dungeon at the garrison."

"I'll help you build one."

His lips twitched, yielding to that slow sweet smile of his. He gathered my hands into his. "You truly do not intend to marry the prince?"

"How could you believe that even for a moment? I have told you many times I have no interest in becoming a princess."

"And yet, I do keep stumbling upon you kissing royalty."

I winced because there was a certain amount of truth to Horatio's accusation. At the ball, he had caught me out on the balcony embracing Prince Ryland. That had not been my idea, but I had not exactly been resisting either. I had been curious to see if any feeling remained within me for the faithless lover I had once known as Harper.

"It is not my fault if the princes in the kingdom are far too free and loose with their lips, arrogantly believing that any maiden can be theirs for a kiss." I complained. "Do you really think that I could forsake you that easily?"

"Not easily, perhaps. But I would understand if you

preferred Florian to me." His smile faded, the somber expression stealing back into his eyes. "I had already begun to have my doubts that there could ever be any happily ever after for you and me."

"How can you say that? After declaring your love for me only hours ago?"

"I meant every word of that, but the most that I will ever be able to offer you is a name that is not even my own, a tainted bloodline."

"Don't mention that foundling nonsense. I told you I don't care about that."

"You should. I come from an unknown parentage, while Florian can trace his lineage back through many generations."

"Probably all conceited fools like him or tyrants like his father," I muttered.

"But you would live in a palace. You and your family would never want for anything again."

"You sound just like my stepmother," I said impatiently.

"You should listen to her. You would have servants, beautiful dresses, jewels and - and books. More books than you could read in a lifetime. You would have so much more than I could ever give you. You could have everything."

"Everything. Except for what I want most."

"What would that be?"

"This!" I seized him by the collar of his uniform and yanked his head down to a level with mine. He emitted a startled *oof* as my lips collided with his. Fueled by my exasperation, the kiss was more rough than romantic until Horatio wrapped his arms around me. He kissed me with a tenderness that left me breathless. I reached up to stroke his beard-roughened cheek.

"I hope this puts an end to these stupid thoughts you have been having."

"It does. So long as you never accuse me of being too free and loose with my lips." He teased me, a rare thing for Horatio.

I laughed. "Never! So long as I am the maiden you are making free with."

The conversation I had had with Em earlier rose unbidden to my mind. I could not help wondering...

I fiddled with the topmost button of his uniform while asking, "Horatio, do you happen to know anything about siren kissing?"

His brows arched upward in surprise, but a hint of a smile touched his lips. He bent to kiss me again, but this time in a way he had never kissed me before. His lips coaxed mine apart, deepening the embrace. Horatio did know quite a lot about siren kissing and my stepmother was right. When a man knew how to do it well, the siren's kiss could be... enervating.

I was flushed and panting when we finally broke apart for air.

"Oh, my!" I breathed.

"Yes," Horatio agreed. I could feel how hard his heart was racing as he held me close, burying his lips against my hair.

I drew back to gaze up at him tenderly. "Now do you still think I would ever allow that foolish prince to come between us?"

"Not the prince, but someone else perhaps."

When I gave him a puzzled frown, Horatio caressed my cheek, a rueful expression stealing into his eyes. "Ella, you have not yet asked me what I am doing here."

"Why, rescuing me as usual. Although now that I think about it, I am a bit surprised that you should turn up here at The Hawk's Nest."

My voice trailed off, my gaze flashing down to the hilt of his sword. Horatio did not wear his weapon on the ordinary course of his rounds. My breath hitched in my throat.

"You have come to arrest Mal. I knew this was bound to happen eventually. I have been waiting, dreading that this day would come."

"Calm down, Ella. I merely want to question him. I am not arresting him yet."

Yet? How could one small word sound so ominous?

"Then why did you bring your sword?" I demanded.

"Because your friend Hawkridge has a reputation for being a difficult and dangerous man, extremely reluctant when it comes to respecting authority."

"Mal may be a bit of a rogue, but he is not some desperate, hardened criminal."

"So you keep telling me. If that is the case, he should not mind giving some honest answers."

"I am sure he wouldn't. But he is not here."

When Horatio gave me a skeptical look, I said, "Truly, Horatio, Mal is away. I was seeking him myself. Look! His boat is gone."

I gestured toward the empty dock. "When the *Ella Marie* is gone, that means Mal is, too. He never lends his precious skiff out to anyone."

"Hawkridge named his boat after you?"

"Yes, we have been close friends for a very long time."

Horatio frowned but made no further comment. He stalked toward the end of the garden and studied the vacant shoreline, almost as though he expected to find the boat hidden among the reeds or even Mal himself skulking there. He inspected the garments on the wash line, fingering the socks, testing them for dampness as though he could determine how long ago Mal had left.

Horatio's movements were brisk and efficient, reminding me of something his kisses and tenderness had allowed me to forget. He was the Commander of the Midtown garrison, sworn to uphold the king's laws and Horatio could be rather inflexible at times. The way he prowled about Mal's garden, seeking clues caused my pulse to skip a beat.

"Where do you think Hawkridge has gone?" he asked.

"I have no idea."

Horatio leveled a searching gaze at me. "Would you tell me if you did?"

"I-I don't know," I faltered. "It depends on what you want him for."

"I told you. I have questions."

"About what?" I trailed anxiously after Horatio as he tried to peer into Mal's kitchen window. "Is it something to do with that Elixir of Love?"

"The what?"

I bit my lip. Perhaps I should have remained silent. Horatio had obviously not heard about Mal's elixir, but he would soon enough. I continued. "You are going to receive a lot of complaints from women accusing Mal of defrauding them. I warned him not to go around peddling that potion. But really, that stuff was quite harmless."

"Ella," Horatio tried to stop me, but I rushed on.

"There was nothing magical about it, just some infusion of herbs so no laws were broken. I am sure Mal made it clear to his customers that all that the potion would do is make them feel more confident and desirable. And if they felt that way, it would surely show and make them seem more attractive."

"Ella—"

"All right, Mal probably was not entirely honest. Maybe he did let all those ladies believe that if they drank his potion, a prince would fall in love with them. And that was wrong of Mal, very wrong. It is not as though he kept the money for himself. Mal is always helping his poorer neighbors here in the Bottoms."

"While I applaud his generosity, he ought to confine his charity to money he has earned through honest, legal means," Horatio said sternly.

I sighed, having told Mal that same thing, many times. But I feared that my reckless friend took far too much pleasure in defying the king's laws.

"What will Mal have to do?" I asked. "Make restitution to the ladies. Pay a huge fine? Spend time in the garrison gaol?"

"As reprehensible as I find the chicanery he practiced upon

those gullible young women, that is not the reason I am looking for him," Horatio replied gravely. "I am investigating a crime of a much more serious nature. A theft."

I felt as though my heart stopped, the orb I had stolen for Mal weighing heavy on my conscience. I had the replaced the orb with an identical fake one. Had the substitution somehow been discovered? I was in such a panic, it took me a moment to register what else Horatio was saying.

"Someone broke into Quad Hall last night."

"Oh!" I breathed out, so weak with relief that my knees nearly buckled. "That explains why the hall is all closed up and heavily guarded."

"What? "

"When I tried to find you at the garrison, I crossed paths with the king's wizard. Mercato would allow no one to enter the hall. He even had the portcullis lowered. "

"That frapping fool! " Horatio growled.

I was startled. Horatio seldom swore, especially not in the presence of a lady. I was even more surprised that he would speak so disrespectfully of the king's chief wizard.

Horatio dragged his hands down his face in a wearied, frustrated gesture. "I warned that man not to do anything that would create a stir or spread alarm through the town. "

"I am afraid he ignored you. Mercato also denied ever telling you he would secure the release of the Midtown citizens. "

"Pay no heed to that. I told you it will all be happily resolved."

"But the Hansons still have not returned home. "

"They will very soon but the matter had to be delayed. I have been informed that the king became ill after the ball last night. Apparently, something he ate or drank did not agree with him."

Probably that same cheap wine which had had such a bad effect on my sister, Amy, I thought wryly.

"Sidney Greenleaf promised me he will discuss the release of the Hansons with the king as soon as his majesty is feeling well enough." Horatio summoned up a tired, but reassuring smile. "All right?"

I nodded, but I felt uneasy and confused. Horatio was one of the few people I had ever heard that dared to refer to the wizard by his real name. He had called Mercato a fool, and yet Horatio seemed to place great faith in the man. At times, it felt as though he was talking about two entirely different people. It made no sense, but I had far more pressing worries.

"Exactly what did happen at Quad Hall last night?" I asked. "How does it concern Mal?"

Horatio sighed. "I had hoped to keep all this quiet until I completed my investigation. Thanks to Mercato locking up the Hall, the entire kingdom will be buzzing with gossip and speculation. I will tell you, Ella, but you must keep this information to yourself. Can I trust you to be discrete?"

"Of course," I murmured, although I squirmed a little. I was not sure how far I could be trusted, not if it became a question of protecting Mal. But my answer must have satisfied Horatio for he continued.

"The annual royal ball has always been an occasion of great celebration, especially this year since for the first time Midtown citizens were permitted to attend."

"Yes, if they purchased tickets at a ridiculously exorbitant cost," I grumbled.

Horatio ignored my interruption and went on, "Because I attended the ball, discipline at the garrison was relaxed. A barrel of rum was delivered to the barracks, purportedly from me. My officers should have known better, but they all imbibed a bit too freely and were not as alert as they should have been. During changing of the guard, someone gained access to the Aura Chamber and smashed the Mirror of Collection. They also stole a huge sack full of the icicles."

"Icicles?"

"Those odd, shaped prisms in which the rays of your aura get stored."

My blank expression must have alerted Horatio I had no idea what he was talking about.

"You must remember how the collection process works," he said.

"I was very young at the time," I started to lie and then stopped. I was constantly concealing things from Horatio, and I hated it. How could our relationship ever deepen and grow if I was always deceiving him?

I took a deep breath and confessed. "The truth is I have never been in the Aura Chamber. I was six years old when Mercato invented it and we were all told that it was designed for our protection, to help the king search for us if we ever got lost. For some reason, I never understood, my father avoided registering me. Perhaps he was suspicious of the king's motives or he simply thought it was all nonsense. All Papa told me was that I was far too clever of a girl to ever get lost. I have never complied with the law."

I braced myself for Horatio's stern reaction. I was surprised when he only smiled.

"You don't need to look so guilty. I was never registered either."

"You weren't?"

"When I was adopted from the Foundling Asylum, I lived with my parents in the outermost reaches of the kingdom. Since they had already registered their son that died and then gave me his name, they never bothered traveling all the way to Midtown to have my aura collected.

"After arriving here to take up my duties as the new garrison commander, I have been far too busy to bother with the Aura Chamber. I only recently complied with the registration law myself. Promise me you will do the same as soon as Mercato is able to repair the Mirror of Collection."

I hesitated, although I was not sure why. Everyone I knew had been to the Aura Chamber and had their aura registered, even my lawless friend, Mal. Why was I so reluctant? Perhaps because my father had never wanted me to do it and going against his wishes felt like an insult to his memory. Such a qualm on my part was rather absurd. I had certainly defied Papa often enough during my teen years when I was stealing away for my forbidden trysts with Harper.

But Horatio was still waiting for an answer. I looked up at him and forced a smile.

"I promise. But all of this is very strange, Horatio. Why would anyone destroy the mirror and steal those prisms?"

"I don't know." He frowned. "I fear this may be the work of a group of dissidents I have been trying to unmask for some time. They call themselves The League of the Lost Heir. There have long been rumors that when the Helavalerians took over the kingdom, a grandson of the old queen, Althea, was hidden away."

"Those old tales? What nonsense." I scoffed. "I have read the history of Queen Althea the Magnificently Wise many times. She was my childhood hero, but there is no mention in that book of any lost heir. It is nothing more than a legend."

"Unfortunately, this league believes in this legend. They are determined to find this heir and mount a rebellion to put him on the throne."

"Merciful fairies! And you think Mal might be part of this League?"

"Worse than that. I suspect he might be its leader."

"Malcolm Hawkridge! A rebel leader?" I gave an incredulous laugh. "Mal is no warrior. He is far too pragmatic to get swept up in such a risky cause. Mal's only ambition is to become a great magician like his grandfather. Hiram Hawkridge was once the king's chief wizard. But he offended his majesty and lost his post. After that, all Hawkridges were denied licenses to practice magic or ever come within a mile of the royal palace."

"That strikes me as a mighty good reason for Malcolm

Hawkridge to harbor a grudge against the king and want him gone."

"Perhaps Mal does resent King August," I admitted. "But not enough to get involved in any mad plot to depose him. Mal hopes to amass a fortune so that he can bribe - er - I mean persuade the king to sell him a wizard's license. That is all Mal desires."

Well, that and one other thing. Me. After being friends for so many years, Mal had taken this notion into his head that he was in love with me, but I kept that information to myself. It certainly wouldn't make Horatio any better disposed toward Mal.

He was already looking unconvinced by my defense of Mal. I said even more vehemently, "I swear to you, Horatio. Mal is no rebel. We have been friends forever. I *know* him."

"Perhaps you do not know Malcolm Hawkridge as well as you think. I can understand why you wish to believe him innocent, but— "

"I don't understand why you are so determined to think him guilty. What proof do you have? Oh, I forgot, proof is no longer necessary in this kingdom," I added bitterly. "People can be snatched up and flung into the Dismal Dungeons without a trial. That is now the way of things in Arcady."

"But that is not *my* way." There was a trace of hurt in Horatio's voice. "I hope you would know that by now, Ella."

"Of course, I do." I kissed his cheek to reassure him. "But you are alarming me with all of your suspicions about Mal."

"If your friend is as innocent as you believe, there is nothing to worry about. All Hawkridge must do is give me a satisfactory answer regarding his whereabouts yesterday at midnight. That is when we have the changing of the guard at the garrison. That would have been the only real opportunity for someone to gain access to the Aura chamber."

Beaming up at Horatio, I blurted out, "Then it could not have been Mal. I know exactly where he was at midnight. With me."

Oh frap. I realized my mistake the moment the words were out of my mouth.

Horatio frowned at me. "But Ella, you were at the ball and Hawkridge was not. At least, I never saw him there. Did you not just tell me that all Hawkridges are banned from ever coming to the palace?"

"Well, yes and that is why I did not meet Mal at the royal castle. There is an abandoned cottage in the woods just outside the palace grounds."

"That is where you were with Hawkridge? Inside this secluded cottage? Alone at midnight?"

I winced, realizing that this was all sounding worse and worse. "We were not *inside* in the cottage. We just met on the bench outside."

"Why?" Horatio demanded.

Because I needed to hand over that frapping orb I had stolen for him before I was caught with it in my pocket.

I moistened my lips, finding it easier to study the braiding on Horatio's uniform rather than meet his questioning gaze.

"Mal was not able to come to the ball, but he was still concerned about me, wanting to make sure I was enjoying myself."

That excuse sounded weak even to my ears, but I babbled on, "You see, Mal was the one who bought the ball tickets for me and my stepmother and sisters."

"How generous of him," Horatio said wryly.

"My sisters called him our fairy godfather. We could never have afforded to have gone to the ball otherwise, not even after I sold my mother's earrings. He furnished me with a gown and hired a coach as well. But that is so typical of Mal. He has ever been reckless with his money, always confident that he can acquire more."

Horatio started to say something but appeared to think better of it. He finally said, "Hawkridge was with you at midnight. You would swear to that?"

"Yes!"

"Very well. I will take you word for it." But Horatio studied my face in a way that made me acutely uncomfortable. "Ella, do you remember what I said to you the night of the ball?"

I ventured a smile. "That you love me?"

"Yes, there was that. But I said something to you equally important. That I would do anything within my power for you. I also asked you to promise me if you ever found yourself in any kind of trouble, you would come to me. And you promised."

"Yes, I remember."

"Forgive me, but I feel as though there is something you are holding back." Horatio cupped my cheek in his hand, his gaze gentle and reassuring. "You can trust me, Ella. Are you sure there is nothing else you wish to tell me?"

If ever there was a moment to confess about the stolen orb, this was it. My breath hitched in my throat, my heart swelling with the need to unburden myself. I did trust Horatio with my very life.

But not with Mal's.

"No, there is nothing," I forced myself to say brightly, although the lie almost stuck in my throat.

"Very well." He drew me into his arms, his kiss as tender as ever. But perhaps it was my guilty conscience at work. When we parted, I imagined I saw a flash of doubt and disappointment in his eyes.

Four

I saw little of Horatio during the ensuing days. I assured myself this was because he was preoccupied, trying to track down the perpetrators behind the theft at Quad Hall, and not because he was avoiding me. When we did have a chance to meet in town, our exchanges were far too brief and too public to allow for anything more than a touch of our hands.

The warmth in Horatio's eyes was still there, but I sensed a constraint in him. Our opposing views of Malcolm Hawkridge had cast a shadow between us, the tension only heightened when Mal continued to be elusive.

I was sure Horatio did not believe me when I denied knowing where Mal was, but I truly did not. I did not even dare return to The Hawk's Nest to look for him because of my fear of another encounter with Delphine.

Wherever Mal was hiding, I prayed it was somewhere far from Arcady. I was not that worried about his angry customers. Given time, the disappointed ladies' tempers would cool. The break-in at Quad Hall was a far more serious matter. I hoped Mal would have the good sense to stay away until Horatio had apprehended the real culprit behind the attack on the aura chamber.

Although I had vigorously defended my friend, I was not naïve where Mal was concerned. He did have a reckless disdain for the law and total contempt for royal authority. Mal had been with me at midnight, but that might not be enough to entirely exonerate him. I am sure that Horatio knew as well as I did that Mal had friends as disreputable as he was, rogues with names like Long Louie and Waldo the Wharf Rat. Perhaps Horatio suspected them all of being part of this League of the Lost Heir.

It did strike me as an odd coincidence that the same night I had stolen that orb for Mal, someone had been busy pilfering aura prisms from Quad Hall. But I could not see how the two events could be connected, any more than I could believe Mal could be part of this mysterious league and weaving mad plots against the king. I would feel better about all this when I did see Mal and was able to question him. Besides wanting his reassurance, I quite simply missed my friend.

It was ironic that the two men whose company I longed for were absent from my life, while the man I had no desire to ever see again kept popping up like an evil sprite.

Just as he had pledged that he would, Prince Florian had started his wooing. Wooing? It was more like being stalked. I could scarcely set foot out of doors without the prince springing up before me. He trailed after me whenever I went to the market, insisting upon carrying my basket. Unless I wanted to engage in an undignified scuffle, I was obliged to let him. Florian would toss back his golden mane, accompanying me on my rounds to the baker's, the fishmongers, and the vegetable sellers. As I picked over the produce, Florian regarded me with soulful adoration, heaving deep longing sighs. It was enough to entirely put a woman off her turnips.

Florian never called upon me at home. I might have been grateful for that if he had not insisted upon making his wooing a public spectacle. He absolutely loved the crowds that he drew when he pursued me through the marketplace. To the Midtown folk, Florian's courtship was as entertaining as a troop of strolling players performing, "*The Noble Prince and the Coy Maiden,*" a play in three acts. Myself, I would have been inclined to entitle the piece, *The Irritating Idiot and the Frustrated Female.*"

I have always preferred to lead a quiet existence, but the prince's antics were turning me into the most notorious woman in the kingdom. The sighing, the distraught pressing of his hand to the region of his heart were bad enough, but Florian penned off reams of bad poetry which he recited aloud to me over the flour and sugar bins. Epics like "Ode to Ella's Bright Blue Eyes which hath cruelly slain me." Or "To Ella's rosebud Lips that so stingily deny me her kiss."

I bore this all with what patience I could muster, until the afternoon he composed the ode to my nose.

"Oh, pert adorable nose! Wherefore dost thou sniff with scorn at thy loving prince?"

"Stop!" I groaned. "Please! No more poetry. I do not think Your Highness would find my nose all that adorable when I have a cold and strings of mucus dribble out of my nostrils."

Florian looked thoroughly revolted. I experienced a brief flicker of hope that I had finally managed to repulse him enough to leave me alone. But to my horror, the prince dropped to one knee. Setting my basket down, he clasped his hands together in an imploring gesture.

"Pardon me, my dearest. I can see that my wretched paeans have offended you. I was only trying to express the depth of my love. If you do not say that you forgive me, my poor devoted heart will break in two. I vow I shall not stir from this spot until you do."

This earned the prince a loud chorus of 'aww' from the watching crowd, especially the ladies. Everyone glared at me as though I was a monster.

I gave a weary sigh of defeat. "I forgive you. Now will you please stand up?"

Florian leaped triumphantly to his feet to embrace me, and the crowd applauded. When he tried to kiss me, I turned my head so that he only succeeded in licking my cheek. This garnered me some hisses and boos until Florian silenced the crowd with a magnanimous sweep of his hand.

"Hush, my friends. No lady worth having was ever easily won. I am confident that my steadfast affection will soon thaw my Ella's cold, cold heart."

More applause for the prince, more nasty looks for me. I slunk away as soon as I could, not even bothering to retrieve my basket from Florian. I was fast acquiring a reputation as the most heartless, obstinate woman in all of Arcady. But everyone, especially Florian, believed I would relent in the end. What sort of madwoman would continue to spurn the love of such a devoted and handsome prince?

This was all so frustrating and embarrassing, I would have happily barricaded myself in my library, becoming as much of a recluse as my father had ever been. But I was finding little peace at home either.

Rhufawn Smythe, the royal herald assigned to our district, arrived on my doorstep at least twice a day, bringing me gifts from the prince: nosegays, chocolates and love letters that were even worse than his poetry.

Far worse than the gifts from the prince were the other packages delivered to my door. After the word spread throughout Midtown that I had been chosen as Florian's bride, the merchants fell over themselves to curry favor with their future princess. Shopkeepers who had taken scant notice of me before, were now eager to extend unlimited credit.

I was dismayed to discover my stepmother had taken advantage of this offer. Growing up as the only child of a wealthy man from the Heights, Em had never learned to be practical or good at managing money.

When my father died, he left control of his modest legacy to me, even though I was so young at the time, barely eighteen. It was quite a burden to place on my youthful shoulders, but I quickly realized the wisdom of my father's decision. If Em had been left in charge, we would have ended up bankrupt long ago and reduced to living in one of those wretched cottages in Misty Bottoms or worse. If one grew too poor to afford even that sort of mean dwelling, the next step was banishment. King August abhorred beggars. Unfortunate souls who could not pay their taxes were routinely rounded up by the Border Scutcheons and driven into the mysterious fenland beyond the Conger River, never to be seen or heard from again.

Every time the king devised some new levy or raised our taxes, I had nightmares about this happening to my family and redoubled my efforts to stretch our income. Em often grumbled that I pinched our pennies until they shrieked. Consequently, when I discovered that Em had been on a spending spree, our parlor heaped with costly bolts of silk, reams of lace and caskets of jewelry, I finally exploded.

"Em! What were you thinking? You know we cannot afford all this stuff. Everything must be returned at once."

"Oh, pooh, my dear," Em said, unpacking one of those ridiculously over-priced bonnets from Martha's Millinery. "Time enough to worry about paying the bills after we are settled at the palace. I am sure you don't want me and your sisters turning up at your wedding looking like charwomen."

"How many times do I have to tell you?" I shouted. "There will be no wedding. I am never going to marry that frapping fool."

I regretted my outburst immediately when my stepmother's lip quivered. Em has always been a sensitive soul, wilting beneath a raised voice or harsh word.

"I am sorry for shouting at you, Em," I began, but she shrank from me, tears spilling down her cheeks.

"I don't know what is wrong with you, Ella," she said. "The

prince is all any woman could desire, kind, considerate, handsome, intelligent and extremely heroic."

I longed to point out that was a far better description of Horatio Crushington, but such a remark would only have added to Em's distress.

"Instead of only thinking of yourself, think of the good that would come to your family if you wed the prince. I n-never imagined you could be so selfish."

Sobbing, she fled from the parlor, leaving me to deal with the dismal task of packing up all this costly finery and returning it to the merchants. I felt more like sagging down upon the settee and weeping myself. Think about the good of my family? When had I ever done anything else? I reflected bitterly. Ever since my father had died, I had done my best to look after Em, Netta and Amy, managing our household, doing more than my share of cooking and cleaning when we could no longer afford a maid. Doing without things myself so I could delight them with a few indulgences, new parlor furniture for Em, a harp for Netta, miniature ponies for Amy.

I did not mind it, truly I didn't. My world had been shattered when my mother died, and my father had become so distant. I felt so alone. After my father married Em, I had a family again and I loved them dearly.

That is why when Em accused me of being selfish, it hurt me deeply. The more so because I wondered if she was right. It *would* make all the difference to my family if I wed the prince. Luxury and security for all of us, the prospect of good marriages for Amy and Netta.

But what about Horatio? Things were strained between us now, but I did not yet despair of our 'and they lived happily ever after.' How could I throw away what might be my last chance of finding true love? The answer was, I couldn't. Perhaps I was being selfish, but that was simply one sacrifice I was not prepared to make.

Still, I hated the discord that had sprung up between me and Em. I would have found it almost unbearable but for the unexpected support of my two sisters. Netta and Amy might well have joined their mother in urging me to marry Florian, but instead they took quite the opposite view.

"If you do not love the prince, certainly you should not marry him," Netta told me solemnly. "Far better to wed a beggar if he is the man you adore."

"Or a certain young sergeant of the guard," Amy teased Netta, causing her to blush. But Amy echoed her older sister's sentiments.

"Netta is right, Ella. You must not pay any heed to Mama. She is simply too old to remember what it is like to be in love. Besides, we only need one princess in the family. When I am wed to my beloved Dashiel, you and Netta shall marry whomever your heart desires. *I* shall decree it."

Amy had been so earnest when she said this, it had brought a lump to my throat. I knew that she donned her best frock every morning, waiting for a prince who was never going to come. It was foolish of her to believe that she had found her true love in one night and to continue to put faith in a prince's empty promises. But I saw so much of myself in Amy, the innocent and romantic girl I had been at the age of seventeen when Ryland had cruelly deceived me. It pained me that I could do nothing to shield my little sister from the heartbreak that awaited her. I could only be there to hug her and dry her tears.

Four days had passed since the fateful ball that had brought all this misery down upon my head. It felt like more than four months to me. I often found myself in my bedchamber, brooding over those glass slippers Mal had given me, wishing they really did have the power to make me invisible.

But no matter how wretched one feels, dust still gathers on the furniture, clothes require washing and supper needs fixing. By now, I had absolutely come to dread my visits to the marketplace, but I had no choice unless we were going to eat chocolates for dinner. (Although in my current state of mind, that did not seem such a bad idea.)

I trudged through the front hall in a thoroughly foul mood. Just as I reached the door, someone knocked loudly for admittance.

"Frap!" I swore and grimaced. I realized I had been swearing a great deal lately.

I yanked the door open and snarled, "What do you want?"

An elegantly attired older gentleman was standing on my front stoop, a nosegay of yellow flowers clutched in his hand. He reared back at my surly greeting. "Why, I am sorry, Miss Ella. Have I called at a bad time? I was hoping to see your stepmother and to give her these fresh from my garden." He held out the small bouquet. "I recall how much Imelda always liked primroses."

My face flushed with embarrassment as I recognized Em's old beau. "Chuffy! I - I mean Lord Redmond. Pray forgive me. I did not mean to be so abrupt. I thought you might be someone else."

"Prince Florian, perhaps? I had heard His Highness was courting you."

"Yes, you could call it that." I sighed, bracing myself for the usual hearty congratulations.

But Lord Redmond frowned. "I hope you are not planning to accept his offer of marriage."

"No, I most certainly am not," I stammered in surprise.

"Good. I know all the girls up in the Heights think Florian, handsome and dashing and all that, but he really is a worthless young man, spoiled and selfish like most of the king's sons. I am glad that you are too sensible to be charmed by him."

Chuffy patted my hand in an approving fashion. "You could do much better for yourself. What about that splendid officer I saw you with at the ball?"

"Commander Crushington?"

"Yes, that's the chap. I got the distinct impression you rather fancy him?"

"Well, I... " The blush that stole into my cheeks was more than answer enough.

His lordship chuckled. "And why not? He struck me as an intelligent, honorable sort. Very useful, the way he helped after your sister imbibed too much of that cheap swill our king calls wine." Chuffy winked at me. "And I am sure it doesn't hurt that the commander is quite a good-looking chap, eh?"

I grinned at his lordship, suppressing a mad urge to hug the man. With the entire kingdom expecting me to marry Florian, Lord Redmond was like the gust of a fresh wind. I stood there beaming at him like an idiot for several seconds before I recollected my manners and invited him inside.

"Let me show you into the parlor," I said. "And I will fetch Em for you. I know she is going to be delighted to see you, absolutely delighted."

I was nearly babbling in my eagerness, almost like a desperate spider, luring in a fly. But it occurred to me that this old beau of Em's could prove my salvation. Lord Redmond and my step-mother had been in love once. What if the romance of their youth was rekindled and his lordship asked Em to marry him? I had a feeling that his lordship would prove to be a delightful stepfather. I would no longer need to feel the least bit of guilt for refusing Florian. My family's financial worries would all be over and—

I brought myself up short, realizing I was doing what I often accused my younger sisters of, letting my imagination run away with me. Lord Redmond's visit might portend nothing more than a desire upon his part to renew an old friendship or engage in a light dalliance.

After all, this was the same Chuffy of Em's summerhouse trysts, the rakehell her father had mistrusted, the young man with the tongue so skilled in delivering those enervating siren kisses.

Beneath that thatch of graying hair and mutton- chop whiskers, I could detect a roguish twinkle in his pale blue eyes. If he continued to call upon my stepmother, I would have to corner his lordship and demand to know his intentions. But for now, I was pleased to settle him in the parlor while I announced his arrival to Em.

* * *

Lord Redmond's visit enthralled Em to the degree that her unhappiness with me was, for the moment, forgotten. I hoped Chuffy's intentions were honorable. But if they were not, at least my younger sisters were there to act as chaperone. In addition to that, we didn't have a summerhouse.

My own mood was much improved as I headed for town. I still dreaded being pounced upon by Florian, but I had come up with a plan. Instead of venturing to the markets at my usual hour, I would delay until it was almost time for the shops to close. Not only might I strike a better bargain with the vegetable sellers at that hour, but surely Florian would grow tired of waiting around for me to appear.

In the meantime, I intended to pay a visit to the Midtown Garrison in hopes of finding a few minutes alone with Horatio. I longed to kiss him and mend our disagreement about Mal. Not that we had actually quarreled, but perhaps a great deal of kissing would prove a remedy against future discord.

The trick would be getting past the crossroad that led to the shops without stumbling into Florian. By lucky chance when I reached that part of my walk, one of those absurd pumpkin-shaped carriages came lumbering down the road. It was moving at such a sedate pace so I was able to trot alongside of it, thus blocking any view of me from the market area.

The occupants of the coach peered out the windows at me. I grimaced when I recognized the Vanderwix girls. Priscilla beamed at me and waved enthusiastically. Ardelia lifted one hand in a half-hearted gesture, her pinched nose thrust into the air.

I could easily imagine what she was thinking. *There goes our demented future princess, running again. What does Prince Florian see in her?*

I managed to smile and wave back, but I feared the young ladies might order their coachman to stop and offer me a ride to my destination. I had no desire to be cooped up in that carriage with Priscilla's giggles and Ardelia's probing questions.

I lifted my heels and bolted until I outdistanced the plodding coach. Truly I was getting so good at running, I might have had a fair chance of winning a prize at the foot races held during the annual Festival of Flowers. That is if those races had not been unfairly restricted to men only.

I paused to catch my breath when I reached the town square, scooping up a cupped handful of water for a quick drink from the fountain. Quad Hall had returned to normal since my last visit. No armed Scutcheons patrolling the walls, no lowered portcullis barring admittance.

Horatio had managed to convince Midtown citizens that the closing of the Hall had been nothing more than a safety inspection required by the king. A few people had remained suspicious— I heard a whisper of gossip here and there. For the most part, everyone was satisfied with Horatio's explanation and far too diverted by Florian's courtship of me to give the matter any further consideration.

The Midtown garrison was located at the back of Quad Hall. I followed a well-worn footpath that led around the building until I came to the stable yard. I saw Scutcheons marching out for their patrols. A small group of privates were engaged in sword practice under the tutelage of the earnest Major Frackles.

I did not like to interrupt him, but I was completely unfamiliar with this area of Quad Hall. I had never had occasion to visit Horatio in his headquarters and needed directions. I started hesitantly toward Frackles when I was overjoyed to spot Horatio, himself.

He was standing beneath a covered walkway adorned with a

series of stone arches. Shaded from the afternoon sun, I could barely make out Horatio's features, but I would know that tall, broad-shouldered silhouette anywhere.

I rushed toward him only to pull up short when I realized he was not alone. I was close enough to recognize who was with him, a hunch-backed man with pointy features and tufts of white hair. Withypole Fugitate ran a small shop in Misty Bottoms, crammed with an odd assortment of things that he bought from people desperate for money. I had been to Fugitate's Fancies too many times, selling off our family valuables to pay the king's ruinous taxes. I had even sold my mother's emerald earrings and it had nearly broken my heart. But Mal, wonderful friend that he was, had redeemed them for me.

On my last visit to Withypole's shop, I stumbled across his secret. The man was not really a hunchback or even a human male at all. Withypole Fugitate was one of the fairy folk. His people had been driven out of Arcady a long time ago by harsh restrictions upon the practice of magic and an exorbitant tax on wings.

Fugitate avoided this by disguising his identity, crushing his wings into a sack, and making it appear as if he had a hump beneath his shirt. Why he would submit to such indignity and discomfort to remain in Arcady was a mystery. Most likely, Withypole had been scorned by the rest of the fairy world for becoming a 'gleaner.'

From my father's book on fairy lore, I had learned that gleaners were fairies who became obsessed with amassing anything that humans valued, jewelry, paintings, musical instruments, furniture, even toys. Fairies who were above collecting such worldly goods only turned into gleaners after suffering some sort of heartbreak.

Whatever tragic event lurked in Fugitate's past, I had no idea. I did know that besides gleaning goods, Fugitate kept his sharp eyes and ears open, gathering information about suspicious activities in Misty Bottoms which he shared with Horatio.

I had once been angry with Horatio about this, accusing him

of coercing Withypole into acting as his informant. But the truth was, Withypole volunteered his cooperation. I could not begin to fathom the reason for this tale bearing, except that perhaps the fairy took some spiteful pleasure in it.

Horatio and Withypole were so deep in conversation, neither of them noticed my approach. Who was Withypole informing upon this time? I prayed it was nothing to do with Mal.

Badly as I wanted to eavesdrop, I did not want Horatio to think I was spying upon him. I ducked beneath the nearest arch, waiting for him to finish his meeting with Withypole. Horatio's back was toward me, but Withypole's gaze appeared to flick in my direction. I could swear I saw his nose twitch as though he could sniff me out. Were fairies gifted with a powerful sense of smell?

I decided not to take any chances. I retreated further down the shadowy walkway until I came to an arched doorway at the base of one of the towers. This was a part of Quad Hall that was more familiar to me. The Registry office was the place one went to apply for licenses to wed, to open a shop or to obtain a permit to practice magic. The latter permit was never issued these days, not unless one possessed a small fortune to bribe the Royal Registrar.

Beyond the door to the registry, a curving stone stair stretched upward to the infamous Aura Chamber. Considering what had happened, I was surprised not to find it more heavily guarded. Perhaps no one expected the thief to return to the scene of his crime, at least not in broad daylight when Quad Hall was humming with activity. I wondered if Mercato had managed to fix the Mirror of Collection.

Stepping closer to the foot of the stairs, I tried to peer upward, but I could see nothing beyond the first spiral. I recalled the promise that I had made to Horatio, that I would comply with the registration law. Perhaps this was one small thing I could do that might ease the tension between us, but I had mixed feelings about it.

My father's avoidance of the Aura Chamber filled me with

unease. Yet even as a child, I had experienced an overwhelming curiosity about the magic device. I placed one hand upon the wrought iron banister. My heart thudding with a mixture of trepidation and excitement, I began to mount the stairs.

As I rounded each curve, I was reminded of a bedtime story that my stepmother had once told me and my sisters. All about a princess who had climbed to the top of a mysterious tower she had been forbidden to enter. Em had been a very good storyteller, and my little sisters were round-eyed, hanging on her every word. Even I was on the edge of the bed, shivering with anticipation of something truly terrible waiting in that tower, a dragon perhaps or an ogre with a mouthful of hideous teeth.

"And when the princess arrived at the top, she found," Em paused for dramatic effect. "A spinning wheel!"

"Oh!" Amy and Netta sighed, but I scowled with disappointment.

"A spinning wheel? What's so scary about that Em?"

"It was an enchanted spinning wheel. Now the king, her father had told the princess she must never go near such a thing. But overcome with curiosity, the princess touched the spindle. She pricked her finger on the needle and immediately collapsed into a death-like sleep."

My little sisters gasped, but I shook my head in disgust.

"Stupid princess! What kind of idiot girl goes around touching something she shouldn't?"

Em heaved a long-suffering sigh. "Hush, Ella, dear. Please just let me finish the story."

I could not help smiling at the memory of my cynical eight-year-old self. What a trial I must have been to my poor Em. I had not thought of that story in years. The recollection had been triggered by me wending my way up a tower, not knowing exactly what to expect at the top. Only knowing this was an action my father had forbidden.

Well, no. Papa had never actually *forbidden* me to visit the

Aura Chamber, I soothed my conscience. He had only ever implied that it was not necessary for me to follow the law and— All right, I was hedging. My father had made it quite clear he did not ever want me to have my aura registered, but this would hardly be the first time I had ignored Papa's wishes.

I paused at a bend in the stairs to catch my breath from the long climb. One thing I did know. If I got to the top and found that this mysterious Aura Chamber was no more exciting than that stupid spinning wheel, I was going to be bitterly disappointed.

Gripping the handrail, I started up the last few steps, only to freeze, listening. A low rumbling issued from the regions ahead of me. The kind of warning sound that might emanate from a large, dangerous dog, or an aura cat. That last possibility made the most sense. It would explain the absence of any guards below if the chamber itself was being patrolled by one of those eerie, hairless beasts. When the rumble came again, I almost turned to flee.

But having come this far, I hated to turn back now. Besides, if there was an aura cat nearby, there surely would have to be a handler as well. Perhaps it might even be Sgt. Ned Wharton, that nice young palace guard who had captured Netta's heart.

The rumbling sound stopped as abruptly as it had begun. I trudged up the last few steps at a more cautious pace until I arrived at the top. Bracing myself, I prepared to run if I was menaced by a ferocious aura cat slipping its leash. I peeked into an antechamber, furnished with a small writing desk and a plush throne-like red velvet chair.

There was no sign of a large ugly beast about to pounce, but something just as alarming. I stifled a gasp as I saw The Great Mercato slumped in the chair, his head flopped to one side, his eyes closed and his mouth hanging open. He was so still I could not even see the rise and fall of his chest as he breathed. For one awful moment, I thought he was dead.

Then he emitted that loud rumble I had heard earlier. The mighty wizard was snoring and what a formidable snore it was.

Enough to rattle the windowpanes if there had been any. But the chamber was only lit by narrow arrow slits open to the sky.

I stepped inside the room as quietly as I could, but Mercato appeared so sound asleep, I don't think I could have awakened him, even if I had been tromping around wearing heavy hobnail boots. Most people in our kingdom were awed and terrified by this man, but no one could have found the wizard formidable at this moment.

His sorcerer's hat had fallen off, tumbled onto the stone floor next to his golden staff. Despite his glittering robes, Mercato looked like someone's ancient grandfather, his hearty snores stirring the whiskers of his long, gray beard. I watched him sleep, uncertain as to what I should do next.

I had never given much thought to the person who oversaw the Aura Chamber. But considering that Mercato was the one who had devised the Mirror of Collection, it was logical to assume that he must be the one who did the aura collecting.

Should I attempt to wake him and announce that I had come to have my aura registered? That idea had little appeal for me. I doubted Mercato would thank me for startling him out of a sound sleep. He might be furious that I had stumbled upon him in such a vulnerable state.

Just behind the wizard's chair, I spied a gilt-trimmed door. This had to lead to the Aura Chamber itself. What would it hurt if I just had a quick look inside before taking the final step of having my aura collected?

Holding my skirt close, I slipped quietly past the sleeping wizard. As I reached for the door handle, I feared I might find the chamber locked. But the knob turned easily in my hand. As I inched the door open, the hinges squeaked in protest. I cast an anxious glance back at Mercato. He shifted position, but his eyes remained closed as he muttered in his sleep. "No, no sweetheart. I promise you my beard won't tickle."

I grimaced, unwilling to speculate what the old wizard might be dreaming about. I eased the door open just enough so I could slip inside. I did not bother closing it behind me for fear of making more noise.

The Aura Chamber was smaller than the room where Mercato slept. But it was better lit owing to the dome of glass that formed the ceiling. I could clearly discern the only objects in the room, an oddly shaped object covered with a white cloth and the Mirror of Collection.

Or perhaps it would have been more accurate to say *mirrors.* The aura gathering device consisted of three full length mirrors, those to the right and left conjoined to the central one at a slight angle. Horatio said that the Mirror of Collection had been damaged, but I saw no sign of it, not a single crack anywhere. Just three silvery surfaces, perfect mirrors in all respect, save one.

I couldn't see my image in any of them. Creeping closer, I stood at the apex of the mirrors. I should have been facing three Ella Uptons, all of them frowning back at me in puzzlement. Instead, there was nothing, not the glimmer of a reflection of any kind. I might as well have been invisible.

I backed away, not knowing what to make of it. Perhaps the Mirror of Collection *was* still damaged and Mercato had been unable to use his magic to fix it. Exhausted from his struggles, he had sat down to rest and fallen into a deep slumber.

That seemed the most logical explanation, but I felt unnerved by this weird phenomenon. Retreating further, I bumped into the only other thing in the room, the veil-covered object.

The white cloth shifted enough for me to perceive what it concealed. I blinked in astonishment. Could this get any stranger? I whipped back the cover to expose an ice cream churn.

Or at least something that resembled the device I used on those rare occasions I was able to treat my family to a lovely sorbet. This churn was a great deal larger, the barrel rising as high as my waist. An absurd thought flitted through my brain: Mercato must have an enormous, sweet tooth. Except that I was reasonably sure this apparatus had nothing to do with churning ice cream.

It was far more ornate than the one I had at home. Although the barrel was constructed of wood, it was banded with thin strips of silver etched with mysterious symbols like the ones that glittered on Mercato's robes. The crank attached to the side was also fashioned of purest silver. A chute protruded from the bottom of the barrel. Was this how auras were distilled, this unusual churn somehow working in conjunction with those mirrors?

I should have flung the cloth back over the apparatus and sneaked back out of the Aura Chamber. I have often scolded my sister Netta for being too inquisitive, but it was a trait that I shared with her. I stared at the churn until I was unable to resist giving the crank an experimental turn. When it shuddered beneath my touch, I snatched my hand back, but it was too late.

I watched with horrified fascination as the churn's lid slid back, revealing a diamond-shaped crystal. It pulsed with light, directing a ray toward the central looking glass. All three of the mirrors began to shimmer, rippling like the surface of a pond ruffled by a strong wind. Suddenly, I could see my reflection, three Ellas gaping back at me, with their mouths hanging open.

What had my foolish curiosity set into motion? I didn't know, but the answer to one question was now clear. What kind of idiot girl messes about with something that she should never have touched?

Me.

Five

I tried not to panic. Perhaps if I gave the handle another crank, I could shut down the aura collector. Before I could make the attempt, I was dazed by a powerful glow emanating from the mirrors. All the images of myself became silhouetted with light. Was that what an aura looked like?

The light became so intense, my vision began to blur. Three rays shot from the mirrors, converging into a single beam aimed straight at me. I gasped as the light went through me like a fiery arrow piercing my heart. It should have been incredibly painful, but it wasn't except for my eyes. They were dazzled by the fierce light.

I closed them and tried to move, but I couldn't, as though the arrow of light pinned me in place. Shivering from chills, the icy sensation that swept through me was indescribable. I felt all my memories, my hopes and dreams, everything that made me Ella Marie Upton, being drained from my body. My knees started to buckle, and I feared I was going to faint.

Then suddenly, it all stopped, the chamber quiet except for my ragged breathing. It took several moments more before I ceased feeling dizzy and was able to open my eyes. I glanced down at my body, frantically patting the region of my heart, dreading to find some gaping wound.

But there was nothing, no light passing through me, no rays emanating from the looking glasses. The mirrors had stopped rippling, the surfaces no longer displaying my reflection. But there was another image in the mirrors, a fairy whose gossamer wings seemed at odds with his tall, strong body. Tall and proud, his face was almost unbearably beautiful with finely chiseled cheekbones and delicate brows arched over his silver-blue eyes. Triplicate warrior fairies and all three of them were glaring at me.

Gasping, I spun around to find Withypole Fugitate standing behind me, but in his usual hunched over disguise. I blinked and stared at him, then back at the mirror images that did not match the person with me in the room.

"What the frap?" I faltered.

"Shh!" Withypole hissed at me.

He turned away from me, studying the aura churn. The lid had closed, covering up the diamond-shaped crystal. He inspected the device as though assuring himself it truly had shut down. Something protruded from the chute at the bottom of the barrel. I caught a glimpse of what appeared to be a broken off shard of icicle. Withypole pocketed it before I had a chance to get a good look.

Seizing me by the wrist, he growled, "Come on! You need to get out of here."

I was too dazed to resist. I doubt that I could have in any case. Withypole might bear the aspect of a wizened little man, but his strong grip was more like that of the warrior fairy I had glimpsed in the mirror.

He dragged me out of the Aura Chamber, only pausing as we passed by the sleeping wizard. To my dismay, Mercato was startled awake. Sitting up in his chair, he rubbed his eyes and squinted fiercely at me and Withypole.

"What's this?" the wizard demanded. "What's going on here?"

"Nothing. You have seen nothing." Holding his palm beneath his chin, Withypole blew a soft gust of air in Mercato's direction.

The wizard's head jerked back as though Withypole had socked him right between the eyes. Mercato slumped down on his chair, tumbling back into sleep with a low murmur. "Nothing... there was nothing there."

I stared at the wizard as he resumed snoring, but Withypole left me no time to gawk. He yanked my arm, pulling me toward the stairs. We descended at such a rapid pace, I stumbled in my efforts to keep up with him. I still felt weak from my strange ordeal in the aura chamber. By the time we reached the last few steps, I could go no further.

"Stop!" I panted. "I need to rest."

"You can rest when you are safe at home," Withypole snapped.

I wriggled free of his grasp and sank down upon one of the lower steps. Withypole tried to haul me back to my feet, but I thwarted him by locking my arms behind my back.

He glowered at me, and I glared right back.

"I am not stirring another step until you explain," I said. "What happened up there?"

"*You* happened, that's what! Blundering about in the aura chamber, setting that accursed device into motion. If I hadn't chanced along when I did—"

"Chanced along! You followed me."

"No." Withypole pursed his lips together and then admitted, "All right, so what if I did? What else did you expect when I noticed you acting all shifty?"

I gave an indignant gasp. "Shifty? I am sure that I have never in the entire course of my life acted—"

"Shifty!" Withypole reiterated with a certain amount of relish. "I saw you lurking about when I was talking to Commander Crushington and I said to myself, 'that Upton girl looks ripe for mischief.' As soon as I was able to make my excuses to the commander, I went looking for you. I lost your trail for a while because I thought you couldn't have been foolish enough to sneak into the aura chamber. But lo and behold, there you were."

Withypole shook his head in disgust. "As if it wasn't bad enough that you went poking about where you don't belong, you turned on that cursed thing. What were you thinking, girl?"

My cheeks flamed beneath the fairy's contempt. I don't know why I felt obliged to excuse myself to him, but I said, "I was curious, and I only gave the crank one turn. Before I knew what was happening, there was all this shimmering and piercing light and, well, it was all sort of an accident."

Withypole snorted. "Good thing I was there to *sort of accidentally* put a stop to it. You should be thanking me."

"Perhaps," I said grudgingly. "But it was all so strange. What did you do to Mercato to make him fall back asleep? Why couldn't I see my image in the mirrors when the device was turned off? Why could I still see yours?"

"Full of questions, aren't you?"

"Yes, and I would like some answers. Why was your reflection in the mirrors so different?"

"I have no idea what you're talking about."

"Yes, you do." I lowered my voice to a whisper even though there was no one about to hear. "The Mirror of Collection showed your real reflection."

When Withypole regarded me blankly, I made a fluttering motion with my hands. "Your true self with the wings. "

Something flickered in Withypole's eyes. Whether it was fear or irritation, I could not tell. He growled, "Being in that aura chamber must have addled your brain. You were seeing things."

"I was not! " I stopped, realizing the futility of this argument. Once before, I had accused Withypole of being a fairy, but he had fiercely denied it. I could not blame him for that. If his identity was ever exposed, he would be arrested and flung into King's Royal Prison. I had heard dreadful rumors about what happened to fairies there. Their wings were crushed and removed. I am not sure if I believed it. Could even King August be that cruel?

My musings distracted me. Enough that Withypole was able to seize hold of my shoulders and jerk me to my feet. His grip was strong, and I cried out in protest.

"Ow!"

The fairy ignored me as he scolded, "You need to go home and stop being such a wicked disobedient daughter. Your father never wanted you anywhere near that the aura chamber.'"

"I *know* that but, how do you?"

Withypole avoided my gaze as he muttered, "I was acquainted with Julius Upton. I told you all about that the last time you visited my shop."

"No, you told me next to nothing."

"All you need to know is that your father did not want your aura collected."

"But he never gave me any good reason for that. Just some nonsense about me being too clever to ever get lost."

"Is that what you think that thing does? Records your aura to find silly little lost girls. Bah! They have those great ugly aura cats to hunt down missing people. The king doesn't need some magical mirror for that. That is not the true purpose of the aura chamber."

"Then what is?" I demanded, although I hardly expected him to answer me. Withypole Fugitate had a frustrating tendency to drop intriguing bits of information in my path and then refuse to elaborate.

After chewing on his bottom lip for a few moments, he said, "That aura chamber is the most diabolical device I have ever come across in all my days. It probes a person's mind and heart, draining their very essence. Could you not feel that happening to you?"

"Yes. At least, I think so." I was disturbed to realize that my recollection of what had occurred in the aura chamber was already growing vague.

"That device registers everything about you, all your secrets, your dreams and all your memories."

"All of them?" I faltered. *Even the moment when I had stolen that orb*?

"Everything," Withypole confirmed, much to my dismay. "Every thought, feeling, and memory you had from the moment you were born. Even things that you were too young to recall. It is the perfect way for the king to spy upon his subjects. All that information about you gets distilled into one of those crystal icicles to be deciphered by the king's chief wizard. Sidney Greenleaf!" Withypole all but spat the name.

I rubbed my arms, chilled by the fairy's words. "Is that why Papa didn't want me to enter that chamber? I was only six years old. I had no dark secrets to conceal, except for when Mal and I raided Mrs. Biddlesworth's strawberry patch. What could I have ever known that would make my father so afraid?"

"I don't know," the fairy said.

I was not sure I believed him. I felt more uneasy than ever. "I don't think anyone else in the kingdom is aware of what the aura chamber really does. How did you and my father learn the truth?"

"That is not important. Just stay far away from that aura chamber and the wizard who built it. Good day, Miss Upton."

Withypole turned to go, but this time I was the one who seized his arm.

"Wait a minute."

Withypole cast me an impatient look. "What now? I have explained to you all that I could."

"Not by half, you haven't! There is one important thing you neglected to mention. You took something from that churn that looked like a broken icicle. I am assuming that it contained information about me?"

"Only a little because I stopped the machine."

"And you took it."

He shrugged. "Yes, I did. What of it?"

"What of it! By rights, that shard should belong to me."

"It will be safer in my hands. Trust me."

"You will pardon me if I don't think so." I held out my palm. "Please give me my icicle."

"No."

"Hand it over, Mr. Fugitate. Right now."

"NO!"

"Give it to me or - or else."

"Or else what?"

By this point, we were standing nose to nose, glaring into each other's eyes. I realized that it was rash to threaten someone with the power to render me asleep with a puff of his breath. I have no idea what might have happened next if we had not been interrupted by a discreet cough. Startled, Withypole and I glanced around to see we were no longer alone in the stairwell. At some point, we had been joined by the king's majordomo.

The bland little man's gray uniform made it seem like he could have faded straight out of the walls. How long had he been standing there observing my argument with Withypole? For that matter, what was the king's servant even doing here?

Before I could react to his sudden appearance, the majordomo said, "Pardon me, Miss Upton, but I was passing by on my way to the Registry Office and I could not help noticing you appear to be in some distress. Has this person stolen something from you? Shall I summon the Scutcheons?"

"That will not be necessary," I said. "We were merely having a small disagreement."

The majordomo raised his eyebrows. "Disagreement? This stranger appeared to be menacing you."

"He is not a stranger. He is—" I hesitated. I could not exactly call Withypole a friend of mine. "He is an acquaintance. This is Mr. Fugitate and he is—"

Gone.

I turned to introduce Withypole to the majordomo just in

time to see the last of the fairy's coattails as he disappeared beneath the arch leading back to the garrison. Vanishing with the shard of my memories tucked in his pocket. But which ones? Did Withypole possess the same magical capability as Mercato to read that crystal? What would the fairy do if the icicle revealed I had stolen that orb for Mal? Run straight to Horatio with the information?

Trust me. Withypole had said, but I didn't. I had to get that shard back, but I could not chase after the fairy with the majordomo's suspicious gaze fixed upon me. Even though I was angry and frustrated with Withypole, I did not want to risk the majordomo raising an alarm that might get the fairy thrown into the Dismal Dungeons.

I forced a smile, saying, "It appears Mr. Fugitate was in a hurry to return to work. He keeps a very interesting shop down in Misty Bottoms."

"I see." The majordomo regarded me with a concerned expression. "You will forgive me for saying so, Miss Upton, but this Fugitate strikes me as a disreputable sort. Not at all the kind of person with whom a future princess should consort."

"Since I have no intention of ever becoming a princess, that is not something I have to worry about."

"I'm very disappointed to hear that," the majordomo said.

"Are you? I was under the impression when the prince proposed to me, you did not approve."

"My approval is of no consequence. I am only the king's servant." He folded his hands in front of him, but the humbleness of his pose was belied by something sharp and cunning in his eyes. From the moment I had first met this little man, I had the impression that there was far more to him than was apparent in his meek demeanor.

I should have excused myself to the majordomo and scurried off to find Withypole. But by doing so, I might be throwing away an opportunity to learn more about this enigmatic man who had known my father.

"Only the king's servant?" I repeated. "Somehow, I suspect you are far more than that. More like the king's confidant, the keeper of his secrets."

The majordomo gave a light laugh. "What secrets do you imagine I might be keeping, Miss Upton?"

"The last time we met, you implied that you knew my father well."

The little man nodded politely.

"Mr. Fugitate also appears to have been well acquainted with my father. In fact, the entire kingdom seems to have known Papa far better than I ever did."

"Perhaps not the *entire* kingdom," the majordomo said with a wry smile.

When I glared at him, he apologized. "I am sorry. I did not mean to make light of your feelings. I can tell you are greatly distressed. How can I help?"

"By telling me something about my father. Anything!"

"What would you like to know?"

"The last time I visited his shop, Mr. Fugitate let slip that my father was once an advocate in the royal courts. Is that true?"

"Indeed, it is. Julius Upton was the most brilliant orator I have ever met, fierce and passionate when it came to seeking justice."

"My father? A brilliant orator? Papa was so quiet my step-mother was always astonished when he strung more than two sentences together."

"Julius was very different in his youth, as so many of us were." The majordomo sighed. "Your father was an affable and charming man. Despite their differing views of justice and the law, he and King August were friends."

"Yet now the king blanches at the mere mention of Papa's name. What caused them to fall out with one another? Was it because of some prisoner that my father sought to defend against the king's laws?"

"No, my dear. It was over something that often causes discord between two ardent young men. A beautiful woman."

"My mother," I murmured. I didn't need the majordomo's nod to confirm this. I had already suspected as much. The night I had broken into the king's treasury to steal the orb for Mal, I had discovered a miniature portrait of my mother, tucked in among the hoard of gold coins and glittering jewels.

"So, the king was in love with my mother," I said. "But he could never have married her. She was only the forest warder's daughter."

"Ah, that did not matter to our young king. August would have happily forsworn any wealth he could have gained through an alliance with a princess from another kingdom, the acquisition of new lands or a huge dowry. But the fair Cecily never had eyes for anyone except your father. When she spurned the king's offer of marriage to wed Julius Upton, Cecily crushed the king's spirit forever. August never recovered."

"I rather think that he did," I replied tartly. "He was married three times, wasn't he? All to women of great rank and wealth."

"Obviously, he needed to father an heir."

"Which he accomplished by wedding Princess Caroline of Northland. She gave the king five sons."

The majordomo smiled. "You know your kingdom's history, Miss Upton."

"Indeed, I do. After Queen Caroline died, King August went through two more wives. So, he could not have been too distressed over the loss of my mother."

"But none of the king's marriages ever brought him the happiness and contentment that he craved."

"No, but they certainly brought a great deal of wealth to the royal coffers, didn't they?"

The majordomo's brows rose slightly at my acid tone. I pressed my lips together, knowing I should mind my tongue. Even the slightest criticism of the king could result in heavy fines or imprisonment. But it was difficult to check my irritation at the way the majordomo appeared to blame my mother for the king becoming such a miserable wretch.

The majordomo regarded me gravely. "No doubt like many in our kingdom you think of our king as a tyrant, greedy, unreasonable and cruel. But August was not always thus. He was a kind generous man before your mother broke his heart."

"That is no excuse." I snapped. "Many people are disappointed in their first love." *Myself among them*, I thought. "Not everyone who suffers a broken heart turns nasty and spiteful."

"Some hearts are not as resilient as others. Your own father for instance."

I bridled. "What about my father?"

"After your mother died, I heard that Julius never recovered from her loss. He became a recluse, didn't he? Even though he still had a young daughter who needed him."

I had often resented the fact that my father had become so closed off after my mother died. But I would be cursed before I allowed anyone, especially not this king's toady, to criticize Papa.

"My father did his best to provide and care for me. When he remarried, it wasn't for wealth, but to give me a loving mother and two sisters. There is no comparison between how my father dealt with his grief and the horrid way the king behaved."

"You do not understand the depth of his majesty's feelings, my dear. King August more than loved your mother. He adored her, worshiped the very ground she walked on."

"There is nothing *more* than love. It is our highest and best emotion. Anything beyond that is a selfish obsession. Perhaps the real reason that the king wanted my mother so much is because she was the one thing he could never have, just like—"

I broke off, checking the thought. I had already said enough to be slapped with a hefty fine.

But the majordomo filled in softly, "Like Prince Florian? Alas, I fear that you find our prince a bit less than charming."

A bit? It was all I could do not to snort.

The majordomo went on, "Florian is his father's favorite. I must admit that August has spoiled and indulged his oldest son to the detriment of the prince's character. But if you came to know him better, you would discover that Florian is a very vulnerable young man, very unsure of himself."

The majordomo stepped closer, leaning toward me in a confidential manner. "I am going to tell you something, Miss Upton, which I trust you will allow to go no further. Our king is extremely ill. He may never rise from his bed again. This will devastate Florian because he is very close to his father. The prince might become king before any of us ever expected and I fear that he is not ready."

"Will he ever be?" I retorted.

"He could be, with the right woman at his side."

"Then I hope he finds her."

"I believe the prince already has." The majordomo smiled at me.

"Oh, no, no, no!" I said, flinging up my hands and backing away from him.

"At first, I was not convinced that the prince made the right choice, but now I am." The majordomo stepped closer. "The lad is so smitten with you, Miss Upton. If you break his heart as your mother did with the king, I foresee the same tragic consequences. But if you reward our prince's devotion, you could make such a difference in the kind of king Florian will become."

"That is not fair to put such a burden upon my shoulders."

"You are old enough to realize by now that life is not always fair, my dear."

I took another step back, but the little man cornered me against the wall. "You could be such a great influence upon Florian. Only think about it. All the good that you could do for this kingdom if you were its queen."

The majordomo captured my hands. His skin felt as brittle as paper, cool and dry. But his voice was soft and coaxing. "You would rule Florian's heart and all of Arcady as well, bringing about a golden age that this kingdom has not seen since the days of Queen Anthea the Magnificently Wise. You could be a greater advocate for justice than your father ever was. The power would lie entirely in your hands. *Think about it.*"

He looked deep into my eyes, his own such a pale gray as to be almost colorless. His gaze was mesmerizing except— Did I only imagine it or was there something predatory deep in those misty gray depths?

"Let go of me!" I snatched my hands from his grasp.

He backed off immediately. "Forgive the impertinence, my dear. At times, I am overzealous in my duty to the royal family. A loyalty that would be yours should you become my queen."

"I have already made my feelings quite clear. I will not marry the prince." I was surprised when my voice shook a little, not sounding nearly as firm as I intended.

"Of course," the majordomo said soothingly. "All I ask is that you *think* about all that I have said."

His smile was all that was humble and affable, but I could not even bring myself to bid him farewell as I turned and fled.

Six

I stumbled out of Quad Hall into the main courtyard before I even realized where I was. The majordomo's persuasive voice continued to whisper through my mind.

"You could make such a difference in the kind of king Florian will become. The power would lie entirely in your hands. Think about it."

I did not want to think about it. I shook my head, clearing away the cobwebs the majordomo seemed to have spun through my mind. It was as though the man was some pale little spider seeking to entangle me in his web. A ridiculous image and as I breathed in the fresh air and felt the sunlight warming my skin, the more absurd it seemed.

There was nothing sinister about the majordomo and his attempt to convince me to marry the prince. The servant's motives were either inspired by his loyalty to the royal family or something more self-interested. If the king was as close to death as the majordomo claimed, the servant would need to curry favor with the heir apparent. How better to do so than by winning me for the prince's bride?

It was bad enough that I felt guilty for not securing my family's future. Now the majordomo wanted to place the fate of the entire kingdom upon my shoulders. I would not stand for it. Selfish I might be, but I refused to be coaxed or coerced into sacrificing all hope of finding happiness with Horatio.

Horatio! I crossed beneath the front gate before I realized. I had been so consumed by the agitated thoughts the majordomo had put into my head, I had completely forgotten my original purpose for going to Quad Hall, to find Horatio and steal a few moments in his arms.

I half-turned to go back when I was pounced upon by the Vanderwix girls.

"Ella!" Priscilla emitted one of her ear-splitting squeals. "Here you are at last."

"We have all been waiting for you forever," Ardelia added with a disapproving sniff.

"Waiting for me for what?"

"For the concert in your honor." Priscilla giggled.

"What are you talking about?" I faltered as I noticed the sea of people stretching before me. When I had passed through the square earlier, the place had been nearly empty. Now it was thronged with Midtown folk, merchants, housewives, and laborers, rubbing elbows with more elegantly attired people from the Heights.

Word of my arrival spread quickly, many heads turning in my directions, whispers being exchanged behind hands. I had a very bad feeling about all this as people nearest me began to step back, opening a path, everyone smiling and nodding, some even dipping into obsequious curtsies and bows.

I stood frozen or tried to, but the Vanderwix girls propelled me forward until I arrived within view of the fountain. Four musicians had set up to play, two lutes, a fife and violin, poised in readiness. My heart sank when I saw Prince Florian pacing impatiently in front of the quartet.

I tried to dig in my heels, but it was too late. Florian spotted me and his brow cleared as he flashed me his blinding smile.

He raised his hands in a gesture to silence the crowd before announcing, "My true love has honored me with her presence at last. Now we may commence."

Striding toward me, he seized my hand and dragged me to the front of the crowd.

"Your Highness, what is all this?" I asked.

"This is the day that I finally win your heart."

He shook back his long blonde hair and leapt up, balancing himself on the rim of the fountain. Standing in the shadow of his stone likeness, he beamed down at me. He signaled the musicians to strike up a tune and then drew in a deep breath.

Oh no, I thought, horrified. Please, please don't let him be about to sing to me. But apparently, I was not born under a wishing star, because my fervent prayers were never answered. I cringed as Florian began to belt out an old love ballad.

"*Oh, my beloved. Come into my arms and reward my steadfast heart.*"

My cheeks flamed bright red. Florian's efforts to woo me with poetry had been embarrassing enough, but this serenade made me want to melt into the paving stones.

I had congratulated myself upon my clever plan to avoid Florian in the marketplace, but the prince had outmaneuvered me. It had to have taken him some time to arrange all this, to have gathered such an audience for his latest spectacle. But how did he contrive to make sure I would be present or even know where I was?

Could the prince have someone spying upon me? The thought was deeply disturbing, but something for me to worry about later. Right now, I needed a way to escape. I took a step back but was surrounded by a crowd of young women looking enraptured, although I could not understand why.

Florian's voice was adequate, hitting all the right notes. I might even have considered his singing pleasant if I had not once been wooed in similar fashion by the prince's younger brother, Ryland.

I did not wish to remember, but my mind turned unwillingly back to that day I had first seen Ryland performing in the square. He had been attired in his humble disguise as Harper, a strolling minstrel, with only his lute to accompany him. But he wouldn't have even needed that. The magic was in Ryland's voice, golden tones that the fairies would have envied him. His singing had vibrated with passion, stirring the soul, and stealing my heart. Ryland's eyes had met mine across the square, sweeping us both into a magical world where his song was for me alone.

I was surprised when the memory caused a lump to form in my throat. I believed myself long over any feelings I had ever entertained for Ryland. But my eyes stung with tears for the trusting girl I had once been, with her dreams of a love that had proved as ephemeral as mist.

I wiped the moisture from my eyes, an unfortunate gesture because Florian noticed. A look of triumph stole over his face, and he sang with more verve. Some of the young ladies near me, including Priscilla, looked ready to swoon.

I hoped she would not because of the Scutcheons threading through the crowd. The garrison soldiers must have been assigned to keep order and protect the prince from any dire threats such as fainting ladies.

Standing at the edge of the crowd, I spotted Commander Crushington. Horatio stood almost a head taller than anyone else, making it easy for his gaze to meet mine. I longed to send him a pleading glance, begging him to rescue me. But I knew he could not intervene, without offending the prince and putting himself in jeopardy. Yet I did not want Horatio to think I was enjoying this. I conveyed my feelings by shrugging and rolling my eyes. A slight smile touched Horatio's lips.

I had to bite back a smile lest the prince see. I counted the moments until this ordeal would end and I could slip away from Florian and make my way to Horatio's side.

But when the prince's song finished, he was greeted with such enthusiastic applause, he launched immediately into another. The majordomo's persuasive voice whispered through my mind again, *"If you came to know him better, you would discover that Florian is a very vulnerable young man, so unsure of himself."*

But when I looked at the prince, all I could see was his arrogance and vanity. My hands twitched. If he began one more song, it would be difficult to quell the impulse to push him into the fountain.

"I know what you are thinking, Ella," someone murmured in my ear. "Much as I sympathize with the urge, you had better restrain yourself." The amused voice sounded remarkably like Mal.

Startled, I twisted around to discover an old man had worked his way to stand behind me. He leaned upon a gnarled cane, his long gray hair spilling over the shoulders of his woolen brown tunic, the kind that hermits wore. A full, bushy beard obscured most of his features. Even his brows were thick and gray, but beneath them, Malcolm Hawkridge's roguish eyes twinkled at me. My heart leapt, torn between joy and alarm at the sight of him.

"Mal!" I gasped. "Are you mad? What are you doing here?"

"I'm glad to see you, too," he replied wryly.

"Of course, I am glad to see you. I've missed you dreadfully, but—" I stole a nervous look around. Fortunately, everyone's attention, including Horatio's, appeared to be focused on the prince.

"You should not be here," I muttered to Mal. "Do you have any idea of the number of disgruntled women who want to see you tarred and feathered?"

"Relax, Ella. My own grandmother would never have recognized me in this disguise."

"I hope you have not been experimenting with hair potions again because that didn't turn out so well last time."

Mal had resorted to magic to cure his prematurely receding hairline. As with most of Mal's attempts at magic, it had gone awry. His hair had fallen out in tufts, rendering him completely bald.

Mal scowled at the reminder. "No, it is only a wig and false beard but it's very effective, don't you think?"

"As long as no one takes a good look at your hands," I pointed out. Instead of the wrinkled skin of an old man, Mal's strong, tanned fingers revealed his true age, a detail Mal had overlooked when planning his disguise.

Mal swore, tucking his hands out of sight, but not before I glimpsed a series of angry red scratches.

"What happened to your wrist?" I asked. "Did some of your unhappy customers catch up with you?"

Mal grimaced, "No, that was Delphine. I caught her trying to sneak into my bed again, disguised as Ebony. I picked her up by the scruff of her neck and told her I was wise to her tricks. I was starting to feel foolish, scolding a cat and wondering if you were mistaken about her ability to transform. But then she turned into a hissing, spitting fury and scratched the frap out of me. As if that wasn't bad enough, she coughed up a hairball on my grandmother's best quilt."

"Cats are known to do that."

"She did that after she turned back into Delphine." Mal shuddered. "It was truly disgusting."

I clapped a hand to my mouth to smother my mirth.

Mal shot me a disgruntled look. "Oh, yes, it is all right for you to be amused. You were not the one with a furious, naked witch hocking up slimy balls of fur in your bedchamber. I wished that she had stayed a cat."

A laugh escaped me. I couldn't help it. Some of the ladies shot me indignant looks and Ardelia Vanderwix shushed me. My pleasure in seeing Mal had caused me to become reckless. I realized our conversation was attracting attention. Florian was too wrapped up in his performance to notice, but Horatio stared in my direction, a slight frown creasing his brow.

I focused my attention on Florian. Out of the side of my mouth, I said to Mal, "Are you aware Commander Crushington has been looking for you?"

"Why? Has our fierce commander been overwhelmed by women demanding my head?"

"No doubt he has been, but he needs to speak to you about something far more serious. Someone broke into Quad Hall at midnight during the Royal Ball. The thief made off with a sack full of aura crystals."

"I heard rumors about that. So what?"

"The commander suspects that you were somehow involved."

Mal gave a snort of suppressed laughter. "You know where I was at midnight. I am a clever fellow but not clever enough to be in two places at once."

"Then it would be best if you met with the commander to allay his suspicions."

"Are you mad? Do you want to see me chained up in the Dismal Dungeons?"

"It would not come to that. Commander Crushington told me he only wants to question you."

"Oh, aye, with a barbed whip applied to my back and a hot spike shoved up my arse."

"Horatio would never do anything like that. He is a fair—"

"*Horatio?*" Mal interrupted. "You are calling him Horatio now?" He leaned forward so he could peer into my face. "Never tell me you have been kissing and flirting with The Crusher again."

Shrinking away from him, I tried not to blush. I dreaded telling Mal that my feelings for Horatio had deepened well beyond flirting. I knew Mal was not going to take it well, but now was not the time to get into all of that.

"Horatio Crushington has been kind to my family," I said.

"He helped me to save Amy from disgrace the night of the ball, so I consider him to be a friend."

"A friend! He's a frapping Scutcheon Commander, Ella."

"But he is not a swaggering bully like some of the others. Horatio is an honorable man."

"Which makes him even worse to deal with because he is not susceptible to an honest bribe. He is rigid and duty bound when it comes to upholding the most petty and unreasonable laws. Crushington is the king's loyal henchmen through and through and you are a fool if you ever let yourself believe otherwise."

Our voices had become heated, drawing attention to us again. We were shushed on all sides. Florian looked annoyed by the disturbance, but he only sang louder. Horatio, on the other hand, had stiffened to attention and was slowly making his way in our direction. Mal noticed this as well.

"Frap!" He growled. "I must get out of here. We will continue this discussion later."

"Fine!" I snapped. "I will meet you at the back of your shop."

"No, you need to stay out of the Bottoms. Delphine is furious with you, too."

"I know that. I crossed paths with her when I was looking for you and she threatened to curse me with boils or a mustache."

"Don't worry about that. She'd have to force a potion down your throat. I am certain she can't just hurl curses out of thin air."

"Just like you were certain that the prince would never remember me from the ball. Pardon me if I am not reassured." I cut off the rest of my retort. Horatio was maneuvering his way closer, with a grim look on his face.

"I'll come to you soon," Mal whispered in my ear.

He squeezed my hand before trying to melt into the crowd, but we were hemmed in on all sides. Unless Mal wanted to draw more attention by shoving people out of the way, his progress was slow.

Horatio however approached at an alarming rate. He barked out a terse command. "Out of the way!"

The crowd fell back clearing a path for him. To make matters worse, someone else in the crowd must have recognized Mal. A shrill voice shouted. "Thief! Stop that villain."

The prince's song faltered to silence and the musicians cut off in mid-note. Confusion and consternation erupted through the crowd. Some of the ladies began to shriek.

I could not see if Mal had managed to get away, but Horatio was closing in fast.

After an agony of indecision, I did the only thing I could. I hurled myself at Horatio, flinging my arms about his neck. It was like colliding with a stone wall. I stumbled and would have fallen if Horatio had not caught me. He held me for a moment and our eyes met, mine apologetic, his stern and accusing.

Before Horatio could set me out of his way, the prince descended upon us shouting, "What do you think you are doing, Commander? Unhand my beloved at once."

Florian was flushed with anger, but Horatio ignored him as he scanned the crowd, looking for Mal. To my relief, there was no sign of my friend.

I turned to the prince, anxious to defuse his fury with Horatio.

"This was entirely my fault," I said. "I stumbled into the commander's way."

"Only because the man was charging like a bee stung bull. What is the meaning of this commander? How dare you interrupt my performance!"

I watched Horatio struggle to swallow his frustration at Mal's escape. He bowed to the prince.

"Forgive me Your Highness. I believed I saw a notorious criminal lurking in the crowd."

"Here is the villain right here!" A voice bellowed, the same shrill one I had heard earlier.

My heart skipped a beat. Had Mal not managed to get away

after all? I whirled about as a huge man struggled through the crowd. Arno Warrington, wealthy owner of the Midtown counting house was a respected Midtown citizen who had an unfortunately high-pitched voice for such a big man.

People scrambled out of the way as Warrington pushed his way forward, dragging someone in his wake. But it was not Mal who struggled in the man's meaty clutches, only a small boy.

Warrington tried to say something to Horatio, but the excitement and curiosity of the crowd had risen to a fever pitch.

"Silence!" Horatio called out with an unmistakable ring of authority that reduced the hubbub to a murmur.

As soon as Warrington could make himself heard, he said, "Commander, I caught this young rogue picking pockets."

"Did not!" the boy cried, kicking out and struggling in a futile effort to be free. Warrington gripped the child by one arm, nearly yanking him off his feet. Women near them shrank away as though the man dangled some sort of vermin by the tail.

"Lemme go, you big oaf!" the boy shouted. Beneath his bravado, I detected the fear in his voice.

I gasped as I recognized a familiar mop of brown hair, scrawny legs poking out from his coarse woolen breeches. It was the same lad that Mal had employed to deliver my earrings when he had redeemed them from Withypole. The boy remembered me as well.

He directed pleading eyes toward me. "Miss Ella! Tell them. You know me. I'm no thief."

"Silence. You little liar," the prince snarled. "How would my beloved be acquainted with such a grubby—"

"But I do know him." I smiled encouragingly at the boy. "His name is Tom Piper, and he is a young man of great enterprise."

Warrington snorted. "For stealing."

"I didn't steal nothin'!"

"Impudent whelp! I caught you with your hand in my pocket." Warrington gave Tom a rough shake. When the boy cried out in pain, Horatio ordered the big man to release his grip.

Keeping a firm hold on the boy's shoulders, Horatio hunkered down beside him. If I had to guess Tom's age, I would have said somewhere around ten years, although there was a shrewdness in his eyes that made him seem far older.

Confronted by the Commander of the Midtown Garrison and with the prince glaring down at him, any other boy would have been shaking with terror. Although Tom's lower lip quivered, he met Horatio's stern gaze with defiance.

"If you were not stealing, what were you doing, Tom?" Horatio asked.

"Passin' out my cards. I tried to get the fat feller's attention, but he paid no 'tention so I just snuck one into his pocket. Tell him to look. He'll find it."

Keeping one hand on the boy's shoulder, Horatio straightened and addressed the counting house proprietor. "Mr. Warrington, if you will oblige us?"

"He certainly will not!" Florian spluttered. "Of all the outrageous—"

"Your Highness, please. It will be the quickest way of clearing up this matter."

The prince fumed and Warrington rolled his eyes, but he complied with Horatio's request. The man delved impatiently inside the inner pocket of his brocade frock coat. His eyes widened with surprise as he produced a slightly wrinkled and grubby square of paper. He frowned as he examined it and suddenly his huge shoulders shook with laughter.

Warrington handed the card over to the commander. By standing on tiptoe and craning my neck, I was able to make out the crudely lettered words.

Tom Piper. Man of busYness.

Errands Run, Packeges Deelivered.

No service too big or small. Reasonable rats.

Utmost diskretion.

Horatio's lips twitched as he read the card out loud. Ripples of laughter spread through the crowd. The only ones who did not look amused were the prince and Tom who appeared indignant that his card would be a subject for mirth.

Still chuckling, the portly Warrington accorded Tom a mock bow. "I do beg your pardon, Mr. Piper. I am sorry for the misunderstanding."

His wounded pride mollified by the man's apology, Tom shrugged, "'s all right, mister."

"This is far from all right," Florian snapped. "Commander, I want this young villain clapped in irons."

"But Tom has done nothing wrong," I protested.

"He's a public nuisance, creating a disturbance and disrupting my performance."

"Oughta give me a medal for that," Tom grumbled, but Horatio quickly clapped a hand over his mouth before the prince could hear him.

Florian continued to grouse. "Perhaps a good thrashing and a day confined in the yoke of shame will teach the whelp some manners."

"Oh, no! Please, Your Highness, the boy meant no harm." I rested my hand on Florian's sleeve and gazed up at him. "Surely he does not need to be dealt with so harshly."

Florian's mouth set in a mulish line, but when he glanced down at me, something in his expression softened. "It would please you if I pardoned the boy?"

"It would indeed,"

"But someone must pay his fine."

"How much would that be?" I asked anxiously, aware of how little coin I had in my purse.

Florian's lips curved into a sly smile. "The merest trifle. Just a kiss."

"I ain't kissin' you!" Tom said, producing another spate of amusement from the crowd. Even Florian gave a reluctant smile.

"Not you, imp. The lady!" The prince took my hand in his

and smiled at me expectantly. I felt my cheeks heat, aware of all those eyes trained upon me, everyone waiting to see what I would do. I stole an uneasy look at Horatio and sensed the tension in him. His jaw was locked at a rigid angle, his hand clenched at his side.

How could I kiss the prince under Horatio's very nose? And yet how could I not, I thought as my gaze shifted to Tom and imagined the lash of a birch rod against his thin backside. Surely Horatio must understand.

Tipping my face up toward Florian, I braced myself for another of his sloppy kisses. To my surprise, Florian pressed his lips to mine in a way that was respectful, almost tender. The kiss lasted far longer than I would have wished, but never had the prince embraced me so gently.

The crowd erupted into applause. When our lips parted, the prince was beaming at me. I risked a glance at Horatio, fearing to see the anger in his eyes. His expression had hardened into a mask of stone.

Florian grinned and reached down to tousle Tom's hair. Sensing his deliverance was at hand, Tom bore the patronizing gesture with good grace.

"Well, young man, this is indeed your lucky day," Florian said. "You are free to go."

"Thanks, Your Highness."

The boy wriggled out of Horatio's grip, but Horatio immediately collared him.

"Not so fast, Mr. Piper."

The prince frowned. "What are you doing, Commander? I have pardoned the boy. Release him at once."

"I am afraid I cannot do that."

"I gave you an order."

"With all due respect, Your Highness, I am pledged to uphold your father's laws. Only he can issue a pardon."

Horatio executed a stiff bow and dragged the boy away,

heading back to Quad Hall. Tom did not try to resist. The lad looked stunned by Horatio's actions, and he was not the only one.

The prince's jaw dropped as though he could not believe anyone, even a Scutcheon commander would dare defy him. I was likewise gaping in disbelief. Horatio could be stern about his sense of duty, but he could have easily acceded to the prince and let the boy go. Was Horatio jealous about the kiss and taking his anger out on poor Tom? That was not at all like the good and decent man I knew.

Angry mutterings spread through the crowd. As a Scutcheon Commander, Horatio was not exactly a popular person in Midtown, but he had always been accorded a great deal of respect. Now a few even dared to boo as he hauled Tom through the Quad Hall gate, while the prince was being heaped with praise for his kindness to the lad. Everyone but me seemed to have forgotten it was Florian who had ordered the boy arrested in the first place.

I felt as though I had been tossed into the middle of some mad play where everyone had their parts all wrong, Florian appearing as the hero while Horatio transformed into a villain.

The prince was performing his part nobly, tossing back his hair and shaking his fist in the air while he railed against Horatio. "What a hard-hearted wretch. Arresting a poor unfortunate little waif! I vow that when I become king, I will remove that arrogant commander from his post and send him crawling off to patrol the swamps."

Florian's speech was greeted with applause. Although I was dismayed by Horatio's actions, I leapt to his defense.

"Please, Your Highness," I cried. "I am sure Commander Crushington meant no disrespect. I daresay he was only trying to do his duty. He is a very loyal servant of the crown and... " I trailed off as I realized my defense of Horatio was not playing well with the prince. Florian regarded me with a mighty scowl.

I have never been good at pandering to anyone's vanity, but I tried to assume a flattering smile. "Commander Crushington was vexed with the boy for interrupting your performance. We all enjoyed your singing so much. Perhaps young Mr. Piper does need to be taught a lesson, but I am grateful to you for being so magnanimous to him."

The ire faded from Florian's eyes. He was quick to seize the advantage, stealing his arms about my waist.

"Grateful enough to marry me?" he murmured.

"Um – no."

My response elicited gasps of disbelief and disapproval from the crowd, especially the ladies.

"What is wrong with that girl?" one exclaimed.

"I tried to tell all of you," Ardelia Vanderwix spoke up. "She is completely mad. She actually enjoys *running.*"

I expected Florian to be vexed as well, but he grinned. "Still being coy, Ella? And yet you cannot deny I have been making inroads upon your heart."

No, not so much as a single paving stone, I could have assured him.

"That was quite an enthusiastic kiss you gave me." He smirked.

I grimaced. What the prince mistook for enthusiasm had merely been relief that no tongues had been involved.

"Perhaps another kiss and a few more love songs and you will be mine."

"No!" I braced my hands against his chest as he tried to draw me closer. "Surely Your Highness must have more important things to do than sing to me all afternoon."

"No, my entire day, indeed my entire life is at your disposal."

His words elicited sighs from the women close enough to hear.

Florian bent lower. He clearly meant to kiss me again in front of half of Midtown. From the ardor in his gaze, I feared there would be tongue this time.

Squirming to get free, I blurted out, "But what about your father?"

I flung out the words in sheer desperation, not expecting them to have any effect. But Florian halted mid-pucker. He drew back, frowning.

"What about my father?"

"I heard that the king is very ill." Aware that these were not tidings the palace wanted bruited about, I lowered my voice to a whisper. "Perhaps even dying?"

"Who told you that?"

"The king's own majordomo."

"That man is entirely mistaken! My father is not dying, but yes, I do admit he is quite ill."

"Then should you not be with him?"

I sensed this was not a subject Florian cared to discuss. His hands dropped from my waist, and he averted his gaze.

"Perhaps I should be at his bedside," the prince said. "But I find it unbearable seeing him so weak and ill. I may have always been my father's favorite, but we do not get along that well. I have no idea what to do or say to bring him comfort."

Florian blinked hard as though trying to hold back tears. I believed it to be the first genuine emotion I had ever seen in the man.

I pressed his hand gently. "It might bring the king comfort just to have you there. I realize it is hard, but if you do not spend time with him now, you will regret it. Believe me, I know. I often quarreled with my own father. When I wanted to tell him how sorry I was, it was too late. He died without ever hearing how much I loved him."

Florian fell silent. I could not guess what he was thinking. At last, he said. "You are right, Ella. I shall be guided by your wise counsel and go to my father at once."

The prince raised my hand to his lips. "Until tomorrow then, my beloved."

As Florian strode away from me, I was aware of the bewilderment spreading through the crowd. Our conversation about the king had been too low to be overheard. No doubt that everyone watching us had surmised our intimate whispering to be romantic in nature. Our eager audience had probably expected to hear that the prince had prevailed and there would be an announcement of our forthcoming wedding.

There was a sense of disappointment in the air when the prince mounted his horse and rode away. As the crowd dispersed, I was aware of the annoyed and indignant looks being cast my way. I paid them little heed, too busy dealing with my own feelings, relief that Florian had left, astonishment that I had been able to persuade him to do so.

Once more the majordomo's words came back to haunt me. *You could be such a great influence upon Florian. Only think about it. All the good that you could do for this kingdom.*

I still did not want to believe that was true. It would only make me feel guilty for not marrying the prince.

Seven

By the time I was able to return to Quad Hall, Horatio and his unfortunate young captive were nowhere in sight. I had no idea how prisoners were processed. I assumed there must be some sort of official documentation required.

But perhaps all Horatio needed to do was unlock a cell and fling Tom inside. I found it painful to imagine Horatio treating a child so harshly.

Crushington is the king's loyal henchmen through and through and you are a fool if you ever let yourself believe otherwise. Mal's warning resurfaced in my mind.

I banished that disturbing thought as I directed my footsteps toward the garrison headquarters and the local gaol. Happily, up until this point in my life, I had never had any personal acquaintance with this grim facility. But like most Midtown citizens, I was all too aware of the massive iron doorway that led to the cells.

No guards were posted because the door could not be opened from the outside. Anyone needing admittance had to summon the warder by tugging on a heavy bell rope.

I approached the forbidding portal, wiping my hands on my skirt. There is something about a gaol that causes even the most innocent person to sweat, especially in our kingdom where it was so easy to run afoul of the law.

I gave the rope a light tug. Annoyed by my own timidity, I yanked harder. I heard a loud peal resounding on the other side of the door. A moment later, a panel slid back. The face of a grizzled old Scutcheon glared at me through the grate.

"Who goes there?" he barked.

"Um… me. Ella Upton." I sketched an awkward curtsy then felt foolish for doing so. "Are you the warder?"

"No, I am the sweet dreams wishing fairy. Of course, I am the warder, you silly girl. Master Sergeant Gravel. Now what do you want?"

"I have come to inquire about one of your prisoners."

"Well, you can't."

"Why not? Is there some sort of protocol I need to follow?"

"You can't because there's no one here."

"The boy would have been admitted a little while ago," I insisted. "I saw Commander Crushington arrest him with my own eyes. The lad's name is Tom Piper."

"And I'm telling you there are no Toms here. No Dicks or Harrys either. Just me and the spiders. I've been a proud Scutcheon for nigh on fifty years, even fought in the Border Wars. Been the Master Warder of this gaol for the last decade and now how do I spend most of my time? Wielding a broom and sweeping out empty cells. Under our old commander—"

"That will do, Master Sergeant," Horatio's stern voice cut him off.

Coming upon us so unexpectedly, the commander startled both me and Sergeant Gravel.

"Aye, Commander," the old man muttered, but I could hear Gravel still grumbling as he closed the panel.

I turned to face Horatio and flinched when I saw his expression, his mouth set in a grim line, his eyes icy.

"Is there something I can help you with, Miss Upton?"

Miss Upton?

I swallowed, concealing my dismay. "I just wanted to know what happened to Tom Piper. The warder says all the cells are empty."

"That's right. I have the boy chained in my private dungeon."

"What! You told me you didn't have a dungeon."

"I took your advice and built one."

"I was only jesting and how could you manage to build one so quickly?"

"For frap's sake, Ella!" Horatio's cold façade cracked, revealing his exasperation with me. "Did you really think I was going to lock that boy up? I was tempted to, especially when I could not get him to confess what he had done. Although it was against my better judgment, I gave him a stern lecture and sent him on his way."

My relief was mixed with remorse for having misjudged Horatio so badly. "I am sorry if I misunderstood. But when you hauled Tom away, you looked so angry. You still do. What did you expect him to confess? Do you think he really was picking pockets?"

"No. From what I know of young Mr. Piper, he is a canny lad, too clever to risk putting his hand into a wealthy citizen's pocket for any reason. The disturbance he created struck me as being rather too convenient. I suspected he might have been paid to cause an uproar should it become necessary."

"Necessary for what?" I asked but I feared I already knew the answer.

"Necessary to facilitate the escape of a certain *old man.*" Horatio said, laying sarcastic emphasis on the last two words. Before I could reply, he added, "Since you all but tackled me to make sure your good friend Hawkridge got away, please don't insult me by pretending you don't know what I am talking about."

"I wasn't going to," I replied. "But I am sure you are wrong about Mal paying Tom to create a distraction. Mal would never put the boy at such risk."

"Why not? Hawkridge certainly never seems to mind risking you."

"Mal does not *risk* me." I protested. "I am quite capable of making my own choices."

"You tend to make some cursed bad ones where that man is concerned."

I flinched beneath Horatio's steely gaze, that stolen orb weighing upon my mind. But the more time that passed since the ball, the more I began to believe that Mal and I had gotten away with the theft. Since by rights that orb did belong to Mal, I did not regret what I had done.

"If Hawkridge is as honorable as you claim, why is he skulking around in disguise to avoid me?" Horatio demanded.

"Mal is mostly trying to avoid all those women dissatisfied with his love potion. He is aware that you want to ask questions about the break-in at the Aura Chamber. I advised him to come and see you to clear his name, but he doesn't trust you."

"Evidently, neither do you. Now if you will excuse me, I have an important matter to attend." Horatio executed a curt bow. As he stalked away from me, I hugged myself, feeling miserable.

I wanted to follow him, but I hesitated. Mal's wise old grandmother had once advised me, "*When your man is in a rage, my dear, best leave him alone to cool down. No good ever comes from trying to scold or cajole him out of his temper fit.*"

Granny Hawkridge would have good cause to know, her husband being of an irascible nature. But when Horatio had walked away from me, I had glimpsed a flash of pain beneath his anger. I had obviously hurt him deeply and I could not let matters rest thus between us.

I hurried after him out the door leading to the yard behind Quad Hall. His long legs propelled him far quicker than I could move, hampered by my petticoats. By the time I closed the distance between us, Horatio had already vanished inside the stables.

The Midtown Garrison was not a mounted unit like the

Heights Scutcheons or the palace guards. Our local stable was a low-slung building, capable of housing no more than four horses. It was not difficult to find Horatio once I slipped inside the barn. The stable might have been small, but it was a well-kept facility, smelling of fresh hay and horse.

All the stalls were empty except for the largest one which held Horatio's magnificent roan gelding. He leaned into the stall, stroking the horse's mane and it responded by lipping playfully at his sleeve. Horatio had a magical way with horses, and I had had many occasions to observe the bond between him and the gelding appropriately named Loyal.

Loyal was responsive to Horatio's slightest command as if the two of them thought and moved as one. The gelding appeared to sense its master's dark mood and sought to comfort him. As Horatio rested his brow against Loyal's neck, the horse nuzzled Horatio and emitted a low whickering. I imagined the gelding was trying to tell him that women were more trouble than they were worth and the only one a man could really depend upon was his horse.

I felt oddly intrusive and might have retreated but Loyal detected my presence, pricking his ears. Horatio noticed my approach as well but chose to ignore me. I ventured close enough to rest my hand against his back.

"I am sorry," I murmured.

For a moment Horatio remained rigid beneath my touch and then his shoulders relaxed. When he came about to face me, there was no lingering anger in his eyes, only a deep sadness.

"I am sorry, too," he said, gathering me into his arms. I buried my face against his chest and felt him brush a kiss against my hair.

"Oh, Ella," he groaned. "Why could you not have even a little bit of faith in me? Why did you feel that you had to kiss that prince to save Tom? You should know me well enough not to imagine I would be capable of so harshly punishing a child. Do I seem like such an ogre to you?"

"No, of course not," I said, drawing away from him. "But to be fair, Horatio, how many times have you told me you have sworn an unbreakable oath to enforce the king's laws?"

I did not want to renew the discord between us, but I could not help reminding him. "It was only a month ago that I watched you arrest that poor farmer whose only crime was trying to evade that ridiculous tax on working dogs."

"I kept Farmer Gray locked up for one night in gaol and let him off with a light fine. No matter how much I disagree with many of the king's laws, I must be seen to enforce them, or the king will appoint someone who will. Do you wish to see me dismissed from my post?"

I shook my head, but I could not help thinking how much less complicated our romance would be if Horatio were not a Scutcheon commander. "I understand that your position means everything to you."

"Hardly *everything*," Horatio said, caressing my cheek. "I admit it is important to me. You know my background, Ella. Becoming commander of the Midtown Garrison is no small achievement for someone who spent their early years in the Foundling Asylum. If I had not had the good fortune to be adopted by the Crushingtons, who knows where I would be? Likely slaving away in the silver mines.

"There are not many people who would have risked accepting a scruffy boy of unknown ancestry and raising him as their own. I was determined to prove myself worthy to be their son. I only wish they had lived long enough to see me attain the rank of commander. My father especially would have been so proud, but sometimes... " Horatio trailed off, lapsing into a troubled silence.

He moved away from Loyal's stall and sank down upon one of the tack benches. I settled myself beside him.

"Sometimes?" I prodded gently.

"Sometimes I wish I had not been so ambitious. When I first came here, I was bursting with enthusiasm to make Midtown the safest part of the kingdom, free from all lawlessness and disorder. I never imagined that would involve arresting downtrodden farmers and impudent small boys. Perhaps I would have been better off staying out of the military. It was certainly not what I dreamed of when I was a foundling lad."

I tucked my hand around Horatio's arm and rested my head against his shoulder. "I remember. You told me all you desired was to become a stable hand so you could always be near horses."

Horatio entwined his fingers through mine. "I might have been happier leading such a simple life if I had never come here to Midtown."

I lifted my head to regard him with consternation. "And never met me?"

He smiled sadly. "No, I can never regret that. I love you, Ella. I always will even if I do not foresee a happy ending to our story."

"We *will* be happy," I insisted. "I know right now the prince is being a royal pain. Who would have ever imagined Florian could be so persistent?"

Horatio stopped my protestations with a light kiss. "My dear, you know as well as I, that the prince is not our real problem."

I wanted to deny it, but I couldn't.

"Mal." I sighed.

"Mal," Horatio agreed grimly.

I slumped against his shoulder, and he wrapped his arms around me, resting his chin atop my head. "You never asked me how I recognized Hawkridge today."

"With everything happening so fast, I didn't think about it. Mal's disguise was quite good. I hardly recognized him myself, so, how did you?"

"It was you who gave him away."

"Me?" I shifted my head so I could look up at him in puzzlement.

"The expression on your face," Horatio said. "From the first day that I arrived in Midtown, I noticed you, Ella, though I don't think you ever looked twice at me. You were always so intent upon getting on with your marketing. You often seemed tired, burdened with cares, but not when I saw you with Hawkridge. You looked happy and relaxed. You smiled and laughed more.

"Your face lights up whenever that man is around," he added wistfully. "And it makes me jealous in a way that the prince never could."

"Silly!" I gave a lock of Horatio's hair a playful tug. "You needn't be jealous, just because Mal knows how to amuse me. We have been friends since we were children."

"Forgive me, but it is a friendship I don't understand. Hawkridge strikes me as being an unconscionable scoundrel, a man who has no regard for anyone or anything beyond his own selfish interests."

"That is because you don't know him!" I pulled out of Horatio's arms and stood up. My hands fluttered in agitated gestures as I struggled for a way to explain the complicated man that was my friend Malcolm Hawkridge.

"I admit that Mal can be reckless and exasperating. He has little respect for the law and no faith in the king's justice. There have been many times I have wanted to strangle him myself. But he can also be tender-hearted and compassionate, although he would scoff and jest and never admit it, even to me.

"He does what he can to help his neighbors in Misty Bottoms. Most of them are too poor to afford a doctor, but Mal freely distributes his herbal potions. He would make an inept wizard, but he is a very skilled apothecary."

"If he would confine his activities to dispensing medicine, I would have no problem with him," Horatio said.

"Then he wouldn't be Mal," I said ruefully. "Despite his roguish ways, he is the most loyal friend I have ever had. I was very young when I lost my mother and I felt as though I had lost my father as well because Papa was consumed with grief. Mal was only a boy, not much older than me. But he was the one who held me and comforted me when I cried.

"My stepmother never liked Mal either. She always accused him of leading me into trouble when we were children. But Mal never led me anywhere. We were equal partners in mischief. I was the one who thought it was a good idea to climb old Farmer Brimstead's fence and steal one of his pumpkins. I never dreamed he'd send his hunting spaniel chasing after me. I was sure that dog was going to tear my leg off, but Mal leaped in between us."

I recalled how we had managed to get away from the dog, but not before Mal had been savagely bitten. I had tried to bind the wound with my handkerchief, but the blood had soaked through the linen. Mal had leaned on me, limping as we headed for home, me sobbing and scolding all the way.

"*You big stupid idiot. Why did you have to do that?*"

"*Oh, stop blubbering and making such a fuss, Ella. I am not dying.*"

"*No, but you will have to get stitches and you'll have a wicked scar and it is all my fault.*"

"*But that scar will look so much better on me than you.*" Mal grinned through his pain. "*Think of all the girls I'll impress. I'll tell them I got it fighting pirates.*"

I chuckled as I related the incident to Horatio, but he only regarded me somberly. I held out my hands in a pleading gesture. "Don't you see? Mal is like the brother I never had."

Horatio stood and gathered my hands into his. "So you keep telling me, but *only* a brother, Ella? I wonder if you truly know your own heart."

"Certainly, I do. I will always care deeply for Mal. He is my dearest friend, but you are the man that I want. I - I love you." I stammered.

I had often implied as much, but I realized this was the first time I had ever dared speak those three simple words aloud. Not since Prince Ryland had broken my heart and those words had lost all meaning for me until now.

"I love you," I repeated more softly, almost wonderingly.

"And I will love you until my dying breath, but that may not be enough. I wish I could accept your view of Hawkridge. But I still suspect he is behind the vandalism of the Aura Chamber and it is part of a plot to overthrow the king. I am going to have to order posters put up, offering a reward for any information regarding the whereabouts of Malcolm Hawkridge."

"Please, don't do that," I begged. "You will make Mal a wanted man through all of Arcady."

"I don't want to, but he has left me no choice. I must solve the Aura Chamber vandalism and discover who is behind this League of the Missing Heir or I may be broken in rank and sent to patrol the northern borders."

Horatio regarded me gravely. "The North is a harsh and dangerous region. No place for a man to bring a wife and family. I could never ask you to—"

He broke off, swallowing the rest of his words, but I understood him well enough.

"We would be parted forever," he said.

"No," I cried. I could not allow such a thing to happen anymore than I could allow Mal to be arrested. I wracked my brain, seeking some solution to this dilemma. "What if I could find Mal and persuade him to help you?

"Hawkridge help *me?*" Horatio made no effort to conceal his skepticism. "How?"

"Mal may have resources that you don't have." I bit my lip, trying to find a way to explain how well-connected Mal was with the less reputable citizenry of Arcady. A way that would not confirm Horatio's worst suspicions of my friend.

"Mal lives in Misty Bottoms. He knows the area far better than you ever could and he is clever. I am sure he could solve this mystery for you."

"Why would he do that?"

"Because Mal would do anything for me, so please." I draped my arms around Horatio's neck. "Just give me a little more time."

Horatio heaved a deep sigh, but he was not proof against my pleading gaze. "Very well. I will hold off putting up the posters for another day or so."

"Thank you." I began, but Horatio interrupted, admonishing me. "But if I do not hear from you or Hawkridge soon—"

"You will. I promise I will fetch Mal to you myself and we will prove his innocence by revealing the real culprit."

I tightened my arms about him, kissing away his doubting frown. Horatio gathered me close, returning my kiss with a fervor that left me breathless, making me forget everything, even the rash promise I had no idea how I was going to keep.

Eight

I had only three goals when I set out that morning: avoid Florian, do some marketing and steal a few kisses from Horatio. Instead, I had been subjected to an embarrassing serenade, nearly witnessed my closest friend getting arrested and had a shard of my aura snatched by a belligerent fairy.

As for Horatio, yes, I had had my kiss, but it might well be the last embrace I would ever have from him unless I could find a way to keep my promise about Mal. Little wonder that I felt bludgeoned as I trudged homeward.

I was unlatching my gate before I realized I had completely forgotten the marketing, but I lacked the stamina to return to the shops.

"Looks like it will have to be turnip stew for dinner. Again." I muttered as I let myself in the front door. I dreaded the barrage of dismay I would receive from my family over this menu. No doubt Em would point out to me we would all be dining on golden plates at the palace by now if only I would stop being so obstinate about marrying Florian.

Fortunately, I did not have to deal with my stepmother. Em was taking a nap, perhaps worn out from the excitement of the visit from her former beau. I just hoped it had not been *too* exciting and my stepsisters had succeeded in playing chaperone.

Amy was likewise up in her bedchamber, perhaps blissfully dreaming of the perfidious young prince who was never going to come for her. The only one awake was Netta, plucking out melancholy tunes on her harp in the parlor.

I left her to her music, refusing her offers to help me with preparing supper. Netta was grace personified when playing her harp, but a bit of a disaster when in the kitchen. We could not afford anymore broken crockery.

However, in my current distracted state, I was as much of a danger to our dishes as Netta, to say nothing of my fingers as I pared the turnips. I kept wracking my brain for some way to prove Mal innocent of the Aura Chamber theft. Alas, the best and most direct way of doing that was lost to me. I should have confessed to Horatio a long time ago about the stolen orb. Maybe he would have understood. Now it would lead to Mal being promptly arrested and perhaps me as well.

Since proving that Mal was elsewhere that night was out of the question, the only other solution was to find the real culprit behind the theft and vandalism of the Aura Chamber. How I was going to do that, I had no notion. I hoped Mal would have some idea.

Thinking about Horatio and my recent visit to the garrison stables reminded me of another chore that had been added to my list since the night of the ball. Amy's infatuation with her prince had led her to neglect her beloved miniature ponies. She remembered to feed and water them, but Pookie and Pippa were accustomed to so much more attention from their young mistress, little treats, daily brushings and walks along the grassy field behind the stables. It fell to me to make up for her absence and although I have never been that good at handling Amy's cantankerous ponies, I did my best.

As I made my way to the barn, I peeked over Mrs.

Biddlesworth's fence. My neighbor had always had a nasty habit of spying upon me, trying to catch me out in some wrongdoing. I felt like her beady eyes had been upon me more than usual of late, ever since the prince had proposed marriage.

When I satisfied myself that Mrs. B. was nowhere lurking about, I leaned across her fence and snitched a couple of her tart summer apples for Pookie and Pippa. Dreadful of me perhaps, but I was annoyed with the woman for threatening to accuse me of witchcraft if I didn't marry Florian. Shoving these treats into my apron pocket, I dragged open the rickety barn door.

When I was a young child, our stables had served as a coach house for several horses and a small gig. A groom whose name I could no longer recall— I believe it might have been Jeremy— lived above the stables. I vaguely remember he had a large bristling mustache and called me 'Miss Filly.' Whenever he fed the horses sugar lumps, he also gave one to me.

It has been a long time since we were able to afford luxuries such as owning a carriage and horses or employing servants. Now the only occupants of the stable were Amy's Caballettes, a breed of ponies not much bigger than a sheep-herding dog.

As I slipped inside, the barn was cool and shadowy compared to the bright warmth of the day. My nostrils were assailed by a mingling of hay, horse sweat and dung. Too much dung. The ponies' stall needed mucking out, a chore that I was not looking forward to since their enclosure comprised a large portion of the barn.

Their pen had been fashioned by combining several stalls and replacing the doors with a knee-high wooden fence. This enabled them to bed down together in their nests of straw while having room to move about.

At my approach, Pookie and Pippa thrust their shaggy brown heads over the top rail. They had learned to tolerate me over the past few days, no longer flattening their ears back and threatening to snap. While they eagerly accepted the treat I offered, crunching down the small green apples with gusto, their dark eyes regarded me with reproach as though demanding, *"Where is our Amy? What have you done with Amy?"*

"Sorry fellas," I murmured, "I promise she will come to her senses and return to you soon and she will need your comfort more than ever."

I bent down to stroke Pippa's mane. His ears pricked up and he shied away from me, stomping, and blowing a loud snort through his nostrils. Pookie also began to act strangely, shifting about in the stall and emitting a shrill whinny. For one dreadful moment, I wondered if Mrs. B had noticed my habit of stealing her fruit for the ponies and had done something to poison the apples. I would not have put it past the woman.

But as Pookie and Pippa became more frantic, I realized their movements were inspired by alarm, a fear that I shared when I detected a furtive footstep behind me. I whirled around to confront a man garbed in a midnight blue cloak, the hood pulled forward to conceal his features. Too short to be Horatio or Florian and not Mal's lean frame either. This was a stranger creeping into my barn for what sinister purpose I could not imagine.

My heart hammering, I backed away, seizing the pitchfork from the hay bale. Brandishing it at him, I demanded, "Who are you? What do you want?"

His hands were encased in leather gauntlets. He flung them upward, assuming a defensive posture.

"Ella, please. Don't be alarmed. It's me."

That low musical voice reverberated through me, striking a chord from my past. Using his left hand, he swept back his hood, revealing familiar features, the aquiline nose, the sensitive mouth, the light blue eyes, and dark blond eyebrows the same shade as his chin length hair.

"Harper!" I quavered. I recollected myself enough to add. "I mean Your Highness."

"Please, you don't need to call me that," Prince Ryland said.

"Even though I know you have good reason to run me through, I would greatly appreciate it if you could lower that pitchfork."

The pitchfork wavered in my hands as I sucked in a deep breath, struggling to recover from my shock. For seven long years, this man had vanished from my life, only to start popping up again. First at the ball and now here in my barn, rising before me like some pernicious spirit I believed I had exorcised. I lowered the pitchfork, jabbing it into the hay bale with more force than necessary.

"What are you doing here?" I demanded.

"I just needed to see you again. Talk to you."

"We said everything that needed saying the night of the ball."

"No, we didn't. We were interrupted by Florian."

"Then you simply ran off and disappeared. Something you make a habit of doing."

His face flushed. "I am sorry, but I was ashamed. I never wanted you to know about this."

He held up his right hand, the gesture stiff and awkward. His long leather gauntlet concealed the fact that his hand was carved of wood strapped to his lower arm. He had lost his limb during a battle with a dragon, a painful fact that had been revealed to me at the ball when Florian and Ryland had gotten into a scuffle. Florian had done no more than ask me to dance, but Ryland had astonished me by flying into a rage. When I had known him in his guise as Harper, Ryland had been the gentlest of men. But he had set upon his brother, trying to shove Florian away from me. During the ensuing struggle, his wooden appendage had been torn off, exposing the stump where his real hand had been.

Ryland lowered his arm, tucking his false hand out of sight beneath his cloak. "When you saw what had happened to me, you looked so horrified, I couldn't bear it and I fled. I have always been something of a coward in my dealings with you."

"Yes, you have," I began, but he looked so wretched that I

stopped and gave a wearied sigh. "Just say whatever it is that you came to tell me, and then go."

He tried to answer me but was distracted by the ponies who were still objecting to his presence by stomping and whinnying. Pippa reared up as though trying to scale the fence while Pookie whirled, kicking at the boards with his hind legs. The ponies would never settle while Ryland remained in the barn.

He raised his voice. "Is there no private place that we might go?"

There was and he knew it as well as I did. There was a woodland behind the barn where we had held our midnight trysts so long ago, but it was the last place I wished to revisit with him. But to refuse might make it seem like I still cared. Which I did not.

I turned without a word, shoving my way out of the double doors that led out of the back of the barn. I did not even look back to see if he was following me as I crossed the grassy verge where Amy exercised the ponies.

At one time, this had been a carriage track winding behind our stable and others in the neighborhood. But the king's taxes had made owning a coach something only the wealthy people in the Heights could afford. Consequently, the track had become overgrown. The path wound through a modest woodland and over a footbridge suspended above a burbling brook.

It was a secluded area, a popular place for young lovers to hold a moonlit tryst. I had met Ryland there often during that long-ago summer. I questioned my sanity in returning there with him now.

The sound of the water flowing beneath the bridge brought back a host of bittersweet, painful memories. Perhaps it was the same for Ryland because by the time I reached the bridge, he was lagging.

Turning back to look for him, I noticed he was limping.

"Did you hurt your foot?" I asked, trying to sound cool and indifferent.

As he closed the distance between us, he grimaced. "It's nothing. Just a bit of a sprain. I tripped and fell over a shoe this morning."

"A shoe?"

He nodded. "Priscilla Vanderwix hurled one of her shoes at me. All the girls from the Heights seem to be afflicted with madness lately. I can scarcely take a walk about the palace grounds without having to dodge footwear flying over the fence."

I bit down hard on my lip to restrain my smile, but I could not manage it.

Ryland eyed me suspiciously. "Now why do I suspect that you might somehow be behind this hail of lady's slippers?"

I made no effort to deny it. I just laughed.

Ryland smiled. "That is one of the things I have missed most about you, Ella. The sound of your laughter."

I sobered at once, scowling at him. "If that is the sort of nonsense you have come to spout, I am leaving."

I tried to brush past him, but he caught hold of my arm.

"No, I am sorry! I realize there is no longer any hope for you and me. But being near you again, I just couldn't help myself. But I promise I won't—"

I yanked my arm free of his grasp, preparing to stride back to the house, but Ryland begged, "Please, Ella. Don't go. I have something of great importance to tell you. Please?"

I emitted a heavy sigh as I relented. "Very well. Just make it quick. I have more pressing chores awaiting me."

I stalked to the center of the bridge and peered over the side at the water eddying over the rocks. The rill looked sluggish and choked with leaves more than I remembered from all those nights when the moonlight had rendered the waters dark and mysterious.

Ryland joined me on the bridge and positioned himself, his shoulder within inches of brushing up against mine. Once upon a time long ago, we would have already been in each other's arms, exchanging kisses fervently with all the longing of a first love. Now we stood as stiffly next to each other as two strangers.

"What is it you need to tell me that is so infernally important?" I demanded.

"I have come to warn you about my brother, Florian."

I gave an incredulous laugh. "A bit too late for that, don't you think?"

Ryland paled. "Too late? Oh, Ella, you cannot accept his proposal!"

"What right do you have to tell me what I can or cannot do?"

"None, except I still care about you too much to see you wedded to that monster."

I arched my brow. "I realize from the way you behaved at the ball, that there is little brotherly affection between you and Florian, but to call him a *monster?* Isn't that rather strong?"

Ryland shook his head vehemently. "You have no idea what he is really like. No one does. Every foolish maiden in this kingdom melts over his good looks and charming smile, but I had hoped you would be wiser."

"I am fully aware of your brother's flaws. He can be vain, arrogant and I suspect he is more than a little spoiled. But I have glimpsed an entirely different side of him."

"Such as?"

"Well... " I paused, wondering why I had any temptation to defend Florian. I could easily have allayed Ryland's fears and assured him I had no intention of marrying his brother. But after the callous way Ryland had trampled over my heart, I felt no urge to put an end to his misery. Petty of me, perhaps, but I have never claimed to be a sweet kind of girl.

"Only this afternoon, I was surprised to discover how vulnerable Florian can be. When he told me about your father's illness, he was so distressed, fearing for the king's life. He clearly values my opinion. When I urged to him to spend time with the king before it was too late, Florian rushed back to the palace."

Ryland rolled his eyes. "He rushed back home to boast to me

about how he was winning your heart, serenading you with *my* songs. Then he went hunting."

"But Florian had tears in his eyes, and I would swear they were genuine."

"My brother can feign tears as easily as his charming smiles. He would have made a better strolling player than a prince."

"So would you," I retorted. "Deceit appears to be a trait that comes naturally to your family. Did you know on the night of the ball, one of your wretched twin brothers convinced my little sister Amy that he had fallen in love with her to seduce her? Now she spends every day dreaming Dashiel will come and sweep her away on a white charger to live happily ever after."

Ryland had the grace to look ashamed. "If Dash did that, I am sorry. I fear we are all a despicable lot, except my brother Kendrick who is kind and gentle. Almost too much so. But Florian is the worst of us. You must believe me when I tell you that."

"No, I don't," I replied coldly, staring down at the rill where a little doe had crept out of the woodland for a drink.

Although he winced at his sore ankle, Ryland, in his agitation, took to pacing. The clatter of his boots striking the bridge startled the doe into darting back through the trees.

Ryland halted and faced me, demanding, "Were you surprised when Florian chose you over all the other ladies who attended the ball? Did you ever stop to ask yourself why?"

I thought that Florian's choice had been inspired by the amount of pixie dust he had snorted. That and my rejection of his suit had presented the prince with an irresistible challenge.

But I said, "Florian declared that he fell in love with me at first sight or do you find such a thing impossible?"

Ryland gave me a longing glance. "No, Ella. I know how easily a man can lose his heart to you. But Florian is incapable of loving or being true to anyone but himself. Only last year he declared himself smitten with Princess Ermengarde of Bryngar, writing her love poems, singing beneath her window, following her everywhere. He pursued her so relentlessly, his courtship amounted to persecution.

"When the princess persisted in her refusals, Florian climbed into her bedchamber one night. When Ermengarde awoke to find him groping her, she screamed for the guards. Florian claimed she was under a sleeping curse and he was just trying to awaken her. The incident caused such outrage, it took all the Great Mercato's skills in diplomacy to keep our two kingdoms from going to war."

I gripped the handrails of the bridge, unwilling to let Ryland see how much this story about Florian disturbed me. Except for the part about sneaking into the bedchamber, it sounded too uncomfortably like Florian's courtship of me. Yet for all I knew, a *story* was all this was.

"How strange," I remarked. "If Bryngar and Arcady were so close to war, not a single rumor of it ever reached this kingdom."

"That is because my father and his wizard have always been very good at suppressing any word of my brother's transgressions."

A bitter expression stole into Ryland's eyes, and he absently rubbed his false hand as he continued, "Florian behaved so badly abroad, my father decided the only way to get my brother safely wed was to invite all the women of the kingdom to this year's ball."

"Really? I thought the king's true aim was to fleece us all out of our money purchasing those exorbitant tickets."

Ryland hung his head, once more looking ashamed of his family. "That is partly true," he admitted. "My father did hope Florian would find a bride, but it was my fault that he chose you."

"*Yours?*"

"Florian always suspected that I had fallen in love with a Midtown girl, but he was never able to discover who it was. When you turned up at the ball, I should have stayed away from you, but I was too weak. When I followed you out onto the balcony, I betrayed how much I loved you." He swallowed. "How much I still do. That must have been when Florian decided he had to have you."

"Why?" I asked scornfully. "Because he figured out there had been some sort of romance between us? He asked me to marry him merely to what?"

"To hurt and torture me."

Incredulously, I shook my head. "I understand little of this kind of sibling rivalry you describe. Granted, I only have younger sisters and I have always felt like more of a mother to them. But it strikes me as ridiculous that a man would choose a wife merely to spite his brother."

"Nevertheless, it is exactly the sort of thing Florian would do. Oh, when we were small children, my brother and I were close, the best of friends. But my father's doting indulgence ruined his character. The king scorned me for being a weakling and he encouraged Florian to bully me, smash my things and steal my toys."

"*Your toys?*" I repeated in a strangled voice.

One look at my stony expression and Ryland realized his mistake.

"I am sorry, Ella," he stammered. "I didn't mean to imply that you were—"

"One of your playthings? That is exactly what I was." A leaf fluttered down from the trees, tangling in my hair. I brushed it angrily aside. "I thank you for your warning, Your Highness. But no one is stealing me. I will be quite pleased if I never see you or your brother ever again."

I tried to storm off the bridge, but Ryland blocked my way. "It won't be that simple, Ella. Now that he has made up his mind to have you, Florian will not give up. You have presented him with a challenge, and he always must win. He is a very dangerous and ruthless man."

Ryland hesitated and then held up his false hand. "Do you know how this happened to me?"

I had started to brush past Ryland, but I stopped, taken aback by this unexpected question.

"I was told you lost your hand, foolishly fighting a dragon."

"No, that was merely another tale concocted by my father and Mercato and they forced me to go along with it. The truth is that I let Florian goad me into a duel. I was never very good with a sword, especially not when I was angry. Florian was enjoying himself, taunting me into such a rage, he easily slipped past my guard. The next thing I knew my hand was dripping with blood. The wound became infected and there was nothing the court physician or Mercato could do. My hand had to be amputated. Florian shed some of his fake tears, claimed that it was an accident, that he never meant to hurt me."

"Perhaps he didn't," I faltered. "To deliberately maim his own brother, Florian would have to be a - a—"

"A monster," Ryland said quietly.

I pressed my hand to my brow, uncertain how much of this terrible story to believe. Ryland sounded truthful and sincere, but he had seemed that way all those years ago when he had broken my heart.

The prince took advantage of my distraction to claim hold of my other hand. "Please, Ella, you must listen to me. You have got to get as far away from Florian as you can."

"Exactly how am I supposed to manage that?"

Ryland drew in a deep breath and blurted out, "Run away with me."

"What! Are you quite mad?" I tried to pull my hand free, but he clung to me.

"It was our dream, remember? To flee to some far-off kingdom where we could marry and live happily ever after."

"The dream of a strolling minstrel and a romantic young maiden."

"I am still your Harper and I love you." He raised my hand to his lips, pressing a kiss against my knuckles.

"But I am not that girl anymore and I don't love you," I cried. "Now let me go."

He released me, but he looked so devastated by my rejection, I could not help but pity him.

"I am sorry," I added in a gentler tone. "For too long I felt hurt and betrayed when you abandoned me the night we were supposed to elope. Now that I am older and wiser, I believe it was a good thing you did not have the courage to defy your father. We both would have lived to regret it."

"You might have. I never would." Ryland frowned. His brow furrowed as though wrestling with some decision. "I swore an oath never to tell you this, but I think you have a right to know."

He looked straight into my eyes. "Ella, it was not my father that forced me to give you up. It was yours."

"What!" Any sympathy I had been feeling for Ryland dissolved into exasperation. I shook my head at him in disgust. "You almost had me believing all your wild stories about Florian, but you go too far when you start lying about my father. Papa was a quiet, gentle man. He could never force anyone to do anything."

"Perhaps force was a poor choice of word. But he did come to me the night before we were going to elope. He cajoled, argued, and reasoned with me, told me that if I truly loved you, I would never see you again. He kept at me until I promised to do just that."

This sounded slightly more creditable. Although I found it difficult to imagine, I had been told that my father had once been a brilliant advocate and orator at the king's court.

I conceded reluctantly. "My father did not approve of my romance with you. Now that I am older, I can understand that. My father believed you to be an itinerant musician, not what any parent would consider an eligible suitor."

Ryland regarded me sadly. "No, Ella, you understand nothing. Your father knew exactly who I was."

Nine

Our evening meal proved to be dismal. Both my stepmother and Amy pleaded with headaches and retired to their rooms early. I was not surprised. The prospect of turnip stew for supper can have that effect on people and my latest batch turned out more unappetizing than usual.

Distracted and unsettled by my visit from Prince Ryland, I added too much salt and scorched the bottom of the pan. Netta and I sat down in the kitchen to dine upon this unappetizing mess, the aroma of charred turnip lingering in the air.

I made a poor supper companion for my sister, my head too full of Ryland's revelation about my father being the one to put an end to my youthful romance, even though Papa had known all along that my 'Harper' was a prince in disguise. I hadn't wanted to believe Ryland. He had seemed like he was truthful, but he had always had that ability to convince me of his sincerity, even while concealing his identity. I did not want to fall under the spell of his earnest blue eyes again.

"Why would my father have done such a thing?" I had demanded.

"He was certain that our marriage would only lead to disaster and danger for you."

"Danger? What danger?"

"I don't know. Perhaps he was thinking of my father's volatile temperament. All I know is that your father was very convincing, and he persuaded me that the noblest thing I could do was to vanish from your life."

"Noble!" I had cried. *"Forsaking me without a word of explanation?"*

I had become so angry and upset with him, I had ordered Ryland to go and never seek me out again. Now I wished I had not been so hasty. I should have pressed him for more details, but I doubt I would have received satisfactory answers. If my father had interfered in my youthful romance, I didn't care what Papa's reasons might have been.

I had been devastated by Ryland's disappearance, my faith shaken in the very idea of love and in my own judgment. My heart had not fully healed until I had fallen in love with Horatio. It seemed Ryland and my father had arbitrarily decided what they thought best for me, without consulting my feelings. I felt completely betrayed by both.

"I think the turnip is dead, Ella." Netta's quiet voice broke into my agitated thoughts. I glanced down and realized I had been absent-mindedly stabbing a singed piece of turnip.

"Sorry," I muttered, lowering my fork. "What a wretched mess."

I was referring to more than our dinner, but my sister took me quite literally.

"It's all right. I wasn't that hungry anyway." Netta summoned up a wan smile as she pushed her plate away from her.

I really looked at my youngest sister for the first time that evening. Netta was pale, with faint shadows rimming her eyes. She appeared as miserable as I felt.

"What is the matter, sweetheart?" I asked. "Are you coming down with something?"

I leaned across the table to test her brow for fever, but her skin felt cool to my touch.

Netta gave a sad shake of her dark curls. "No, I am quite well, but I am very worried about Mama and Amy."

"I am sure they are both fine. My stew is enough to make anyone take to their beds."

"It is not your stew, Ella. Mama has been in the dismals most of this afternoon."

No doubt because of my continued refusal to marry Prince Florian. I had hoped the visit of her old beau, Chuffy, would provide a welcome distraction.

"What happened?" I asked. "Em seemed so happy when Lord Stanhope came to call."

"I think they had some sort of quarrel."

"What about?" I drew in my breath sharply, remembering Chuffy's roguish reputation. "His lordship didn't attempt to do anything inappropriate, did he?"

"Certainly not!" My little sister looked shocked by the very idea. "I am sure Lord Stanhope behaved like a complete gentleman. I don't know why they quarreled. It happened while I was in the kitchen preparing tea. His lordship stalked out of the house in high dudgeon, not even bothering to say goodbye and Mama took to her bed weeping."

"I am sorry to hear that," I said. I truly was, although my motives were not entirely unselfish. I had hoped that if Em reconnected with her old beau, she might end up happily wed to Chuffy, thus ending our financial worries and any guilt I had for not accepting Florian's offer.

I emitted a deep sigh which Netta echoed.

She continued, "Amy has been crying most of the day as well."

"Over Chuffy?"

"No, she has finally realized her prince is never going to come.

She sent a love note to the Prince Dashiel asking when he would keep his pledge to her. She received a very cold reply from His Highness, saying that he did not remember her."

"Did not remember the girl he lured down to his father's wine cellar and attempted to seduce? That is highly unlikely," I said angrily.

"Amy described her tryst with Dashiel in far more romantic terms. But perhaps she was dazzled from being pursued by a handsome prince."

"No, Amy did not have so many stars in her eyes as she did wine fumes in her head. That young villain had our sister quite drunk. If I had not come upon them when I did, who knows what would have happened next?"

Netta winced at my bluntness. "I am sure Amy would never have allowed him to... " She trailed off, blushing. My youngest stepsister was so naïve, such immodest behavior was beyond her comprehension.

She continued hopefully, "If Amy was befuddled, perhaps she sent her letter to the wrong prince. Dahl and Dashiel are identical twins. Maybe it was Prince Dahl who was with Amy and he really does love her."

I cut Netta off with a firm shake of my head. "No. Well, I mean yes, it really was Dahl who was in the cellar with Amy, but he was pretending to be his brother. I have heard the princes enjoy doing that, fooling people by switching identities. It doesn't really matter which twin it was because they are both lying wretches. Amy will recover in time and realize she had a narrow escape. I am sure her pride has been wounded more than her heart and she will feel better the next time Mr. Bafton comes to call and brings her chocolates."

Before Amy's head had been turned by the prince, her favored beau had been Fortescue Bafton, the tailor's son.

"Fortescue can be a rather foolish young man," I went on. "But he does seem to genuinely adore our Amy."

Netta gave me an odd look. "Don't you remember? Fortescue was one of the Midtown citizens arrested after the brawl at the palace, along with our neighbors, the Hansons. None of them have come home since the night of the ball."

"Of course, I remember," I said. But I sank back into my chair, feeling guilty. I had been so caught up in my own problems that I had spared little thought for my neighbors.

I hastened to assure Netta, "Commander Crushington spoke to Mercato who agreed to take care of the matter. The only reason their pardon has been delayed is because the king has been too ill of late. I am sure as soon as His Majesty is well enough, he will be persuaded to give the order for the release of our neighbors."

At least, I tried to sound sure for Netta's sake. But the major-domo had implied that the king might not recover. If Florian ascended to the throne, could he be induced to show mercy to the Hanson and Bafton families? Not according to his brother. Ryland insisted Florian was a monster. The majordomo painted a far different picture of a prince who was spoiled, but unsure of himself, needing only the guidance of the right woman to help him become a good king. While I prayed that the majordomo was correct, I did not want that woman to be me.

Netta looked so relieved by my assurance, I kept my doubts to myself. My sister was such a tender-hearted girl, more concerned about the welfare of other people than her own. I reached across the table and pressed her hand.

"You are so kind to worry about Amy and your mother and the Hansons. But how are you faring, my dear?"

Netta hunched one shoulder. "Oh, I am fine."

"Are you? Have you had any word from your handsome Sergeant Wharton?"

Netta's eyes lit up at the mere mention of his name. "Ned *is* handsome, isn't he? He has such kind, gentle eyes, something you would never expect to find in a soldier. I had the most magical time with him at the ball."

I had to bite back a smile. Netta's evening would have been a far cry from what most girls considered magical. While the other maidens like Amy had danced and pursued princes, Netta had spent her time in the palace gardens, with a sergeant of the guard and his ugly aura cat.

"Ned shares my love of music and quiet afternoons. He feels as shy and awkward in new situations as I do. I have never met a man so easy to talk to or one who seemed to understand me so completely." The light in her eyes dimmed. "But I do not expect to ever see him again. His duties keep him bound to the palace and Mama would never approve of him as a suitor. But at least, I will always have the memory of one wonderful night."

She pasted on a brave smile as she helped me clear away the remains of our miserable supper. Somehow Netta's sad resignation affected me more deeply than all of Amy's and my stepmother's angst.

My spirits were quite low as I wound my way up to bed that night. After the day's events, I should have been exhausted enough to flop down on my bed and pass out. I was tired but I could tell that sleep would not come easily. Not with my head so crowded, a veritable tournament of worries and problems battling it out inside my brain.

I attempted to clear my mind as I brushed out my hair and bathed my face. I had not bothered to heat the water for my basin, but the cool water felt soothing. It was going to be a very warm night. My bedchamber already felt stifling. After I donned my nightgown, I moved to open my window, only to freeze, Ryland's warning about his brother coming back to me.

"When the princess persisted in her refusals, Florian climbed into her bedchamber one night. When Ermengarde awoke to find him groping her, she screamed for the guards."

Open my window? I should be nailing it shut. I started to back away only to rebel at spending the night, tossing, and sweating in a stuffy, airless bedchamber. I had no reason to believe anything

Ryland said. For all I knew, he had made up the entire story out of jealousy of his brother.

But what if he hadn't?

When I flung up my sash, I was horrified to realize there was someone lurking in the bushes below. Lit by moonlight, I could just make out a dark cloaked figure starting to scale the vine-covered walls.

Florian! My first impulse was to flee but something inside of me snapped. I was furious. I had had enough of his relentless pursuit of me. Regardless of the consequences, I looked about me for something to throw. My gaze fell upon the porcelain basin still filled with tepid bath water. Not exactly boiling oil, but it would have to do.

Hefting the basin, I sloshed water over my gown. Florian was already halfway up the wall. I dumped the rest of the water over the prince. The basin slipped from my hands, bonking him on the head as well.

Florian emitted a startled gasp.

Losing his footing, he scrambled for purchase but ended up falling back into the shrubs. Watching him flail about in the rose bushes, I grinned with a fierce satisfaction until a familiar voice called out.

"What the frap, Ella!"

My smile faded. I leaned further out the window, squinting into the darkened garden. "Mal, is that you?"

Still swearing, Mal regained his footing. "Of course, it is me. Who else would it be?"

"I thought you were Prince Florian."

"Oh, certainly, because we look so much alike." Mal shoved back the hood of his cloak, exposing his bald head.

"I am sorry, but it is dark down there and I could not see your face."

"Is that still any reason for you to douse me?" Mal paused to sniff at his cloak. "Er - that was only water you threw at me?"

"Yes, you idiot." Grimy and soapy, but still only water. I started to ask what Mal was doing, creeping around outside my window, and scaring me out of my wits. But a low moan carried to me from the adjacent bedchamber which belonged to my stepmother.

Fearful of waking Em, I hissed at Mal to meet me in the back garden. Closing my window, I tiptoed through the silent house. Entering the kitchen, I paused long enough to light a lantern from the oven embers. I grabbed up a towel and stole out the back door in the garden to find Mal waiting beneath the pergola.

He had stripped off his cloak and laid it across the garden table to dry as I hung up the lantern. When I gave him the towel, he handed me my basin. I was pleased to find the porcelain bowl still intact.

"It is not even chipped," I exclaimed. "Your head must not be as hard as I thought."

"Very amusing." He gave me a disgruntled look as he toweled off his face and head. "I guess I should consider myself lucky to have escaped with a bump on the head. You could have made me break my neck."

"Serves you right. What were you doing sneaking about my window like some sort of brigand?"

"I told you this afternoon, I would find a way to come to you."

"By climbing the wall into my bedchamber?"

"I used to visit you that way all the time."

"When we were children. You gave me a terrible fright. I thought you were Florian."

"Why would you think it could be him? He's an arrogant moron, but surely not even he would be bold enough to creep into a lady's bedchamber."

"According to his brother Ryland, he is."

"Prince Ryland? When did you see that wretch?"

I could not conceal my distress as I gave Mal a brief account of the unexpected visit from my former lover. Mal pulled a wry face.

"Good grief, Ella. You are positively infested with princes. You need an exterminator." He lifted one foot and then the other as though trying to avoid the royalty scurrying about my garden.

He made me laugh which had been his intention. At least, it started out that way. Perhaps because I have had so little to laugh about of late, I could not regain control of myself. I laughed until tears flowed down my cheeks and somewhere mid chuckle, I found myself crying in earnest.

"Hey! Hey, now," Mal protested. "What's all this?"

He took the basin from me before I dropped it again. Setting aside the porcelain bowl, he drew me down onto the bench beside him and gathered me into his arms. He smelled like a combination of sweat and soapy water, but I burrowed my face against his shoulder, making it even wetter with my tears. All the stress and exhaustion of the past few days poured out of me as if a dam had burst.

I have always hated to cry in front of anyone. My family relied upon me so much to be the strong, sensible one. I never felt free to display any emotion that would distress them. Much as I loved Horatio, I was not yet comfortable enough to reveal my weaknesses. But Mal knew all my flaws and vulnerabilities. He had been my comforter since we were children. His shoulder had often provided me with refuge, a safe place to vent my misery.

Mal rocked me in his arms, murmuring. "There now, my brave, beautiful Ella. Tell me. What has happened to overwhelm you like this?"

"Everything!" I sobbed out the tale of all my recent woes. I was crying so hard, I wasn't sure how much was comprehensible to Mal, but he patted my back, making soothing noises as I jumbled together the day's events.

"And - and now Florian is p-persecuting me with - with music and Ryland s-says to stay away from his brother because there never w-was a dragon and W-Withypole took some of my memories and put them in his pocket. And I had to kiss him in the square in front of everyone to keep him from having Tom Piper arrested."

"You kissed the fairy!"

"No!" I hiccupped. "Florian. You told me when he woke up from his pixie dust binge, he would forget all about me, but he didn't and now I cannot set foot out of the house without him plaguing me with flowers and bad poetry and marriage proposals. I have no peace at home either because Em cannot understand why I won't leap at the chance to marry such a handsome prince. Now Ryland is warning me how ruthless his brother is, and I don't know whether to believe him or not. I am just so exhausted by all of it."

The words poured out of me in a breathless flood. Mal cuddled me close as I finally managed to regain control of myself. I drew away from him, groping for the towel to dry my eyes and wipe my nose.

"Sorry for falling apart on you and sniveling all over your shirt," I mumbled.

"I was already wet, and I'd take your snot over Delphine coughing up hairballs on my bed any day."

I gave a watery chuckle. "How I have missed you, Hawkridge."

"And I you. I would have found a way to come to you much sooner if I had realized you were on the verge of losing your mind." Mal drew me back into arms, resting his chin on top of my head. "I am here now so don't fret any more about either of those idiot princes. They will be taken care of soon enough."

"What do you mean by that?"

"Why, nothing." I felt Mal shrug, but there was an edge to his voice that filled me with foreboding.

I shifted in his arms, trying to peer up at him. "Mal, please tell me you are not planning to do anything reckless to protect me from Florian."

"Reckless? Who? Me?" Mal laughed.

I pulled away from him. "I am serious. Commander Crushington still suspects that the League of the Missing Heir was behind the theft in the Aura Chamber and he thinks you are part of that."

"How very unfair of him," Mal drawled. "Just because I happen to be missing my hair to accuse me of joining up with some league of disgruntled bald men—"

"Stop it, Mal! This is nothing to jest about. You know right well I am referring to that secret group of madmen plotting to overthrow the king."

"You think they are mad?"

"Certainly, they are. They would have to be, to believe in some old fairy story about a long-lost heir. I have had to work very hard to convince the commander you are far too sensible to ever be involved with such a thing. I even had to tell him where you really were the night of the ball."

"You what!"

"Well, not the part about us stealing the orb. Just how we met up on the grounds outside of the palace at midnight."

When Mal rolled his eyes, I added defensively, "I *had* to tell Horatio at least part of the truth to persuade him you were not responsible for the attack on the Aura Chamber."

"Have I never taught you anything, Ella? Rule number one. Never volunteer information. And if you are accused of something, rules two, three and four."

"*Obfuscate. Obfuscate. Obfuscate,*" I repeated along with him.

Despite how worried I was, the word brought a reluctant smile to my lips. Mal and I had been messing about in his grandfather's forbidden magic workshop. When we had broken some of the potion flasks, Mal had invented a fanciful excuse for how the accident had occurred. Hiram Hawkridge had angrily accused Mal of obfuscating.

Mal and I had become entranced with the word. *Obfuscating* sounded nicer than lying. It had a certain elegance to it. We had merrily obfuscated our way out of trouble for many of the misdeeds of our childhood.

My smile faded as I set the memory aside.

I regarded Mal anxiously, "You are too sensible, aren't you? To ever get involved with this League of the Missing Heir."

"How long have you known me, Ella? Well enough to realize I am far too cynical and selfish to ever espouse any cause but my own. I am a lover, not a fighter."

I wished the lantern light had been bright enough that I could have read his eyes, but I had to be satisfied with his answer. Mal might lie to everyone else, but he was not in the habit of obfuscating with me.

Mal brushed my tangled curls back from my cheeks. "What more can I say to convince you?"

"It isn't me you have to convince. Horatio was ready to post a wanted poster for your capture. I persuaded him to wait by promising that you would help him find out who was really behind the attack on the Aura Chamber."

Mal snorted. "You truly have lost your mind. Why would I agree to do Crushington's dirty work for him?"

"Oh, I don't know. Let me see. Possibly to save your own neck!" I softened my sarcastic tone to a pleading note. "And because I am asking you to help. You are often aware of what skullduggery is afoot among the less respectable people in our kingdom. Could the culprit possibly be one of your unsavory friends? Perhaps that pirate, Waldo the Wharf Rat?"

Mal cut me off with a shake of his head. "I swear to you, Ella. Neither I nor any of my friends had anything to do with that break-in."

"Surely you must have heard some rumors about who did."

"No, I haven't. Whoever pulled off that theft has been very clever about covering their tracks. Even if I did know who it was, I would be more inclined to applaud their daring instead of betraying them to the Crusher."

"I have asked you not to call Horatio that," I snapped. "He is a good man, kind and caring, honorable and true."

My defense of Horatio was so heated, that Mal frowned. He tipped up my chin to scrutinize my face.

"Exactly how far did you go to convince *Horatio* not to swear out a warrant for my arrest?" Mal laid sarcastic emphasis on my intimate use of the commander's name. "Never tell me you have been kissing him, too."

I pushed Mal's hand away as I felt my cheeks flame. Even in the lantern's dim light, it must have been obvious.

"Frap, Ella, why must you run about kissing every man in this kingdom? Every man but me."

He wrapped his arm around my waist. He hesitated before drawing me closer, his head lowering to mine. Before our lips could meet, I shoved him away and leapt to my feet.

"Don't, Mal."

"Don't what, Ella? Want you? Need you? Tell you how much I love you?" His voice was rife with frustration.

When he stood up and tried to take my hand, I backed away from him.

"I am sorry, Mal. I have tried and tried to tell you. I will love you always as my dearest friend. But please stop hoping I will ever feel anything more. Especially not when... " I faltered and plucked up my courage. "I have fallen in love with someone else."

"You can't mean Horatio Crushington?"

"Yes!"

I had not meant to blurt it out like that, but perhaps there was no gentle way of telling him.

A choking sound escaped him something between a curse and groan. He paced away from me, clenching, and unclenching his hands, only to wheel back to confront me again. "No! You can't possibly be in love with such a man. I will grant you that the Crusher is more honorable than most, but he is still a Scutcheon

Commander, sworn to uphold the king's tyrannical laws. Have you entirely forgotten that?"

"Of course, I have not. I heartily wish Horatio was not in the king's service. But he tries very hard to be merciful and just. I love him for that and for so much more."

Mal's face fell. I could feel the weight of his despair and I hated hurting him this way.

"I am sorry," I whispered.

Mal swallowed thickly. "Has he asked you to marry him?"

"He wants to, but he can't. If he does not find out who robbed the Aura Chamber, he could be broken in rank and sent to patrol the Northern border. He says it is a wild region, no place for a man to bring a wife. If that happens, I will likely never see Horatio again."

"Good riddance," Mal said. But when a single tear escaped to cascade down my cheek, he sighed. "No! Please don't start crying again, Ella. I still think Crushington is not right for you. There is far more of the pirate than the princess about you, my beloved friend. Your upright commander will never be able to understand or appreciate you the way I do. But if the blasted man gets exiled to the north, you will never realize that. You will pine for him the way you did for that stupid Prince Ryland all those years and I will be cursed if I allow your heart to be broken a second time."

Mal heaved a deep sigh. "Fine. I will help him find out who broke into the Aura Chamber."

"Oh Mal, thank you," I began, but he dismissed my gratitude with a curt gesture.

"Mind you, I can't promise you I will succeed in unmasking the culprit. I have been preoccupied trying to figure out how the orb works."

"Have you had any luck?"

"No. When my grandfather lost his post as the king's chief wizard and was forbidden to practice magic again, all his potion books and grimoires were destroyed. If only the old man had trusted me enough to explain the secret of the orb." Mal's lips set in a bitter line. "But of course, he despised me too much."

"No, I am sure your grandfather loved you after his own gruff fashion."

"Did he? I was very young when my father died, but I remember how it was. My grandfather grieved so deeply, he shut himself away, even from my grandmother. But I was playing outside his study window the day he finally allowed your parents to call. Your mother was always so kind and gentle. She tried to console my grandfather by reminding him he still had a grandson who loved and needed him.

"I'll never forget the bitter look on my grandfather's face or his words. *'That worthless imp? I would rather he had died instead of my son.'*"

"Oh, Mal, you never told me about that."

He shrugged. "Because it wasn't important. I never cared what the old man thought of me."

I knew that wasn't true. Mal's problem was he had cared too much. He had spent his youth both defying his grandfather and longing for his approval. I suspected that was what had made Mal so desperate to recover that orb from the king's treasury. Yes, he believed the orb could lead to some fabulous treasure that would be the salvation of all of us. But I think he was equally motivated to prove to himself that he was worthy to be Hiram Hawkridge's successor.

My heart ached for Mal. I wanted to hug him, but such gestures had become awkward between us. I folded my arms instead as I asked, "If your grandfather left no clues about the orb, how will you ever learn how to use it?"

"I didn't say there were absolutely no clues. I found references to the orb and the lost treasure in an old diary my grandfather kept. There was a page ripped out which might have held more information. I have torn the Hawk's Nest apart, thinking maybe my grandfather hid it somewhere. But I found nothing. I wondered if he could have given it to a friend for safekeeping. But the old man was so cantankerous, he didn't have any friends except for your father."

I frowned, a memory surfacing in my mind, like something that had been buried under a thick layer of cobwebs for years. Late at night in our library, Hiram Hawkridge trying to give Papa something. Something Papa didn't want.

The memory disappeared as quickly as it had come, causing me to doubt the recollection. But I said, "It is remotely possible your grandfather might have trusted my father with such a thing. But after Papa died, I had to go through all the papers and ledgers in his desk. I saw nothing about any mysterious orb."

"Your father would not have left such valuable information just lying about, would he? He would have tucked it away somewhere. Perhaps in a secret compartment."

"I am sure if there was any secret compartment in our library, I would have stumbled it across it by now."

"Then what about between the leaves of one of the books?"

"Mal, my father owned hundreds of books!" I sighed, thinking it would be a waste of time to mount such a search. But after Mal had agreed to help Horatio, how could I not offer to do so?

I said reluctantly, "I don't expect to find anything, but I will search the library if you wish."

"Could you, Ella?" Mal brightened. "I realize it would be an enormous task, but I could come and help."

"No! My stepmother would have an apoplexy if we were closeted alone together in the library."

"What?" Mal grinned. "I thought since I had provided those ball tickets, the woman adores me."

"Em was grateful, but not enough to want you within a mile of me. She has always been terrified I would take into my head to run off with you someday."

"Maybe you will," Mal murmured with a suggestive lift of his brows. He tried to make it sound as if he was teasing, but I could tell he still cherished hopes of prevailing with me in the end. I felt too weary to continue trying to convince him this would never happen. Mal could be incredibly stubborn. He would keep on hoping until I married Horatio if that happy day ever came.

I promised to start my search of the library first thing after breakfast and Mal agreed to begin his quest to expose the Aura Chamber burglar. As he donned his cloak, I tucked the basin and towel under my arm. I retrieved the lantern to light the way back to my garden gate.

"I will return to you to tomorrow to report what I find," Mal began but I interrupted him.

"No, it will be safer for me to meet you in Misty Bottoms."

"Safer? With Delphine prowling about, still looking for revenge?"

"I will be on the lookout and take great care to avoid her."

Mal scowled, still not liking the idea. But I could not risk a confrontation between him and Horatio. Horatio had agreed to wait a few days, but if he stumbled across Mal in the meantime, he would feel obliged to arrest him.

Mal and I argued the entire way to the gate, our voices getting louder. I was alarmed to notice the bushes rustling in my neighbor's garden. But surely Mrs. B would not rouse herself to spy upon me at this hour.

I hushed Mal, peering over her fence, until I satisfied myself it must have been nothing more than a stray dog or garden mole.

Mal finally gave in and agreed to my plan. We arranged a time to meet at the Hawk's Nest around two the following afternoon. Ordinarily we would have parted with a hug. But Mal's unrequited feelings for me and my love for Horatio had put a strain on our friendship as I had feared it would. What were we supposed to do now? Shake hands? Bow to each other?

Mal solved the problem by planting a kiss on my cheek and then he disappeared into the darkness. As I turned to head back to the house, I tensed, noticing a candle flicker in my neighbor's kitchen window. I had not been imagining things. Mrs. Biddlesworth was awake and spying upon me. Had she been watching me and Mal the entire time? I doubted she could have seen or heard much, but it still made me vexed and uneasy. I held up the lantern, so she could see me glaring in her direction.

The candle was hastily snuffed out.

Ten

I woke to an overcast sky the next morning, but at least breakfast proved to be a more cheerful meal than our supper had been. I was surprised to find both of my sisters up before me and Netta had prepared oatmeal. It was a little thin and lumpy, but I praised Netta for her cooking. I was pleased to see her looking much happier than she had last night.

As I helped her dip the oatmeal into bowls, she confided to me in a whisper, "Wonderful news, Ella. Amy seems so much better and guess what? Early this morning, I peeked out my window and saw the Hansons had returned home."

"That is indeed excellent news," I said, my own spirits lifting. Perhaps this was a sign that the entire day would go well.

Mal would unmask the Aura Chamber thief and exonerate himself to Horatio's satisfaction. I might find that missing page for Mal and he could use the orb to find the lost treasure. And who knows? Maybe Florian would decide I was not the right bride for him and cease his pursuit. Horatio could openly declare his love for me, and we would all live happily ever after. I smiled at my wild imagination. But if one was going to be optimistic, there was no point indulging in half measures.

"The Bafton family must have been released as well," Netta continued in a low voice as she glanced at Amy. My other sister was seated at the kitchen table, stirring a dollop of honey into her tea. "Since Amy has stopped weeping over Prince Dashiel, I thought of suggesting that we call upon the Baftons. But perhaps it is too soon for her to turn her affections back to Fortescue."

"I think it might be," I said. While Amy appeared resigned to the loss of her romantic dreams about her prince, she was not her ebullient self either.

But she ate her lumpy oatmeal without complaint. As soon as she had finished, she rose from the table and announced, "I need to go exercise Pookie and Pippa. I have been neglecting them shamefully."

She rose from the table, inviting Netta to accompany her. The two girls left the kitchen, whispering to each other. Netta made some remark that caused Amy to giggle. The sound of their girlish laughter gladdened my heart. After the disruption the royal ball had created in our lives, I felt there was a chance that our household might finally return to normal.

That hopeful thought lasted until my stepmother straggled into the kitchen. Em was usually most particular about her appearance, but she had buttoned her dressing robe on crooked. Her lace cap sat askew atop her wilting curls, her face pale and forlorn.

She declined the oatmeal and sat across from me, sipping her tea and emitting heavy sighs. All my attempts to engage her in conversation elicited monosyllabic replies until I ventured to mention Lord Stanhope.

"That odious man," Em snapped. "I have no wish to talk about him!"

Knowing Em, I realized that was exactly what she did want to talk about. After a great deal more of her sipping and sighing, I finally coaxed her to tell me what had happened during his lordship's visit.

"Chuffy had the impertinence to tell me I needed to stop

pestering you about marrying the prince." Em gave a wounded sniff, looking very much like a plump dove that had her feathers ruffled. "Pester? I am sure I have never *pestered* anyone in the entire course of my life. I could not believe Chuffy could be so unkind or so lacking in good sense. He had the temerity to suggest that Commander Crushington would make you a better husband. A foundling of unknown origins instead of a prince of royal blood! I told Chuffy he must be mad, but he has a poor opinion of all the princes. He called them a parcel of arrogant, selfish brats. Can you imagine that he would dare to say such a thing?"

"I am sorry that his lordship should have expressed himself in a manner you found distressing, Em. But I am gratified to hear that he is on my side in all of this."

"*I* am on your side, Prunella Upton," my stepmother regarded me fiercely. "Charles Stanhope never had any children of his own so he has no right telling anyone else what he thinks is best for her daughter and so I said to him."

"Oh, Em." I groaned. "I cannot believe you quarreled with your devoted old beau over that wretched prince."

Em affected a careless shrug. "It does not signify. I daresay I was just making a fool of myself. I had no business seeking to rekindle a romance at my age when my only concern should be the welfare of my daughters."

Em reached across the table and caught my hand firmly in hers. "Ella, dear, are you sure you could not learn to love Prince Florian? He is every young maiden's dream."

"More like a recurring nightmare," I muttered.

"I simply don't understand you, child." Em released my hand, regarding me with sad, bewildered eyes. "Even if Commander Crushington claims to have had proper parents, the rumors persist that he was a foundling. If the truth about that was ever revealed, my dear, you have no idea what it would be like to marry a man who might bring you into disgrace and cause you to lose everything and put the very future of your children in jeopardy."

I realized from the anguish in her voice that Em was no longer talking about me but recalling her own disastrous marriage to Albert Wendover. Her eyes filled with tears.

"It would quite break my heart to ever see you suffer such a fate."

"I promise you that I won't, Em." I rose from my chair and bent down to give my stepmother a hug. "I don't care about Horatio's background, whatever it might be. I only know what kind of a man he is, honest, brave, and true. I love him with all my heart, and I would be honored to be his wife."

Em rested her head against me with a resigned sigh. "At least he is a Scutcheon commander and not a common soldier. And I would be able to stop worrying you might elope with that scoundrel, Malcolm Hawkridge."

"You never did need to worry about that."

Em wiped her eyes and drew away from me. "But everyone in Midtown is bursting with pride at the thought that one of their own will be crowned queen, chosen above all the aristocratic ladies of the Heights. If you do not marry the prince, I do not know how any of us will ever dare show our faces in town again."

"I am very skilled with a needle. I will cut up my ballgown and sew us all the most elegant sacks to put over our heads."

"Wicked teasing girl," Em grumbled, but her lips tilted in a reluctant smile.

"Now I want you to go up to your room and write Lord Redmond a charming note," I said. "Tell him how much you regret your misunderstanding. Invite the man to tea."

"What if he does not wish to come?" Em asked anxiously. "I was so very cross with him."

"He will come. I'll wager he is as unhappy about this foolish quarrel as you are," I said as I escorted her to the door. When she attempted another protest, I silenced her with a kiss on her cheek. "Go do it, Em. Or I vow I will write the letter for you and send it myself."

After I succeeded in urging her out the door, I expelled a deep breath, silently cursing Prince Florian. How much more havoc would that man wreak in my life before I could be rid of him?

* * *

As soon as I cleared away the breakfast dishes, I headed straight for the library. This room had always been as much of a refuge for me as it had been for my father. But as I closed the door behind me and looked around at all those book-lined shelves, I felt daunted. Could there be anything more overwhelming than mounting a search for something that there was only the slimmest likelihood of finding?

But I had promised Mal that I would try, so I shoved back my sleeves and began. I started with Papa's writing desk, even though I was thoroughly familiar with its contents. When my father had died and named me as his executor, I had been obliged to sort through all his account books and legal papers. But I combed through the desk again, tapping on drawers, even examining the ornate legs in case there was some secret hiding place I had missed. There was not.

That only left the books. The hundreds and hundreds of books. For the first time in my life, I wished Papa had not been such a prolific reader. I knelt and began my search on one of the lower shelves, planning to work my way up.

I pulled out book after book, rifling through pages, shaking each volume to dislodge any paper that might be hidden between the leaves. My search was hampered when I stumbled across some favorite passage. I would become distracted and start to read, until I reminded myself of what I was supposed to be doing.

I wasted nearly an hour in this fashion without discovering anything beyond the fact my library shelves needed cleaning. Searching in this random way would take me forever. Rocking back on my heels, I dusted off my hands, wracking my brain for a more logical approach.

If my father had secreted something inside a book, which one would he have chosen? One of his favorites that he kept close at hand near his wing back chair? The problem with that theory was those books were my favorites too. I had read them as often as my father did. If he was going to hide something, it would make more sense that he would select a book he seldom read, one that he even disliked. One candidate leapt readily to my mind.

The 'sack witches' book.

As a child, I had thought the book looked dull and uninteresting. Too many big words and no pictures of any kind. I was surprised to discover that my father felt the same way.

"If you don't like the book, why don't you just burn it up in the fireplace, Papa?" I remembered asking.

"Because that would be sacrilege."

"Sack witches?" I had echoed, puzzled.

My father's lips twitched. He seldom smiled after my mother died, but he did so then.

"It means that I think it wrong to destroy any book, especially one that was a gift from a friend."

Could that friend have been Hiram Hawkridge? Was it possible that this search was not so futile after all?

I scrambled to my feet, scanning the shelves with new interest. As a little girl, I had thought of that volume as the 'sack witches' book. I did not remember its title. I had only a vague recollection that the book was some sort of history.

I concentrated my search on the upper shelves where Papa's least favorite books had been consigned. Moving the library step ladder from stack to stack, I finally found it. The thick ancient volume was crammed between taller books so that it was all but obscured from view. This had to be it, the 'sack witches' book. Its title was as ponderous as the tome itself.

The One Complete and True History of the Most Noble Kingdom of Arcady.

It was stuck between the other books so tightly, I had to tug hard to pull it free. I dislodged a cloud of dust, sending me off into a sneezing fit. I dropped the book, clutching at the bookcase to keep myself from falling as well. As soon as I recovered, I used the back of my hand to dash the moisture from my watery eyes.

I blinked hard. I do not know whether it was finding the 'sack witches' book or perhaps the violent sneeze. Something jarred loose in my brain, the return of that elusive memory I had had when I was with Mal in the garden last night. A childhood memory long forgotten.

I had a habit of creeping out of bed at night after my stepmother and sisters were asleep. I would sneak downstairs to the library where I knew my father would be settled in his chair by the hearth, reading. By crawling on my hands and knees, I was able to escape detection. I would hide behind his chair, selecting a book of my own, while congratulating myself on being so stealthy and clever. I have realized since then that my father must have been quite aware of my presence but chose to indulge my misbehavior.

But one night, something very different occurred. When I inched open the library door to peek inside, I discovered my father was not alone. Someone had been with him... Mal's grandfather! My father had appeared agitated and—

My mind threatened to cloud over again. I gripped the stepladder hard, fighting my way through the fog to retrieve the memory of Papa's voice.

"No, Hiram! My beloved Cecily is gone. I will not risk endangering Ella or my new wife and daughters by proceeding any further."

"We are all taking risks, Julius," Mr. Hawkridge replied. *"If you—"*

"Julius is right to be cautious," another voice interrupted.

Someone else had been there, seated in Papa's chair. But who?

I pressed the heel of my hand hard against my forehead, but I could not remember. All I could recall was a pair of long legs and a slender white hand positioned atop the arm rest, the sound of the man's calm, reasonable voice.

"The time is not yet right, Hiram and you know it as well as Julius and I do."

Mal's grandfather paced before the hearth, fuming, until he flung up his hands in defeat.

"All right," he growled, "But you have got to hide this book for me. The king's blasted Scutcheons have already raided my house. Among my other magical objects, they have confiscated the orb."

My father paled. "What!"

The quiet man in the chair spoke up, "Don't worry. We will find a way to get it back. And the king has no idea what the orb does or how to use it."

"All the more reason, this needs to be kept safe." Mr. Hawkridge thrust a heavy volume into my father's hands. "I have hidden—"

He broke off. In my eagerness to see and hear, I had pushed the door too far, betraying my presence.

My father spun toward me looking horrified. "Ella!"

Mr. Hawkridge glared at me, and the stranger hidden in the chair started to rise...

"Ella? Ella!"

My sister's voice snapped me back to the present. I had been so lost in my struggle to remember that I had not noticed Netta enter the library. She stood at the foot of the stepladder, gazing expectantly up at me.

"What do you want?" I asked.

Netta flinched at my sharp tone. I had not meant to snap, but I had been so close to recalling the identity of that stranger. The cloud descended over my mind again and the memory was lost.

"I am sorry to have disturbed you," she said. "But there is a royal herald at the door. He has brought you flowers and a message from Prince Florian."

I groaned. "Fine. Tell the herald I will be there directly."

My sister started to retreat when she noticed the 'sack witches' book. When the volume had slipped from my hands, it had fallen face down, the pages flattened against the carpet.

"You dropped one of your books and it is coming apart," Netta said, bending down to retrieve it.

"No! Be careful!" I cried.

Netta snatched her hand back, gaping at me with wide-eyed consternation. I scrambled down the ladder and lifted the book. The binding had come loose, the front cover hanging askew. I could see what appeared to be a scrap of ancient parchment protruding from the binding.

I hugged the book close, concealing it from my sister as best I could. After what I had just remembered, who knew what sort of dangerous secret this book might contain?

My poor sister stared at me as if I was losing my wits as I babbled, "Just an old book, too fragile, need to fix it. Why don't you just run along and get the message from the herald?"

"Mr. Smythe insists he can only deliver the message to you. Do you want me to escort him into the parlor?"

"No!" The last thing I needed right now was a royal herald lurking about the place.

"I - I mean no, "I said in a calmer voice. "Just tell him to wait on the doorstep. I will be there as soon as I can."

I could tell Netta thought I was behaving very strangely. I lifted one hand from the book to shoo her on her way, while summoning a reassuring smile. Netta left to do my bidding, but she cast me an anxious glance on her way out of the room.

As soon as she was gone, I hastened to lock the door behind her. I carried the book over to the desk and laid it down carefully. I kept stumbling on one revelation after another about my father, each more troubling than the last. Had I really remembered Papa being involved with Mal's grandfather in what? Some sort of conspiracy against the king? Something that involved that mysterious orb? And who was the third person in the room that night?

The answers to these disturbing questions might well lie with whatever was hidden inside that old book. Whatever it was, I wasn't sure I wanted to know. It took me a moment to summon the courage to ease open the book. Because the binding had cracked, I could see where a piece of parchment had been concealed beneath it and the cover flap. My fingers trembled as I tried to tug the paper free, but it was so ancient, it threatened to tear apart. Taking a deep breath to steady myself, I reached for the letter opener and carefully inserted it inside the binding. I enlarged the gap until I was able to retrieve the parchment.

The paper was brittle with age. It crackled as I slowly unfolded it and perused the contents. The ink had faded with time, but the writing was clear enough that I could have read it if the words had not been penned in a foreign tongue. I could not begin to decipher it, but I was able to hazard a guess this was the ancient language of the fairies.

Beneath the writing was a sketch of a small orb positioned atop a circular disk that looked like a sundial. I refolded the parchment with a mixture of frustration and unease. It had provided me with no answers, but I was convinced of one thing. There was more to that orb than Mal or I had ever suspected. We had no idea what its true power or purpose might be, but I wagered it had nothing to do with finding some great lost treasure. Mal was experimenting with the thing, oblivious to what power he might unleash. He had not been able to activate it thus far, but I had to warn him about what I had discovered as soon as possible. I wanted to rush to his shop at once, but it was still four hours before we had agreed to meet. In the meantime, I still had to deal with the royal herald and find a good hiding place for the parchment.

I decided the safest course was to keep it on my person. I wrapped the parchment carefully up in my handkerchief and tucked it inside my bodice. I dusted off my hands and composed myself as I prepared to greet the royal herald, doing my best to look innocent. Not at all like the daughter of a man who might have plotted against the king.

* * *

I hoped the herald might have given up waiting for me and gone away, but no such luck.

Rhufawn Smythe awaited me on the doorstep, prancing from foot to foot, his round face apprehensive beneath his mop of red curls. I had acquired an unfortunate reputation for my surly treatment of royal heralds, 'accidentally' dropping buckets of water on them or slamming doors on their feet. In my defense, they seldom brought good news, usually some announcement of the king's newest petty law or tax.

Rhufawn was braver than our former herald who had retired to join the Loyal Order of Hermits. But he was still wary enough to hold the bouquet of red roses he carried out in front of him like a shield.

"Flowers, Your Highness." He bowed. "A small token of Prince Florian's love and adoration."

"I am not 'Your Highness,'" I replied. Seizing the flowers from him, I tried to close the door, but Rhufawn managed to wedge one foot in the opening.

"Please, Miss Upton. There is a message as well. Prince Florian wishes to convey his regrets that he will be unable to wait upon you today, but he is obliged to tend to his official duties. Otherwise, nothing else would keep him from your side."

I doubted that Florian had any official duties. Perhaps he was spending time at his father's bedside as I suggested or more likely, he had felt an urge to go hunting or was recovering from another pixie dust binge. I did not care where he was or what he was doing if he was not stalking me. It would make slipping away for my rendezvous with Mal so much easier.

I was so relieved and delighted at the prospect of a Florian-free day, that I laughed.

Rhufawn eyed me dubiously. "Er - the prince hopes you will not be too disappointed."

"Oh, I am. Completely devastated." I said with a broad grin.

"By way of consolation for his absence, the prince has written you another love poem."

My grin faded as Rhufawn rummaged in his pouch and produced a small scroll. I eyed it with distaste and held out my hand. "Fine. Give it here."

"Oh, no. I am obliged to read it to you."

"Rhufawn... " I growled as I tried to seize the scroll, but the herald was too quick for me.

Rhufawn danced out of my reach, whipping the scroll behind his back. "Please, Miss Upton. The prince's instructions were most explicit. I am to recite the poem for you and with great feeling." He fluttered his lashes and added coaxingly. "There are only seventeen verses."

"Seventeen!" I squawked.

"Perhaps closer to twenty, but they are short ones."

I scowled at him but before I could argue further, I was distracted by a commotion in the lane. Rhufawn and I both turned to stare as a troop of mounted Scutcheons surged past my gate. Clad all in black and wearing unadorned helmets, these grim-faced men presented a fearsome aspect.

"Border guards," I murmured. "But they never leave their assigned post unless..."

"Unless the king has ordered an eviction." Rhufawn filled in the thought that I was reluctant to complete.

A chill swept through me as I watched the troop rein to a halt before the Hanson residence and dismount. Leaving one man to tend to the horses, the others marched upon the house, led by a burly Scutcheon, who bore the single epaulette of a sergeant on his shoulder.

I shoved past Rhufawn and hurried to my fence, craning my neck to get a better view. The sergeant hammered on the Hanson's front door and bellowed, "Open in the name of the king."

When there was no response, the impatient sergeant appeared ready to give his men the order to break the door down. But it opened a crack and Myrtle Hanson peered timidly out. The Border Sergeant forced the door open further and brandished some sort of notice. I saw Myrtle shake her head and try to close the door. But the sergeant dragged her outside. He flung her to one of his men to guard and motioned the rest of his troop to follow him. As they surged inside, I was already heading out my gate.

Rhufawn rushed after me protesting, "Miss Upton, do you really think you should... "

The rest of his words were lost as I raced across the lane, but I had no difficulty completing the rest of his thought. Did I really think I should attempt to interfere with a royal order of eviction? No, definitely not. But I could not stand aside and do nothing as the rest of the neighborhood was doing.

Usually, any sort of commotion in the lane brought people spilling from their houses, but as I hurried toward the Hansons, I was the only one foolhardy enough to try to help, even though I did not have the least idea what I could do.

Myrtle struggled in the grip of her captor. When she spotted me, she broke free. Rushing across her front lawn, the girl hurled herself into my arms, sobbing.

"Myrtle, what is this? What is going on?"

The girl was weeping too hard to answer me. Her guard, a tall, grim, looking man with heavy brows and a thick mustache, closed in on us. When he tried to yank Myrtle away from me, I cried, "Leave her alone."

It was a command born out of desperation. I never expected him to obey me. I was astonished when he stopped, stared at me, and then bowed. "Your pardon, Miss Upton."

Apparently even the Border Scutcheons were aware that Prince

Florian had marked me as his future bride. I wondered if I might be able to use that to my advantage to aid the Hansons, but I was disabused of that notion as the guard continued, "I am sorry, miss, but you cannot interfere with a household's removal sanctioned by the king."

"A removal of the entire Hanson family? To where?" I demanded. "Misty Bottoms?"

The guard shifted his feet, looking uncomfortable. It was Myrtle who recovered enough to answer me. Lifting her head from my shoulder, she wept, "N-no. We are being exiled."

"To the swamp lands?" I gasped, training my horrified gaze upon the guard. "But why?"

The man shrugged. "Not our place to ask the king for explanations, miss. We just carry out our orders."

Myrtle pulled away from me, swiping her damp cheeks with the back of her hands. "It is all my fault. For swooning in front of the prince."

"Nonsense! Surely that would rate a heavy fine, at most."

"Yes, but remember? My brothers tried to rescue me and attacked the king's guards. Our whole family was arrested that night at the ball, even Mama and Papa and Fortescue Bafton and his sister. Oh, Ella, we were all chained up in the Dismal Dungeons. Such a horrible place and I was so scared."

"But I thought Commander Crushington had successfully pleaded your case with the king's wizard."

"He did. The commander got us all released yesterday evening. He sent us home and said that Papa would pay a fine and that would be the end of the matter. But now the Border guard has this writ, saying we must leave at once and we are only allowed to take one bundle of our belongings and —"Myrtle dissolved into tears again.

"This has to be some dreadful mistake," I said. "I will go find Commander Crushington at once. He will straighten everything out and put a stop to this."

Myrtle regarded me through tear- drenched eyes. "Oh, Ella, can you?"

"Yes. Don't lose heart. I will be back with the commander directly." I gave the girl a fierce hug and tore off running toward town.

With my skirts hiked up so I could run faster and my hair flying wild, I must have looked like a madwoman if there had been anyone to notice or care. As I passed through town, I saw another contingent of the Border guard swarmed around the tailor's shop, rounding up the Bafton family. A few of the Midtown citizens watched in helpless disbelief, but most had retreated inside the shops. I caught glimpses of alarmed faces peering out windows.

We all heard the disturbing tales of poor folk from the Bottoms being driven out of the kingdom for failure to pay taxes, forfeiting their meager homes to the exchequer. It was against the law to be homeless in Arcady. Our king wanted no beggars littering his streets.

This was the first time a writ of exile had been passed against anyone from Midtown. And all because of such a trivial matter— a foolish young girl trying to attract the notice of the prince by swooning. Small wonder if Midtown folk were unsettled and seeking security by cowering at home. I clung to the belief that this had to be some ridiculous error and Horatio would be able to see everything put right.

By the time I reached Quad Hall, I was panting for breath, a stitch blooming in my side. Pressing my hand against my ribs to dull the ache, I stumbled toward the quadrant that housed the garrison office and gaol. The interior of this part of the towers was dark and cool with unvarnished stone walls and floor. My halting footsteps set up a lonely echo as I crossed the outer hall. Most of the Scutcheons were on patrol at this time of day. I prayed that Horatio was not gone as well. The only one in sight was the sentry that guarded the stairs leading up to the commander's office.

I was relieved to see that it was the amiable Major Frackles. I had no time to get into a lengthy explanation or argument with some overzealous Scutcheon about my need to see the commander *immediately.*

At the sight of me, Frackles abandoned his soldier-on-important duty pose. The young man looked startled by my sudden wild-eyed appearance.

"Miss Upton!"

I had to pause to recover my breath before I could gasp out, "Commander Crushington. I must see him. Is he here?"

"Yes, miss. He is in his office."

"Thank the heavens." I breathed.

"In fact, he wishes to see you as well. I believe the Commander sent Private Benton to fetch you only a few minutes ago."

He had? Why had Horatio not come to call upon me himself instead of sending one of his subordinates? But this was hardly the moment to wonder about that. Even now the Border Scutcheons could be marching the unfortunate Bafton and Hanson families through the streets, toward the bridge that crossed the Conger River, leading to the dismal wilderness beyond.

"If you just wait a moment, I will go up and tell the commander you are here," Frackles began, but I cut him off with a shake of my head.

"Sorry. I have no time to waste."

The major frowned as I brushed past him, but he made no effort to stop me. Gripping the rail, I climbed the stairs as fast as I could. I was badly winded by the time I reached the top, but I did not pause. Not even bothering to knock, I flung open the door and staggered inside the commander's office.

The garrison commander's office was as austere and unadorned as I would have expected it to be, the only furnishings, a scarred oak desk and several uncomfortable looking chairs. A hanging lantern suspended from a chain provided sparse light for late night working hours.

On the wall behind the desk was the obligatory portrait of

the king that hung in all government offices. A flag stand bearing the pennant with the Helavalerian coat of arms stood nearby. The only personal touch that marked the office as being Horatio's domain was a set of prints depicting fine thoroughbred stallions. Although obviously not the work of any of the great fey masters like Peccano, the sketches were pleasing in their simplicity and reminded me of the foundling boy that Horatio had once been. The child whose humble dream had been to become a stable boy so that he could always be near the horses that he so loved.

Horatio stood near the narrow window. His back turned toward me, his arm against the wall as he stared down toward the courtyard far below. He appeared too lost in his thoughts to notice my arrival.

I shoved the door closed and rushed toward him. "Horatio, there has been some dreadful mistake. The Border Scutcheons don't realize that the king pardoned the Hansons and the Baftons. They are being rounded up and—"

"I know," he interrupted, without turning around.

"You know? Then you must hurry back to the palace and—"

"The king appears to have changed his mind. There is nothing more I can do."

His curt reply filled me with dismay. "But I thought you had influence with the Great Mercato. Can you not go to the royal wizard and have him speak to the king?"

"I *said* there is nothing more I can do." Horatio swung around to face me. "I cannot fix everything, and you would do well to realize that."

I was taken aback by his harsh words, but his anger seemed to be directed more at himself than me. His eyes were shadowed with such a look of exhaustion and defeat, my heart ached for him.

"I am sorry. You did everything you could. I did not mean to imply otherwise." I wrapped my arms around his neck. "Was this why you wanted to see me? To tell me this?"

"No." His face lit with a brief longing, but then his features hardened with such a stony expression, it sent a chill through me.

He seized hold of my hands and forced me away from him.

"Prunella Upton, I am obliged to inform you. You are under arrest."

"W-what?"

Before I could fully absorb the impact of his words, the man I loved slapped a pair of iron manacles about my wrists and locked them.

Eleven

I stared at the manacles locked about my wrists, too stunned to speak. I gazed up at Horatio and faltered, "Is this a jest?"

"Do I look as though I am jesting?"

No, he looked like a man ready to march me downstairs to the gaol and fling me into the nearest empty cell. He seized hold of my arm. His grip was firm as he guided me around his desk to a straight-backed chair positioned in front of it.

"Sit down."

The chair was lower than usual, and my legs started to tremble, making it difficult for me to comply. Because of the manacles, I could not use my hands for support. I held my burdened wrists up to Horatio.

"Are these things necessary? I am hardly any dangerous criminal."

"That remains to be seen." But he helped ease me down onto the chair before taking his own seat behind the desk.

This could not be happening. My head reeled with disjointed thoughts. What was this about? The orb. It had to be about that strange orb. Horatio had found out that I had stolen it. But how? Why had I ever helped Mal to take the blasted thing? And how had my father been involved with all of this? The mysterious parchment I had tucked inside my bodice seemed to burn against my skin. Would I be searched?

I wished I had left the note hidden in the library. I wished I had never looked for it in the first place and - and my family. What about them? What would become of Imelda, Netta and Amy if I never returned home? Could Horatio really charge me with a crime and send me off to be locked away forever in the King's Royal Prison?

I looked up, feeling more distanced from him than an expanse of wooden desk. I searched his face for the warmth I was accustomed to, some trace of the man who held and kissed me so tenderly yesterday, promising to love me forever. I didn't find him because it was not Horatio sitting there, only the formidable commander of the Midtown garrison.

Mal had tried to warn me so many times. *"You can't trust him, Ella. He's a Scutcheon. The king's man through and through. His first duty and loyalty will always be to the crown."*

I hadn't wanted to believe that. I still didn't, but I was daunted by Horatio's dispassionate expression. He avoided my gaze while he shuffled through some paperwork on his desk. The silence that stretched between us felt stifling.

Was this a tactic Horatio used to unnerve criminals, wielding silence like a weapon against them? Or was he finding his duty so hard and painful he needed time to steel himself to act against me? I prayed it was the latter reason.

He leaned back in his chair at last, steepling his hands in front of him. His voice was soft, but it was the softness of steel sheathed in velvet.

"Your reaction to being arrested surprises me, Ella. Most people either loudly declare their innocence or at least demand to know what the charges are."

He was still calling me Ella and not Miss Upton? I tried to draw some comfort from that.

"I assumed you would get around to telling me."

"Can you not guess?"

The orb.

I squirmed. The parchment secreted in my bodice seemed to crackle loudly enough for Horatio to hear. More likely it was my own guilty conscience.

I moistened my lips and said, "I don't know. Perhaps my neighbor filed a complaint accusing me of practicing witchcraft without a license. She has long threatened to do so."

"Mrs. Biddlesworth? As a matter of fact, she did, not long after I took up my post here in Midtown. She has tried to file several complaints. I finally told her to stop wasting my time with such nonsense."

I regarded him with wonder. "You have been protecting me all this time?"

"A rather thankless task. I should have listened to Mrs. Biddlesworth's accusations. You certainly managed to bewitch me."

For the first time, I glimpsed a crack in his rigid armor, the hurt and turmoil roiling beneath. I leaned forward in my chair.

"Horatio, you can't really believe I cast some sort of love spell on you. I am not a witch."

"No, but it seems you are a thief."

I flinched. So, this *was* about the orb.

Horatio recovered his rigid commander's façade as he continued, "You have been accused of breaking into the king's treasury room on the night of the ball. You stole a valuable artifact, a glass orb that you replaced with a fake. Do you deny doing this?"

Mal's voice shouted inside my head. *Admit nothing. Obfuscate.*

But as I looked deep into Horatio's eyes, I could not keep lying to him.

"No," I whispered.

Horatio pressed his hand to his eyes as though he had taken a blow. I realized how badly he had wanted me to deny it, convince him it was not true.

"How did you find out?" I asked. I expected him to tell me that it was because of Withypole Fugitate, that the fairy had managed to recover my memories from the shard of my aura he had pocketed.

"You were seen, Ella! Sidney Greenleaf fashioned some sort of magical device that guards the king's treasures and captures images of any intruder invading the chamber."

A magical device? My thoughts flew immediately to the massive carved dragon head mounted on the treasure chamber's walls. I remembered the eerie sensation I had had, that the dragon's glassy eyes were watching me. I had dismissed the notion at the time, as a mere product of my nerves, but it seems I had been right.

Who would have believed such a thing possible? Except this was the king's wizard we were talking about, the magician who had designed the Aura Chamber with its diabolical mirror. The elderly wizard often seemed ridiculous, with his arrogant posturing and flamboyant robes, trying to hide the fact that his true name was something as mundane as Sidney. His magical powers, however, were terrifying. But part of Horatio's explanation did not make sense to me.

"It has been over a week since the ball. If Mercato realized that I had taken something from the treasury room, why did he not have me arrested at once?"

"Because he has been much preoccupied with the king's illness and when Greenleaf did have a chance to visit the treasury room, he could not discover anything was missing, so he was reluctant to take any action against you."

"Why?" I demanded again.

"He told me it was partly because of Prince Florian's desire to marry you and partly because of the wizard's friendship and regard for your late father."

"His what!" I nearly came up out of my chair.

Horatio's brows lifted in surprise at my reaction. "You did not know that Sidney Greenleaf and your father once were friends?"

I shook my head numbly. My quiet father friends with someone as strutting and arrogant as the Great Mercato? The wizard who had abetted our tyrant king in his repression and cruelty? There had been a time I would have scoffed at such a suggestion, but I wondered if I had ever known my own father at all.

Could Mercato have been the third person in that late-night meeting with Hiram Hawkridge and my father? The man I had been unable to remember? My head throbbed painfully as I struggled to recall. I was dimly aware that Horatio was speaking, but I did not look up until he rapped his knuckles against the desk to regain my attention.

"The important point is that this morning Greenleaf inspected the treasury room again and realized that someone had switched the king's orb and replaced it with a fake. The only one who could have possibly done that was you."

"Yes, I already admitted that I did."

"Why would you do such a thing, Ella? I would never have taken you for a thief."

"I am not! That orb did not belong to the king. It—" I choked back my words before I declared that the orb had belonged to Mal's grandfather. I had already made a huge mistake by admitting as much as I had. I did not want to make matters worse by betraying Mal.

I swallowed and continued, "That orb was not the king's rightful property, and I wanted it back."

"During the ball, when I caught you down in the forbidden hall near the treasure chamber, I suspected you were up to something. You claimed you were there looking for your sister and I believed you. What a lucky coincidence that must have been for you, her turning up drunk. Unless Amy faked her inebriation to distract me, and she was in on the plot with you."

"No!" My heart leapt in panic at the idea of my little sister being arrested as well. "Of course, she wasn't. You carried Amy back upstairs. You could tell how drunk she was."

"Then you claim to have acted entirely alone in this burglary."

"Yes!" I struggled to hide my fear behind a show of defiance.

Horatio's gaze drilled into mine. "I don't believe you."

"Then what are you planning to do? Torture the truth out of me?"

"You must know I would never do a thing like that," he replied impatiently.

"I never thought you would clap me in irons either." The chain rattled as I held up my hands, displaying the manacles weighing down my wrists.

Horatio stared at them for a moment before swearing under his breath. He stood up and marched around the desk. Fitting a small key into the lock, he removed the manacles from my wrists. The heavy iron had already chafed my skin. I started to rub the sore spot, but Horatio seized hold of my hand. He lifted my hand to his lips and blew lightly against my wrist.

I would have found this behavior odd, but he had done this once before when I had been injured by Iggy Burt in Misty Bottoms seeking to rob me. I had barely known Horatio at that time and had been astonished when the gruff commander took my hand so gently and breathed against my skin. He had told me he had learned this trick of blowing the pain away from his mother. Surprisingly it worked.

"I am sorry," he said. "It was not my intent to hurt you. I only wanted to scare some sense into you."

"You certainly managed to do that."

"I sincerely doubt it." Horatio heaved a deep sigh. "Do you know Ella, I don't mind so much that you keep trying to make a fool out of me."

He gave a bitter laugh. "Yes, I do mind quite a lot, but that is not important now. What matters isyou have gotten yourself into such deep trouble, I can't help you. Especially if you persist in lying to me."

I withdrew my hand from his grasp. "I am not lying. I—"

"Don't!" Horatio brought his fist down upon the desk with such force that I jumped. I watched him struggle to master his anger and frustration.

"Don't, Ella," he said in a quieter tone. "If you tell me the truth, there is still a chance that I can save you. The king knows nothing about the theft. Greenleaf told me he would be willing to overlook what you did, for the sake of your late father and because of the prince's love for you. All you must do is return the orb to him."

It was an incredibly generous offer, and I would have leapt at it except for two reasons. I did not trust the Great Mercato the length of his ridiculous beard. Hadn't the wizard promised that he would see that the Hansons and the other Midtown citizens were pardoned? And now they were all being exiled. Mercato's word meant nothing.

The second reason obviously was Mal. Recovering that orb had meant so much to him, he would not willingly surrender it. Neither would he allow my life and freedom to be put at risk. He would be bound to come up with some reckless plot to rescue me that would end up getting him killed.

What was I going to do? I felt like an eel caught in a sniggler's trap, desperately trying to find a way to wriggle free. As I considered my options, I was silent for so long that Horatio grew impatient.

"I don't see why you are being so hesitant, Ella. Just give the orb back."

"It is not as though I have the blasted thing with me," I protested.

"Where is it then? Back at your house? Hidden in your bedchamber?"

"Y-yes."

"Good. Just tell me where and I will send Major Frackles to fetch it."

"It would be quicker if you trusted me to go."

Horatio leaned back against the desk and folded his arms. "I don't think so, my dear. I don't believe that orb is hidden at your house, any more than I believe you would have undertaken such a lawless scheme all on your own. Someone planned this theft very carefully and persuaded you to take part. I can think of only one conniving person who holds such influence over you.

"Hawkridge!" Horatio pronounced Mal's name with loathing.

Although my heart missed a beat, I shook my head weakly.

"You already told me that you met him out in the forest after the ball. Was that so you could hand the orb over to him?"

I shook my head again, avoiding Horatio's gaze. I have never been as good at obfuscating as Mal. I gripped my hands together and stared down at the floor, but Horatio cupped my chin, forcing me to look at him.

"Are you truly prepared to accept all the blame for this while Hawkridge slinks off into the shadows? The man is a contemptible coward."

I shoved Horatio's hand away and shot to my feet. "Mal is no coward! As soon as he learns of my arrest, he will come—"

I broke off, realizing too late Horatio had deliberately goaded me.

"Hawkridge will do what, Ella? Come forward and confess?"

I bit my lip, wishing I had kept my mouth shut. Mal would never have been so easily tricked. I sank back down on the chair, regretting that I had not followed my impulse to tell Horatio about taking the orb before he had to discover it this way. I had plenty of opportunities. If I had confided the truth to him voluntarily, perhaps I could have made him understand. Now it was far too late, but I still had to try.

"The king is the one who is the real thief," I said. "That orb does not belong to His Majesty. It was the rightful property of Hiram Hawkridge before King August confiscated it and locked it up in his treasure vault along with all the other objects he had snatched from his subjects. That orb means nothing to our greedy king, but it means the world to Mal, a cherished reminder of his late grandfather."

Horatio gave a contemptuous snort. "That is how Hawkridge convinced you to steal the orb? With some sad sentimental tale about a family heirloom that had been taken from his grandfather. Your good friend lied to you, Ella.

"That orb never belonged to Hiram Hawkridge and it is far from being some harmless memento. It was fashioned by the fairies and possessed of some deep older magic. Even the king is unaware of the orb's true power, but Greenleaf knows. He refused to tell me exactly what that orb does, but he insists that in the wrong hands, that orb could have the ability to rain destruction down upon this entire kingdom."

I felt myself go pale. I would have refused to believe the king's wizard except that the proof was tucked inside my bodice. That ancient parchment with its sketch of the orb and words written in the language of the fairies. There was also my disturbing recollection of that mysterious meeting between my father and Hiram Hawkridge.

Could Mal possibly have known about all of this and lied? Mal, my lifelong friend, always able to make me smile when I wanted to sink with despair, always ready to offer me a shoulder to cry upon. He was the only person I had ever allowed to see the real Ella with all her flaws and weaknesses, knowing that no matter what I did, whatever mistake I made, Mal would forgive me. If I found out that Mal had deceived me— No! I refused to allow Horatio to shake my faith in my friend.

"If what Mercato says is true, Mal has no idea how dangerous the orb is," I said.

Horatio's brows arched with skepticism. "Are you so sure about that? Such a weapon would be quite useful to a man plotting a rebellion against the king."

"I already told you. Mal is not the leader of the League of the Missing Prince or whatever the blasted thing is called. He told me so himself. He might have his faults, but he would never lie to *me*. Especially not about something this important. He truly believes that orb belonged to his grandfather and that it is the key to finding some fabulous lost treasure."

"The man might well be nothing more than a greedy fool, but that doesn't excuse his crime."

"It may have escaped your notice, Commander," I retorted. "But being poor is considered the worst crime in this kingdom nowadays."

"I have noticed," Horatio said. A deep weariness settled over his face. But his expression hardened again as he straightened, stepping away from the desk. "I don't care what Hawkridge's motives are. He should never have gotten you involved in this."

He strode across the room to where his sword was sheathed in a belt hanging from the wall. I watched in alarm as he lifted it down from its wooden peg.

I rose from my chair and hurried toward him. "What are you going to do?"

Horatio didn't answer me, his mouth compressed in a taut line. As he girded the belt around his waist, he said. "You are free to go. Under guard of course. Frackles will escort you home. I can't have you running off to warn him."

"Warn Mal? Of what? Horatio! What are you planning to do to him?"

"What I should have done a long time ago. Find Hawkridge even if I must kick in every door in Misty Bottoms. Arrest that miscreant and recover the orb." Horatio angled a sidelong glance at me. "I suppose it is useless asking you to make this easier by telling me where Hawkridge is."

"I don't know."

"Of course, you don't." Horatio gave me a frustrated look.

"I don't!" I took a deep breath before adding, "But I could help you find him if you allow me to go with you."

"Not a chance!"

"I realize I have given you no reason to trust me, but—"

"No, you certainly haven't."

I winced at his bluntness. "Even if you tell Mal what Mercado said about how dangerous the orb is, Mal won't believe you. He'll fight to keep it."

"That would be a huge mistake on his part."

"Horatio, please. You feel betrayed and angry with me and you have every right to be. But don't you see going after Mal this way is going to end in some horrible confrontation and it doesn't have to be that way. Let me talk to Mal. He will listen to me."

Horatio shook his head, his expression as obdurate as stone.

"You'll never find him on your own. You've tried before."

Horatio scowled at the reminder. "Misty Bottoms teems with poor folk and rogues desperate enough to sell their own mothers for a single coin and yet for some reason I cannot begin to fathom, they are as blindly loyal to Hawkridge as you are."

"That is because there is another side to Mal you are unwilling to see." I sighed. Horatio had once told me that he viewed the world in black and white until I had brought color into his life. I despaired of ever getting him to understand the subtle shades of gray that existed in Mal. Any more than I could ever persuade Mal to understand Horatio's stern code of honor.

"Please," I said, clutching at Horatio's arm. "I love both of you. I could not bear it if either one of you was hurt."

"A little late for you to be worrying about that now," he said, pulling away from me. "I don't understand why you keep defending that criminal. Why do you love him so much when it is obvious, he does not care a frap for you? If he did, he would never have asked you to steal that orb. If he truly loved you, he would have protected you."

"Mal might have asked me to help, but it was my choice. He tried to keep me safe by giving me these magic shoes that were supposed to turn me invisible."

"Magic shoes? For mercy's sake, Ella! How gullible are you where that man is concerned?"

My mouth twisted wryly. "I should have known the shoes wouldn't work. Mal's magic invariably never does. When I arrived at the ball that night and saw how well guarded the door leading down to the treasury was, I was ready to abandon the plan. Mal would have been disappointed, but he would have understood."

"Then why did you still go through with it?"

"Because when Myrtle Hanson was arrested for swooning and the fight broke out, the door was left unguarded. I saw my chance and took it."

Horatio stared at me with a mixture of incredulity and bewilderment. I gave a helpless shrug, knowing it was useless to explain further how nervous and frightened I had been. But after I had stolen the orb and believed I had gotten away with it, I had felt a surge of excitement, a rush of triumph. That same thrill I had experienced with Mal when we had succeeded in pulling off some mischief during our childhood.

There is more of the pirate than the princess about you, Mal had told me, and I feared he was right. It was a shade in my character that my honorable Horatio would never understand and that thought made me unbearably sad.

"Mal didn't compel me to do anything," I said. "He has never regarded me as some helpless damsel. He sees me as his equal, strong, and resourceful."

"I see you that way too, Ella. But I will always strive to keep you safe. I would die for you."

The anguish in Horatio's eyes matched what I felt in my heart as he turned away from me, pacing back to the window to stare outward. His voice was thick with exhaustion as he said, "Unfortunately, my ability to protect you could be coming to an end. Greenleaf has given me until sunset to retrieve that orb from you. I have already been unable to catch the person who vandalized the aura chamber. If I fail the king a second time, the wizard has made the consequences of what will happen very clear. I will be dismissed from my command and banished to patrol the northern border."

I didn't know if there was any chance at all that the shattered trust between me and Horatio could ever be mended. But if he was sent north, I would never see him again. I felt stricken with a mingling of despair and guilt. Mal and I were the ones who had chosen to steal that orb. It was not right that Horatio should suffer because of our reckless folly.

"Please let me help you find Mal and recover the orb." I followed Horatio to the window. "I said I didn't know where Mal is right now, but I know where he will be. We agreed to meet later this afternoon."

Horatio whipped about to face me. "When and where?"

I hesitated, fearing that I could be making a huge mistake by telling Horatio this. But if I ever hoped he might trust me again, I needed to start by being honest.

Exhaling a deep breath, I said, "Two o'clock at the Hawk's Nest. But if you arrive there without me, Mal will bolt before you have a chance to say a word."

"Not if I take him by surprise," Horatio said.

I shuddered, overcome with visions of a violent confrontation between the two men I loved.

"I can reason with Mal if you let me speak to him first. Please, Horatio, let me help you."

Horatio gazed down at me, and his stern expression wavered. "If I do agree to allow you to come, you will make no effort to warn Hawkridge. You will obey my orders, do exactly as I say, when I say it."

I nodded vigorously.

The muscles in Horatio's jaw tightened, a sign of his inward struggle. But at last, he sighed. "Very well."

"Thank you." I looked up at him, gratitude welling in my eyes. "You are a good man, Horatio Crushington."

"No. What I am is a frapping fool," he said. "Let's go. Before I change my mind."

Twelve

T he sun disappeared behind the clouds, the air heavy with the scent of oncoming rain. The overcast sky matched the bleakness of my mood as I trudged along beside Horatio. I was accustomed to covering the distance to the Bottoms on foot, yet I had thought Horatio would want to fetch his horse from the stables. But he feared if Mal spotted Loyal tied up outside the Hawk's Nest, Mal would be likely to flee.

Horatio's plan was to conceal all evidence of his presence. He had even brought along a hooded black cloak which he carried slung over his shoulder.

I could not refrain from pointing out, "That cloak will not prove much of a disguise."

"It is not intended to be." Horatio gestured toward the lowering sky. "I brought it in the event we are caught in a rainstorm."

He showed far more foresight than I had. When I had seen the Hansons being dragged from their home by the Border Scutcheons, my one thought had been to find Horatio as quickly as possible. I had not paused for anything, even to fetch a shawl. Getting wet was the least of my worries.

However, we had not gone far, when I realized Horatio had not brought the cloak for himself. Commanding me to halt, he swirled the garment about my shoulders.

"No," I protested. "My gown is old and faded, but your uniform could be ruined."

"My uniform has survived far worse things than rain."

I persisted in trying to remove the cloak, but his hand closed over mine to stop me.

"Leave it, Ella. You agreed to do as you are told, remember?" he said sternly.

I sighed and stood like an obedient child while he fastened the cloak about my neck. But I squirmed inwardly with shame and guilt. Despite how I had deceived him and brought all this trouble down upon his head, Horatio was still striving to protect me.

I mumbled my thanks as we resumed our trek. The cloak which would only have reached the top of Horatio's boots hung to my heels. I had to hug the garment tightly about me to keep from treading upon the hem.

I hoped I had done right by telling Horatio where to find Mal, the only thing I could do to prevent disaster from overtaking all three of us. I still felt wretched about it, fearing I was betraying my dearest friend to a terrible fate.

I glanced up at Horatio but could glean no comfort from his rigid profile.

"If I persuade... " I paused and amended, seeking to inject a more confident note into my voice. "*When* I persuade Mal to give back the orb, I suppose you will still feel obliged to arrest him."

"Of course."

I swallowed. "And send him to the King's Royal Prison?"

"No. I would not send my worst enemy to that place if I could avoid it. But I do intend to incarcerate your friend in my gaol for a long stretch until I am convinced, he is ready to abandon his illegal activities and earn his bread as an honest apothecary."

I breathed a deep sigh of relief, even though I suspected Mal enjoyed defying the king's laws. If there was more pirate than princess in me, there was more of the outlaw than apothecary in Mal. I envisioned him locked up in the Midtown gaol, arms defiantly locked across his chest until his beard grew long and gray. It was still a better fate than being choked to death at the hands of the Royal Garrotter.

I expressed my gratitude to Horatio for his leniency, adding, "I hope that Mal will have enough sense to be grateful as well."

"I don't give a whit about his gratitude. I am not doing it for him."

Horatio's reply was curt, but my gaze flew to his face, hoping to find some lingering trace of his love for me. I could not read anything into his stony expression. It was probably too late to explain or excuse my part in all of this, but I had to try.

Taking a deep breath, I said, "The night of the ball when you caught me in the forbidden part of the castle after I had stolen the orb, I was only beginning to know you. I liked and respected you. I was even starting to fall in love with you, but I was very aware you were a Scutcheon commander, your loyalty pledged to the king. I still hated deceiving you, hated it even more after you declared your feelings for me. There were so many times I wanted to tell you the truth, trust that you might somehow understand."

"You should have trusted me, Ella. I told you if you were ever in trouble, you could come to me. If you had, I might have been able to do something to avoid this dire situation. But you chose to keep silent to protect that miscreant Hawkridge."

"Protecting Mal was only part of the reason for my silence. I was so afraid of losing your love which is exactly what I had done. I realize there is no longer any hope that one day you and I... " I had to pause to blink back my tears. "But at least, do you think you ever will be able to forgive me?"

Horatio came to an abrupt halt. "I already have."

I gaped up at him in surprise.

Horatio frowned as he continued, "I admit that I am angry,

hurt, and disappointed in you, but you must have a very poor opinion of me to think that my feelings for you could be so easily set aside. When I said that I would love you forever, I meant it." His gray eyes softened with a look that was both tender and sad. "I love you even though I believe your heart really belongs to Malcolm Hawkridge."

"No. *No!*" I stomped my foot for emphasis. "I have told you and told you—"

"He is only your friend," Horatio finished the sentence for me. "The friend you are willing to risk your life for." He shook his head with a look of weary resignation. "You don't know your own heart, Ella."

But I did. I longed to fling my arms about his neck and prove it to him, but it was going to take far more than kisses to convince Horatio. I did love Mal, my lifelong friend, but there was only one man that truly held my heart. I hoped, given enough time, I would be able to prove to Horatio that my love was as deep and true as his. But first, we needed to survive this disaster of a day.

As we resumed walking, a silence settled between us as heavy as the darkening clouds overhead. The closer we drew to Misty Bottoms, the more anxious I became, the less confident of my ability to control the situation when we arrived at the Hawk's Nest.

Mal was convinced that orb was the key to a treasure that would save us all and he could be unbelievably obstinate when he took a notion into his head. I also feared he would not submit tamely to being clapped in irons. Horatio, in his own way, was equally inflexible.

I straightened my shoulders, trying to imbue myself with the fortitude of my childhood heroine, Anthea, the Magnificently Wise. It was part of that great queen's legend that she had once rounded up all the women of the kingdom and lead them in between two armies to prevent a war. If Queen Anthea could do that, I could surely manage to stop two hard-headed men from coming to blows, couldn't I?

My brief spell of confidence and bravado lasted until Horatio and I passed the first few tumbledown cottages. We found the lane ahead of us blocked by a gathering crowd. Horatio and I both halted, surprised, and uneasy at the sight. Bottoms dwellers tended to keep to themselves, never pausing in the streets to exchange friendly greetings or gossip the way Midtown people were wont to do.

Horatio frowned and moved closer to me as we drew nearer to this ragged crowd. Scrawny bare foot lads jostled for space next to burly ruffians and stooped old men with straggly beards. There was also a scattering of women in the crowd, housewives as worn looking as their much-mended gowns, even gray-haired beldames leaning on their canes. Male, female, young or old, they were alike in one respect, the degree of resentment in their faces, a suppressed anger that appeared as ready to erupt as the threatening skies overhead.

Ordinarily the approach of the commander of the Midtown garrison would have caused these people to duck their heads and scuttle off to their homes, but no one even noticed Horatio. All attention was focused on whatever was happening in the lane ahead.

I could hear the distant ominous beat of a drum and someone shouting. Craning my neck, I tried to see over the cluster of heads. Horatio, being that much taller than me, had a far better view. Whatever he saw caused him to tense and swear.

"What is it? What's happening?" I asked anxiously.

"That cursed fool Bluntvale!"

"Bluntvale?"

"The commander of the Border Scutcheons. I can't believe that pompous ass is fool enough to flaunt his prisoners in front of this angry mob."

"Prisoners?" I faltered. "You mean the Hanson family and the Baftons?"

Horatio didn't answer me. He hooked his arm about my shoulders, propelling me in the opposite direction. "You need to get away from here, Ella. Right now."

"But—"

"Don't argue with me. Head for the Hawk's Nest and wait for me there."

When I tried to hang back, he gave me a shove.

"Go!" he snapped before pivoting on his heel and heading toward the crowd.

I stared at his retreating back, dumbfounded by his command. I did not flatter myself that Horatio had suddenly decided he could trust me. His concern for my safety overrode any fear he had that I would betray him by helping Mal to escape.

I loved the man for it, loved him so much my heart ached. But I did not stir a step even though I promised Horatio to heed his every command. Well, not promised exactly. I had merely nodded my head. Even if I had sworn obedience on my beloved mother's grave, there was no way I would skitter away like a frightened mouse.

I waited until Horatio was far enough ahead of me before following him. As he thrust his way forward, some people in the crowd became aware of his presence. They grudgingly moved aside, but the sullen glares cast in his direction chilled me to the marrow. I could still hear the relentless beat of that drum. Thump, thump, thump, setting up a fearful echo in my own heart.

If this crowd did break out into violence, they would never distinguish between a Midtown commander with good intentions and the hated Border Scutcheons. It was ridiculous of me to think that I could do anything to protect Horatio from an angry mob, but I was prepared to die trying. Queen Anthea certainly would never have abandoned the man she loved.

As I wove my way through the crowd, I could have encountered some hostility myself. There was little affection or respect between the rough, poor folk of the Bottoms and the more prosperous law-abiding Midtown citizens. But garbed as I was in my old gown and Horatio's travel-worn cloak, with my unbound hair a tangled mess, never had I looked less like a daughter of Midtown.

Little notice was taken of me as I worked my way to the front of the crowd. One toothless old woman shifted aside to make room for me. My breath hitched in my throat when I was finally able to see my neighbors, their misery and humiliation cruelly put on display. The Hanson and Bafton families had been herded together by the troop of Border guards wielding pikes and halberds.

Mr. Bafton hung his head in shame, looking as though he could not believe such a thing was happening to a respectable tailor like himself. His daughter, Ivy stood close to him, her cheeks bright red, but her small chin jutted out in defiance. They both carried small valises. The only one empty- handed was Amy's erstwhile suitor, Fortescue Bafton. I had always regarded the young fop as being something of an ass, vain and foolish. When I had danced with him at the ball, I was surprised to realize that his love for Amy was genuine. Even more astounded when the fight had broken out and the dandy had leapt in, fists flying to defend his fellow Midtown citizens from the Heights aristocrats and the palace guards.

Fortescue must have offered some resistance when the Border Scutcheons had turned up at the tailor shop to evict his family. His cheek was badly bruised, his jaw swollen, one eye nearly closed shut. Despite all of this, he had decked himself out in his finest apparel, tight bright yellow pantaloons, and a chartreuse waspwaisted jacket with enormous gilt buttons. His hands were encased in kid gloves, his high crowned beaver hat tipped at a jaunty angle. He should have looked utterly ridiculous, enough to inspire mockery from the watching crowd. But not a single jeer was hurled, perhaps because Fortescue carried himself with remarkable dignity. Any angry mutterings were directed at the Border Guards.

The Hanson family crowded close to the Baftons. Myrtle and Flora looked terrified, clutching small bundles of whatever belongings they had been allowed to take. Their father hovered protectively near the girls, one arm draped around his weeping wife, his other hand gripping a heavy satchel. Their brothers, Payton and Toland brought up the rear, limping, their faces streaked with dried blood.

The grinning border guard continued to beat his drum. I don't know whether the annoying sound was meant to make this dismal proceeding seem more like some bold military action or perhaps it was intended to convey a warning to the watching crowd. The first thing Horatio did was to bear down upon the drummer and command him to cease his infernal racket.

The Border Scutcheon looked taken aback to be receiving orders from a Midtown commander. When he drummed out a few more taps, Horatio wrenched the stick from his grasp and flung it to the ground.

The action elicited some gasps from the watching crowd and a few faint cheers. Myrtle Hanson broke past the guards. She hurled herself at Horatio's feet, hugging his knees and crying.

"P-please, Commander Crushington. Help us."

"I am sorry, Miss Hanson, I—" Horatio broke off as he was surrounded by the rest of the Hanson family and the Baftons, clamoring and pleading, their faces lit with the hope he had come to offer them a reprieve.

Horatio looked sick as he was forced to disillusion them. I know how hard he had tried to save these people. The weight of his failure rested heavily upon his shoulders and my heart ached for him as much as it did for the families.

The guards closed in, roughly herding the Hansons back into line. One grabbed Myrtle, trying to pry her away from Horatio.

Horatio shoved the man back before gently drawing Myrtle to her feet.

By this time the commander of the Border Guards had recovered from his initial astonishment at Horatio's arrival on the scene. Bluntvale appeared to be an arrogant, swaggering sort of fellow, despite his double chins and large stomach flopping over his military belt.

His face as red as his brick-colored hair, he stormed toward Horatio, bellowing.

"Crushington!"

Horatio swung about to face him. If Bluntvale possessed any sense at all, he would have halted in his tracks. Horatio had drawn himself up to his full height. With his broad shoulders, he cut a formidable figure and never had I seen my beloved look so angry.

Good sense was clearly not among Bluntvale's virtues (if the man had any). Jabbing a pudgy finger at Horatio, he said, "This is a Border matter and none of your concern, so what the frap are you doing here?"

"Trying to stop you from causing a riot, you fool. What were you thinking, man? Making such a spectacle of these unfortunate people."

"I am following my orders directly from the palace."

"What? The king instructed you to behave like a frapping idiot."

"No. I was told to make an example of these miscreants. Especially to this lawless rabble here in the Bottoms."

A low rumble sounded, almost like distant thunder but it was coming from the mob. I was surprised that this ragged crowd would care about the fate of anyone from Midtown. But I recalled that most evictions were carried out in secret. This was likely the first time the Border Scutcheons had dared flaunt their cruel actions publicly.

Giving Bluntvale a disgusted look, Horatio faced the crowd, holding up his hands in a peace-making gesture. "Good citizens of

Misty Bottoms," he called out. "I sympathize with your anger and outrage, but you can do no good here. You cannot help these unfortunate people. If you try to interfere with the king's justice, you will only bring his wrath down upon yourselves and your families. Go back to your homes and your shops."

No one moved but I sensed a subtle shift in the mood of the crowd, an uncertainty. Perhaps it was because Horatio had won a modicum of respect from this rough crowd from the way he had challenged Bluntvale. Perhaps it was something more elemental than that.

Horatio Crushington was one of those rare men who seemed born to lead and command. When the fistfight had erupted at the ball, he had seized control of the situation and restored order. He might have succeeded here in Misty Bottoms if not for Bluntvale.

The volatility of the situation appeared to have finally penetrated his thick skull, but jealousy over having his authority usurped caused Bluntvale to push his way in front of Horatio.

"I can take it from here, Crushington," he said. Hitching up his breeches he snarled at the crowd, "All right. The show is over. Enough gawking. Clear off, the whole stinking lot of you."

Bluntvale's command was greeted by a heavy silence more ominous than the rumble of anger. No one retreated an inch. One old man in the front stubbornly stood his ground and spat in the dirt.

Incensed by this defiance, Bluntvale shouted, "All you all deaf? I said go home!"

The Border Guard commander was foolish enough to unsheathe his sword. I could sense the anger swell around me. Some of the burly, grizzled men pushed forward wielding cudgels, while the younger lads advanced, armed with nothing more than their fists. Even the old lady next to me smacked her gums and waved a rusty dinner fork.

The surge forward was countered by the Border Scutcheons bracing themselves, prepared to drive back the crowd with lowered pikes. Horatio cursed, ordering them to put up their weapons, commanding the crowd to fall back, but no one was listening to him.

This ragged angry mob would be no match for the well-trained Border guards with their fearsome weapons. I was sick with terror at the thought that I was about to witness a massacre. I felt so useless, not knowing what to do, longing to rush to Horatio's side. I began tugging at the women nearest me, begging them to go home.

Some of them were frightened enough to listen. Encouraged by even this small success, I kept at it until I noticed there was someone else moving along the back of the crowd, doing the same thing.

I heard a low voice rapping out orders.

"Get back to your homes and shops. You can accomplish nothing here today except get yourself killed. This is not the time."

I twisted around, catching a glimpse of a figure in a gray woolen cloak, the hood pulled forward. I could not see his face, but I recognized the voice. Mal! He cuffed ears, jerked on collars, yanked at arms, all the while urging retreat. I was astounded to find him here issuing such commands, even more surprised to see that these rough-hewn men reluctantly obeyed him.

Mal's grandmother had always said that Mal could charm a pixie into surrendering her dust and it was true. I had often seen Mal work his roguish magic upon women, but I would never have imagined he could exert such influence over a mob of angry ruffians. I had to be mistaken. The man in the cloak could not be Mal. What would he even be doing here when we were supposed to be meeting at his shop later? Mal had a firm policy of steering clear of any trouble that might involve confrontations with armed Scutcheons.

"I am a lover, not a fighter," he often jested.

Whoever the cloaked man was, I felt grateful to him for achieving what the Border commander and Horatio could not.

The crowd began to melt away, except for one rash boy. I was startled to recognize Tom Piper.

His young face a mask of fury, he drew back his arm to hurl a rock, but was prevented by the man in the cloak. He seized hold of Tom. As the boy struggled and kicked, the man's hood fell back. It *was* Mal.

As I absorbed this fresh shock, Mal lifted Tom off his feet, hauling him away amid the dispersing crowd. I whirled about looking for Horatio. He had succeeded in gaining control of the Border Guards, persuading them to raise their pikes, but he was locked in another furious argument with Bluntvale.

With the angry crowd's retreat, Horatio was no longer in any danger other than losing his temper and flattening the pompous Border commander. I should alert Horatio and tell him that I spotted Mal. But Horatio would be vexed that I had disregarded his command to seek safety. By the time I managed to explain to him and offer my excuses, it might be too late.

From the direction Mal had taken, I realized he was not heading toward his shop. Mal had to have seen Horatio in the lane with the Border Scutcheons. Perhaps he had even seen me arrive with Horatio and guessed that something had gone wrong with our plans. Mal might consider his best course was to disappear and return to meet me another day when it was safe.

I couldn't allow that to happen, not if I was going to persuade Mal to relinquish the orb in time for Horatio to get it back to Mercato before sunset. If I took off after Mal, Horatio would feel as though I had deceived and betrayed him. *Again.* Yet what choice did I have? Mal could vanish at any moment and getting that orb back was my only chance of saving all three of us.

With one last despairing glance toward Horatio, I hurried in the direction I had last spotted Mal. As I threaded my way through the straggling remains of the crowd, I craned my neck, fearing that I had dithered too long. Much to my relief, I glimpsed Mal's gray cloak not too far ahead. He still had Tom in tow. Before

I could overtake him, he hauled Tom out of sight behind a cobbler shop.

Seizing the boy by the shoulders, Mal gave Tom a brisk shake, admonishing him in a low terse voice. I was not close enough to hear what Mal was saying. Tom continued to look defiant before subsiding into tears. Mal bent down and enveloped the boy in a fierce hug.

Undoing his purse, he slipped a coin into Tom's hand, imparting some further instruction. The boy mopped away the last of his tears and nodded. He raced off down an alley behind the shops. Mal hurried in the opposite direction from where I approached.

"Mal!" I shouted, but my voice was lost in a sudden clap of thunder.

Mal glanced up at the sky, scowled and tore off running. I groaned as I raced after him. I tripped on the hem of Horatio's cloak and fell hard onto my hands and knees. Although my kneecaps throbbed with pain and my palms stung, I scrambled to my feet. Hitching the cloak up higher, I staggered after Mal. Misty Bottoms was a maze of twisting lanes and alleys. Mal was familiar with all of them and could disappear at any moment.

I panted with my efforts to overtake him as the sky grew darker. Mal hastened down a worn path that led to the river. Why was he headed there? Surely Mal would not be mad enough to take out a boat in this weather.

"Mal!" I called out to him again, but my words were whipped away by the rising wind.

He came to a halt at the end of a small fishing pier, the only building in sight, a forlorn-looking cottage. I was too out of breath to shout again. The wind whipped at my cloak, and I had to fight to keep my grip on the woolen folds lest the long garment trip me up again.

After his rush to get to this deserted spot, Mal stood there, staring out across the river. I could not understand what had brought Mal here until I was close enough to see what drew his gaze. The pier offered a perfect view of the bridge that spanned the Conger River.

I could discern a troop of figures moving along it, the Border Guard driving their prisoners across the bridge. From there, the Hanson and Bafton families would be forced out into the wild swamp lands beyond, forbidden to ever return to Arcady. I clenched my teeth, blinking back angry tears as another clap of thunder sounded, closer this time. Could not that wretched Bluntvale have given those poor people a reprieve until the storm had passed? I could see Horatio among them, arguing with Bluntvale, no doubt trying to buy the Hansons and Baftons some time. But from this distance, I could not tell how much success Horatio was having.

Mal dragged his hand across his bald pate, something he often did when frustrated. The gesture was familiar to me. The expression on his face was not. It was a hard, angry look I had never seen before on Mal's carefree features, his eyes as turbulent as the river waters slapping against the pier.

I felt unsettled by it, recalling the way Mal had moved among all those rough men in the crowd, ordering them to retreat.

Now is not the time.

It was what I recalled the stranger saying during my father's midnight meeting with Mal's grandfather. My memories of that night were fragmented but vivid enough to make me fear that Papa had been involved in some conspiracy against the king.

Horatio had long suspected the same thing about Mal, that he was the leader of a rebel group plotting to overthrow the kingdom, but I had refused to believe it. I knew Mal's faults well enough. He had no qualms about breaking the law, dabbing in illegal magic, brewing fake elixirs, smuggling and other kinds of mischief.

Mal had denied being part of the League of the Lost Heir and he certainly would never have tricked me into abetting such a dangerous enterprise, I told myself. But it was getting harder and harder to believe that. I felt as though I was walking along a cliff's edge that threatened to crumble beneath me at any moment. I clung desperately to my faith in Mal with both hands.

"Mal?" I stumbled closer, recovering my breath enough to choke out his name.

He started at the sound of my voice, his grim expression dissolving into one of complete dismay. "Ella! What are you doing here?"

"We arranged to meet. Have you forgotten?"

"You came too early. I just sent Tom Piper to your house to warn you to stay home. This is a bad day for you to be here in the Bottoms."

"I know. I was there when the riot almost broke out."

Mal seized me by the shoulders, regarding me with concern. "Are you all right?"

"For the moment, but—" The wind tangled my hair in front of my mouth.

"Thank the fairies for that!" Mal hugged me. "Cursed Bluntvale! His brutes usually just kick in doors and haul folks away from the Bottoms in the middle of the night. Bluntvale always had enough sense not to flaunt people being exiled. The oaf is either getting stupider or bolder."

Fighting to brush my hair back, I nodded in agreement. "But, Mal, I need to tell you—"

"And this time it is all because some foolish girl broke the king's petty law against swooning in front of the prince. Could things possibly get any worse in this kingdom?"

"Mal! Listen," I cried in frustration. But I was cut off again by a loud peal of thunder. A jagged bolt of lightning cut through the clouds. The skies opened and started to pour.

"Frap!" Mal seized my arm and propelled me toward the only shelter available, the dilapidated cottage.

The door hung half off its hinges. We pushed through the opening and darted inside. I had not had time to fling up the hood of my cloak. Rainwater trickled down my cheeks from the wet ends of my hair. I brushed the moisture away, my eyes adjusting to the dim interior of the cottage. The windows had been boarded over in haphazard fashion, allowing the rain to blow inward.

Mal urged me toward the fireplace in the middle of the room where it was relatively dry. The cottage reeked of decay and neglect, the hearth filled with ashes and dried leaves. Little trace remained of the former occupants— a rough-hewn wooden table, a lopsided chair, a shelf dangling half off the stone wall, some shards of broken crockery.

The family that had lived here must have fallen victim to the Border Scutcheons carrying out a royal order of exile. Huddling beneath my cloak, I stared at the rain cascading outside the half-open doorway, another peal of thunder shaking the very foundations of this abandoned cottage. My heart ached at the thought of the Hanson and Bafton families being driven out of the kingdom in the middle of this storm. I worried about Horatio, hoping he would take shelter somewhere and not try to make his way to the Hawk's Nest, only to find me gone.

"Now what were you trying to tell me?" Mal's voice cut into my anxious thoughts. He stood near the hearth, using the sleeve of his shirt to wipe the rain from his face and head.

I had to wait for another rumble of thunder to pass before I could blurt out, "Mercato found out that I switched the orbs."

"What! Impossible!"

I assured him that it wasn't, giving him a somewhat disjointed account of what had occurred in Horatio's office. "I tried not to betray you, but Horatio guessed that you had to be involved and—"

"Ella!" Mal interrupted me with a groan. "You should have told the commander immediately that I was the one behind the whole thing and convinced him that I coerced you into helping."

He hugged me. "Foolish woman! What did you think I would

do when I heard? Hide out in my shop while Crushington locked you up?"

I rested my head against his damp shoulder. "No, I was afraid you would hatch some foolish and dangerous scheme to rescue me."

Mal chuckled. "You know me so well."

Did I? I drew away from him, wished the storm was not making the light in the cottage so dim. Mal smiled at me, but it seemed a mere shadow of his usual roguish grin.

When I told him about Mercato's demand for the immediate return of the orb, I was not even sure Mal was listening to me. His brow furrowed, his mind churning with some swift calculation.

"Mal!" I said sharply. "You know what we have to do."

He nodded. "The orb is hidden back at my shop. As soon as the storm lets up, we'll go and get it."

I had braced myself for a long and fierce argument to persuade him to surrender the orb. His capitulation caught me by surprise. I was so relieved, I could have wept, until Mal added, "We are going to have to flee the kingdom, Ella. I know you'll hate leaving your family, but we have no choice. We must get that orb someplace safe."

My jaw dropped open. "Have you not heeded a word I have been saying? That orb never belonged to your grandfather and it's not the key to some fabulous treasure trove. That cursed thing was fashioned by the fairies. It's imbued with some dark magic and it's dangerous!"

"Only to Mercato and the king," he muttered.

"W-what?" I faltered. "What did you say?"

The room lit up with a flare of lightning, casting an eerie glow over Mal. It was as though I was staring at a stranger, the truth evident in the hard lines of his face, a truth I should have seen if I had not been so blinded by love and loyalty.

"You *knew*," I accused. "You have known all along what that orb really is."

Mal compressed his lips together and I expected him to deny it. I prayed that he would, but all he said was, "Yes."

No apologies, no excuses, just *yes*.

With that one simple word, Mal broke my heart. I reeled, feeling as though the storm battering at the cottage was causing the walls to collapse around me.

"Horatio was right," I choked. "You have been lying to me all this time."

"I didn't lie to you precisely, just obfuscated at bit."

"I am your closest friend. You are not supposed to obfuscate with me!" Seized by a pain and rage, the like of which I had never known, I slapped Mal across the face as hard as I could. He staggered back, as stunned by the violence of my action as I was. I clutched my stinging palm.

Mal rubbed his cheek, the red imprint of my hand staining his cheek. "I guess I deserved that."

"You *guess?*" I snarled.

"You should have just socked me in the nose. Did you forget how I showed you to throw a punch?" he asked, trying to coax a smile from me.

When I glowered at him, he sighed and abandoned the effort.

"I am truly sorry, Ella," he said, reaching out to me, but I shrank away from him.

"Don't! Don't you dare touch me or I swear I will rip off your arm and pound you over the head with it."

Mal had the good sense to retreat.

"I never wanted to deceive you," he began.

"Then stop doing it. You tell me the truth right now, Malcolm Hawkridge. How dangerous is that orb? Exactly what does it do?"

"Just what I told you. The orb was designed to find that which is lost."

I swore and doubled up my fist. I would have hit him again, but Mal grabbed my hand to stop me.

"I allowed you to believe that the orb would lead us to some fabulous cache of riches. The treasure is not a pot of gold or a chest of jewels." Mal paused for effect, before announcing dramatically. "It is a man. The orb is the key to locating Queen Anthea's true heir, our long-lost prince."

"No!" I cried in outraged disbelief. "You let me risk my life to help you steal that orb, all to pursue some ridiculous old myth?"

"It is not ridiculous. Many people believe in the legend, including me."

"Frap, Hawkridge! How old are you? Two? Do you still believe if you catch a mermaid, she will grant you a wish?"

"No, she'd more likely try to drown you. I discovered that the hard way one time when I— but never mind about that. The benevolent mermaid story *was* a myth, but the tales of the missing heir are true."

"So, you *are* part of this league of the Missing Heir, just one more thing that you lied to me about. I suppose you were also behind the break-in at the Aura Chamber."

"No, I swear I didn't lie about that. I had nothing to do with that nor did any of my men."

"As if I will ever believe another word that you say." I sank down upon the rickety chair, feeling sick. Mal's ability to influence those rough-looking men in the crowd suddenly making so much more sense. Horatio's suspicions about Mal were all correct.

"*Your* men," I said hollowly. "You are the leader of this league."

"As was my grandfather before me." Mal flexed his shoulders, the gesture a mingling of pride and defiance. "From the notes in Grandfather's diary, I think your father was also part of the league."

I had already suspected as much from that strange memory I had recovered, but I said tartly, "Is there anything else you failed to mention to me last night? No wonder you were so eager to accept my offer to search my father's library for that missing page."

Mal hesitated before asking, "I don't suppose you found anything yet?"

I looked away from him, conscious of the parchment hidden in my bodice. Ordinarily, I would have been eager to tell Mal about what I had remembered and shown him the missing page, but I could no longer trust him. The thought left me feeling bleak and empty.

I locked my arms across my bosom and said, "If I did find anything, I would never give it to you now."

"Ella," Mal protested. He tried to approach me again but a black look from me stopped him in his tracks.

"No. This madness of yours must stop."

"My grandfather and your father didn't think it was mad. They believed in the legend."

"Then they were as deluded as you are. Why didn't he and Papa use the orb to find this lost heir years ago?"

Mal frowned. "I am not entirely sure, but my grandfather made some reference in his diary to the time not being right. I imagine it meant that the prince was too young to assume his rightful place. But he must be a man fully grown by now."

"If he even exists."

"He exists." Mal struck his fist against his chest. "I feel it here."

"Then why hasn't this mythical hero of yours already come to save us all?"

"I have a theory about that too. I believe he has been raised somewhere in obscurity. I daresay he does not even realize himself he is our lost prince."

"Will you listen to yourself, Mal?" I demanded. "You imagine this, you believe that. I always thought you were one of the most practical men I knew. How could let yourself get swept up in this fantasy?"

"Because I must have faith in something, Ella or everything would seem truly hopeless. There are rumors floating about that the king is dying. I would rejoice except for one thing. Prince Florian! Arcady has suffered enough under King August's tyrannical rule. How much worse will it be when Florian assumes the throne? Even his own brother accused him of being a monster."

"Ryland lies as well as you do," I said. "He could have spoken out of jealousy or spite. The king's majordomo paints a far different picture of Florian. He views him as a spoiled young man who could learn to be a good king with the right guidance."

"Do you really believe that, Ella?"

No, unfortunately I didn't, but I argued, "What makes you think this mythical lost prince of yours would be any better than Florian?"

"He has to be," Mal said. "He has the blood of Queen Anthea the Magnificently Wise flowing through his veins and according to the legend, one day her true heir will return to save Arcady from tyranny and ruin."

"And what do you expect Florian to do if, by some miracle, this did happen? Hand over the crown, saying, *oh, sorry, I didn't realize this really belonged to you.*"

"Of course, not. The League is prepared to fight. We have been amassing weapons, recruiting more men to our cause."

Mal's words sent a shiver of apprehension up my spine. A horrible thought struck me as I recalled Tom Piper's distress and anger as he had prepared to hurl a rock at the Border Scutcheons.

I glared at Mal accusingly, "Never tell me you have been heedless enough to get that poor boy, Tom Piper involved with this mad league of yours! He is only a child."

"I could not have kept him out of it if I tried," Mal said. "Tom stopped being a child the night he came home from foraging for food and discovered Bluntvale had dragged his parents and little sister off to the swamps." Mal gestured angrily around the empty cottage. "This used to be the Pipers' home before Tom's father was injured and unable to work and the family fell behind on their taxes. Ever since that night, Tom has been living in a room above Long Louie's livery stables, hustling about the kingdom, trying to earn what he can in hopes of being able to rescue his family from exile. I have done what I can to help him, employing him for odd errands, but the lad is fiercely independent, too proud to accept charity."

I had seen the same traits in Tom myself. I had first met the boy when I sold my mother's emeralds to Withypole Fugitate to obtain money for my family to attend the ball. When Mal had redeemed the earrings for me, he had sent Tom to bring them to me. Mistaking him for a beggar, I had insulted the boy by offering him food. Tom had thrust out his thin chest, informing me indignantly that he was respectable man of business.

I had always been amused by the boy's cocksure, strutting attitude. Although, I could never have guessed what heartache lay behind his saucy grin, I felt dreadful about that.

Nonetheless, I admonished Mal, "You need to try harder to keep Tom away from this insane league of yours. You are going to end up getting him arrested or even killed."

"I have no intention of allowing Tom to fight when the time comes," Mal replied. He looked hurt and offended that I would even suggest such a thing. "I have enough able-bodied men for that."

"Oh? Exactly how many would that be?"

"There must be at least three dozen of us fully committed to the cause."

"*Three dozen!*" I squawked, coming up out of my chair. "Against all the king's scutcheons and the palace guard? You truly have run mad, Hawkridge!"

Mal flushed. "As soon as I find our lost prince, others will join us. After what happened to your neighbors, I wager there will be plenty of people in Midtown ready to flock to our banner."

"If you think that, you don't know Midtown very well. When the Hansons and Baftons were rounded by the Border Scutcheons, everyone in Midtown cowered in their homes. By tomorrow, they will all be back to shopping and gossiping in the town square, desperately pretending nothing ever happened. They have too much to lose by defying the king. And if you think anyone if the Heights will lift a finger to fight on your side, you have lost your wits."

"Those pampered aristocrats?" Mal sneered. "They have never borne the brunt of the king's unjust laws. We never expected any help from them. And if the Midtown folk are such cowards, we don't need them either. Here in the Bottoms, we have nothing left to lose."

"Except your lives!"

"The legend claims the league will prevail."

"Oh, frap your stupid legend." I gripped my hands together to keep from shaking some sense into Mal. "Why can you not see that your pursuit of this will lead to nothing but a disastrous war in which a lot of innocent people could be killed?"

"Innocent people are already dying, Ella. What do you think happens to all those Arcadians driven out into the swamp?"

My cheeks heated because I was ashamed to admit I had no idea. Helpless to save any of them, I hadn't wanted to think about it, mainly because of my fear that if I didn't manage our money carefully enough to pay our taxes, my own family might experience that grim fate.

I faltered, "I hoped that the exiles found a way to make a new life for themselves somewhere else."

"Out in the swamp teeming with predatory beasts and the yellow gnats carrying the dreaded spotted fever? The lack of food or decent shelter? Our wretched king has decreed it illegal for anyone in Arcady to have any contact with the exiles. The old tyrant doesn't want it known what has happened to those wretched people, because the fairies forfend, someone might start to care. But none of those people would survive if it wasn't for members of our league smuggling what blankets, food, and medicine we can."

"So that is where you have disappeared to when I thought you were just larking about with your pirate friends? Why couldn't you have just told me the truth, Mal? Why did you have to deceive me?"

Mal dragged his hands down his face and sighed. "Don't you think I have hated deceiving you? I wanted to tell you the truth so many times, but I knew you would not have been willing to listen. If I had confessed what I really wanted that orb for, I didn't think you would ever have agreed to steal it."

"No, I wouldn't have! I would have been willing to risk helping you take supplies to the exiles, but this missing heir league is pure lunacy and outright treason. It is far too dangerous, and I have my own family to think of. I lost both my parents, Mal. Em, Amy and Netta are all I have."

"You have me," Mal said, holding out his hand to me.

But I backed away. "You? I don't even know who you are anymore."

His hand dropped back to his side. A heavy silence fell, both of us wearied by this argument that was getting us nowhere. I became aware that the storm was passing, the deluge outside the cottage reduced to a steady light rain.

Mal drew up the hood of his cloak, moving toward the doorway. "I cannot afford to linger here any longer," he said. "Are you coming with me or not?"

"Yes." As I pulled up my own hood, Mal's eyes lit up with hope. A hope I dashed when I added, "I am only coming to retrieve the orb and see that is returned to Mercato."

Mal shot me an incredulous look. "You are the one who is mad, Ella. What do you think that old buzzard will do with the orb if he gets his hands on it again?"

"He'll likely just stick it back in the king's treasure chamber to gather dust. I don't think he'll try to destroy it, or he would have done so years ago."

"Why do you imagine that is, Ella? Mercato obviously knows what the orb is for. He may even know how it works because otherwise how could he tell the one you put there was a fake? His power comes from serving the Helavalerians. Mercato has probably just been biding his time until he can find the true prince and slay him."

"If this prince exists and Mercato did know how to use the orb to find him, the wizard would have done it by now. In any event, it doesn't matter because we have no choice. If we don't give back the orb, both of us could end up in the Dismal Dungeons and Horatio will lose his command."

Mal's lips tightened. "I might have guessed that your beloved Crusher would be your first concern."

"He is a good man, and he doesn't deserve to pay the price for what we did. He does his best to protect people from the king's unjust laws."

"Considering what happened to those Midtown people, Crushington's best is not good enough. He would do far better to join our league."

"Horatio would never do something so reckless, and neither will I. Will you please be sensible, Mal and just give back that orb?"

"No!"

"You might not care what happens to Horatio, but what about me? Will you really allow me to be arrested?"

"As soon as I get the orb to safety, I will come back for you."

"Don't bother. I will never want to see you again."

Mal sighed. "You don't mean that, Ella."

"I have never meant anything more," I said. "If you walk out that door, I am done with you forever. Our friendship is at an end."

Mal hesitated in the doorway. When he finally looked at me, his eyes watered with fierce tears. "I love you, Ella. I would do anything in the world you asked of me, but I can't do this. I am sorry, but saving that orb is our only hope."

He ducked through the doorway, vanishing into rain. I emitted a cry and started to go after him, only to halt, overcome by the sheer futility of overtaking Mal and forcing him to be reasonable.

My shoulders slumped in despair. Never in my life had I felt so helpless, abandoned and alone. As I stepped back from the rain blowing in through the doorway, I trod upon something soft. Stooping down, I retrieved a dirty cloth doll that must have been forgotten by Tom's little sister when the Piper family had been dragged from their home.

The ragged doll stared forlornly up at me with her remaining button eye. I hugged her to my heart and started to cry.

Thirteen

The skies were clearing, the rain tapering to a fine mist when I left the Piper cottage. I had stopped crying, but my eyes were raw and swollen. I felt as battered as the reeds and river grasses that had been flattened by the storm.

The Conger River was still a bleak shade of gray, but the waters had calmed. Mal would have no difficulty launching the *Ella Marie* and escaping with the orb. I wanted to hate him for the way he had betrayed and abandoned me, but my anger had burned itself out, leaving an aching hollow inside me.

Stepping out onto the pier, I saw some fishermen downriver, working their way along the muddy banks to inspect their boats for storm damage. My stomach knotted when I spied activity on the bridge as well. The brief reprieve the storm had afforded my neighbors was over. The Border Scutcheons were herding the Hanson and Bafton families through the final barrier that led to the fen lands.

I caught a glimpse of Horatio still moving among them, likely trying to ensure Bluntvale did not treat his captives too roughly. As soon as he accepted there was no more that he could do, I knew Horatio would hurry to the Hawk's Nest looking for me and Mal.

I needed to intercept Horatio and tell him what had happened, but I dreaded facing him. He would probably think I had deceived him again and warned Mal. My heart was so heavy, it was all I could do to put one foot in front of the other. The path leading away from the river had become a morass of mud. I slogged my way through it, heedless of the way it caked my shoes and stained the hem of Horatio's cloak.

I arrived back on Rock Gunnell Street to find it nearly deserted. The rain must have helped to disperse the last of the angry mob and cool tempers. The few Bottoms folk who had emerged from their homes wore their usual downtrodden expressions. An exhausted looking young woman brushed past me, leading a little girl by the hand. With her matted curls and pale pinched features, the child reminded me painfully of the ragged doll I had found in the Piper cottage.

After the storm in Midtown, many mothers would be scolding their offspring to keep them from splashing joyously through puddles. This little waif trotted listlessly by her mother's side. It occurred to me that I had never actually seen children in the Bottoms playing.

Raising my head, I looked around me. I had not been oblivious to the poverty of this region of the kingdom, but never had I been so aware of the number of abandoned cottages. What few shops remained were so dilapidated they appeared in danger of tumbling down. Something Mal had said echoed through my mind.

"I wanted to tell you the truth so many times, but I knew you would not have been willing to listen."

Those words stung me more than I wanted to admit. Maybe I was not as bad as the rest of the Midtown folk, hiding behind their shutters, completely ignoring the terrible things happening in our kingdom. But I had always been too overwhelmed caring for my own family to do more than try to survive.

The exile of my neighbors had forced a harsh truth upon me. The tyranny and injustice in our kingdom *were* growing worse, but

I was helpless to do anything about it. Our signs falsely proclaimed Arcady to be the kingdom of happily ever after. If I could have conjured up the magic to make it so, I would have done it in a heartbeat. But no matter what Mal believed, such magic did not exist.

"Ella!" The sound of Horatio calling my name drew me out of my tormented thoughts. I turned to find him approaching from the end of Rock Gunnell Street that led from the Border Guard garrison.

He appeared to have been soaked during the rainstorm, his dark wet hair curling across his brow. As he closed the distance between us, he scowled. "What are you doing out here? I told you to take shelter at The Hawk's Nest. You agreed to follow my orders."

He broke off, his anger fading as he took in the sight of my tear-ravaged face.

"What's happened? What's wrong?" he demanded.

"Mal!" I choked out his name and nearly burst into tears. But I feared if I started crying again, I would dissolve into a puddle deeper than the ones gathered in the rutted lane. I hitched a deep breath and managed to tell Horatio how I spotted Mal in the crowd and followed him down to the river.

"Mal wouldn't listen to a word I said. He has run completely mad. He won't give back the orb. He thinks it has the power to find the lost prince and he and that stupid league of his are going to start a war. He's gone back to his shop to fetch the orb and disappear. It's too late to stop him and— and you were right. I never should have trusted him. He lied to me about everything."

I hung my head, bracing myself for Horatio's reproach. But when he crooked his fingers beneath by chin and obliged me to look up at him, his eyes were soft with tender regret.

"Oh, Ella, I am so sorry he has hurt you this way."

Horatio's sympathy nearly undid me. I had to swallow hard before I could speak.

"You feel sorry for me after all the trouble I have brought you? My blind faith in Mal is going to cost you everything."

"Hush, my dear. Don't worry about me. I will come through this somehow and I will make sure that you do, too." He drew me into his arms, and I rested my head wearily against his damp shoulder. "Now do you have any idea where Hawkridge might be going?"

I blinked back the tears from my eyes and tried to think. "I have heard him mention some pirate friend of his named Waldo the Wharf Rat and I think sometimes they sail to the Isle of Lothmara. But he also spoke of traveling to some place in the swamps where the exiles have set up camp or he could—"

I pulled away from him, shaking my head. "I have no real idea. I thought I knew Mal so well, but I don't know him at all." I gazed up at Horatio despairingly. "What are we going to do if you can't return the orb to the king's wizard by sunset?"

"Perhaps I will be able to persuade Sidney Greenleaf to allow me a little more time." Horatio gave me a reassuring smile, but I could see the worry clouding in his eyes. "I'll go to the Hawk's Nest. Maybe there's still a chance I can intercept Hawkridge and thrash some sense into him. Or at least find some clue to where he is headed."

I snuffled and nodded. "I'll come."

"No. There is nothing more you can do, Ella. Now you must let me handle things my way." His voice softened as he added, "You have been through quite enough for one day. Go home and wait for me there. I'll come to you as soon as I can."

He caressed my cheek. I could tell that he was loath to leave me in such a state of distress. With one last regretful look, he hurried off down the street. I stood there and meekly watched him go, making no attempt to follow. Because what good could I possibly do? I set off in the opposite direction, feeling utterly useless.

There was little left of the Ella who had strode into Misty Bottoms, scarcely an hour ago, fancying herself like the brave

Queen Anthea, believing I could recover that orb, prevent Mal and Horatio from fighting and somehow set the entire world right again.

I was nothing like Anthea the Magnificently Wise. I was Ella the Pathetic. Ella the Defeated. Ella the Obfuscated! Deceived not just by the man I had considered my closest friend, but by my own father as well. How many secrets had Papa kept from me over the years, his career as a royal court advocate, his rivalry with King August for my mother's love, the part he had played in ending my romance with Ryland.

My father should have told me about his participation in this rebellious League. Mal's grandfather had thought Mal too feckless to trust with any secrets. It hurt to think that Papa might have had a similar view of me. But I immediately rejected that notion.

He had often called me his clever girl and he had had enough faith in me to leave me in charge of his will. So why had he never breathed a word to me about his past, his connection with that strange orb and the search for the missing prince? Had he considered me too young to be burdened with such dangerous knowledge? If he had not died so suddenly, perhaps he would have told me everything, especially about that mysterious scrap of parchment hidden in the 'sack witches' book.

My fingers strayed to the bodice of my gown, checking that the page was still safely tucked away. I was convinced that I had been right not to share what I had found with Mal, not wanting to encourage his mad obsession with the orb.

Once I would have been prepared to swear that Hiram Hawkridge, my father, and Mal were all the most sensible of men. I didn't understand how they could have been seduced by this legend of a long-lost prince. The orb was reputed to have been designed by the fairies, yet I had not sensed anything magical about it when I stole the little glass globe from the treasury room. Of course, I had handled it only briefly and I had been wearing gloves at the time.

As I reached the outskirts of Misty Bottoms, the first shadow of a doubt crept into my mind. What if Mal, his grandfather, and my father were not wrong? What if there was some truth to the legend?

I tried to shake off the absurd notion. But once I allowed myself to entertain one doubt, others followed, nipping at my heels like a parcel of hungry river rats. What if Mal's belief in this missing prince was not just wishful imagining? What if the orb could lead us to Queen Anthea's true heir, the one prophesied to save our kingdom?

If the idea was absurd, why *did* the Great Mercato want that orb back so badly? If Horatio managed to retrieve the orb from Mal and return it to the king's wizard, would that be a huge mistake?

I didn't know, but if I could not obtain any answers to these questions, I was doomed to be haunted by doubt for the rest of my life. I pressed my hand to my brow, trying to recall all that I had witnessed in my father's library, the identity of the stranger seated in the chair. If only there was some way to recover the rest of that memory.

But perhaps there was.

My breath caught in my throat as I thought of the one person who might be able to help me. The same person who had stolen that shard of my aura, who would be capable of translating the page torn from Hiram Hawkridge's diary. Withypole Fugitate.

I had long suspected the irascible fairy knew a great deal more about my father's past than he was willing to tell me. I had not had much luck in compelling information from him. But as the sun broke through the clouds, it ignited a spark within me, of determination and rebelliousness. I had allowed myself to be obfuscated for long enough. Time to get some answers.

I pivoted and headed back to the Bottoms, aware that I was once again ignoring Horatio's orders. But if there was any chance for us to have a future together, there was one thing that my beloved would have to understand about me. I was not a just-go-home-and-wait kind of girl.

* * *

Fugitate's Fancys was little more than a shack, unfortunately located next to the Snigglery. The strong odor emanating from barrels of pickled eels assailed my nostrils as I worked my way around the puddles barring my path. As I approached the shop, I tried to formulate my plan of attack. Withypole usually resisted giving any answers to my questions. My best chance for gaining information from him would be to employ a ruse. I would reveal that I had found that missing page and imply that I knew far more than I did about the orb and my father's role in the league in hopes of tricking Withypole into telling me more.

Preoccupied with rehearsing what I would say and avoiding the mud, I nearly collided with a customer leaving Withypole's shop. I looked up to find Delphine blocking my path, her hair at its deepest black, her eyes snapping with malice.

I reeled back, swearing softly, "Frap!" As if this day had not already been bad enough.

"Well, look who it is." The witch sneered. "The very person I was hoping to see. You and I have unfinished business, missy."

Delphine raised her arms, curling her fingers in a menacing fashion, clearly expecting me to flee in terror. But Mal had told me she could not cast spells out of thin air. Even if she could, I was beyond caring.

"Go ahead. Curse me with warts or boils or whatever," I said. "Just do it, then get out of my way because I have no time to waste."

Looking puzzled and disappointed by my response, Delphine lowered her arms. She peered intently at my face and frowned.

"You have been crying," she accused, pointing at my eyes. "You have Mal and a prince dangling after you. What have *you* got to be so miserable about?"

"I am not miserable. Sometimes I cry when I am furious, so you would be well advised not to trifle with me today. And as for Mal, if you want the wretch, you are welcome to him. I am done with the man. Our friendship is entirely at an end."

Delphine folded her arms, her raised eyebrows revealing her skepticism. "Really? What did the rogue do to get your drawers into such a twist?"

"He obfuscated with me."

Delphine gasped, her astonishing hair fading to a shade of deep green. She moistened her lips, her expression an odd mingling of envy and longing. Leaning closer, she asked in a low, confidential tone, "So how was it? I mean, wasn't it good for you? I have heard that Mal has exceptional skills in the boudoir and—"

"Oh, for frap's sake, Delphine." I reared back from her, rolling my eyes in disgust. "*Obfuscated!* It means to confuse or deceive. Mal lied to me."

"Oh!" She rocked back on her heels, her lips curving in a somewhat sheepish smile. "Well, what did you expect? The man is such a wicked rogue, wily and seductive." Delphine brought herself up short, giving a haughty sniff. "But who cares about that? I certainly don't. I am done with him, too, the ungrateful wretch. I deserve much better, perhaps one of those rich lords from the Heights. Or maybe I'll even land myself a prince like you have done."

"Wonderful. You can have Florian." I tried to skirt past her, but unless I wanted to wade through a very deep puddle, it was impossible.

"That conceited yellow-haired dolt? No thank you. I have concluded younger men are best. Get one at the age when he can still be trained to be obedient. Now those rascally twin princes are both quite delectable."

"I recommend Prince Dashiel," I said. After the shabby way he had treated Amy, it would serve the treacherous youth right if the witch pursued him.

Delphine tipped her head to one side as though considering my suggestion. She sighed. "But Prince Dahl is equally handsome. It is so difficult to choose between them."

"Then bewitch them both," I advised, impatient to bring this conversation to an end. "Why break up a matching set?"

Delphine stared at me and much to my surprise, she burst out laughing. Not the sort of cackle one might expect from a witch, but in a manner that was light and feminine, almost musical. Her hair turned a silvery hue of blonde, her eyes sparkling with mirth.

"I do like the way you think, Ella Upton. Mal always said you and I could become good friends if only I got to know you better."

"Perhaps someday when I have more time," I murmured, making another effort to get by her. "Will you please let me pass? I need to see Mr. Fugitate on a matter of urgent business."

Delphine shrugged and stepped aside. "Go on, then. But you needn't be in such a hurry. The shop's closed."

I was dismayed to see that she was right. A closed sign hung in one of the windows. When I tried the door, it was indeed locked. Cupping my hands around my eyes, I tried to peer through one of the grimy windows. If I saw any sign of Withypole moving about in there, I was prepared to hammer at the door until he was obliged to admit me.

As though she guessed what I was thinking, Delphine said, "That won't do you any good. The fairy's not there."

I whipped about to stare at her. "Then you *know* what Withypole really is?"

Delphine smirked. "My dear, I am a witch who can transform herself into a cat. No one's secrets are safe from me."

Including Mal's. Considering the amount of time Delphine had spent lurking about The Hawk's Nest in her guise of Ebony, she probably knew far more about Mal and his plans than I ever had. On the night of the ball, she had turned up at the palace to ensure that I succeeded in stealing the orb for him. Because of Mercato's witch-warding detector, she had been unable to get much further than the castle gates. I wondered if Delphine knew where Mal would be likely to go if he had to flee the kingdom.

But when I attempted to question her, she cut me off with a scowl. "It's no use asking me about anything Mal might be up to lately. Since you had to go blabbing about me being able to turn into a cat, the man won't let me anywhere near him. Besides," she added slyly. "I thought you said you were done with him."

"I am," I said. "It's just that— oh, never mind. Can you at least tell me where Withypole has gone?"

"That's an easy one. When Fugitate is not at his shop, he can be found at the Winking Goblin. He falls into these morose moods and tries to alleviate his misery by downing thimbles full of whiskey. A very bad idea. Fairies have a notoriously low tolerance for strong spirits. One of these days, he'll probably get so drunk, he'll forget himself and go flapping about the kingdom."

I stared at Delphine, aghast. "And you have never made any attempt to dissuade him? Do you know what would happen to Withypole if the royal authorities ever found out he is a fairy in disguise?"

Delphine shrugged. "What do I look like? His fairy godmother?" She broke into another of her silvery laughs. "The fairy's fairy godmother! Oh, that is amusing."

Shooting her a disgusted look, I pushed past her, heading away from the shop.

"Wait! Where are you going?" she asked, falling into step beside me.

"To the Winking Goblin. To find Withypole."

She caught hold of my arm to stop me. "Have you lost your mind? The Winking Goblin is a dreadful place where the worst thieves and cutthroats in this kingdom gather."

"I am fully aware of how dangerous the tavern is. Mal has warned me to stay away from there many times, but I have no choice." I yanked free of Delphine's grip. "I told you that it is urgent for me to speak with Withypole."

She regarded me wonderingly. "You are either very brave or quite deliciously mad. Being a bit mad myself, I admire that in a person. I am beginning to believe you and I really might become fast friends." She paused, her brow furrowing as she mulled something over and then nodded. "In the spirit of our new accord, I will lend you this."

Delphine unhooked something from her belt and handed it to me. It was a small leather sheath holding a knife not much bigger than what I used at home to peel potatoes.

"Um... thanks." I tried to sound grateful, but couldn't help adding, "I don't suppose you have something a bit larger I could borrow. Like a sword?"

"That little knife is much better than any sword. It is one of my finest magical creations," Delphine informed me proudly. "I call it a Fear Blade. The spell will not affect the one who wields it, but I guarantee that anyone you threaten with that knife will cower away from you, begging for mercy."

I studied the tiny knife with a great deal of skepticism. When I started to unsheathe the blade, Delphine seized my hand to prevent me.

"Stop, you foolish girl! Never draw the blade out when it can be struck by the rays of the sun. Don't you know what happens to fear in broad daylight? It tends to evaporate."

Not wanting to offend Delphine, I tucked the sheathed knife into the pocket of Horatio's cloak, although I had little faith in the blade's power or Delphine's claim that fear could not survive in daylight. If that were true, I wouldn't be experiencing these chills of apprehension at venturing inside the Winking Goblin. Despite my display of bravado, I dreaded entering that den of iniquity alone.

I had never imagined the day might come when I would seek help from Delphine, but the company of a woman known for being a witch could prove a much greater deterrent than her dubious Fear Blade.

Since Delphine appeared to be in such a generous mood, I suggested tentatively, "Since we are now friends, perhaps you would come with me to the Winking Goblin."

The witch snorted. "Sweetie, we are not that good of friends, yet. If Withypole Fugitate has been drinking too much, he will be far more dangerous than any villain in that tavern. He can play tricks with your mind at the best of times and when he is not fully in control of his own power— well, watch out! I may be a touch mad, but even I am not insane enough to go anywhere near an inebriated fairy. But I wish you the best of luck, Ella Upton."

Delphine chuckled as she turned to walk away. "Don't forget to return my blade to me when you are done. That is if you can still remember anything, including your name."

Fourteen

T he memory of Delphine's laughter did little to bolster my confidence as I approached the Winking Goblin. The tavern was a low-slung building, faced with rough wooden shingles, half of which had fallen off. The sign that creaked above the door depicted an ugly goblin's head. His eye appeared to be engaged in an evil squint more than a playful wink. Beneath his bewhiskered chin, someone had scratched out the words LAW ABIDERS NOT WELL COME HERE.

Since I was not exactly a 'law abider' myself, that warning need not apply to me. I squared my shoulders, trying to convince myself I was as bad and dangerous as anyone in there. After all, I had burgled the king's treasury and I was armed with a Fear Blade, although I harbored more than a few doubts about that. If Delphine was seeking her revenge, what could be more perfect than tricking me into threatening some ruffian with a weapon that was nothing more than a paring knife? Given her wicked sense of humor, I was sure the witch would find that hilarious.

I glanced around, half expecting to find myself being trailed by a sleek black cat, snickering in anticipation, but I was quite alone. I took a deep breath and stepped closer to the tavern. The windows were too begrimed with years of pipe smoke and dirt for me to see inside. But the burst of coarse drunken laughter that carried to my ears was far from reassuring.

My pulse skipped a beat as I reached for the door handle. I hesitated, recalling the piece of parchment tucked inside my gown. Struggling to remove that page from inside my bodice under the leering gaze of the Goblin's patrons was a bad idea. I paused beneath the tavern sign to retrieve the parchment as surreptitiously as I could. I tucked it inside the cloak's pocket along with the Fear Blade. Pulling the hood up to conceal my face, I hoped that would give me a menacing and mysterious aspect.

I took a deep breath and entered, quietly closing the door behind me. Peeking out from beneath my hood, my eyes struggled to adjust to the dim, smoky interior. The Winking Goblin reeked of stale food, ale, and masculine sweat. Because of the closed windows and low ceiling, the taproom felt overly warm and stuffy. I could already feel beads of perspiration gathering on my brow but that could have been due more to my nervousness than the heat.

The tavern held some half dozen tables crowded with the most disreputable lot of men I could have imagined, swilling tankards of ale, puffing on pipes, playing cards, or dicing. An individual with a bulbous nose was passed out on the floor. At least I hoped he was merely unconscious and not dead. None of his companions appeared concerned. One scrawny fellow leaned back in his chair and used the inert man's swollen stomach for a footstool.

The Goblin's proprietor with his long sallow face and greasy hair was as ill-favored as his customers. He worked behind the bar, cleaning tankards by spitting into them and polishing them with a dirty rag. Dismayed to realize I was the only woman in the place, I looked anxiously about for Withypole. I spotted him sitting alone at a small table in the far corner.

Keeping my head down, I headed in his direction, wincing at

the crunch of grit beneath my feet. It was a sound I should not have been able to hear with all that cacophony of harsh voices.

But the tavern had gone unnervingly silent. I risked a glance around to discover dozens of bloodshot eyes trained in my direction. Swallowing hard, I suppressed an urge to turn and run, but I kept going. I heard a chair scrape back and my way was suddenly blocked by a burly fellow with a bushy gray beard and an eye patch.

"Afternoon, stranger," he drawled.

I nodded by way of greeting and tried to sidle past him, but he barred my way with his long thick arm.

"Not too friendly, are you? Here at the Goblin, we don't much care for the quiet sort who try to hide their faces, do we lads?"

His question was answered with a rumble of agreement, the proprietor chiming in, "We surely don't, Waldo."

I shrank back as the man named Waldo attempted to peer beneath my hood.

"For all we know, you could be a Scutcheon spy," he said.

"I am not." I tried to make my voice sound as gruff as possible.

"Then why are you hiding your face?"

"Be - because it's hideous. You would shudder to see—"

I broke off with a gasp as Waldo wrenched back my hood. My cheeks flamed at the chorus of catcalls and whistles.

"Well, looky here," Waldo chortled. "It's a wench and she's not at all hideous. We don't customarily get females in here."

"Not unless they come to sell something," A leering bald man called out.

"If she's selling, I'm buying." Waldo winked at me.

I backed away, my heart hammering. "I am not selling anything. I just came in to have a quiet word with Mr. Fugitate."

"Fugitate?" Waldo snorted. "That crabbed old man won't appreciate a pretty girl like you. Why don't you just come over here and sit on my knee and let me buy you a drink?"

"No, thank you." My hand trembled as I groped in my pocket

for the Fear Blade.

"Aw, now don't be so standoffish, missy." Waldo grinned.

As he reached for me, I dodged him, whipping the sheathed blade out of my pocket. "Leave me alone," I cried.

I tried to sound fierce, but my command was met with a round of coarse laughter and someone shouted, "Careful, Waldo. She's got herself a right big knife."

"Oooh, I am so scared." He smirked at the way my fingers shook as I unsheathed the blade. It looked so ridiculously small, I expected Waldo to dissolve into guffaws. But his jaw dropped, his face draining of color.

He stumbled away from me, holding up his hands in a defensive stance. "N-no. Please."

I stared dumbfounded at the little knife. I had not expected the Fear Blade to work, at least not in such a spectacular fashion. Waldo was not the only one shaking in his boots. The proprietor had ducked down behind the bar, peeking at me with terrified eyes. The other men leaped up from their seats, clutching at each other and huddling as far away from me as they could get. A few hid under the tables and a faint whiff of urine alerted me that someone had wet his breeches.

Waldo collapsed to his knees, almost sobbing as he begged, "Please, don't hurt me."

I squared my shoulders, wielding the Fear Blade with a new confidence. "No one will get hurt as long as you all sit back down and keep to yourselves." I grimaced as I stepped in something sticky. "Although you could clean up this place. It's filthy."

"Yes, ma'am. Right away, miss. Whatever you say, ma'am."

I was answered by a dozen quivery voices. Waldo's head bobbed up and down as he scrambled away from me. As I made my way to the back of the tavern, I maintained a stern expression with great difficulty. I wanted to grin with relief as I murmured to myself, "Delphine, I utterly adore you."

Not only had the witch given me the power to fend off these

ruffians, but I also had in my hand a weapon that could compel Withypole to tell me anything I wanted to know. I strode over to the table where Fugitate sat, hunched over a glass that was not much bigger than a thimble.

"Mr. Fugitate?"

He glanced up at me with bleary eyes. I brandished the blade, waiting for him to cower in terror. He merely eyed the knife and gave a contemptuous sniff.

"A Fear Blade. Don't know how you managed to get your hands on one of those, but you might as well put your little trinket away, girl. Witch's magic doesn't work on fairies."

A fact that Delphine had failed to mention to me, I thought with a disgruntled sigh. So much for my hope of forcing any truth from Withypole. But I recalled what Delphine had told me about a fairy's inability to cope with strong liquor. Perhaps the drink might loosen Withypole's tongue. He had already admitted he was a fairy, something he would have never done when completely sober.

Ignoring me looming over him, he refilled his glass from a bottle of some murky liquid labeled Knock You Dead Lightning. Badly as I wanted information from him, I didn't want him getting so recklessly drunk he endangered himself or anyone else.

"How many thimbles full of that stuff have you already had?"

"Not enough and it's no concern of yours. This is no place for a girl like you. Get out."

"I need to talk to you."

"Don't feel like talking," he grumbled. He raised the glass and downed the contents in one big sip.

He glowered at me as I plunked myself in the chair opposite him. I laid the Fear Blade down upon the table. Despite the fact it had no effect upon Withypole, I was too wary of the tavern's other occupants to put the knife away. A glance over my shoulder revealed that my suggestion that the taproom needed cleaning had been taken as an order.

Two of the ruffians stirred up dust as they wielded brooms while others busied themselves scrubbing down tables and chairs. Lacking any sort of cloth, Waldo was trying to clean the windows by rubbing his broad bottom against the panes.

I turned back to Withypole who was on the verge of pouring himself another drink. I grabbed for the bottle. As we struggled for possession of it, he growled at me. "Let go and leave me in peace. If you have come to pester me about that piece of aura I took from you, I won't give it back. The shard is much safer with me. It's for your own protection."

"Since when have you been worried about protecting me?"

"Since the day your father asked me to—" Withypole choked off the rest of his words.

Stunned, I let go of the bottle. "My father asked *you* to protect me? Why?"

"Because the foolish man trusted me." Withypole's hand trembled as he measured himself out another drink. "If anything happened to him, I promised to look out for you. But I have made poor work of it, miserable useless creature that I am."

"I knew you were acquainted with my father, but I had no idea you were his friend."

"I am not a good friend to anyone. Leave me alone."

"Mr. Fugitate... Withypole, please. I have so many questions and you could give me the answers. Especially about this."

I retrieved the piece of parchment from my cloak and slapped it down on the table between us. Withypole froze in the act of raising his glass to his lips. His eyes bulged, his face draining so white I feared he was about to faint.

"Where did you get that?" He lowered his glass and tried to snatch the paper, but I was quicker, drawing it back out of his reach.

"I found it in a book in Papa's library. I remembered the night Hiram Hawkridge gave it to him."

"What? You should not have been able to recall anything about that night. Your memory was befogged. I—"

"You what?" I prompted.

Withypole refused to look at me, clutching his face in his hands. Suddenly it was as though the last wisps of mist clouding my mind vanished. I could clearly see the man who had been concealed in Papa's wing back chair, rising to his feet.

"It was *you*," I cried. "You were the third person at that midnight meeting."

"No, no!" Withypole made a muffled denial from behind his hands. I pried one of them away, obliging him to look at me.

"I remember everything, Mr. Fugitate."

Withypole regarded me with anguished eyes. "Why can I never do anything right? I was sure I had succeeded in erasing your memory."

"Why would you do such a thing to me?"

"Because you were only a little girl and there were things too dangerous for you to know."

"Like about the fairy orb and the missing heir?"

"Keep your voice down," Withypole hissed.

I looked behind me. The men in the tavern continued to sweep and scrub, although they were not achieving much beyond shifting the dust and dirt from one corner to another. Despite their fear, I detected a curiosity in their eyes as they stole wary glances at me and Withypole.

I shoved to my feet, waving the Fear Blade.

"Enough cleaning!" I commanded.

Everyone froze, the proprietor making an absurd attempt to hide behind his broom.

"It is time for you all to clear out of here and go home to your wives."

"But I haven't got a wife," the little bald man wailed.

"Then go find one," I snapped.

"Yes, miss. Right away, miss."

The ruffians nearly tripped over each other, pushing, and

shoving in their haste to get out the door. The tavern's owner backed away trembling, wielding his broom like a shield until he was able to vanish through an arch behind the bar. The only one left in the taproom was the drunk sprawled out on the floor and he showed no sign of stirring.

As I resumed my seat, Withypole said, "You realize that witch's spell is going to wear off as soon as those rogues get far enough away from you. They'll wonder what happened and come creeping back."

"I will be ready for them if they do," I said, laying the blade on the table. I was dismayed to realize the parchment was missing. Withypole had used my momentary distraction to seize it.

"Give me back the parchment."

"It's of no use to you. Unless you can read the fairy language, you have no idea what it says."

"I can guess. It explains how to use the orb, doesn't it?"

Withypole compressed his lips, then muttered. "Nothing about the orb should ever have been written down. That stupid Hiram Hawkridge. I was the designated keeper of the orb and all its secrets. But Hawkridge got me drunk one night and took the orb away from me. Arrogant man thought I was unworthy to be trusted."

Withypole sniffed. "He was right, but he was no better than me. He allowed the orb to fall into the king's hands. It has been locked away in the royal treasury ever since."

"The orb is not there any longer."

"And just how would you be knowing that, missy?"

I hesitated before confessing, "Because on the night of the ball, I managed to steal it."

"What!" Withypole squawked.

Swiftly I explained about the plot that Mal and I had hatched, enabling me to get into the royal vault and steal the orb.

"But Mal deceived me," I said, my heart still aching with bitterness. "He led me to believe the orb was some harmless magical object that had belonged to his grandfather. I had no idea what the orb really was or what it did."

"Stupid, gullible girl!" Withypole groaned. "If you had to attend that wretched ball, why couldn't you have just danced and flirted like any another maiden?"

I gave an apologetic shrug. "I am not a dancing and flirting kind of girl."

"So where is the orb now?" Withypole demanded.

I sighed and told him the rest of it, about Mercato discovering the orb was missing, the deadline he had given Horatio for the orb's return, how Mal was trying to flee the kingdom with the orb in his possession with Horatio hard on his heels.

Withypole grew more and more agitated with each word I spoke. Wrapping his arms about himself, he rocked back and forth, moaning. "No, no, no! Stupid Hawkridges. The boy is as misguided as his grandfather. I had heard rumors that young Malcolm had revived the League and was searching for the lost heir. So long as he didn't have the orb, I believed there was nothing to worry about.

"But Hawkridge could ruin everything because the time is not yet right. It's not right!"

"That's the same thing you said that night in Papa's library. *The time is not right.* But what exactly does that mean?"

Withypole didn't answer. Slumping forward, he rested his arms upon the table and buried his face.

I prodded his shoulder. "Withypole! What does it mean?"

He was silent for so long, I feared he had passed out. I poked him again until he finally mumbled, "It explains how to use the orb when the time is right for Queen Anthea's true heir will be revealed. Only then will Arcady be restored to peace and happiness."

"So the legends about the missing heir are really true?"

Withypole raised his head enough to regard me blearily. "Of course, it is all true."

I leaned back in my chair, feeling dazed and guilty for the way I had so fiercely dismissed Mal's claims.

"But that is not what all the history books say," I protested weakly. "They claim that Queen Anthea died, leaving no descendants."

"The history books are wrong. All falsehoods concocted by the Helavalerians to bury the truth."

"Then unbury it for me."

When Withypole reached for the bottle again, I seized his tiny cup to stop him refilling it. "Please. Mal could well blunder his way into starting a war or if Horatio recovers the orb, he will give it back to Mercato. If you care anything about the fate of Queen Anthea's heir, you've got to tell me what you know."

Withypole stared at me for what seemed like forever. I could almost see the battle being waged behind his large, luminous green eyes. At long last he sighed, "Very well. But if there is to be a confession of sins and crimes, I need my fortification."

"Whose sins and crimes?"

"Mine." He took a long swallow directly from the bottle. He hiccupped on another sigh and began his tale. "A long time ago, there lived a distant cousin of our good Queen Anthea."

"Cuthbert Helavalerian," I said. "My history book said that because the queen had no issue, when she was dying, she invited Lord Cuthbert to assume the throne."

Withypole snorted. "Invited? The queen had no choice. Cuthbert was a scheming, ambitious man. When he raised a large army, Anthea realized she could not prevent Arcady from falling into his evil hands. Her grandson was a mere babe. The only way to protect the infant from Cuthbert was to allow the world to believe the child had died. The queen's last act before she perished was to consign her beloved grandchild to the care of the only beings powerful enough to protect him."

"The fairies?"

Withypole nodded. "Guardianship of the child was assigned to

Marigold Stufflebeam, the most beautiful and gifted of all the fairies. She could cure suffering with the touch of her hand or ease the worst of pain with but one sweet breath. Marigold had even mastered the art of prophecy. She foresaw the future and predicted it would be several generations before the throne could be reclaimed for Queen Anthea's bloodline."

Withypole swallowed thickly. "I completely adored Marigold and hoped one day she would accept me for her mate."

"Wait!" I said. "You were alive during Queen Anthea's time? How old *are* you?"

"Time passes differently for fairies than you mortals. We can live for centuries. I was not quite a hundred years old in your years when the queen died. A mere lad."

I gaped at him. Ordinarily I would have been bursting with questions about all the history Withypole must have witnessed, especially regarding my heroine, Queen Anthea the Magnificently Wise. But I needed to keep Withypole focused on his tale. As he took another swallow from the bottle, his eyes glittered. Was that how a fairy looked when he was becoming hopelessly drunk?

I longed to wrestle the bottle away from him, but feared if I did so, Withypole would stop talking or worse, curse me with one of his mind-altering fairy spells. Gripping my hands tightly together, I urged him to go with his tale.

"We fairies hid the young prince and obscured his heritage. Marigold devised the orb so we could prove the true heir's identity when the time was right. Decades passed and the prince grew to manhood and fathered a son and in turn, his child had a child and so forth. Meanwhile, dark days fell upon our kingdom, especially for the fairies.

"Cuthbert had ever been suspicious about the existence of a rightful prince and the fairies' role in concealing him. The king began to persecute my folk with harsh laws, condemning many of us to the dread punishment of having our wings crushed."

Withypole shuddered and took another swig from the bottle.

He rubbed the hump upon his back where his own wings were concealed. "There is nothing worse you can do to a fairy. It would be far kinder to kill us outright."

I nodded sympathetically. "My father often read to me from a book on fairy lore. I was so angry and disappointed when Papa explained to me why there were no more fairies to be found in Arcady. I desperately longed to meet one."

I must have been regarding Withypole rather wistfully because he cringed.

"You don't need to be pleased to make my acquaintance, girl," he said dourly. "I am a very poor specimen of my race."

He took a long swallow from the bottle and hiccupped. I feared Withypole might be reaching that stage of drunkenness that Mal had always referred to as 'pickled brain.' The fairy's eyes had become as glassy as a frozen pond, but as he continued his tale, his speech remained astonishingly clear, except for the hint of a slur.

"Even after Cuthbert died, his heirs continued their persecution of the fairies. The exorbitant tax placed upon our wings was the final insult. One by one, the fairies all fled to live in a hidden realm far north of Arcady. Marigold was forced to remain to fulfill her duties as guardian of the heir and the orb. And I was unwilling to abandon my beloved."

"Marigold and I were forced to live in disguise, but each day brought us closer to the time when the true heir could be revealed. I could scarce contain my impatience because as soon as Marigold's duty to the heir was at an end, I intended to reveal the depth of my feelings and beg her to be mine."

Withypole heaved a great sigh. "What a happy, glorious day that would have been. We formed a group to prepare for Anthea's heir reclaiming the throne. The league consisted of me, Marigold, your father, Hiram Hawkridge and Sidney Greenleaf."

"Greenleaf?" I echoed in astonishment. "The Great Mercato?"

Withypole snorted. "He wasn't the great anything then, merely Hawkridge's apprentice, a wizard of little ability."

"Modest?" I protested. "He invented the Aura Chamber and the witch-warding staff and -and that secret device for spying in the king's treasury room."

"Bah. Those were all of Hiram's designs. Greenleaf stole them. He pretended to be aligned with the goals of our league, but at some point, he decided his road to power lay with the Helavalerians rather than any unknown heir. He began by removing one obstacle to his ambition, Hiram Hawkridge. You may not be aware, but at one time Hiram was King August's chief wizard."

"I know. Mal told me how his grandfather lost his post when he was accused of putting truth serum in the king's drink. Mr. Hawkridge claimed it must have been an accident, but—"

"It was no accident," Withypole said fiercely. "Hiram might have believed that, but I suspected all along that somehow Sidney Greenleaf was behind it. He got Hiram ousted and took his place. Thus, the Great Mercato was born."

Withypole startled me by reaching across the table and seizing my wrist in a painful grip. "No matter what happens, Ella, you must never, *never* trust Mercato. Even if he pretends to be your friend."

"Of course, I won't, but—"

Withypole's fingers dug into my skin. "Promise me!"

"Ouch! I promise! Now let me go."

Withypole released me. As I rubbed my bruised wrist, he swayed dangerously, appearing on the verge of tumbling out of his chair. But he gripped the edge of the table, steadying himself.

"You must understand about Mercato. He's a fake, a..."

The fairy's voice trailed off as though he was losing track of his words. He lifted the bottle and squinted inside it as though he expected to find his missing thoughts swirling there.

"That old wizard is what?" I prompted. "A liar? A trickster? A betrayer?"

"Betrayer, yes." Withypole latched on to the last word. His eyes filled with tears. "No, that was me."

"Who did you betray?"

"M-my darling Marigold. Oh, I can't speak of it. Too ashamed."

I took his hand, saying gently, "It is all right. Please just tell me."

He pulled away from me and grabbed his bottle. Nothing remained of the brew except for a few drops which he lapped up desperately with his tongue.

He moaned. "If only I had ever found the courage to declare my love to Marigold, maybe it never would have happened."

"What? What happened?"

"Marigold. She fell in love with someone else. A mere mortal. He was nothing but a lowly Scutcheon, but Marigold was completely besotted. She was willing to surrender everything to become his bride, her wings and all her fairy magic."

"Was such a thing possible?" I asked in astonishment.

"Yes, the king of the fairies could have granted her wish, but she would have been condemned to live out her days as a mortal. I would have had to watch her age and die. She would have been lost to me forever, so I knew I had to stop her." Withypole fixed me with a piteous gaze. "You must understand, I loved her so much. I became crazed with despair and jealousy, or I would never have done anything so terrible."

I dreaded to ask. "What did you do?"

Withypole's breath hitched with a suppressed sob. "I tricked Marigold's lover into meeting me at this tavern. I sought to erase all memories of Marigold from his heart, b-but I had had too much to drink. My magic went awry, and I completely shattered the man's mind. He ran totally mad and ended up taking his own life."

"Oh, Withypole." I exclaimed. "And Marigold, what became of her?"

"She - she died of grief." Tears poured down Withypole's face faster than he could check them, even though he tried to stem the flow with his sleeve. "So sweet and generous was Marigold, she forgave me on her deathbed, b-begged me to protect the orb and Anthea's heir. And I promised her. But I am so weak. I became a wretched gleaner."

I knew from Papa's book that was the peculiar fate of a fairy who suffered some great loss, an uncontrollable compulsion to acquire and hoard the kind of material objects most fairies disdained. Withypole's shop bore mute testimony to his obsession, crammed from floor to ceiling with furniture, old clothes, musical instruments, books, even toys.

Giving way to his grief, he shook with sobs that were dreadful to hear. I slumped back in my chair, helpless to comfort the distraught fairy.

What he had done was terrible and his love for Marigold had proved to be of a most selfish kind. But he had paid a heavy price for his actions, and I could not help but pity him.

"I - I failed so badly. I let the orb fall into the king's hands and I b-broke my promise to Marigold, to your father to l-look after the children."

He was crying so hard, his muffled words punctuated by such sobs and hiccups, I barely understood him. But one word stood out clearly, causing me to bolt upright in my seat.

"*Children?*" I repeated. "You mean me, but who else? The missing prince? Do you know who he is? Where can we find him?"

Withypole raised his tear-streaked face and opened his mouth as if to speak. But his eyes rolled back, and his head clunked down upon the table. I tugged frantically at his arm, but he appeared to have succumbed to all the cheap whiskey he had consumed. All my efforts to rouse him were in vain.

I bit down upon my lip, fretting over my next course of action. My first impulse was to find Horatio and warn him. If he had managed to seize the orb from Mal, I had to stop Horatio from giving it to Mercato. But I could hardly abandon Withypole in such a state, especially without discovering the identity of the lost prince.

What should I do? Before I could decide, the door to the Winking Goblin burst open. Fearing the return of the tavern's rough patrons, I leaped up from my chair, wielding the Fear Blade.

But the short man who stumbled inside was not a stranger to me. I recognized him at once as Long Louie, a friend of Mal's who had been engaged to drive our coach the night I had attended the ball.

"Help!" Louie panted, striving to catch his breath. "It's Mal. Something terrible has happened to him. The League has been betrayed. We've got to hide the weapons before they come for the rest of us and - and where is everybody?"

He gazed about him, taken aback to find the tavern deserted. He appeared even more confounded when he caught sight of me.

"Miss Upton?" he squawked.

I closed the distance between us, demanding, "What's happened to Mal?"

The Fear Blade caused Louie to shrink away from me, reducing him to a state of babbling incoherency. I hastily sheathed the knife and repeated my question.

Louie blinked as he shook off the effects of the magical blade. He still looked a little trembly as he blurted out, "Two men! They must have ambushed Mal in his shop. Shifty, the tinker saw the whole thing. These brutes slung Mal over the back of a horse, and they rode off with him."

"Who did? Who were these men?"

Louie shook his head. "Two great, tall fellows dressed in ordinary working -clothes. But Shifty suspected they were Scutcheons in disguise. He caught a glimpse of one of their swords. It had a gilt emblem like all the soldiers carry.

"Mal was unconscious, bleeding." Louie gulped. "Shifty said they killed him."

"No!" I gasped.

"I am sorry, Miss Upton." Louie's eyes filled with tears. "I am sure Mal must have put up a good fight but—"

I didn't wait to hear anymore. I shoved past Louie and rushed out of the Winking Goblin. As I raced down Rock Gunnel Street, my heart pounded out a denial with every beat. Mal dead? No, no, no!

Scutcheons in disguise... Shifty said they killed him.

Long Louie's words echoed through my mind, but they made no sense. Horatio had gone alone to confront Mal and there was no way Horatio could have summoned men in time to ambush Mal unless...

Unless that had been Horatio's plan all along. Before he had traveled to Misty Bottoms with me, Horatio could have already set this trap into motion, all the while pretending he would let me try to reason with Mal. Even when Horatio had held me in his arms, comforting me after my quarrel with Mal, Horatio could have been concealing his plot to ambush Mal.

No, my heart swiftly rejected this painful idea. Horatio Crushington was far too honorable of a man to have deceived me in such a cruel way. If it had been his intention to capture Mal in such a brutal fashion, Horatio would never have risked me being there to witness it.

I slowed my pace, catching my breath, allowing reason to master the panic that had consumed me. As I approached Mal's shop, I tried to convince myself Long Louie's story of Mal's death had to be based upon nothing but a wild rumor. After all, how much faith could one place in the account of a tinker named Shifty? And The Hawk's Nest looked so quiet and undisturbed.

There was a closed sign posted on the front window, but the shop door stood slightly ajar. My stomach knotted with apprehension as I pushed the door open. I stumbled across the threshold, greeted by a scene of utter chaos. Potion bottles shattered on the floor, a broken shelf barring the way to the counter, the fireplace cauldron tipping over, spilling some green liquid over the hearth, all bearing mute testimony to some terrible conflict.

"I am sure Mal put up a good fight," Long Louie had said.

Perhaps he had believed I would derive some comfort from that thought. I didn't.

Picking my way carefully to avoid stepping on shattered glass, I retrieved a garment discarded in front of the apothecary counter. Mal's cloak, the one he'd been wearing when I had last seen him. The gray wool was still damp from the rain.

My fingers trembled as I inspected the garment. The braid that fastened the cloak had been snapped as though the cloak had been wrenched from Mal's neck. Near the hem, the wool was stained with a large splash of something dark crimson. Blood.

"Mal." I breathed his name in a despairing whisper. Hugging the cloak against me, I felt as though I was going to be sick. I swallowed hard, my mind struggling to reject the evidence of my own eyes.

A rattling sound alerted me that I was not alone in the shop. I tensed, listening. A floorboard creaked in the adjacent room. Someone was moving about in Mal's kitchen. I tiptoed in that direction, torn between fear and hope that contrary to all reports, Mal had somehow survived the ambush and eluded his captors. Or perhaps it was Horatio and he would take me in his arms, reassuring me that my worst dread was untrue.

But when I reached the doorway, I halted in shock at the sight of the man in Mal's kitchen, the last person in the world I would have wanted or expected to find.

Prince Florian had made himself quite at home in Mal's kitchen. Rocking on the back legs of a wooden chair, he unscrewed the lid from the jar of Mal's favorite sweets. Glancing up, Florian did not appear in the least surprised to see me frozen in the doorway.

He calmly popped a peppermint in his mouth, crunching it between his teeth before drawling, "Ah, my beloved. You have finally arrived for your tryst with this Hawkridge rogue." He ate another mint and regarded me with a dreadful smirk.

"Well, my dear, I am afraid you are a bit too late."

Fifteen

I stared at the prince, unable to believe my eyes, my mind in such a whirl, I wondered if this was what it felt like to snort pixie dust. Florian seemed to have sprung up out of nowhere, reminding me of a story that Mal and I shivered over during our childhood. The Tale of the Malicious Imp, all about a wicked sprite that would appear to torment bad children by breaking their toys and stealing their sweets. I believe the story had been concocted by Mal's crusty old grandfather to induce us to behave. It had never worked.

It spoke volumes about the disordered state of my wits that I would recollect such a thing at this moment. When I finally recovered my voice, I blurted out, "*You!* What are you doing here?"

I stalked forward, brandishing the gray cloak. "Where is Malcolm Hawkridge? What have you done to him?"

"So many questions," Florian mocked. He munched another peppermint, eyeing the cloak. "Is that blood? Tsk, tsk. You'll never get that stain out. Might as well throw the cloak away. It is not as though Hawkridge will be needing it."

A surge of fury rushed through my veins. Florian was still rocking on the rear legs of the chair. One good shove was all it would take to send the prince flying over backward. Perhaps he discerned something of that angry thought in my eyes. He leaned forward, the chair settling back on all four legs with a loud clunk.

"Where is Mal?" I repeated through gritted teeth. My voice cracked a little as I added, "Is - is he dead?"

"No, he is still alive... for the moment."

I breathed a sigh of relief. It was fleeting, tempered by my fear of what had befallen my friend. Florian smirked, clearly enjoying keeping me in suspense. He dipped his fingers into the jar scrounging for another peppermint.

Casting the cloak aside, I wrenched the jar from Florian's grasp. It was all I could do to keep from smashing it over his head. But I needed to remain calm until I wrung some answers from this infuriating oaf.

"I don't understand why you are here. Did you attack Mal?" I demanded. "Where is he now? Explain yourself!"

Florian scowled. I doubt that anyone had ever dared speak to the prince this way, let alone a woman. He uncoiled himself from the chair, towering over me. "I did warn you, Ella. I will not tolerate any rivals for your affection."

"Rivals? What are you talking about? Mal is my friend."

"Don't be ridiculous. A proper friend for you would be another girl to shop with and gossip, giggle and fuss over hair ribbons. Just as I would seek out another man for companionship, to hunt and drink with. But a man and a woman can never be just friends."

"How would you know?" I snapped. "I doubt you have ever had a true friend in your entire life."

"Careful, Ella. You are sounding shrewish, and I really don't like that in a girl." Florian seized my chin in a hard grip, something ugly surfacing in his eyes. My heart missed a beat as I recalled Ryland's warning about his brother.

"Florian has mastered the art of appearing charming, but you have no idea how dangerous he can be."

I was suddenly aware of how alone I was with the prince. No adoring audience of Midtown citizens to ooh and ahh over Florian's every word and smile. He had no inducement to behave in a noble manner. I swallowed nervously, but I sensed that displaying any fear would be a great mistake. Neither was it wise to deliberately provoke him. Pushing his hand away, I muttered an apology although I nearly choked on it.

Florian's expression lightened. "It is all right. I shall attribute your nasty remark to a natural state of distress. I know how prone you women can be to fits of the vapors. Thus, I will forgive you this time."

Vapors? I thought, grinding my teeth. I was far closer to a state of volcanic eruption. I bought myself time to martial my wits by putting the lid back on the peppermint jar and replacing it on the kitchen shelf above the coal stove. Florian's unexpected assault upon Mal appeared to have been motivated solely by jealousy. The prince did not seem to know anything about the stolen orb, and I was grateful for that. But if I had any hope of saving my friend's life, I needed to tread carefully.

As I turned back to confront Florian, I was able to keep my voice level. "Because you considered Mal to be a rival, you did what? Challenged him to a duel?"

"A duel? With a lowborn creature like that?" Florian snorted. "You forget I am a prince. I would not stoop to soil my hands with the blood of such a ruffian. I had my personal guards give the wretch a sound thrashing and then haul him off to King's Royal Prison. Or the Dismal Dungeons as I have heard the peasants call it. A fitting sobriquet for such a dreadful place, the dank cells, the stench, the rats." Florian gave a mock shudder.

I felt the blood drain from my face at the thought of Mal, badly injured, chained up in one of those fetid cold dungeons. How long could he survive in such grim circumstances? I had warned my friend so many times he would wind up in King's Royal Prison someday because of his reckless disregard for the laws against smuggling and the practice of illegal magic. It was a cruel irony that Mal had ended up incarcerated through no fault of his own but because I had inadvertently inspired this stupid prince's infatuation.

"How did you even know I was supposed to be meeting Mal here today?" I asked. "Have you been spying on me?"

"No!" Florian struck his palm against his chest, trying to appear wounded that I would suggest such a thing. The effect was ruined when he chuckled. "I didn't have to when you have such an obliging neighbor so eager to give me information about your rendezvous with this rogue."

"What neighbor—" I began, but I knew at once who he meant.

"Mrs. Biddlesworth," I grated her name with loathing. I had not been imagining things when I thought the woman had been spying upon me and Mal last night.

I swore. "That miserable, nosy, old cow."

"Now, now, my dear." Florian interrupted, wagging a reproving finger at me. "You must not be vexed with that good woman. Mrs. Biddlesworth has only your best interests at heart."

No, that awful woman wanted to be rid of me because she hated my untidy garden and believed that I was a witch. Fortunate for her that I was not, because I could think of any number of horrible curses to inflict upon her. I had to content myself with vengeful thoughts of decapitating every one of her prize roses.

Florian strutted about the kitchen as he gloated about how he had sent the royal messenger to delude me into thinking he would be gone for the day so I would feel free to keep my meeting with Mal. Then the prince had arranged to arrive at The Hawk's Nest well ahead of time hoping to catch us in a lover's tryst.

Florian looked so pleased with his own cleverness in setting this trap, it was all I could do not to slap him. But his smug expression faded as he added, "I had hoped you would be here to witness your lover getting the thrashing he deserved. But you spoiled everything by being late and then Commander Crushington blundered in, attempting to interfere."

"Hor—" I managed to check myself before I blurted out his name. If Florian suspected one tenth of what I felt for Horatio, I could end up with both men I loved chained up in the Dismal Dungeons. Keeping my expression as neutral as I could, I asked, "Commander Crushington? How did he come to be here?"

Florian gave an irritated shrug. "No idea. He had some lame excuse about being summoned to investigate a disturbance of the peace. Crushington arrived just in time to see my men lashing Hawkridge to the back of a horse to convey him to the prison. That upstart of a Scutcheon attempted to stop me."

"Did he?" I breathed. I had to lower my eyes to conceal how much I adored Horatio for that. I realized Horatio had needed to gain custody of Mal himself to retrieve the orb. But my heart whispered that Horatio had another reason for trying to save Mal from Florian. He had done it for me.

Florian continued in an aggravated tone. "The commander had the impertinence to tell me that I had no authority to arrest Hawkridge. Only the king can issue such a writ."

I seized upon this eagerly. "That is true, isn't it?"

"But I will be king very soon. My dear Papa is dying."

"I heard that the king was doing better."

"He had a sudden relapse. I fully expect him to be dead by morning." Florian apparently recollected he should be sad about this. He managed to squeeze out a sigh. "Alas, I am devastated, but we all must die sometime."

"But the king has recovered before. Surely he—"

"No, he won't. Trust me. There is absolutely no hope of that."

The deadly calm way Florian spoke those words unsettled me. How could he be so certain his father would not recover unless... A chilling suspicion swept through me. No, surely not even Florian could be that vile as to poison the king. I shivered as I remembered Ryland's harrowing tale of Florian maiming his hand. If a man could do that to his own brother, would he have any qualms about murdering his father?

The answer was all too clear in the cold, calculating expression in Florian's eyes. "I explained to Commander Crushington that my father was no longer capable of issuing commands before I ordered him to return to his barracks and cease meddling in matters that were none of his affair."

Was that where Horatio was now? Or had Florian also aroused his suspicions and Horatio had rushed to the palace to alert Mercato and check on the king? Perhaps Horatio had gone to my house, looking for me to soften the blow as he explained what had happened to Mal. All I knew was that Horatio was too far away to help me now.

As Florian stalked closer, I backed toward the rear door that led to Mal's garden. The prince stroked his chin and mused, "That Crushington can be a most annoying fellow. He'd best learn to be more respectful or when I am king, I will assign him to a new duty, scrubbing out the palace latrines."

Florian gave a silky laugh. "But I have a far more important matter to deal with right now." His lips tilted in a sinister smile. "My faithless sweetheart, what am I going to do with you?"

My heart leapt into my throat. I had no idea what dire fate Florian intended for me, but I was not waiting to find out. I flung open the back door and rushed outside, with no notion of where I was going, only somewhere as far away from Florian as I could get.

Perhaps if Mal's boat was docked down in the reeds, I could reach the *Ella Marie* and— But I drew up, short, dismayed to find my way barred by the prince's equerry. The burly man held the reins to his own mount and Florian's. He was allowing both horses to trample all over Mal's carefully tended herb garden.

Before I could register my shock and anger at this, Florian was upon me. He seized me from behind, whipping me around to face him. He clucked his tongue in scolding fashion as his thumbs dug into my shoulders.

"Ella, Ella! Why are you running from me? I would never hurt you."

"You *are* hurting me," I cried. "Let me go."

To my surprise, he did. An aggrieved look crept into his eyes as he complained, "I don't understand you at all. What sort of woman would reject a prince like me for the likes of that wretch Hawkridge? He is nothing but an apothecary, a lowlife from Misty Bottoms and on top of everything else, he's *bald.*"

Florian ran his hand caressingly through his long, golden mane.

"I already told you," I said, rubbing my sore shoulders. "Mal is my friend. I have known him since childhood. He is like my brother."

Florian frowned over this and then his face lit up with sudden comprehension. "Oh! He is your father's bastard. That explains everything."

No, you ignorant cretin, I nearly shrieked. My father had been a completely honorable man. He would never have betrayed the love he felt for my mother in such a fashion. To even imply such a thing was an insult to Papa's memory, and yet it might offer a way to save Mal.

Forgive me, Papa, I thought. Swallowing the lump of guilt that lodged in my throat, I said, "You have guessed the truth. Mal is indeed my illegitimate brother. Now that you know he is not your rival will you please release him from the dungeons?"

Florian nodded his agreement, but only long enough for my face to light up with hope. A hope he quickly dashed with a huge grin and a laugh.

"No, you silly girl. Of course, I won't release him."

I released a deflated breath at the same time my hands balled into fists. Never had I experienced such a tangle of emotions, fear, anger, despair, frustration, and a sense of complete helplessness.

Except that I wasn't. Not entirely. A rustle emanated from the bushes that separated Mal's property from Delphine's next door.

Out of the corner of my eye, I saw a sleek black cat slinking beneath the shrubbery. Delphine regarded me with large unblinking golden eyes. How long she had been there watching or if there was any chance the witch might come to my aid, I didn't know. But her mere presence reminded me that I was not without power.

In my hasty departure from the Winking Goblin, I had forgotten Horatio's cloak, but I had remembered to bring away something far more important. The Fear Blade. It was still attached to my belt.

As my fingers inched toward the sheath, Delphine went into the most astonishing series of gyrations, twitching her tail, waving her paws, and shaking her head. I ignored her, too intent upon the power I could wield to make Florian's smirk disappear.

Unsheathing the tiny blade, I brandished it at him. "Enough of your nonsense," I growled. "You will give the order to release Mal or else!"

I waited in triumphant anticipation for Florian's knees to buckle in terror. Perhaps he would even wet himself as the rogue in the Winking Goblin had done. But the prince merely stared at my little knife in bemusement.

"Or else what?" he repeated with a sneer. "You are going to pare some apples and bake me a pie?"

The Fear Blade hadn't worked. But why? I was certain Florian did not have even a drop of fairy's blood in his veins. I waved the knife at him again, my motions growing more frantic. Sunlight glinted off the blade. My stomach took a sickened plunge as I recalled Delphine's warning.

Never draw the blade out when it can be struck by the rays of the sun. Don't you know what happens to fear in broad daylight? It tends to evaporate.

I watched the blade shimmer, waves of heat rising off it as though the magic enchantment disappeared before my very eyes. A strange meow sounded from the cat hiding beneath the bushes.

Delphine flopped over on her back, twisting her head to regard me with a look of reproach and disgust. I don't speak cat, but I could not have understood the witch more clearly if she had shouted at me. *How could you be so stupid?*

By this time the equerry had noticed I was menacing the prince with some sort of weapon. He started to intervene, but Florian waved him off.

The prince easily plucked the blade from my grasp. I braced myself for his anger, but Florian appeared more amused than vexed. He contemptuously tossed the small knife aside.

"As entertaining as all this has been, I am a busy man," he said. "I have a funeral and a coronation to plan. Let us quickly come to terms. There is only one way for you to obtain your brother's release."

"And what is that?" I asked in dispirited tones.

"You must agree to marry me."

"What!" I gaped at him. "You suspected me of being of the kind of woman who sneaks off to meet with a lover in the middle of the afternoon. I just threatened you with a knife and you *still* want to marry me?"

"Everyone has their little bad habits. I am sure I can correct yours quickly enough once we are wed." Florian smiled but his voice was soft with menace.

I shuddered. "I would rather die than marry you."

"Alas, that would not be your fate, my dear. But if you refuse to wed me, the next gift I send to your house will not be a box of chocolates. It will be Hawkridge's head in a basket."

"But why are you so determined to marry me? Don't try to pretend it is because you love me so much."

"All right, I won't," he agreed affably. "Though I do find you quite beautiful. At least when you take the time to wash your face and brush your hair. More importantly, the entire kingdom expects me to wed you. I do not intend to start my reign as king with all my subjects secretly laughing at me for being a rejected suitor."

"Whose fault would that be?" I retorted. "You should not have turned your courtship of me into such a public spectacle, stalking me all over Midtown. If you had accepted my refusal when I told you no the first time—"

"I'll wager you never said no to Ryland." The prince sulked.

When I started at the mention of his brother's name, Florian's lip curled in an ugly sneer. "Oh, yes that's right. I know all about your history with Ryland. Thanks to Mrs. Biddlesworth, I even know he sneaked out of the palace to see you recently. Still pining after you, is he? I can't wait I see the anguish on his face when he is forced to watch me swoop you up in my arms and carry you off to our bridal bed."

Florian's eyes glittered with such malice, I could not decide if he was completely mad or simply evil.

"Ryland was right," I cried. "I should have listened to him when he tried to warn me. You *are* a monster."

"No, I am merely a man who doesn't like to lose or come off second best, especially to my sniveling brother." Florian fished inside his pouch and produced a diamond ring.

"I don't have all day for you to make up your mind, Ella. What is it going to be? Your hand in marriage or your bastard brother's head in a box?"

I whipped my hands behind my back, agonizing over a choice that was really no choice at all. My gaze strayed to where I had last seen Delphine crouched beneath the bushes. She was still there, but she was busy grooming her paws, completely impervious to my distress. Perhaps the witch was too annoyed that I had wasted the Fear Blade to try to come to my rescue. I don't know what she could have done to help even if she had been so inclined.

Turning back to Florian, I said, "If I agree to marry you, you absolutely promise Mal won't be harmed?"

"I give you my solemn word of honor as a prince and future

king. I will send my own personal physician to tend to your brother's wounds and see to his comfort until our wedding day when I will order his release." Florian placed his hand over his heart, doing his best to look sincere.

I did not trust him in the least to keep his word, but until I could think of another way to save Mal, I had no other option. I moved my hand from behind my back and held it reluctantly out to Florian.

The prince's eyes lit up with triumph as he jammed the ring upon my finger. The diamond was enormous enough to make most women gasp with delight. But I felt as though Florian had just fastened a chain around my neck.

"There now," he crowed. "You are already learning to be sensible and obedient. I really like that in a girl."

He seized me about the waist and yanked me hard against him. His tongue snaked out to moisten his lips as he prepared to assault me with one of his disgusting kisses. This time I would be forced to endure it. I closed my eyes, bracing myself when suddenly a blood-curdling yowl sounded from the bushes.

"What the frap!" Florian's grip on me loosened. When I opened my eyes to see what had elicited this startled exclamation, I saw Delphine streaking toward us across the garden. She spooked the horses, leaving the equerry with his hands full as he tried to calm them.

The cat closed in on Florian, hissing and arching her back.

"Be gone, mangy beast," he snarled. He kicked out at her, but Delphine deftly avoided the blow. She bared her fangs. I half-expected her to leap at Florian and try to scratch his face. Instead, Delphine began to emit a dreadful wheezing sound. Her sides heaved in and out as she coughed up an enormous hairball, long, wet, and slimy, all over the toe of Florian's boot.

Florian gagged and turned green. Apparently, our bold swaggering heir to the throne possessed a delicate stomach. He pressed a handkerchief to his mouth to keep from throwing up as he dragged his toe over the grass. His efforts to dislodge the hairball only succeeded in smearing it.

The prince gagged again before gasping to his equerry, "Find that miserable feline and kill it."

I started to protest, but it was unnecessary. The equerry was too busy keeping the horses under control to obey Florian's command and Delphine had already disappeared back into the shrubbery. I doubted that she would be easily found. Florian must have realized that as well.

Swearing and still struggling not to be sick, the prince bent down and scrubbed his boot with the handkerchief. I had to bite down upon my lip hard to keep from laughing. Delphine might not have offered me a permanent reprieve, but she certainly had succeeded in dampening the prince's ardor. At least for the moment.

Kissing me appeared to be the last thing on Florian's mind. He straightened, flinging the soiled linen away from him with an oath of disgust. He still looked pale as he seized my wrist and snarled, "Come on!"

Alarmed, I tried to hang back. "Wait! Where are you taking me?"

Florian paused to give me an impatient look. "To the palace. I mean to swoop you up on the front of my horse and carry you off with the entire kingdom looking on so that everyone will know you are finally mine."

"No!"

When Florian glared and took a menacing step in my direction, I held up both hands to fend him off. "Please, Your Highness. You must allow me to go home first and— and acquaint my family with the news of our engagement."

"They will learn the glad tidings soon enough," he growled.

"But I need some time to prepare myself."

"To do what? Run away?"

"You know I will not do that. Not while you have Mal chained up in your dungeon. Besides where would I go?"

When Florian continued to regard me with suspicion, I rushed on, "And this late in the day most of the kingdom will be in their homes, having afternoon tea or preparing for supper. There will be hardly anyone to watch you carry me off and you surely would not want people to see your future bride looking like this."

Florian's gaze swept over me, from the mud-stained hem of my old gown to the bedraggled tangles of my hair.

"True enough. You are entirely unfit to be seen in my company," he conceded. "Very well. I shall give you a day - no, two, perhaps. I have much to arrange myself."

His expression lightened as he added, "If I plan it well, I could combine the funeral, coronation, and wedding. Then I would only have to outlay enough coin for one feast and celebration."

"Er - yes," I agreed, trying not to roll my eyes. Florian was vain, deceitful, cruel, and otherwise despicable, but at least the prince was thrifty.

Florian stalked over to his equerry, wrenched the reins from the man's grasp. Vaulting up into the saddle, the prince gazed imperiously down at me. "I shall send word before I come to fetch you in the royal carriage, attended by heralds and all appropriate fanfare. Make sure you are ready and well groomed. Look beautiful. And adoring!"

"Yes, Your Highness." I dipped into a curtsy of feigned meekness.

Having delivered this final command, the prince gigged his horse into motion and rode away, his equerry in close attendance. After Florian disappeared, I was finally able to release a tremulous breath. I had been half-afraid that Florian would insist upon escorting me safely home, but something like that would never have occurred to the self-absorbed prince.

Sunlight sparkled on the ring Florian had given me. I wanted to wrench the hateful thing off my finger and fling it into the

Conger River. But other than giving some relief to my feelings of anger and loathing, such a gesture would solve nothing. If the prince had Mal locked up in his dungeon, Florian had me well and truly trapped. I had two days to find a way to rescue my friend, save myself and perhaps the entire kingdom. If Florian were to become king... I shuddered at the prospect.

My mind should have been working furiously. But after all that I had endured today, I felt as crushed and downtrodden as Mal's poor herb garden. I was standing there as frozen as a statue when Delphine poked her head out of the shrubbery. She glanced around as though checking that Florian was gone before she crept out of the bushes. Sinking onto her haunches, she waved her paw at me. Then she turned back toward the shrubbery. Giving me an impatient look over her shoulder, she jerked her head.

It took my numb brain a few moments to decipher what she wanted. The witch was beckoning me to follow her. Quite naturally, I hesitated. There might have been a truce of sorts declared between us, but I would have hardly considered Delphine a friend. Yes, she had come streaking to save me from Florian's kiss, but I had ruined the Fear Blade she had loaned me.

When I did not move, Delphine let out an impatient meow. She beckoned again, with her head, her paw and even her tail, her gestures growing more insistent. She could not compel me to do anything in her cat form, but I was afraid she might decide to transform back to her human self. And I lacked the fortitude to deal with an irritated, naked witch.

With a weary sigh of surrender, I followed the cat.

Sixteen

I had never been inside a witch's house before. I would have expected it to be dark with cobwebs in the corners, something green and sinister bubbling in a caldron, a well-ridden broom parked near the hearth, perhaps even a skull or two adorning the mantle. But Delphine's parlor was bright and cozy, the creamy wallpaper etched with roses and intertwining vines. A fine lace cloth covered the tea table, the delicately carved chairs cushioned with dark rose damask.

Delphine had shifted back into her human form and thankfully had gone in search of clothing, leaving me to pace about the room and question the wisdom of following her here. The parlor was ordinary enough to make me almost forget this was the home of a witch. When I inspected her mantlepiece, I discovered it held an array of porcelain figurines all in the shape of mice. Some dancing, some playing musical instruments. There was even a tiny mouse bride and groom.

I would have dismissed this as a whimsical collection in any other home. But considering Delphine could transform herself into a cat, I found this celebration of mice a trifle macabre. In addition to the figurines, an oil painting hung above the mantel. It depicted a little white mouse nestled in the center of a pink cushion, rather like some delicacy being served up for dinner.

"Do you like it?" Delphine cooed in my ear.

I started, my heart thudding as I spun around to find the witch standing just behind me. She could not have slipped into the room more quietly than if she had still been slinking along on cat feet. Attired in a floral robe that was as soft and feminine as her parlor, her extraordinary changeable hair shimmered ice blonde down her back.

Recovering from my fright, I croaked, "Like it?"

"The portrait of my mama. I painted it myself."

"Your - your mother?" I faltered.

Delphine nodded, looking at the painting with a misty smile. "Wasn't she able to transform into the prettiest little mouse?"

"Er - yes."

"I was obliged to paint her in her mouse form because I really can't remember what she looked like as a human." Delphine's hair turned a soft shade of blue. "She perished when I was very young."

I gave an empathetic nod. "I lost my mother when I was six. She died of the spotted fever."

"Mine was carried off by a hawk," Delphine said. The tips of her hair started to blacken as she added with a scowl. "My horrid Aunt Tilly accused me of being responsible for Mama's death. As if I would devour my own mother. Besides, I was only a kitten at the time! I have always had the most tender regard for mice because of Mama and I have never been a predatory sort of cat.

"But Aunt Tilly succeeded in turning most of my family against me, even Papa. Nasty old bat and I mean that quite literally because that was Tilly's alternative form. I would have had nowhere to go if my Granny Ginger had not taken me in. She died a few years ago and now I am entirely on my own."

Given Delphine's alarming family history, I could not help wondering what Granny Ginger could transform into and how she had died, but I was not about to ask. Delphine looked so forlorn. I wished I could offer some token of comfort. I was trying to decide if I dared risk a hug or at least a pat on her hand, when she stiffened her shoulders and shook back her hair, the tresses fading to a blonde hue.

"Enough," she said. "This is no time for reminiscences. Come, let us have some tea."

I was both startled and dismayed to realize that while I had been studying the mice on the mantel, Delphine had quietly wheeled a tea cart next to the table. The cart was laden with a teapot and matching cups adorned with painted violets, a plate of dainty-looking sandwiches and an even larger platter of gingerbread.

"Delphine, we don't have time for tea either," I protested. "Mal is in terrible trouble. I need to be doing something."

The witch arched one brow at me as she began to fill our cups. "Doing what?"

"Well, I - I don't exactly know, but *something.*"

"When one doesn't know what to do next, I find the best idea is to have tea. It clarifies the mind and fortifies the soul."

After all that I had endured today, my soul certainly needed fortifying. The spicy scent of the tea, a blend of orange and cinnamon wafted across the room, enticing me. When Delphine patted the seat of one of the chairs and ordered me to sit, I reluctantly obeyed. Easing myself down upon the soft cushion, I accepted the teacup and saucer from Delphine. Raising the cup, I sighed, savoring the fragrant aroma.

But as I started to sip the golden liquid, I froze, remembering Mal's warning.

"Delphine can't hurl curses out of thin air, but don't ever let her give you anything to eat or drink."

I hastily set my cup down onto the saucer, pushing the tea away from me. Delphine had settled into the chair opposite me, cradling her teacup in her long, graceful fingers. Observing my action, she laughed.

"I didn't lace the tea with any sort of nasty potion, if that is what you are afraid of, silly girl."

"I am not being silly. You did threaten me with some manner of vengeance."

"But you must remember the old saying. Vengeance is a dish best served with mounds of sticky sweet icing and a cherry on top."

"That is not quite the way I remember that adage."

"What I am trying to tell you is that Mal's plight eclipses my desire to pay you back. So, drink your tea. You are quite safe from me. *For today.*" Delphine added with a mischievous glint in her eye.

I picked up my cup and took a cautious swallow. The tea tasted as heavenly as it smelled, and Delphine was right about it being fortifying. The warmth seemed to rush through my veins, restoring me. Until that moment, I had not realized how drained with exhaustion I was. Perhaps the tea held some magic after all, but of the good kind.

I ventured to try some of the dainty butter and cucumber sandwiches, piling some of the gingerbread on my plate as well. Delphine had cut the dough into the shape of people, the ladies quite demure in their flared skirts. But with her wicked and I might add bawdy sense of humor, she had equipped the ginger-bread men with masculine accoutrements including tiny baked balls of dough. Pretending that one was Florian, I viciously bit his head off.

Not having eaten anything since breakfast, I was quite hungry. As I devoured my food, sunlight spilled through a nearby window and glinted off the diamond on my finger. Delphine frowned. She plied a napkin to her lips, wiping away crumbs, before demanding, "Let me see that."

I was uncertain what she meant until she indicated my ring. I was only too happy to yank off the hated thing and hand it to her. Delphine held the ring up to light, squinting at the diamond, holding it this way at that. She bit down upon the band before tossing the ring contemptuously back down upon the table.

"Fake," she pronounced. "The diamond is nothing but glass. I doubt the gold is real either. It will probably turn your finger green." She snorted with contempt. "I don't mind a bit of wickedness in a fellow. In fact, I rather like it, but I cannot abide a man who is cheap."

"It could be the costliest diamond in the world, and I wouldn't want it. I don't give a frap if the ring is a fake or not."

"You should. That ring is but one more proof of the prince's duplicity. Do you really think Florian will honor his word to spare Mal if you marry him?"

"No," I said. "But if I hadn't agreed to the wedding, Mal would already be dead." I summoned up a bleak smile. "By the way, I never thanked you for the hairball."

"It was my pleasure." Delphine grinned. But she immediately sobered as she added, "Unfortunately, I cannot cough up one large enough to save either your or Mal from the prince."

I placed a half-eaten gingerbread man back on my plate, my appetite gone as I remembered my bitter parting from Mal.

"Mal and I had such a dreadful quarrel today," I said, tears prickling at the back of my eyes. "The last thing I ever said to him was that I never wanted to see him again."

Delphine sniffed. "I think the last thing I ever said was that I hoped his pizzle would rot and fall off."

She dashed her hand across her eyes and rapped her knuckles upon the table, saying sternly. "Enough of these maudlin regrets. We must work on a plan to break Mal out of that horrible prison."

"The Dismal Dungeons?" I exclaimed, drying my eyes with my napkin. "Delphine, no one has ever escaped from there. Even if those League friends of Mal were to join us-"

"Those brainless ruffians!" Delphine interrupted me with a scornful snort. "Don't expect any help from that lot. The word of Mal's arrest has probably spread all over Misty Bottoms by now. Those rogues are all likely scrambling to save their own skins by disposing of any evidence they were ever in league with Mal."

As Delphine refilled our teacups, she demanded, "What about your Commander Crushington?"

"Horatio is not mine—" I began.

"Oh please." Delphine rolled her eyes. "It is obvious the man is besotted with you. Is there nothing he could do to help Mal?"

I considered the idea for a fleeting moment only to reject it with a sad shake of my head.

"But he is a Scutcheon Commander. He could issue a writ demanding that Mal be released into his custody," Delphine insisted.

"Horatio already tried that when Florian seized Mal. The prince refused."

"But the commander could forge an official looking document and trick the Warden at Dismal Dungeons into thinking—"

"No. Mal has broken so many laws, Horatio believes that he deserved to be arrested. Even if Horatio considers incarceration in the Dismal Dungeons too harsh a punishment for anyone, he would not be willing to help Mal escape. Not only would it affront Horatio's sense of honor as a Scutcheon commander, but it would also be far too great a risk for him to take."

"Surely, he would if you begged him. Just flutter your lashes like this." Delphine batted her eyes. "Summon up some tears and bribe him with a kiss or two."

"I can't do that, Delphine. I won't!"

When she glared at me with frustration, I said, "Mal and I have already brought too much trouble down upon Horatio when we stole the orb. I won't endanger him any further."

I sucked in my breath. "The orb! I entirely forgot about the orb."

"That ridiculous bauble." Delphine sneered. "What of it?"

"The orb is not ridiculous. Everything Mal told me about it

was true." Leaning forward in my chair, I related to her all that I had learned from Withypole at the Winking Goblin.

Delphine listened with her arms crossed, appearing unimpressed. Refusing to be daunted by her skeptical expression, I concluded, "I doubt Mal had time to retrieve the orb before he was ambushed by Florian, and I doubt Horatio was able to look for it either. Not with the prince there. The orb must still be hidden somewhere in the Hawk's Nest. If we could find it, maybe we could—"

"We could what?" Delphine cut me off impatiently. "Use the orb to conjure up this mythical prince who is supposed to magically save this kingdom? Even if such a thing were possible, by the time we managed to do so, Mal would be missing a head."

I winced at the terrible image Delphine's words evoked. "I realize that. But Withypole is supposed to be the guardian of the orb. We could offer to return the orb to him if he agrees to help us save Mal. You told me that fairies possess powerful magic."

But Delphine was already shaking her head. "I don't trust fairies, especially that one. Withypole Fugitate has already proven himself to be notoriously unreliable. Even if we could get the cantankerous wretch to agree, he'd probably show up drunk and accidentally obliterate our minds or start gleaning gold buttons off the guards' uniforms."

I sank back in my chair and blew out a frustrated sigh. "Fine! Then what do you suggest?"

"If Mal is going to be rescued, I am afraid it is entirely up to us."

"You mean just me and you?" I stared at her in disbelief.

"Um, no. I mean mostly you." Delphine gave me an apologetic smile.

"What!" I squawked.

"Mercado has conjured a device to keep witches away. The nasty old wizard! If I try to get anywhere near any of the royal properties, I will set off an alarm."

Delphine was right. That was exactly what had happened when the witch had tried to attend the royal ball. She had been forced to transform into Ebony to escape the guard.

"Then you expect me to storm the Dismal Dungeons all by myself, just by waving a sword to strike terror— Wait!" I regarded her hopefully. "You don't happen to have another magical weapon, do you?"

"No!" Delphine pulled a sour face. "If I did, I would not trust you with it. Not after the way you ruined my Fear Blade."

"Sorry," I mumbled. "Can you not just enchant it again?"

"No, you ignorant chit. Do you have any idea how long it took me to enchant that knife? It is a very complicated spell. It took me weeks to perfect it and Mal doesn't have that kind of time.

"Fortunately, I do have a few other bits of magic that will prove useful. Most important of all you have the invisibility shoes Mal gave you." Delphine brandished her teaspoon, leveling me with an accusing stare. "Unless you managed to destroy those as well."

"I still have the glass slippers, but they don't work. Mal's magic never does."

"Mal didn't enchant those slippers. I did and they work just fine."

"No, they don't." I retorted. "I tried the shoes and followed the directions Mal gave me, but nothing happened. That is why I never wore them on the night of the ball."

Delphine gave me the kind of look one usually reserved for the village idiot. "Don't tell me, let me guess. You were alone when you tried on the shoes. You looked at yourself in the mirror and you could still see your reflection."

"Well, yes."

She flung up her hands in exasperation, forgetting she still held the spoon. It went flying across the room as she exclaimed, "Of course you could still see yourself, you foolish girl. Do you have any idea how discombobulating it would be to watch your own body vanish? That was the beauty and cleverness of my shoes. The slippers only render you invisible to everyone else."

"Well, Mal never explained that to me," I said defensively.

"I am sure he didn't. Because as usual he was in a tearing hurry and only half-listening to me when I instructed him about the shoes worked. But you had better pay much closer heed to me if you and Mal are to survive this rescue attempt." Delphine rapped her knuckles upon the table as though to ensure she had my full attention.

"Listen up," she commanded. "Here is what we are going to do."

My jaw dropped as Delphine outlined her plot to free Mal from the Dismal Dungeons. I listened with mounting trepidation because her plan was so audacious. It was reckless. It was dangerous. It was completely mad.

But there was a slim chance that it just might work.

Seventeen

The sun was setting by the time I returned home after what felt like the longest day of my life. And it was not over yet since I had pledged to meet Delphine in Mal's garden before midnight. She had wanted to embark upon our rescue mission as soon as it had grown dark, but I had persuaded her to wait because I had preparations to make.

I needed to fetch the glass slippers and decide how I was going to deal with my family. As I entered my garden gate, I glanced across the lane. The Hansons' home already bore a melancholy and abandoned aspect, the front stoop not swept, the windows shuttered. It was as though the family that had lived there was long gone and forgotten.

I could still picture Myrtle's tear-streaked face as the Border Scutcheons had ruthlessly herded the Hansons and Baftons into exile. It was far too easy for me to imagine Em, Netta and Amy in that dire situation. If something were to go wrong tonight, if I did not return... But I could not allow myself to think that way or I might lose my courage entirely.

I braced myself as I opened my front door, expecting to be confronted by my stepmother in a high state of distress, demanding to know where I had been and did I have any idea how worried she had been. I could hear voices emanating from the back of the house. Good. That would give me a moment to slip up to my room and hide the parcel Delphine had given me.

You need some sensible clothing to wear tonight, the witch had insisted. Given Delphine's eccentric notions, who knew what that might mean. I had not yet taken the time to look, but the mere sight of the bag would be enough to rouse my family's curiosity, eliciting too many questions I was not prepared to answer. For that same reason, I hid my fake engagement ring as well.

But I had no sooner stepped inside the front hall when I was pounced upon by my two stepsisters. They both seized me in such exuberant hugs that I dropped the package.

"Girls! Can't breathe," I gasped. As I pried free of their strangling embraces, I used the toe of my boot to nudge the parcel beneath the hall table. I dreaded that my more observant sister Netta would notice, but she was too preoccupied with staring at me reproachfully.

"Ella! You have come home at last. Where have you been all day? We were so afraid that something terrible might have happened to you like being run over by a carriage or falling into a ditch or being arrested."

"Oh, don't be so silly," Amy said. "Far more likely she would be caught in that awful storm and struck by lightning, but there is no reason Ella should be arrested."

I grimaced. Not unless one counted robbing the king's treasure vault or plotting to help a prisoner escape the royal dungeons.

"There was no good reason the Hansons and Baftons should have been arrested and driven out of their homes either." Tears filled Netta's eyes. "Ella, you said everything would be all right. That Commander Crushington would save them."

"I am sorry, my dear." I brushed a stray tear from Netta's cheek. "Horatio tried his best, but there was nothing he could do."

"Of course, there wasn't," Amy said. "I am sorry for what

happened to those families too, but they brought it upon themselves for behaving so badly at the royal ball."

"Amy!" Netta cried. "The Hanson girls and Ivy Bafton were our friends and Fortescue was your favorite beau until you got all those foolish ideas about marrying a prince. You should be ashamed for saying such a thing."

Amy reddened but muttered, "It is what everyone in Midtown is saying."

Of course, they were, I thought. It was what I warned Mal about when he hoped this latest instance of the king's tyranny would rouse the good citizens of Midtown to join his rebellion. But my neighbors had far too much to lose. It saddened me but I wasn't surprised to learn that they were trying to distance themselves from the exiled families.

"I can't believe anyone could be so callous as to blame our neighbors for their own misfortune." Netta scowled at her sister. "The people of Midtown are mean and cruel, the same as you, Amy."

Amy bridled like a hen that had its feathers ruffled. Before my sisters could fall into a serious quarrel, I hastened to intervene.

"I don't think anyone means to be cruel, Netta," I said, trying to soothe my sister. "If people can convince themselves that the Hansons and Baftons were in the wrong, it makes folks feel more secure, less worried that such a terrible fate could ever befall their own families."

"How can anyone ever be sure of that?" Netta asked, mopping her eyes.

"*We* can. We will never lose our home," Amy insisted. "Not now because of the betrothal."

"B-betrothal?" I faltered in dismay. Had Florian already managed to trumpet to the entire kingdom he had won me for his bride?

Amy beamed. "If Netta hadn't gotten all weepy over the Hansons, I could have told you our wonderful news."

"It is not up to you to tell." Netta sniffed. "You should wait for Mama."

Amy ignored her sister. "You will never guess what has happened, Ella. Lord Redmond called upon Mama this afternoon and—" She paused for dramatic effect. "He proposed and Mama has accepted him!"

My jaw dropped. I had advised my stepmother to mend her quarrel with Chuffy, hoping that perhaps in time, Lord Redmond and Em could rekindle their youthful courtship. I had never expected Chuffy to act so quickly.

Before I could respond to what Amy had blurted out, my stepmother appeared. Shooing her daughters off to the kitchen, she tugged me into the parlor to share the good tidings herself. Em blushed like a young girl as she related how during afternoon tea, Chuffy had suddenly dropped to one knee before her.

"I was so startled I dropped a buttered muffin on his head. He nearly lost his balance and fell over. His knee creaked when I was helping him up." Em giggled. "It was not quite as romantic as when we were young, but, oh, when he kissed me, it was as though all these years we have been apart melted away and now we are to be married at last."

Em faltered, giving me an anxious look. "I hope you do not mind, Ella."

"Dearest, Em, why should I mind?"

"I feared this sudden betrothal might seem disloyal to your father's memory."

"Papa has been gone these five years and more," I reminded her. "He would not have expected you to mourn him forever."

"I know but I always told you such stories about the great love we shared." Em's face fell. "Part of me knew I was fooling myself. I was certainly infatuated with your Papa, but—" My stepmother's eyes grew wistful as she asked, "Do you think he ever loved me at all?"

Not in the way my father had adored my mother, but I told

Em gently, "I believe that Papa cared for you a great deal and he would want you to be happy. Just as I do."

Em gave a relieved sigh and enveloped me in her arms. As I returned her hug, I thought that my stepmother could not be nearly as relieved as I was. My stepmother's betrothal to a wealthy aristocrat would have been welcome news even under ordinary circumstances. Now, no matter what happened to me, I knew my family would be taken care of and that eased a great burden of guilt from my shoulders. It was as though for once, the fates had aligned in my favor. Surely that had to be a good omen for the success of my dangerous mission tonight. At least that was what I sought to convince myself.

When we joined my stepsisters in the kitchen, I was surprised to discover that Amy had done the marketing in my absence. She proudly displayed the supper she had prepared, consisting mostly of pastries, tarts, fairy cakes, chocolates, and a bottle of cherry wine.

My habit of keeping strict track of every penny spent had become so ingrained that I nearly cried out against the impracticality and the extravagance of such a meal. I swallowed my protest, realizing that Em's betrothal made my frugality unnecessary. Taking my place at the table, I tried to join in the merriment over what Amy called our celebratory feast.

But I couldn't help thinking that if my attempt to rescue Mal failed, this could be the last meal I ever shared with my family, the last time I ever saw them. I did my best to suppress this terrible notion. My pasted-on smiles fooled my stepmother and Amy, but more than once I caught Netta giving me a puzzled look.

I was glad when the time came for everyone to retire for the night. When I was sure that Em, Amy and Netta were settled in their bedchambers, I crept back downstairs to retrieve the satchel I had tucked beneath the hall table.

I had darted half-way back up the stairs when I froze. Netta awaited me at the top, a ghost-like figure in her white nightgown. Holding a candle aloft, she peered down at me.

"Ella? What are you doing?" She came down a couple steps, her eyes alight with curiosity. "What's in the parcel?"

"Um, er." My brain scrambled to come up with a convincing lie. "It's only some garments that need mending. You know how I fret over our lack of funds. I thought I would earn some extra income by taking in sewing. But of course, after Em's good news, that will no longer be necessary."

"So that is where you were all day, trying to find sewing customers?"

I nodded. "Now you should scamper back to bed."

"But I have something else to tell you. I forgot because of all the excitement of Mama's engagement. Commander Crushington called here this afternoon."

"Oh?" I tried to sound casual, although my heart missed a beat. "What did he want?"

"*You*, of course. He seemed most distressed and displeased to find you were not at home."

I winced, well able to imagine how worried Horatio would have been, perhaps even a trifle vexed with me. Twice in one day, I had ignored orders he had given for my own protection. I had thought about stopping by the Scutcheon barracks on my way home. There was so much I had learned from Withypole that I needed to tell Horatio, along with my suspicions that Florian might be poisoning his father. I was also worried about how Mercato had reacted when Horatio had returned without the orb.

More than all of that, I longed to cast myself into Horatio's embrace, feel the warm, reassuring strength of his arm about me. But I had been too afraid that I might weaken, blurt out how Florian was using Mal to coerce me to marry him. Horatio would tell me to go home, allow him to deal with the prince, but I did not see how he could without putting himself in danger.

Netta's worried voice pulled me out of my thoughts. "What is really going on Ella? I keep feeling like there is something you are not telling me."

"Nonsense." My denial came out a shade too hearty. I feigned a deep yawn. "It has just been a very eventful day and I am so tired. We can talk more in the morning."

"But—"

"Goodnight, my dear." I linked my arm through hers and hustled my sister up the stairs toward her bedchamber. "Sweet dreams."

Before she could ask any more questions, I bolted to my own room. *Sweet dreams?* I cringed. Never in my life had I cooed such words. My odd un-Ella-like behavior would only fuel Netta's sense that something was not right with me. But I had no time to waste worrying about what my sister might be thinking. I intended to wait until I was sure that everyone was asleep before sneaking out of the house. In the meantime, I had much to do.

Moonlight spilled through my bedchamber window, enabling me to find the tinder box. I dumped Delphine's parcel upon my bed and proceeded to light several candles. Before I unwrapped the package, I had a far more important task. Faced with the very real prospect that I might never return from my mission, I owed my family some explanation for why I had vanished.

Sitting down at my small writing desk, I dipped my pen in the inkwell and started to compose a letter to Em, only to think better of it. If my stepmother awoke to discover me missing tomorrow morning, she would likely dissolve into hysterics. As for Amy and Netta, I still thought of them as my little sisters, whom I had striven for most of my life to protect. They were far too young to have any notion how to handle my disappearance.

I needed someone older, possessed of calm and good sense, to take charge of my distraught family. What little I had seen of Lord Redmond convinced me I should address my letter to him. But how to begin? Dear Chuffy? Although he had once asked me to call him that, it seemed far too impertinent. Dear step-papa? Too presumptuous. I settled upon a more formal tone.

Dear Lord Redmond,

If you are reading this, the worst has happened. I have either been arrested or possibly killed in my attempt to free my dearest friend Malcolm Hawkridge from King's Royal Prison.

I kept my explanation succinct, leaving out any references to the stolen orb or the League of the Missing Heir. The less Chuffy or my family knew about that, the better for their own safety. I described Mal's arrest as being the unreasonable result of Prince Florian's jealousy and his attempt to coerce me into marriage. I knew how much Lord Redmond disliked the prince. He would sympathize with my wish to avoid wedding Florian, even if Chuffy would not approve of my dangerous plan.

I concluded my letter by expressing my joy over Chuffy's betrothal to my stepmother. In the event I was unable to ever return, I begged his lordship to look out for my family and to tell them how sorry I was and how much I loved them.

I blinked hard as I sealed the letter. I was near to tears and that had been the easy one to write. Drawing in a deep breath, I reached for another piece of parchment and began my letter to Horatio. I held my pen suspended over the paper for a long time, dripping blots of ink as I struggled to find the words. Above all else, I needed him to understand how much I would always love him. But I feared I could fill the pages with passionate protestations of my devotion and Horatio would still doubt me.

He had become convinced that I did not know my own heart, that it was Mal I loved. Risking my freedom, even my very life to save Mal would only confirm Horatio in that belief. It would seem like I was choosing Mal over him and perhaps in a way I was.

Even if I succeeded in helping Mal escape, what then? How could I return home, expecting that my life would ever return to its normal course? I could not ignore all that I had learned today, that the legend of the missing heir was true and what a monster Prince

Florian would be if he ascended to the throne. I seemed to have little choice now. I would have to join Mal in his quest to find Arcady's true prince, even if it cost me the man that I loved.

Horatio had already made it clear that he was adamantly opposed to any rebellion. If I threw my lot in with Mal and his League, I would be closing the door upon any sort of happy ending for me and Horatio forever.

When I finally touched my pen to the paper, I was only able to scratch out a few words.

Horatio,

I love you. Forgive me. Yours, Ella.

After staining the letter with a few of my tears, I wiped my eyes with the back of my hand and sealed the note. I set both letters atop my fireplace mantel where they would be sure to be found in the morning. Then I turned my attention to the parcel of clothing Delphine had given me.

I eyed it warily, hardly knowing what to expect. An enchanted corset? A magical pair of drawers? One never quite knew what to expect from Delphine and she had offered me no explanation other than insisting I wear these garments tonight.

Cutting the string, I peeled away the brown paper wrapping. I was surprised to discover not any sort of feminine apparel, but instead a pair of masculine breeches and a black shirt. I now understood why Delphine had been so coy about telling me what was in the package.

I suspected that she had stolen these clothes from Mal, probably off his wash line. The shirt with its flowing sleeves and open neckline with leather lacings looked like something Mal would wear. But why would Delphine have taken them? Perhaps to lay some sort of curse on Mal? The witch had expressed a penchant for taking revenge upon those she felt had wronged her. Yet for all her protestations of hating Mal and being done with him, Delphine was as willing to risk her life to save him as I was.

More likely she had snatched the clothes to have something of his to cherish. The garments still carried a lingering odor of that bayberry soap Mal liked to use. As I breathed in the scent, it conjured up an image of my friend, his ready laugh and teasing grin. My heart ached. What if when I arrived at the prison, I discovered he was already dead? What if I was never able to mend our quarrel, to take back those last terrible words I had spoken to him?

"Stop it, Ella," I muttered. I had to truly believe I would succeed in saving Mal. Otherwise, my mission was doomed before I had even begun.

I quickly stripped out of my own apparel and pulled my hair back from my face as severely as I could, pinning it into a chignon. Mal was not a large man, but his clothing was still too big for me. I had to roll up the legs of the breeches, cinching the garment about my waist with a belt I fashioned out of a blue sash. The shirt hung on me like those castoff tops farmers used to adorn scarecrows. I pulled the neck lacings as tight as I could and stuffed the tails of the shirt beneath my belt. At least that helped to fill out the breeches.

I had often envied Mal for his masculine garments. Despite how ill-fitting his clothes were on me, I liked the new freedom of movement. I swaggered about a bit, fancying myself as a dark and menacing corsair. All I needed to complete the illusion was a pair of knee-high boots, but alas, I knew what I needed to wear, and I was not looking forward to it.

I fetched the glass slippers from their hiding place in my wardrobe. As I eased my feet into the magical shoes, they were as stiff and uncomfortable as I remembered, the heels far higher than I liked.

I minced over to study my reflection in the mirror. Any notions I had about myself appearing as a dangerous brigand were swiftly dispelled. I looked utterly ridiculous like a young lad who couldn't decide what he wanted to be when he grew up, a river pirate or a foppish dancing master.

But if the shoes worked the way Delphine had promised, it

wouldn't matter how I looked. No one would be able to see me. I furrowed my brow, concentrating hard to remember the exact sequence of directions to activate the shoes' magic.

Click your toes together three times.

I followed the instructions, but I could still see myself reflected in the mirror. But according to Delphine, this was to be expected. I should now be invisible to everyone else. The witch had not lied to me about the Fear Blade, so I needed to trust her about the magical properties of the shoes.

I still felt uneasy as I left my room and hobbled downstairs. The heels on my shoes made me awkward and I feared taking a tumble, arousing the entire household. Even if the shoes had made me invisible, they did not mute any noise I made. The heels clicking against the floor of the lower hall sounded far too loud no matter how quietly I tried to move. It was almost impossible to tiptoe when wearing glass slippers, but somehow, I managed to slip out of the house without waking anyone.

Most proper young ladies would not have dared venture out of their homes at such an hour when all decent folk were fast asleep. But I had never been afraid of the night. Most of my trysts with Prince Ryland had taken place at midnight. When Mal and I were children, we had sneaked out of our beds and met up to go hunting for the Dread Gobbledygook, a horrible, fanged monster that was purely the creation of our own fervid imaginations.

Any perils I encountered tonight were not going to be the stuff of fantasy. That realization heightened my senses, making me overly aware of every sound, the hoot of an owl hidden in the branches of our oak tree, the rustle of a mole darting through my overgrown rose bed, even the quick rise and fall of my own breath.

The moon was bright and full, surrounded by a coterie of stars. I could not decide if that was a good or bad thing. The moonlight illuminated the lane that ran past my house, making travel easier but it would also make it more difficult to conceal myself if I met any Scutcheons on night patrol. I could only hope that the shoes were working their magic.

I cringed at the loud creak of my garden gate as I opened it and let myself out into the lane. I closed it as quietly as I could before setting off down the road. But I had not taken many steps when I heard the distant pounding of a horse's hooves. I halted, listening intently as I sought to determine the direction the sound was coming from. When I realized it was behind me, I whipped about to see a horse and rider galloping down the lane, coming from the direction of the Heights and the royal palace. Someone whose broad shoulders and upright bearing, I recognized even from this distance.

"Horatio." His name escaped me in a choked whisper. I froze for a few seconds before coming to my senses enough to stumble to the side of the road. There was no place to conceal myself. I stifled a gasp of dismay when he reined Loyal to an abrupt halt, mere feet from where I stood.

My heart banged in my chest and for one pulse-stopping moment, Horatio seemed to stare straight at me. My mind raced and I almost started to stammer out some lame excuse for my presence. But Horatio's gaze shifted in the direction of my house. I could read his expression clearly by the light of the moon, a combination of weariness and hopeless longing.

Then he dug in his knees, urging Loyal onward. As he rode past me, I had to press my hand to my mouth to keep from calling after him. I forced myself to remain silent even knowing this might be the last time I ever saw him. My heart ached as he vanished from view, but at least now I knew one thing.

The magic shoes worked. I had become invisible, even to the man I loved.

Eighteen

I am an excellent walker, but it took me longer than usual to traverse the few miles that separated my home from Misty Bottoms. I was still growing accustomed to the glass shoes. I continued to tread carefully lest I stumble and twist my ankle. I also did not want to blunder into any of the rough denizens who might be lurking in the narrow lanes of this lawless part of town. But perhaps the full moon discouraged any sort of skullduggery. The only one roaming about tonight with criminal intentions appeared to be me. Except for one other.

I found Delphine waiting for me in Mal's back yard. The witch was draped in a long dark cloak with the hood flung back. She carried a lantern that illuminated her annoyed expression. As she paced along the borders of the herb garden with mounting impatience, I came up behind her.

Tapping her on the shoulder, I announced, "Delphine, I'm here."

She ought to have been expecting me, but she still squawked in alarm. If she had been in her cat form, I think she would have leaped straight into the air, all four paws off the ground. Whirling about, she held up the lantern and groped the air in front of her, her fingers brushing against my shirt.

"Ella?"

I slipped out of the shoes, grinning as I reappeared.

Delphine swore. "Blast you, woman. You nearly scared me out of all my nine lives."

"You actually have nine lives?" I asked in astonishment.

"No. That's just a little feline joke. I only have one life so I would appreciate not being frightened to death."

"Sorry," I muttered, even though I wasn't. Delphine had alarmed me so many times, I enjoyed getting a bit of my own back. I suppose the witch and I were not unlike in that we both had a capacity for delighting in revenge.

"You're late," she snapped. "What took you so long?"

"Sorry," I repeated as I bent down to retrieve the shoes. "It's these awkward glass slippers. I could have got here much faster if you had enchanted something sensible like a nice pair of kid boots."

"You are such a complainer." The witch rolled her eyes as she mimicked my voice. "Oh, Delphine, this is such a nice Fear Blade you loaned me, but couldn't you have made it a sword? And these magical slippers are pretty, but I would have preferred something in leather."

"I don't mean to sound ungrateful," I began.

"Well, you are!" Delphine huffed with exasperation. "You seem to have forgotten I originally designed those shoes for you to wear to the royal ball. You'd have looked rather foolish if I had given you a pair of hobnail boots. Besides, I have experimented with leather. For some reason, it won't hold the enchantment."

She scowled at the shoes I clutched in my hands. "You realize you don't need to take the shoes off to become visible? Just reverse the instructions."

"It is easier just to take them off."

"Suit yourself. But be careful! Those dancing slippers are made of a special kind of crystal. Sturdier than glass, but still breakable and I would be quite vexed if you ended up ruining those shoes the way you did my Fear Blade."

"Yes, ma'am," I said meekly, hugging the shoes to my chest.

"Now, come on. We have no more time to waste."

Still carrying the shoes, I followed Delphine as she set off. I had no intention of putting those slippers back on until necessary. My feet welcomed the respite, the feel of the grass cool and soothing.

I came to an abrupt halt when I realized where the witch was leading me. "Delphine, we are heading toward the river."

"Where else do you expect to find a boat?"

"A boat? That is how we are going to travel to the Dismal Dungeons?"

She paused to throw me an impatient look. "How did you think we were going to get there? In a coach and four with a footman blowing a trumpet to announce our arrival?"

"Of course not." In truth I had not given the manner of our transportation much consideration, leaving all those preparations to Delphine.

"Using Mal's boat will be our swiftest and stealthiest way of getting to the prison," she insisted.

"But I don't have the least notion of how to steer or row a boat. Unless you have some way of enchanting the *Ella Marie*."

"This doesn't require magic. Just a pair of strong arms and a broad back. Happily, I was able to recruit such help."

"You trusted someone else with our plans for tonight?" I exclaimed in dismay. "Who?"

The question died on my lips as a hulking figure lumbered out of the shadows near Mal's dock. Moonlight skimmed over familiar features, a bristling gray beard and an eye patch.

"Evening, Miss Upton," he grinned.

"You!" I cried, backing away.

Delphine's brows arched in surprise. "You have already met Waldo the Wharf Rat?"

"Regrettably I have." I waved one of the glass slippers accusingly in his direction. "This man tried to attack me in the Winking Goblin this afternoon."

"Aw, no, miss," Waldo protested. "I was only after stealing a little kiss."

I glared at him. "I think you were after a great deal more than that!"

"Sorry, miss. But I did obey when you ordered me to stop. I even helped to clean the tap room when you commanded me and my friends to do it." Waldo scratched his head, looking perplexed. "Though for the life of me, I can't understand why we did."

Delphine smothered a laugh. She must have been able to guess that Waldo had been under the influence of the Fear Blade.

The big man continued to whine. "I would never have bothered you at all, miss, if I had known you were Mal's young lady friend."

"You shouldn't have been bothering her no matter whose young lady she is," Delphine said sternly. "Shame on you, you old villain. You have four daughters of your own."

Waldo shrugged. "I didn't come by those four girls without being friendly, Delphie." He leered at the witch and leaned closer. "I still cherish hopes of getting me a son one day with the cooperation of a fine wench like yourself."

Delphine doubled up her fist and bopped him.

"Ow!" Waldo stumbled back, rubbing his nose.

"Don't ever call me Delphie again!" The witch growled. "You should recall what happened the last time you tried to get too familiar with me."

Waldo obviously did from the way he backed off, protectively clutching his privates. Delphine snapped at him to prepare the boat for launch. As Waldo stumbled in his haste to obey, I whispered in the witch's ear.

"Delphine, what were you thinking? That man is completely despicable! Do you really believe we can trust him?"

"Around any pretty girl, no! But he and Long Louie are the two of Mal's disreputable friends who are the most dependable and loyal to him. And no one knows the river like the Wharf Rat."

I almost grumbled that I would have preferred the help of Long Louie, but Delphine would likely have accused me of complaining again.

"Fine!" I muttered. "But I wish I still had the Fear Blade."

Delphine patted my hand. "You don't need a Fear Blade to keep that rogue on his best behavior, sweetie. You have me."

I was not entirely reassured, but I swallowed any further misgivings. Waldo appeared respectful enough as he helped me and Delphine into the boat, although he did give me an audacious wink when he thought Delphine wasn't looking. The small skiff rocked perilously as Waldo cast off and leapt aboard. I clutched my precious shoes tight in my lap, fearful of dropping one.

But for such a large man, the Wharf Rat was remarkably agile. The boat steadied as he took his seat opposite me and Delphine. Manning the oars, he steered us out of the shallows and onto the main course of the river. As we headed downstream, we were travelling with the current which made the rowing smooth and easy.

The return trip would prove more difficult with the addition of Mal's weight on board. After the beating he had taken from Florian's guards, who knew what condition my poor friend might be in. I tried not to think too much about that or any of the difficulties or perils that lie ahead. Stealing a glance at Delphine, I wondered if she was as anxious as I was. I had learned a little about reading her moods from the ever-shifting color of hair.

Tonight, her long tresses were as silvery white as the moonlight. I had never seen that hue on her before and wondered what it denoted. A serene confidence in our success or an utter terror that we were headed for disaster.

She appeared calm enough as she set her lantern down on the bottom of the boat. I had not noticed before, but the illumination came from a curious-looking blue candle that showed no sign of melting or waxing any smaller as it burned. Delphine must have enchanted it somehow. Ordinarily I would have been fascinated, but my attention was claimed by Delphine producing a small pouch.

"Here are a few more things that you will need to rescue Mal," she said. Delving inside the pouch, she retrieved what looked like an ivory darning needle, the thick kind a cobbler would have used on leather. She handed it to me for my inspection.

"What is this? A Fear Needle?" I asked hopefully.

"No, don't be silly. It's a Skeletal Pick. I whittled down a piece of bone and put a spell on it. This will enable you to pick open any lock you encounter."

"Bone? Not a human one, I hope?" I joked weakly.

"Of course not," Delphine started to deny and then she shrugged. "Well, not the bone of anybody important."

"Hey!" Waldo squawked in protest.

Delphine smirked at him. "I bought the bone off of some drunken idiot who thought it was a good idea to perform the Corsair Sabre Dance when he was barefoot and ended up slicing off his own toe."

"And I would happily cut off another one if you'd make me one of those magic lock picks," Waldo said.

"In your dreams, Wharf Rat," Delphine retorted.

I shuddered with revulsion, not wanting to think about the process Delphine had used to transform Waldo's severed toe into the Skeletal Pick. I handed the splinter of bone back to her, dreading to find out what else she might have in her bag of magic tricks.

The next item she produced was not as gruesome. Cupped in the palm of her hand was a cloudy blue marble.

"This is a Mist Pellet," she said. "Fling it at the ground as hard as you can, and it will produce a temporary fog."

"Is that what you used to escape on the night of the King's ball?"

She nodded. "You'll need this to get past the prison guards."

"But I already have the magic shoes."

"The shoes will turn you invisible, but they won't help Mal."

"Invisibility shoes?" Waldo rested the oars long enough to stare wistfully at the glass slippers cradled in my lap. "I'd hack off my whole foot for a pair of those."

"If you cut off your foot, the shoes wouldn't do you much good, numbskull," Delphine said. "Now keep rowing."

Waldo grunted and resumed his labors as Delphine drew forth the last items from her bag, gingerbread cookies cut in the shape of mice.

"You thought I might get hungry?" I asked in disbelief. "Delphine, I assure you I have absolutely no appetite."

"These aren't for you. These are in case you encounter any Aura cats."

"Aura cats?" I gasped. "They have those patrolling the prison?"

"I don't know for certain, but you might just run into one or two. Even though, they won't be able to see you, they will still sense your aura."

"Oh, wonderful," I muttered.

"Don't worry. Just toss them a cookie. These are laced with a powerful sleeping potion. The cat will keel over as soon as it swallows it." Delphine looked pensive. "I only hope the cookies work just as well on the dragon."

"Dragon?" I had to smother my shriek.

"Just teasing." She chuckled and Waldo grinned.

I glared at them.

When Delphine stopped laughing, she conceded, "There are some wild tales about a dragon kept in the dungeons, but I am sure it is nothing but a ridiculous rumor. If you should come across a dragon, there is one important thing you should remember."

"To run very fast?" I asked sourly.

"Yes, that is always a good idea when a dragon is after you, especially since invisibility shoes won't work on magical beings like dragons, fairies, mermaids, or pixies. They might not be able to see you, but they will sense your presence. But I doubt you will encounter anything like that inside the prison."

"No, just aura cats and hordes of nasty prison guards," I grumbled.

"Don't worry, Ella. You are going to be fine." Delphine gave my shoulder a reassuring pat. "You can do this. Just think of Mal and how much he needs you."

Thinking of my beloved friend was the only thing that kept me from diving off the boat and swimming back to shore. Delphine handed me the pouch and I fastened it to my belt. After that, the witch lapsed into silence with no more dire warnings or unsettling jests.

Delphine was obviously more worried than she would admit, and that realization offered me little comfort. The hue of her hair shifted from silvery to stark white. Waldo turned quiet and somber as well. The only sounds disturbing the night were the rhythmic stroke of his oars, the trilling of frogs along the riverbank and the mocking call of a loon.

We had now come further along the river than I had ever traveled with Mal those times we had gone fishing. There was no sign of habitation along the shore, just a forest of trees, dense and black with forbidding shadows. Despite my misgivings about Waldo, I was forced to concede the Wharf Rat knew the river and how to avoid any hazards that could bring a small craft to grief. His shoulder muscles strained as he steered us clear of any rocks or shoals.

I had no way of telling how long or far we had traveled, but the knot in my stomach grew tighter with every sweep of the oars. I was close to demanding how much further we had to go when Waldo guided us toward the shallows and locked the oars into place.

The boat lurched as he clambered out, the water splashing above his knees. Tugging on the rope, the big man hauled us forward until the skiff rested in a thick bed of reeds. He secured the rope to a sturdy low-hanging tree branch before turning to help me and Delphine out of the boat.

When it was my turn, I tensed at the prospect of his touch, but Waldo was respectful enough as he lifted me up and carried me to solid ground at the edge of the forest where Delphine awaited me.

"Thank you," I murmured.

The Wharf Rat grinned and offered me a roguish wink, but his 'good luck, miss,' sounded heartfelt. The plan was for Waldo to remain behind and guard the boat. I worried that he might decide to abandon us should anything go awry. But Delphine seemed to place great trust in the man's courage and loyalty and so must I.

The woods closed around me as I followed Delphine, clutching the magic shoes in my hands. The fir trees loomed above us, the branches so thick with leaves that very little moonlight filtered through. We had only the dim light of Delphine's lantern to guide us. I could feel the dampness of the ground seeping through my stockings and pine needles pricking my feet. But I was reluctant to don the glass slippers and risk stumbling along in those high heels.

Nudging branches out of my way, I kept pace with Delphine as best as I could. We finally emerged into a clearing only to find our way blocked by a massive wall that towered above us and seemed to stretch on forever in either direction.

"Now what?" I groaned, casting a despairing look at Delphine.

"Now *this,*" she said with a smug smile as she set down the lantern and delved beneath her cloak.

By this time, I should have had more faith in the witch's ingenuity when it came to handling obstacles. As she dug into the large pocket of her cloak, I waited breathlessly to see what Delphine would produce. A magical rope ladder or even a flying rug?

I was surprised and perhaps a trifle disappointed when all she retrieved was a jar of some murky liquid. But when Delphine unscrewed the lid and ordered me to stand back, I was quick to obey.

Delphine splashed the liquid over the base of the wall. For a moment, nothing happened and then the stonework began to bubble and blister, emitting a faint hiss. I watched in astonishment as the solid wall crumbled away like a gingerbread cookie dunked in milk, until I was staring at a small gaping hole. If Waldo had been here to see this, I was sure the river bandit would have gone down on his knees to Delphine, offering up more body parts if only she would brew him some of this amazing potion.

Delphine regarded her handiwork ruefully. "I wish I could have made the hole bigger for you, but this wall is so ancient. I didn't want to risk bringing a whole section caving down."

"I am sure I can squeeze through there." I managed to put on a nervous smile. "I guess it's time for me to put my shoes back on."

Bracing myself by leaning against the wall, I dusted any stray pine needles from my feet and eased them into the glass slippers. Delphine fretted her lip as she watched me.

"I'd give my claws and whiskers to be able to go with you," she sighed.

"I know, but if you set off any of Mercato's witch alarms, we'd all be finished. Don't worry. I'll be back with Mal before you know it." I spoke with far more confidence than I was feeling. Sucking in a deep breath, I prepared to turn invisible.

But before I could disappear, Delphine cried, "Wait." She flung her arms around my neck and gave me a fierce hug, whispering in my ear, "Be safe, Ella."

Moved by the unexpected gesture, all I could do was nod. When she released me, I performed the ritual clicks to vanish. Without allowing myself to dwell on the dangers ahead of me, I got down on my hands and knees and crawled through the hole in the wall.

Nineteen

E merging on the other side, I climbed carefully to my feet. I no longer had Delphine's lantern to guide me, but moonlight spilled over a barren landscape formed of black dirt and patches of weeds. Looking around me, I realized the wall I had just breached surrounded the prison yard. The ground sloped upward toward the massive fortress of the King's Royal Prison.

The Dismal Dungeons was a more fitting name. Constructed of a rough gray stone, the rectangular building presented a grim aspect. The windows were no more than narrow slits, the parapets adorned with crenellations that resembled blunt ogre teeth. I could just make out the distant figures of guards patrolling the walkway. How many there were, I could not be sure, but it didn't matter because I was invisible.

The slope of the prison yard was not steep but still presented a challenge to me in my high heels. My breath had quickened by the time I reached a gravel roadway that led from the prison to a small guard shack and a pair of iron gates set into the thick wall. I presumed this was the usual way of gaining access to the prison grounds for those who were unaided by witchcraft.

Two guards lingered outside the gatehouse, their uniforms

nowhere near as dashing as Horatio's. They were clothed in a fabric as dismal gray as the prison walls, their black helmets shaped like small cauldrons. If the effect was intended to make them appear menacing, it failed utterly. They more resembled a pair of drunken men who thought it a fine idea to parade around wearing their wives' cooking pots.

Looking completely bored with their late-night shift, the two men shared the contents of a small flask while stealing wary glances to be sure their misconduct was not being observed. I should have been accustomed to my invisibility by now, but it still felt eerie, passing within yards without either of them being aware of my presence.

My heels crunched against the gravel, and I winced at the amount of noise I was making, but the guards remained oblivious, sneaking sips from the flask. Still, I kept a wary eye on them as I tried to walk on tiptoe. My attention was so focused on the men, I did not notice the real danger in front of me until something prickled against my hand. Something that felt like the bristles of a broom. Or more accurately the whiskers of an enormous aura cat.

My heart stopped as I stared down into a pair of large menacing yellow eyes. The beast was so close to me, I could see the veins pulsing beneath its furless hide, feel the heat of its breath. Smothering my gasp of alarm, I froze until I remembered an aura cat would not be deceived by my invisibility shoes.

As it eyed me, a low rumble issued from its throat. I backed slowly away, whispering hoarsely, "N - nice kitty. Good kitty."

The aura cat flung back its head and roared. The sound masked my own cry of alarm. I suppressed my urge to turn and run, sensing that would be the worst possible thing to do. It wasn't the first time I had ever encountered one of these ugly beasts, although on the other occasion, the aura cat had been leashed on a stout chain held by its handler, Ned Wharton, the handsome young palace guard who had charmed Netta. This cat was much larger than Ned's and completely unrestrained.

My knees quaked as I continued to retreat. The beast prowled after me, its snarls finally drawing the attention of one of the guards at the gate. I fervently hoped he might be inspired to come and take charge of the beast, but all he did was shout, "Mehitabel! Quiet! What are you on about? There's nothing there, you silly beast."

"She probably scented another of those burrow squirrels," the second guard replied. "Stupid old thing is always eating them. No wonder she's getting so fat."

"Aye, but she only likes the ones with the blonde bushy tails." The first guard chortled.

Blonde? Like the color of my hair? I gulped as the men went back to their drinking, ignoring the beast's growls as it prowled after me like a cat stalking its prey.

Surely the beast could tell the difference between me and a burrow squirrel, couldn't it? My heart thudded in my chest as I backed off the roadway, nearly stumbling as I began to retreat down the slope. In my terrified state, it took me a moment to recall the potion laced cookies Delphine had given me. My fingers trembled as I undid the lacings on the pouch. Groping inside the leather bag, I retrieved a gingerbread mouse and flung it wildly at the beast. The cookie bounced off Mehitabel's nose. The creature reared back, blinking in surprise. She emitted another snarl, but she paused to examine the object that had struck her. The cat snuffled the gingerbread mouse where it had fallen in a tuft of weeds. She regarded the cookie with momentary suspicion before gulping it down.

I stopped in my tracks, waiting for the aura cat to keel over as Delphine had promised. But Mehitabel cocked her head to one side. Regarding me with renewed interest, she kept coming closer as I retreated further down the slope, tossing her another cookie. And then another and another. The cat gobbled the gingerbread down greedily. Licking her chops for more, she resumed her pursuit of me.

I had come to trust in Delphine's magic, believing it infallible, but this time the witch appeared to have made some terrible miscalculation. Digging frantically inside the bag for another cookie, I only came up with crumbs and it was too late to run. As the aura cat closed in on me, I closed my eyes and flung up my hands in a feeble effort to ward off her claws and sharp teeth.

But a strange noise emanated from the creature. It almost sounded like she was purring. Daring to open my eyes, I found Mehitabel regarding me with sleepy adoration. She rubbed her massive head against my arm in an affectionate gesture before sinking back onto her haunches. Her golden eyes rolled back in her head before she tumbled over. Her legs twitched for a second and then went still, her sides rumbling with soft snores.

I exhaled a shaky breath of relief, but I could not afford to linger until I recovered from my fright. I didn't know how long the cat would remain asleep or when one of the guards might notice something was amiss with the beast and come to investigate.

Hurrying back up the slope, I passed by the guards at the gatehouse and beneath a narrow archway that led into a small courtyard lit by torches. I could see the door that must lead into the main part of the prison, but much to my frustration, another obstacle blocked my way.

Two men stood just outside the door, engaged in an intense conversation. The taller one was clad in a prison guard uniform, his broad face dominated by a prominent nose, thick lips, and a cleft chin. Unlike the other guards, a pair of silvery epaulets adorned his wide shoulders. I presumed he must be the Chief Warder of the prison.

He completely dwarfed his companion, a small man whose nondescript features sent a jolt of recognition through me. The king's majordomo. What in the world was he doing here? And how was I going to squeeze past him to reach the prison door?

I approached cautiously. Even though I was invisible, I risked exposing my presence if I accidentally bumped up against either man in my efforts to get around them. At least their voices obscured the light tap of my heels against the stone floor.

"The Royal Garrotter knows his business," the Chief Warder was saying. "He's as skilled at the arts of torture as he is at choking the life out of a man. But some prisoners are not easily broken. This rogue is as stubborn as I've ever seen. I realize the Great Mercato will not be pleased."

"No, *he* will not be," the majordomo said. His lips twitched in an odd smile, but the ice in his voice chilled me. I shuddered, wondering what unfortunate prisoner they were discussing, hoping it was not Mal.

"We'll get the rogue to talk," the Chief Warder insisted. "It's only a matter of time."

"Unfortunately, time is running out. I should have known better than to depend upon—" Whatever else the Majordomo was about to say was lost in the distant clang of a bell.

For one dreadful moment, I feared someone had found the unconscious aura cat and was sounding an alarm, but the Warder said, "Ah, someone approaching the gates. We appear to have a late arrival."

"Who would be coming here at this time of night?" the majordomo demanded.

"Most likely His Royal Highness. Prince Florian often comes under cover of darkness to replenish his supply of – er – you know what."

The notion that Florian might be arriving sent a jolt of panic through me. I had to suppress the urge to shove my way past the Warder and the majordomo to get to Mal as quickly as possible.

The majordomo scowled at the warder. "The king has outlawed the selling of pixie dust, even to the royal princes. Not only could you lose your post, but you could also find yourself locked in your own dungeon."

The Chief Warder shrugged, looking unmoved by these threats. "I haven't been selling anything. We arrested Mimsy

Peasecod, the Chieftana of the pixies and imprisoned her, so if Prince Florian comes here to obtain his dust, who am I to tell him nay? Now I should go and greet our visitor in case it is the prince. Will you accompany me?"

"No, if it is Florian, it would be better if the prince remains unaware that I am here."

When the warder's brows lifted in surprise, the majordomo explained, "The king disapproves of his son's little habit. Since I am his father's devoted servant, Prince Florian would be vexed and embarrassed if he knew I was privy to the source of his secret stash. It will be best if I wait in your office until the prince is gone."

"Suit yourself."

I barely had time to shrink out of the way as the warder brushed by me. Disappearing beneath the arch, he headed toward the front gates. The majordomo hammered on the prison door. A panel slid open, and a guard peered out. As soon as the guard realized it was a servant of the king demanding admittance, I heard the click of a bolt and the door swung open. I had barely enough time to hurry after the majordomo and follow him inside before the guard slammed the door closed and bolted it again.

The majordomo exchanged a quiet word with the guard before walking off down a narrow corridor to the left. I presumed that must be the way to the warder's office. Frowning, I watched the little man vanish from view. Something about the majordomo's excuse for not wanting to meet the prince rang false to me. The prince's *little habit* was no secret. Although few dared to speak about it, it was known that both Prince Florian and his younger brother Kendrick were addicted to pixie dust sniffing. I doubted that Florian would have cared if a mere servant like the majordomo caught His Highness coming to the prison to collect his fresh supply of dust.

So why was the majordomo so anxious to avoid Florian? I had no time to worry or wonder about that now. If that was Florian arriving, the sooner I found Mal and spirited him away from here, the better.

But where to go next? In the chamber ahead of me, I spotted what appeared to be the opening to a staircase leading down. Most likely that was the way to the dungeons. But to reach it, I had to creep through a large chamber where the prison guards must have been allowed to relax between shifts. A wrought-iron chandelier hung over a round rough-hewn table, the flickering candles illuminating three guards lounging on stools. Two were playing at cards while the third was engrossed in a book titled, *Naughty Sirens of Lothmara.* The book must have been of a salacious nature because a bit of drool trickled down the guard's chin.

Besides the pikes and swords mounted on the wall, the only other thing in the room was a cage suspended from the ceiling. Whatever sort of bird it contained was concealed beneath a folded pair of faded blue wings. Even though I was invisible, I had no wish to rouse the creature and set it to squawking. I was getting quite good at moving stealthily even in the glass heels. The guards never once looked up from their occupations. But the blue bird's hearing must have been keener.

I was almost at the staircase when the wings shifted and the creature's head poked up, but it was no kind of bird at all. The face that peeked through the bars was human-like, with pale, sharp features. Two pointy ears poked through a stringy fall of dirty blond hair.

I had only ever seen pixies depicted in books before. My breath caught in my throat as I realized I was looking at one now and she was looking straight back at me. My invisibility shoes did not fool her any more than they had deceived the aura cat.

This must be the unfortunate Mimsy Peasecod, the Chieftana of the pixies that the Warder had mentioned. Her demeanor was one of exhaustion and despair, but a spark of hope lit up her almond shaped eyes at the sight of me. Struggling to her feet, her tiny hands circled the bars of the cage as she whispered, "You, there! Are you a witch? Whoever, whatever you are, can you not help me? Please."

I drew closer to the cage and pressed my finger to my lips, trying to warn her to be silent. But Mimsy's pleas only waxed more desperate. "I will reward you. I can pay you anything you ask. Please, please save me. Get me out of here."

The guard reading the book glanced up in annoyance and growled, "Quiet, you! You ought to know by now we can't be bribed."

"I wasn't talking to you, you stupid oaf," the pixie snapped. She lowered her voice, begging, "Help me. Florian had me imprisoned so he no longer has to pay for my dust, but I can't keep making as much as the prince wants. He's draining all the magic from me."

Huge tears trickled down Mimsy's cheeks. But I could not even reach the lock on her cage without standing on one of the stools. If objects in the room started moving about by themselves, even these thick-headed guards would be able to surmise something strange was going on.

"I am sorry," I mouthed to the pixie. "I have to go but I promise I will find a way to help you after I release my friend, Mal, from the dungeons."

"Mal? You mean Hawkridge?"

"Yes, you know him?"

Despite her tears, Mimsy smiled. "Who doesn't know that handsome rogue? Get me out of here and I'll help you find him."

"I am sorry, but I can't." I whispered, casting an anxious look in the direction of the guards.

Mimsy wailed and shook the bars of her cage in sheer frustration. One of the guards playing cards looked up in annoyance and flung his empty cup at her. The tankard banged against the cage and sent it swaying. Mimsy lost her balance, landing on her bottom. All three of the guards erupted into coarse laughter.

I hated abandoning her this way, but I could not risk trying to help her until I freed Mal. The pixie's eyes filled with tearful reproach as I retreated toward the curving stairs that led down to the dungeons.

The worn stone steps had never been designed for a woman wearing dancing shoes made of glass. I had to mince along carefully, my only illumination provided by the flaming torches set at infrequent intervals along the walls. Somehow, I arrived at the bottom without taking a tumble or twisting an ankle.

The dim lighting revealed what looked like an endless corridor of cells. The odor down in the dungeons was a noxious combination of mildew, unwashed bodies, and excrement. I had to fight the urge to gag as I hurried from one cell to the next, peering through the iron bars. Most of the cells were empty except for piles of dirty straw and chains hanging slack from the wall. That didn't surprise me. Most people unfortunate enough to be incarcerated in the Dismal Dungeons were either sentenced to exile or to a far worse fate at the hands of the Royal Garrotter.

I didn't see how anyone could survive long in this miserable place, cut off from sunlight and fresh air. Some of the prisoners I glimpsed looked like the hardened sort of rogue one would dread to meet in a dark alley, but others were enough to break my heart. An old man huddled beneath a ragged blanket, shivering in his sleep. A boy looking barely old enough to sport his first beard, cradled a young lad in his arms. Despite the filth matting their hair and faces, I could detect a resemblance that marked them as brothers.

This was one thing I had not taken into consideration in my plan to rescue Mal, the sorrow and guilt I would feel at abandoning these other wretched souls to their fate. I had to fight the urge to begin unlocking all the cell doors. The only thing that stayed me was the realization that it was going to be difficult enough just getting Mal out of this place alive.

As I hastened from one cell to another without finding my friend, I grew more and more desperate. Finally, there was only one left to check. Gripping the bars, I peered through the semi-darkness at a prisoner who was chained to the wall in such a way that he could not even lie down. He slumped over in a sitting posture, his back braced against the wall. His face was so battered and bruised I barely recognized him.

"Mal!" His name escaped me in a choked cry.

For one horrible moment, I thought he was dead, but he stirred a little, mumbling, "Ella?"

My hands shook as I fumbled to locate the bone pick inside my pouch. I nearly dropped the tiny shard as I inserted it in the keyhole, but the device worked its magic. The lock clicked and I shoved the cell door open, rushing inside.

"Oh, Mal, what have they done to you?" I cried.

He forced his swollen eyes open a slit and muttered, "Scrambled my brain. Making me imagine things, hear voices."

"No, I am really here." Remembering that I was invisible, I slipped off the magic shoes. Kneeling beside him, I caressed his face, brushing a gentle kiss against his cheek.

Mal groaned. "This is a really good dream."

Much to my dismay, he sounded half-delirious. Neither Delphine nor I had anticipated that. Despite his imprisonment in the Dismal Dungeons, somehow, we had expected Mal to be his usual sharp-witted self. I should have brought a flask of brandy or an herbal tonic from Mal's shop in case I needed to revive him. But there was nothing in his barren cell to help me, not even a bucket of fetid water.

"Listen to me, Mal. You are not dreaming," I said as I applied the bone pick to his wrist manacles. "I have come to rescue you."

"That's nice." His eyes fluttered closed. As I released him from his shackles, his hands fell limp to his sides. He would have keeled over if I had not clutched at him, using all my strength to keep him sitting upright.

"Mal," I cried. I dreaded causing him any more pain, but I

needed him to wake. I shook him as gently as I could, repeatedly calling his name.

Mal groaned again, his head flopping to one side.

In sheer desperation, I did the only other thing I could think of to shock him back to his senses. Scooting closer, I cupped his face between my hands and pressed my lips to his in a fervid kiss.

His chest rose and fell with a moan that was a combination of pain and bliss. Suddenly his hands closed over my shoulders, and he was kissing me back with a passion that took my breath away. Mal's skills as a lover were legendary among the women of Arcady. I had always thought the silly females had to be exaggerating. But no man who had been battered half to death should have still been capable of kissing the way Mal was kissing me.

I broke away from him with a gasp, feeling guilty. Not only was it a betrayal of my love for Horatio, but in a strange way of my friendship with Mal. But I could not regret what I had done, not when I saw the lucidity return to Mal's eyes.

He stared at me, saying hoarsely. "Ella, you really *are* here."

I nodded, tears of relief springing to my eyes.

Despite his pain, his mouth lifted in a teasing smile that was pure Mal. "Here in this frapping dungeon, *now* you finally decide to kiss me? I might have known you'd prefer your men in chains."

I choked on a laugh that was part sob. Mal's fingers trembled as he reached up to touch my face. "Your laugh, Ella. Your beautiful, wonderful laugh. I never expected to hear it again."

"I know. I hated the way we parted. I never meant any of those horrid things I said to you."

"Hush," Mal said. He struggled to sit up straighter, although I could tell how much pain the effort cost him from the way he clenched his teeth. "I deserved everything you said and more after the way I deceived you. But that is not important right now. How did you manage to get past the guards?"

I dashed the tears from my eyes. "Have you forgotten about those glass dancing slippers you gave me the night of the ball? You said they would turn me invisible, but I didn't believe you. But you were right. The shoes really do work."

"Ha! Told you so."

"Seriously, Mal? Only you could be beaten to a pulp and still be unable to resist the urge to gloat."

Mal started to laugh, but immediately stopped, flinching as he clutched his side. He sucked in a short painful breath. "Here is what I want you to do. Put those magic shoes back on your pretty feet and get the frap out of here before you are caught."

"I am not going anywhere without you!"

"Yes, you are." Mal's mouth set in that stubborn expression I knew all too well. "No one has ever managed to escape from the Dismal Dungeons. I can't believe you would be reckless enough to try freeing me all on your own."

"I am not alone. Delphine and Waldo are helping me."

"The Wharf Rat and the mad witch who hates both of us?" Mal moaned. "Oh, that makes me feel so much better."

"Delphine is not mad," I retorted. "Well, perhaps a bit. But she doesn't hate us. I believe she adores you and she has become my friend. She has given me all sorts of magical objects to help rescue you. I used up all the mouse cookies, but I still have the mist pellets and the magic lock pick made from Waldo's big toe."

Mal gaped at me. "Mouse cookies? The Wharf Rat's toe? One of us is clearly insane and I don't think it's me."

Ignoring his gibe, I said, "There is no time to argue about this, Mal. Delphine and Waldo are waiting for us with a boat on the river side of the wall. Now come on."

I stood and tugged at Mal's arm, trying to urge him to his feet.

Mal pulled away. "Unless Delphine gave you some potion that will grant me invisibility and wings, there is no way you are getting me out of here. I don't think I can walk. They broke my ankle in the iron boot when they were torturing me."

"Oh, Mal." My eyes burned with tears of fury and anguish at the thought of Mal enduring such a thing. But I pursed my lips with renewed determination. "Then you must lean on me, use me like a crutch. When we get up to the top of the stairs, I will use the mist pellets to cover our escape."

Mal shook his head. "No, Ella, you must see how hopeless this is. You can't save me. Please just go."

I regarded him with dismay, realizing they had broken more than Mal's ankle in this dreadful place. That roguish spark that lit up his eyes was gone, replaced with the shadows of defeat.

Swallowed a thick lump that rose to my throat, I said fiercely, "What kind of foolish talk is this, Hawkridge? The Mal that I know would never give up like this. You have an orb to protect, a rebellion to lead."

I tried to drape his arm about my shoulders, but Mal resisted all my efforts to draw him to his feet.

"That stupid orb," he muttered. "That's why they were torturing me, to find out where I had hidden it."

"Did you tell them?"

"No, but I should have. I should have never persuaded you to steal it in the first place." Mal's lips twisted bitterly. "But I fancied myself becoming this great hero, the savior of this entire kingdom. What a joke! There's no magic in that orb and no hero in me. I have failed everyone and most of all you."

"No, you haven't! Withypole told me that the legends about the lost prince are all true. I believe in it now and I believe in you."

"You shouldn't. I'm not worth it," Mal said wearily. Then he tensed, sitting upright. "Frap, Ella! I think one of the guards is coming. Put your shoes on now!"

The heavy tread of footsteps carried to my ears as well. While Mal struggled to reach his chains to attach them, I scrambled to find my glass slippers. But it was already too late to turn invisible, too late to even close the cell door that I had left ajar.

I whirled, bracing myself to confront the guard, only to go numb with shock at the sight of the man looming in the doorway.

"Horatio!"

Twenty

Earlier tonight when Horatio had ridden past me in the lane, not knowing I was there, I had watched him go with a heavy heart, fearing I would never see him again. I would have given anything to be with him just one more time, to share one last kiss. Now he was so close, I only had to take a few steps to be able to cast myself into his arms. But I found myself wishing for him far away from here.

From the grim expression on Horatio's face, I imagined that he was wishing the same thing about me. Recovered from his first shock, he demanded, "Ella, what in thunder are you doing here?"

"I am rescuing Mal." Daunted as I was by Horatio's unexpected arrival, I squared my shoulders in a posture of defiance. But I could not keep a note of pleading from my voice as I said, "I am sorry, Horatio, but I cannot allow anyone to stop me, not even you."

"No! Ignore her," Mal said. He struggled to get to his feet, only to sink down with a hiss of pain. "She doesn't know what she is saying. She has been bewitched. You can't arrest her. She's completely out of her mind."

"I can easily believe that. Calm down, Hawkridge. I have no

intentions of placing Ella under lock and key." Horatio pulled a wry face. "Although I find it disconcerting how often that seems like a good idea."

He cast me a look that was both exasperated and tender. "Nor do I intend to prevent you from freeing your friend. I am here on the same errand."

I had been marshalling all manner of pleas and arguments to convince Horatio, but his calm statement left me so dumbfounded, all I could do was falter, "You - you are?"

Mal snorted in disbelief. "Why would you ever help me?"

"I wouldn't. I am doing this for *her*."

Horatio closed the distance between us. After a moment's hesitation, he gathered my hands into his. The warm, calloused strength of his fingers was so reassuring, I clung to him, despite being conscious of Mal's gaze upon us, my friend's eyes filled with jealous misery. "I discovered that the reason Prince Florian had Hawkridge arrested was to force you to marry him," Horatio said. "Is it true that you have agreed?"

I gave an unhappy nod. "I had no choice. It was the only way Florian would promise to spare Mal."

"Ella! What by all the cursed fairies were you thinking?" Mal exclaimed. "You should have known I'd rather die before I let you wed that royal idiot. Were you foolish enough to believe his promise?"

"No, I wasn't, Mal," I said. "Why did you think I am so desperate to get you out of here?"

"I can free Hawkridge if he will follow my orders, although your being here certainly complicates matters, Ella." Horatio heaved a deep sigh. "I should have guessed you would attempt something drastic. I just wish that for once you would have trusted me enough to come to me when you were in trouble."

"I *do* trust you. But if you free Mal, everyone will know it was you. You'll be ruined. You will lose everything, your reputation, your position, perhaps even your life." I pulled away from Horatio. "That is why you need to go."

"And what will happen to you if I just turn and walk away?" Horatio demanded. "Look at the condition Hawkridge is in. You'll never get him out of here without my help."

I realized Horatio was right, but I fretted my lower lip, trying to resist the temptation to leap at his offer of assistance, an offer that could only result in bringing Horatio's entire world crashing down upon his head.

The decision threatened to be taken out of my hands by Mal's obstinacy. He compressed his lips and leaned his head against the wall. "I don't want your help, Crushington. Or Ella's. Whatever happens to me, I deserve it."

"You certainly do after the way you have endangered Ella," Horatio said harshly. But something in his face softened as he studied Mal's battered and swollen features.

"No," Horatio said in a quieter tone. "No one deserves to be beaten and tortured this way."

"I don't need your pity, either," Mal replied. "Just take Ella and go. And make sure you protect her from that rotten prince."

"Mal, please," I said.

But Mal closed his eyes, blocking out both me and Horatio.

Horatio regarded him with frustration. "You just intend to stay here and die? Haven't you already caused Ella enough grief? Do you want to break her heart?"

"Do you?" Mal opened his eyes to glare at Horatio. "How do you think she'll feel if you end up getting yourself killed?"

"Stop it, both of you!" I cried, once again torn between the two men I loved. I was desperate to save Mal, yet I hated endangering Horatio to do it. But what choice did I have?

"We do need your help, Horatio." When Mal started to protest, I cut him off. "Shut up, Mal. I can get us all safely out of here if you both follow my plan."

"My plan is better," Horatio said.

"How do you know that?" I stiffened with indignation. "You don't even know what my plan is."

"Considering your usual rash behavior, my dear, I assume your plan must involve something equally reckless."

"Apparently it involves the use of my friend Waldo's severed toe and mouse pellets." Mal put in drily.

"*Mist* pellets," I glowered at Mal as I corrected him.

"Er - as intriguing as that sounds, I think we'd better go with my idea," Horatio said. "That is if Hawkridge is able to swallow his stubborn pride."

The two men locked eyes for a long moment before Mal finally conceded with a wearied sigh, "Fine. Let's hear this brilliant idea."

"First, I need to put these on you." Horatio detached a pair of iron manacles from his belt.

But when he tried to approach, Mal locked his hands beneath his armpits. "I already don't like your plan. I rather trust my fate to Ella's mouse pellets."

"It is necessary for you to act the part of my prisoner, Hawkridge," Horatio explained with strained patience. "I have a writ that remands you into my custody."

"You forged a royal document?" I asked in dismay. "If you are caught, the penalty for that is immediate death."

But Mal regarded Horatio with grudging admiration. "It must have been a frapping good forgery of the official seal to fool the warder. I'm impressed, Crushington. I would have never guessed you had it in you."

"I don't!" Horatio snapped. "The writ was forged in the king's name and sealed by a member of the royal family. The Chief Warder was a trifle suspicious, but Prince Ryland is dealing with him."

"Prince Ryland?" I faltered in astonishment. "*He* is here with you?"

Mal also gaped at Crushington. "You are working with Ella's

former lover? The prince she almost eloped with? Isn't that a bit awkward?"

"Shut up, Mal," I hissed, my cheeks suffusing with heat. But the damage had been done. Horatio absorbed this information in stunned silence. Even after catching Ryland kissing me on the night of the ball, Horatio had no idea of my past relationship with the prince.

"I am sorry, Horatio. I should have told you about Ryland, but it was all so long ago—" I began but Horatio interrupted me.

"It doesn't matter."

But it clearly did. Despite Horatio's wry smile, I saw the hurt and doubt in his eyes. I rested one hand on his sleeve as I sought to reassure him. "Any love that ever existed between me and Ryland was over a long time ago."

"Apparently, His Highness does not think so." Horatio said, drawing away from me. "Prince Ryland was the one who alerted me about Florian's plan to force you into marriage. He didn't know who else to turn to for help saving you. Ryland has always struck me as being such a quiet and cautious sort of prince. Why would he take such risks if he was not still in love with you?"

"I guess Ella should ask him herself," Mal said, nodding his head in the direction of the cell doorway.

I spun away from Horatio. dismayed to find the prince standing behind me. Ryland had come upon us so quietly I didn't know how much he had overheard.

He was attired in a velvet doublet, a short cloak hanging loose about his shoulders. The silver embroidered gauntlets he wore effectively concealed his wooden hand. He appeared to have taken great pains to look regal, most likely to impress the warder with his royal authority. But his diffident expression spoke more of the minstrel Harper than it did a prince.

"Hullo, Ella." Ryland approached me hesitantly. After the angry way I had parted from him at the footbridge, the prince appeared uncertain of his reception.

He started to make a formal bow, only to reach for my hand instead. When he tried to carry it to his lips, I pulled away from him.

"No, no, no. You shouldn't be here."

"I am sorry, Ella. You made it clear you want nothing more to do with me. But when Florian boasted about what he planned to do to you, I had to save you. I failed you a long time ago. Let me make it up to you now."

"Do you realize the risk you are taking? Florian might do far more than chop off your hand if he catches you trying to thwart him."

"I don't care. I am ready to die for you."

Mal gave a derisive snort, while Horatio listened to this declaration in stoic silence. I groaned, feeling as though my head was going to explode. This situation was bad enough with the tension simmering between Mal and Horatio without adding Ryland into the mix. Another woman might have considered herself lucky to have three men ready to profess their devotion. But I felt as though this small cell had become unbearably crowded and they were cutting off my air. If Delphine's magic shoes had the power to transport me, I would have slipped them on and wished myself far away from here.

To my great relief, Horatio reassumed command, saying, "There will be time enough to deal with all of *this* later. We need to get moving."

Prince Ryland dragged his gaze away from me. "You are right. I came to tell you that the Chief Warder is growing suspicious. He demands to see both of us before he will consent to release Mr. Hawkridge."

Mal gave Ryland a disgusted look. "The warder should not dare to demand anything from you. For fairy's sake, man! You are royalty, the son of a king."

"Alas, I am royal in name only. I fear that I made a far better wandering minstrel than I ever did a prince." Ryland directed a sad smile at me which tugged strangely at my heart.

I searched myself for some trace of my old resentment and anger against him, but I could not find it. All I felt was sorrow for this man who was so ill-suited for the role he had been born to play.

"I believe the warder is stalling until he can consult with my brother," Ryland continued. "He is waiting in the outer courtyard, expecting Florian to arrive at any moment."

Horatio choked back an exasperated oath as he bent down to snap the manacles on Mal. "Did you think it might have behooved Your Highness to mention that sooner?"

"Instead of wasting time mooning over Ella," Mal said as he submitted grudgingly to the iron restraints being placed upon his wrists.

Ryland flushed. The prince tried to stammer an apology, but Horatio cut him short. "If Your Royal Highness would be good enough to help me get this miscreant on his feet."

"That's Mr. Miscreant to you," Mal retorted, some of the old spark returning to his eyes. He scowled at Horatio. "Why aren't you wearing a sword?"

"I was obliged to surrender it at the warder's office. Carrying weapons into the King's Royal Prison is forbidden, even for Scutcheon commanders."

"Tell me you at least have a knife hidden in your boot," Mal said.

"No, I am not in the habit of breaking the law by concealing weapons."

When Mal gave Horatio a look of pure disgust, Horatio said, "Prince Ryland and I never intended on fighting out way out of here. Our only hope lies with the success of our deception."

Mal sighed. "Fine. Then before we proceed any further, Ella needs to put her magic shoes back on."

"Ella has magic shoes? What magic shoes?" Ryland asked. As he shifted about the cell, looking for them, I cautioned him to be careful, but it was too late. I flinched at the horrible crunching sound.

Mal swore. "Those magic shoes, you royal dolt."

Ryland lifted his boot and bent down to retrieve what remained of one of my glass slippers. It was not completely shattered, but it had broken sharply in two.

"I am so sorry, Ella," the prince said, balancing the pieces between his good hand and his wood-carved one, as though fearful of splintering the glass any further. Not that it would have mattered if he did. The shoe appeared damaged beyond repair.

I took the pieces from him, staring numbly at the broken parts, making a ridiculous effort to fit them back together as though the glass slipper might miraculously become whole again.

"Delphine is going to kill me," I moaned.

"Delphine is the least of your worries," Mal said. "How are we going to get you out of here now that you can't turn invisible?"

"That's what the shoes did? Rendered you invisible?" Ryland asked in an awed voice.

I nodded miserably.

"I thought you told me those shoes didn't work," Horatio said.

"They certainly won't now, thanks to his royal oafishness," Mal grumbled.

"Oh, be quiet, Mal," I said. Ryland was already looking devastated enough by what he had done. I explained to Horatio, "I just didn't fully understand the magical properties of the shoes before. But when I tried them tonight, they did make me invisible. That is how I got past the prison guards."

Horatio's brow furrowed. "So, you *were* there standing in the lane when I rode past your house earlier."

I regarded him with amazement. "Yes, but how do you know that?"

"I don't know. I thought I had to be imagining things. But somehow, I can always sense your presence. Your scent, perhaps."

A faint smile touched his lips as we exchanged a glance that caused my heart to skip a beat.

"You can sense Ella just by smelling her?" Mal grimaced. "I can't decide if that is rather romantic or completely disgusting."

"Shut up, Mal!" I said, but the tender moment was ruined.

Ryland found my other shoe and inspected it. "This one is intact, Ella. If you slip it on, perhaps the magic might still work."

"Forget about the shoes," Horatio said. "We need to get moving before Prince Florian arrives."

"How are you going to explain to the Chief Warder how Ella appeared out of nowhere?" Mal asked.

"I'll think of something," Horatio said as he stooped down beside Mal. Hooking his arm beneath Mal's shoulders, Horatio struggled to draw my friend to his feet. Horatio was trying to be as gentle as possible, but Mal sucked in his breath with a pain-filled hiss.

Instead of helping, Ryland continued to look devastated with guilt. Cradling my remaining shoe in his hand, he begged. "Could you not at least give it a try, Ella?"

Before I could stop him, the prince dropped to one knee before me, holding up the glass slipper which glowed in the flickering light cast by the wall sconce. It would have been a romantic gesture if we had been in a moonlit garden instead of a dungeon cell, with me attired in Mal's baggy clothes and Horatio scowling with impatience.

Mal gritted his teeth against his pain, but managed to say, "Go on. Try it, Ella. What can it hurt?"

"Besides wasting time we don't have?" Horatio demanded.

I tended to agree with Horatio, but with both Mal and Ryland urging me to make the attempt, I surrendered with a tiny sigh. Tossing the broken pieces of my shoe aside, I braced myself against the rough stone wall and raised my foot.

Ryland eased the glass slipper on me and rose to his feet. If negotiating those heels had been a challenge for me before, wearing just one left me wobbly and lop-sided. Torn between hope and feeling foolish, I stared down at my feet as I executed the steps to activate the shoes' magic. Since I only had one slipper, all I could do was click my glass heel against my foot. Just like before, I had no way of telling if anything magical had occurred. I could still see myself quite clearly.

"Did it work? Am I invisible?" I asked, glancing up to find all three men gaping at me.

"Not exactly," Mal said.

"You are mostly visible except... " Horatio trailed off. I had never seen my stalwart commander look so unnerved.

"Your head is gone!" Ryland exclaimed in a horrified accent.

"What?" I gasped, clasping my hands to my face.

Mal rolled his eyes. "She still has her head, you fool. We just can't see it."

I had no time to process this information before one of the prison guards appeared in the cell doorway. I recognized him as the burly man whom I had seen reading the naughty book.

"Commander Crushington! Your Royal Highness." The guard's stomach doubled over as he bowed to Ryland. "The Chief Warder bade me say that he is still waiting for you in the courtyard. He will not grant you custody of the prisoner until—"

The guard broke off as he caught sight of me. His eyes widened as he stared at the empty area above my shoulders where my head should have been. He shrieked like a tavern wench who had just spotted a rat. Backing away from the cell, he nearly stumbled over his own two feet as he turned and fled.

Mal burst out laughing, even though it cost him. His guffaws were punctuated with pain-filled cries of "Ow! Ow!" Despite the perils of our situation, I could not help chuckling myself. Even Ryland gave an uncertain smile, but Horatio looked far from amused.

"Ella! Take off that blasted shoe before this situation gets any worse. Maybe I can explain to the Chief Warder how a woman mysteriously appeared in our midst, but it will be impossible to account for a headless one."

But my mind raced with the possibilities. The destruction of my magic shoe could prove to be an asset, even better than a Fear Blade.

I pleaded with Horatio, "Don't you see how this could work to our advantage? If I can terrify all the guards into fleeing—"

"No," he interrupted. "Creating such chaos will only make things worse."

"A bit of chaos is exactly what we need. We won't have to waste time arguing with the Chief Warder before Florian gets here and I am not sure how much longer Mal can endure being on his feet."

"Don't worry about me," Mal said. But even with Horatio's support, Mal looked ashen and shaky. Ryland hastened to brace him from the other side.

Before Horatio could protest further, I was out the cell door, hobbling down the corridor with my ungainly limp-step, my single heel clicking loudly. The guard that I had terrified was long gone, but his shrieks had roused the other prisoners. Frightened, desperate faces peered at me through the cell bars as I passed by. I hated abandoning these unfortunate souls in this awful place, but I had no choice.

"Don't worry. Somehow, someday, I will find a way. I will come back to get you," I said.

I guess such vows coming from a headless woman were far from comforting. The inmates shrank to the back of their cells, cowering away from me. I gave over my efforts to reassure them, heading toward the arch that led up to the guard room.

Despite my awkward gait, I had far outstripped my three companions. Supporting Mal between them, Ryland and Horatio had to move at a much slower pace.

"Ella!" Horatio growled my name, ordering me to stop and come back, but I ignored him.

The ascent up the curving stair required all my concentration.

It was even more perilous than coming down had been when I had had two glass slippers to keep my balance. I managed by clinging to the wall and placing most of my weight on my bare foot.

By the time I reached the top, I was sweating and panting from my efforts. Lurking in the shadows of the archway, I fought to still my breath as I peeked inside the guard room.

The burly guard who had come to Mal's cell was still shaking from the fright I had given him. His teeth chattered as he tried to convince the other two guards who were still engrossed in their card game.

"B-but I s-saw it, I t-tell you. A specter with no head."

"What was it doing? Riding a purple dragon?" One of the guards looked up from his cards to jeer.

"You've had too much ale, Smedley," the other one said. "You better sober up before the Chief Warder tosses you in one of the cells."

His words faltered to silence as I appeared from the shadows. Raising my arms, I pronounced in deep sepulcher-like tones, "Villains! Where is my head?"

The card-playing guards froze, their jaws going slack. Smedley whimpered, trying to disappear behind his two companions. I heard a rustling from Mimsey's cage as the pixie emerged from her bed of straw to see what was happening.

I stepped further into the chamber, emitting a blood-curdling howl. "I want my head, or I will take one of yours!"

"Aieee!"

I never realized grown men were capable of such high-pitched screams. Smedley sobbed in terror. The other guards bolted to their feet, upturning the table. Cards and tankards of ale flew everywhere.

Shoving and knocking each other aside, the guards fled in the direction of the prison yard, leaving the outer door gaping open. Mimsey Peasecod doubled over, her thin shoulders shaking with laughter. But she sobered quickly, gripping the bars of her cage.

"Well done, you clever girl. But the Chief Warder is made of sterner stuff. It won't take him long to corral those cowardly fools and force them to return. Release me and I can help you with my magic."

When I hesitated, Mimsey cried, "You promised me!"

I glanced toward the arch that led to the dungeons. My companions had not yet managed to catch up with me, but I could hear Horatio and Ryland struggling to get Mal up the stairs. If I acted quickly, there was surely enough time to keep my pledge to Mimsey.

"All right." I fished the bone pick out of my pouch and then dragged a wooden stool close to the cage. But the stool was a bit rickety. Between its instability and balancing my weight on one high heel, I realized there would be slim chance I could avoid taking a tumble.

There was no help for it. I needed to risk removing my shoe. Easing off the glass slipper, I climbed atop the stool which wobbled beneath me. I shifted my weight. When I was sure I was steady enough, I opened the lock. So eager to be free, the pixie all but knocked me over as she shot out of the open cage door.

I managed to land on my feet as the stool slipped out from under me. Mimsey appeared to be suffering from the effects of her long confinement. Fluttering over my head in a series of lopsided spirals, she stretched her arms and flexed her wings, trying to recover her equilibrium. A hint of color returned to her pointed little face which was more than I could say for my poor Mal.

My friend looked on the verge of collapse as he finally reached the top of the stairs. His featured contorted with pain, Mal slumped between Horatio and Ryland. Horatio compressed his lips as he did his best to shore up Mal and keep his weight off his broken ankle. But as Horatio gazed upward at the open cage and the pixie flitting about the room, his determined expression turned to one of horror.

"Ella, what have you done!"

Surprised by the vehemence of Horatio's reaction, I stammered, "Why, I released that poor creature."

"Poor creature!" Horatio exclaimed. "Mimsey Peasecod is one of the most dangerous and ruthless criminals in all the kingdom, lining her coffers with the illegal sale of the magic dust, enslaving other pixies and forcing them to work for her."

"No, Mimsey is a victim herself, imprisoned by Florian and she promised to help in our escape if I would set her free." But when I glanced up at the pixie, I was startled by the change in her. No trace remained of the pathetic sobbing creature who had pleaded for her freedom. She shot me a wicked grin, thrust her tongue out at Horatio before streaking out the open door and disappearing into the night.

Disgusted with myself for being so easily tricked, I complained, "She didn't even say thank you."

"Never expect gratitude from a pixie," Mal mumbled, his sagging weight nearly causing Ryland to lose his grip.

Struggling to help Horatio keep Mal upright, Ryland said, "We have to let him rest for a few minutes."

"We've no time for that—" Horatio began, breaking off as the distant sound of the bell tolled, announcing a new arrival at the prison gates.

"Florian," I whispered, exchanging an alarmed glance with Horatio.

Ryland paled. "We're never going to make it. Even if Ella dons her glass slipper, it will take more than a headless woman to frighten away my brother. We are all done for."

"No, we aren't," I said, quelling my own panic. "I still have the mist pellets Delphine gave me."

"Ella!" Horatio groaned. It was the despairing sound of a man accustomed to being in charge, to an orderly approach to everything. But I had already reduced his well-laid plans of rescuing Mal to utter chaos. Horatio's face settled into an expression of wearied resignation as I outlined what I intended to do.

When we reached the outer courtyard, I would release the mist pellets. Under the cover of the magical fog, we would make our way back down the hill to the breach in the wall. Horatio insisted that we should try to reach the place where he and Ryland had tethered their horses, but I shook my head. Mal looked on the verge of complete collapse. He'd never survive a breakneck escape by horseback and if we didn't manage to get through the gate before the guards closed it, we would be trapped.

Our best bet lay in reaching the boat, although I did have qualms. I hoped that the aura cat that I had drugged was still unconscious and that Mal's small craft could bear the weight of all of us. My only comfort was the thought that Delphine would be there, waiting. I had seen how resourceful my witch friend could be. Maybe she could conjure up another amazing feat of magic and reseal the hole in the wall, buying us more time to escape. A desperate hope, perhaps, but it was all I had.

I crept through the open door, ducking behind one of the courtyard pillars as I scouted the path ahead. The torchlight near the main gate enabled me to make out the figures dismounting from their horses. It was easy to discern which one was Florian from his height and long mane of golden hair. My stomach clenched at the sight of him and the four palace Scutcheons attending him.

I could also see the three prison guards that I had terrified into fleeing. They cringed before the Chief Warder. Even from this distance, I could tell the guards were receiving a severe tongue-lashing for their cowardly nonsense about headless ghosts. The Chief Warder looked furious, but Florian's jeering laughter cut off the warder's tirade.

I motioned the others to emerge from the shadows of the doorway. My poor Mal had become a dead weight between Horatio and Ryland. Their muscles strained as they half-dragged, half-carried Mal closer to where I crouched behind the pillar.

"Try to stay close to me when I release the mist," I warned them. "Or else we might lose each other in the fog."

"Right," Ryland whispered. Horatio signaled his agreement with a terse nod.

I emerged from my hiding place in the portico, leading the way across the courtyard. I tried to move stealthily but I could not move as quickly as I wished for fear that the three men would not be able to keep up with me.

We were not able to get far before we were spotted. One of the prison guards near the gate shouted out a warning. "'Ware, my lord. Prisoner trying to escape."

Heads swiveled in our direction. My pulse thudded as fortress guards, palace Scutcheons, the warder and Prince Florian began to rush toward the courtyard.

My fingers felt damp with sweat as they closed about the mist pellets. I had to curb a frantic urge to fling them down at once. But timing was everything. I had to wait for the charging force to draw closer, not near enough to capture us, but close enough to be enveloped in the mist.

My heart lurched when I saw Florian draw ahead of the pack. I could not make out his expression, but I swear I could feel the fury emanating from him despite the many yards that still separated us. I had only a second to fix in my mind the path we would need to follow to reach the boat. Unable to wait any longer, I flung the pellets at the ground as hard as I could.

A bright light exploded, momentarily blinding me. The mist seemed to erupt from the courtyard stones as though a dam had burst. Within seconds, we were all enveloped in a thick fog. I could hear bellows of pain and grunts as men blundered into each other. Someone was cursing. I thought it might be Florian, but I couldn't be sure. The mist distorted and confused my senses.

I headed in the direction I believed would lead us down the hill toward the curtain wall, taking care not to outdistance Horatio,

Ryland, and Mal. *Hurry! Hurry!* A voice inside me urged. I had no idea how long the mist would last.

It was still thick enough I could scarcely see my hand held in front of my face. I had no choice but to continue one cautious step at a time. Careful as I was, I was not prepared for the paved stonework of the courtyard to end so abruptly.

I stumbled a few steps down the grassy slope. Losing my balance, I fell to my knees. Although my knees and hands throbbed from the impact, I scrambled up as quickly as I could.

But the fall was enough to make me lose my bearings and my three companions. Groping my way through the mist, I tried to retrace my steps.

"Ella!" I heard Horatio softly calling my name.

I spun around, struggling to pinpoint his location. But my efforts were frustrated by the sounds of other masculine voices swearing and shouting. Much to my horror, the mist was fading. I began to make out distorted shapes moving in the fog, drawing closer.

Although I risked giving myself away, I called frantically, "Horatio?"

"Over here, Ella," a muted voice responded.

I staggered in that direction. A stalwart masculine form loomed in front of me, a pair of strong hands closing over my shoulders.

"Horatio!" I almost sobbed with relief. But as the mist parted enough for me to see the face leering down at me, my heart stopped.

Prince Florian's mouth curved in a triumphant grin.

"Why, Ella, you look truly terrified. I really like that in a girl."

Twenty-One

"Let go of me, you cur!" Recovering from my initial fright, I struggled to free myself from Florian's grip, kicking at his shins. My bare feet had so little impact the prince chuckled.

"Tsk, tsk, Ella. You are so foolish. What did you plan to do if you rescued Hawkridge? Flee the kingdom? You will never escape me that easily."

Rearing up on my toes, I drove the top of my head into the bottom of Florian's chin. I heard his teeth clack together, followed by his grunt of pain. He released me and I staggered away from him, my head throbbing.

The mist had evaporated as swiftly as it had come, revealing a scene of total chaos. The Chief Warder had been tackled by his own guards and was swearing furiously. Prince Florian's Scutcheons had become completely turned around and were stumbling toward the gate.

I searched desperately for my companions. I could not find Horatio and Ryland, but I spotted Mal halfway down the hill, sprawled on his back. Rushing to his side, I tried to gather him up in my arms.

"Mal! Please. You must try to get up."

His eyes were mere slits and it cost him great effort to speak.

"I'm done for, Ella. Go! Save yourself." His eyes closed, his head lolling to one side.

"No," I cried. A pair of strong hands seized my shoulders, pulling me away from Mal.

I almost lashed out when I realized it was Horatio. He hauled me to my feet.

"There is nothing more you can do for Hawkridge. I'll do my best to protect him, but you must run. Get down to the boat."

"No, I won't abandon you."

My protest was cut off as Ryland appeared, adding his urgent voice to Horatio's.

"Go, Ella! Crushington and I will deal with the Warder and my brother."

I shook my head vehemently. It was a futile argument in any case. The Chief Warder had managed to climb out from under his guards and lead them in our direction. The palace scutcheons had recovered their bearings and rushed us as well. We were swiftly surrounded by men brandishing swords and truncheons.

Smedley, one of the guards I had terrified into fleeing, pointed a shaking finger at me. "There she is, sir. The dread headless ghost I told you about."

"She appears to be in possession of her head now," the warder snarled.

"She-she must have grown it back. Or stolen one from some-body else."

"Witless fool!" The Warder clouted Smedley upside the head. "She employed some sort of - of—"

"Witchcraft!" Florian bellowed. "Ella Upton has been prac-ticing sorcery. And without a license."

Considering the far more serious laws I had flouted tonight, the prince's accusation inspired me with an urge to break into hysterical laughter. I stifled it, fearing I might burst into tears instead and I refused to display such weakness.

Shoving his way through the circle of men, Florian tried to grab me.

But Horatio thrust him away from me. "Don't touch her!"

Florian stumbled back a pace. As he caught his balance, he flushed with outrage.

"You dare to lay hands on your prince? I'll have your head for this." The prince glared at Horatio before sneering at me. "Oh, Ella, it would seem you have bewitched even the stolid Crushington into forgetting his duty. What a devastating effect you have on the men in your life!"

I started to retort, but what could I say? It was true. My best friend lay unconscious, perhaps dying only yards away from me, all because of the insane jealousy I had inspired in this treacherous prince. That was bad enough but by allowing Horatio and Ryland to help in my mad scheme to save Mal, I had doomed them as well.

For a moment, I was overcome with a sense of guilt and the hopelessness of the situation. But I forced my shoulders back as I stepped forward to confront Florian.

"You are exactly right. I am a witch. *And* without a license."

This admission elicited a gasp from Smedley.

I raised my hands, hooking my fingers into claws, trying to emulate Delphine when she threatened to cast a spell.

"You all saw what I can do, making my head disappear, conjuring a mist out of thin air. Back off and let us go before I turn you all into slugs."

I must have sounded fierce and convincing enough because the men surrounding us took a wary step back. Even the Chief Warder twitched with apprehension.

But, although he was vain and vicious, Florian was not stupid. Well, not entirely. He folded his arms and dared me, "Go ahead. Do it, then."

"I will. I really mean it." I waved my arms muttering meaningless incantations.

Smedley whimpered and fled back toward the prison. I prayed that the rest would follow, but Florian commanded, "Stay where you are, idiots. If she had any such power, she would have already used it."

The prince's words carried more weight than my useless babble. As the guards closed in on us again, I lowered my arms. Florian snapped his fingers at the head of the prison guards. "Chief Warder. Arrest all the three of these men and my betrothed! Chain them in your deepest, darkest dungeon."

The Chief Warder licked his lips nervously and faltered, "Even your own brother?"

Florian glared at Ryland. "Especially him."

"No, wait," I cried, making one last attempt to save my companions. "I am the only one who should be punished. I enchanted the Commander and Prince Ryland. I forced them to—"

"That is not true," Horatio interrupted. "This escape plan was entirely mine. Ella is innocent."

"No, it was all my idea," Ryland said.

"Shut up! All of you. You will all pay the price for this treachery." Florian shouted. "Warder, carry out my order or I'll have *you* clapped in irons."

I braced myself to be seized but I was more terrified for Horatio and Ryland. They were unarmed, but they looked ready to fight to the death to protect me.

One of the prince's men took a step in Horatio's direction but froze beneath Horatio's steely gaze. Not only did my beloved present a formidable figure, but he commanded a certain respect from most of the kingdom's scutcheons, even the palace guard. As for Ryland, no one appeared eager to be the first to lay hands on a member of the royal family.

"Are all you all deaf?" Florian howled. "Arrest them!"

"Ignore that order," Horatio said. "You all know that the prince has no authority to issue such a command. Only the king can—"

"I *am* the king."

Florian's assertion was met by a stunned silence.

"Or I soon will be. The royal physician has declared my father will be dead by morning." Florian did not bother summoning his usual fake tears. His voice vibrated with satisfaction.

But Ryland cried, "No! If that is true, it is because you have killed him."

Florian looked startled by the accusation, but he rallied. With a forced laugh, he addressed the warder and the men surrounding us. "My poor bewitched brother appears to have run completely mad."

"You are the one who is mad if you think you can get away with this. You have been poisoning our father since he fell ill on the night of the ball."

I smothered a gasp. I had thought much the same thing, but it still came as a shock to hear my suspicions verified.

Florian attempted another sneering laugh, but Ryland's accusation sent an uneasy murmur through the assembled men. The Chief Warder appeared taken aback.

Florian ground his teeth and his hand dropped to the hilt of his sword. "Hold your tongue, brother. Any more of your insane lies and you'll lose more than your hand this time."

"Ryland." I clutched at his arm, trying to caution him. The fury simmering in Florian's eyes unnerved me.

But Ryland shook me off and continued, "It's true and what's more, I can prove it."

"Liar!" Florian unsheathed his sword, his face suffused with fury.

My breath caught in my throat. Would Florian dare to murder his own brother in front of so many witnesses? I believed that he would have if something had not darted between them.

Florian reared back, staring up at the small creature hovering over his head. Mimsey Peascod! Her pointed little face glowed a healthy shade of pink and her ashen wings had been restored to an iridescent blue. Had the irascible pixie returned to help us as she had promised? My heart swelled with hope even though I was uncertain what such a small being could do against a contingent of armed guards and one enraged prince.

Already furious to the point of madness, Florian turned purple at the sight of Mimsey fluttering just out of his reach.

"Which one of you fools freed my pixie?" he howled.

"I am the Chieftana Mimsey Peascod! I am no man's pixie." Mimsey declared. Her lips curved in a wicked grin. "But if you desire my magic dust so badly, you shall have it."

She flew straight at Florian's face. Twitching her wings, she enveloped his entire head in a shower of glittering silver. Florian tried to swat at Mimsey with his sword, but he was blinded by the cloud of magic dust. He choked and was seized by such a fit of violent sneezing, his sword flew from his hand. He tumbled backward, falling on his butt.

Before any of his astonished men could come to the prince's aid, Mimsey flitted among the guards and scutcheons, liberally dispensing her dust without any regard for who she hit.

When she darted past me, Horatio shouted, "Ella, cover your face."

But his warning came too late. I breathed in a snoot full. My eyes watered and I wheezed until my head reeled. I staggered and would have fallen but someone braced me. Horatio, perhaps?

I knuckled my eyes and was finally able to open them. I gasped to find the world transformed into a place of beauty and vibrant color. The night sky sparkled with diamonds. The grim gray stone walls of the prison had been repainted in all the hues of the rainbow. My wondering gaze tracked to where Mal's bald head had sprouted long, luxurious tresses.

"Oh, look, Horatio, Mal has grown his hair back. He will be

thrilled when he wakes up." My brow furrowed. "But maybe he won't like it being green."

"Ella, no." Horatio gave me a gentle shake. He was trying to tell me something, but I could not focus on anything except the delectable shape of his mouth.

I flung my arms around his neck and tried to kiss him. Much to my disappointment, he peeled me off him, capturing my wrists in a strong grip.

"Ella, stop! You are under the influence of pixie dust. You must try to fight it."

"All right." I sighed. But why would I want to do that? I had never experienced such euphoria in all my life, and I was not the only one flooded with joy.

Prince Ryland had told me he had abandoned his music. But my gentle Harper was once more filling the night with song, his voice golden and glorious enough to make fairies weep. A few of the guards were sobbing with emotion while the rest tossed aside their weapons and began to dance. The Chief Warder performed a graceful pirouette. I marveled that such a big man could be so light on his feet.

"Bravo," I said. Freeing my hands from Horatio's grip, I applauded.

Horatio groaned. He was the only one who was not enjoying himself, but my beloved had always been too serious and full of duty for his own good.

"Waltz with me," I begged. But when I reached for him, I grasped nothing but air. I pouted as I watched Horatio head for Ryland instead.

He shook the prince. "Snap out of it, Your Highness. This is our chance to escape."

Ryland ignored him and kept on singing.

Escape? Escape from what? I frowned at a vague memory of being in danger. The recollection threatened to dispel my happy mood, especially when I realized Florian was lurching toward me.

The prince tossed back his golden mane of hair, his tongue snaking out to moisten his lips. His eyes gleamed with a lust-filled expression.

"C'mere, you little vixen," he growled. "Those breeches are not proper for a wench. Take them off."

I giggled and smiled at him as I bent down to retrieve one of the guard's discarded truncheons. It felt all heavy and rough. I was delighted when the weapon transformed into a large golden sunflower with a thick stalk.

I kept smiling at Florian until he staggered within range. There was a loud crack as I struck him across the face with my sunflower. I swung so hard I fell to my knees. Florian went down even harder, blood spurting from his nose. His body twitched violently and then he lay still.

"Yes!" I chortled with triumph. "You are bleeding and unconscious. I really like that in a man."

Someone plucked the sunflower from my grasp, and I looked up to meet Horatio's horrified gaze. "Well, not every man," I hastened to explain. "Just that one."

Horatio pulled me to my feet, and I wrapped my arms around his waist.

Ryland had launched into another lilting ballad. I hummed along, trying to get Horatio to sway with me, but he forced me to stop.

"Ella, please. I need to get you—"

"Naked?" I suggested, waggling my eyebrows in wicked fashion.

I started to undo the buttons of his uniform when I was distracted by the sight of someone who had popped out of nowhere. The majordomo cut a somber appearance contrasted to all the delicious colors swirling before my eyes.

I scowled. "Hey, it's what's-his-name, the king's annoying little servant. What's he doing here? Shoo! Go away."

I waved my hand in a dismissive gesture, but the majordomo ignored me, addressing Horatio.

"Well, Commander, we appear to have quite a dire situation here," he said in that dry tone of his. "The question is what am I to do about it?"

"*You?*" I snickered before Horatio could reply. "You have no power. Who do you think you are, the king's wizard?"

"Hush, Ella." Horatio murmured in my ear. "That is exactly who he is."

"What? Don't be silly." I gave Horatio's shoulder a playful swat. "Everyone knows the Great Mercato is an old man with a long, long, white beard."

"No," Horatio whispered. "The majordomo is the real Sidney Greenleaf."

This was the most ridiculous and amusing thing I had ever heard. I laughed so hard I didn't think I would ever be able to stop. I laughed until my head pounded and my stomach ached.

Groaning, I doubled over, clutching my midsection. "Horatio, I don't feel so good."

My words trailed off as the sky above exploded with a hail of shooting stars. My knees buckled. Horatio caught me just in time before I sagged to the ground, and all went dark.

Twenty-Two

I was having the strangest dream about feeding gingerbread to an aura cat, rescuing Mal from a dungeon, and kissing Horatio. That part of the dream was wonderful before the majordomo popped up to ruin it. But the rest was a jumbled nightmare of Florian turning into a monster and threatening to ravish me.

Moaning, I tossed and turned. I needed to wake up, but lifting my eyelids was like struggling with wooden shutters that were painted shut. I knuckled my eyes until they became unglued enough to open a crack. The soft morning light blurred my vision. I blinked hard until I could focus on my surroundings.

I was tucked up in a bed that wasn't mine, yet the white ash headboard seemed familiar. My bleary-eyed gaze traveled over the low ceiling, the small windows, and their lacy curtains. It was the multi-colored quilt draped over me, along with the faded wallpaper of vines and roses that helped me gain my bearings. I was in one of the attic rooms above the apothecary shop that had once served Mal's grandmother as her bedchamber and sitting room.

How did I end up in Granny Hawkridge's bed and why was I wearing Mal's clothes? Had any part of my dream been real or was it all just a nightmare? Shifting upright, I smothered a groan. As I stretched to ease my sore muscles, I let out a startled squeak.

I was not alone.

A man dozed in the wing-back chair by the fireplace, his long legs stretched out, his boots propped on the matching ottoman. He had to be dreadfully uncomfortable, the chair never fashioned to accommodate his large frame. His dark head slumped to the side, his lips slightly parted, issuing soft sighs.

Horatio! I was relieved and astonished to find him here with me. How could he manage to sleep in that cramped position? The poor man must be exhausted after everything that had happened last night.

I sucked in my breath as memories surfaced of my desperate attempt to free Mal from the Dismal Dungeons, Horatio and Ryland helping me. Where was Mal now? The last I recalled he had collapsed on the hillside, the rest of us surrounded by scutcheons, prison guards and Florian! The prince had been waving his sword about, threatening to kill his brother. My recollections after that were vague, a flutter of iridescent blue wings, Mimsey darting overhead, a shower of silvery particles raining down on me.

Pixie dust! Was I still under its influence and only imagining that Horatio and I were miles away from the Dismal Dungeons, safe at The Hawk's Nest? Flinging the quilt aside, I stood up too quickly. My head reeled. I staggered forward, clutching at the bedpost for support. The noise I made startled Horatio awake. Bolting upright, his hands doubled into fists, he prepared to do battle. When he spotted me, he released a deep breath and relaxed his hands.

"Ella! Thank the fairies you are finally awake. I was so worried." Horatio dragged his hands down his face. "I am sorry. I never meant to fall asleep. What time is it?"

I was unable to answer him. Time had disappeared for me the moment I had inhaled that pixie dust. I marveled that Horatio appeared far less confused by our current situation. When I took a step in his direction, he leaped up to steady me.

I flung myself into his arms. He felt wonderfully solid and real, his presence reassuring. I clung to him, trembling. Horatio held me close, murmuring, "Everything is going to be all right, Ella. You are safe now."

"Am I?" I croaked, my throat feeling as thick and fuzzy as though I had been swallowing caterpillars. "Mal! What happened to Mal?"

"Don't worry about him. Hawkridge is here, settled in his own bed. Miss Delray is looking after him and tending to his injuries."

"Miss Delray? Who is that?"

"Delphine Delray. Hawkridge's witch friend and yours as well?"

"Oh." I had never heard Delphine's surname before. It was odd to think of her as Miss anything and that only added to my bewilderment. The last I remembered she was waiting for us outside the breach in the wall. How did she end up back here at the Hawk's Nest? How did any of us? I experienced a glimmer of hope.

I tipped back my head to peer up at Horatio. "We managed to rescue Mal and escape?"

Horatio brushed tangled strands of hair from my brow. "Not entirely."

"Not entirely? What does that mean?"

"We were permitted to leave the King's Royal prison and return to the Hawk's Nest, but the shop is surrounded by palace guards."

I peeled myself away from Horatio and staggered toward one of the dormer windows. Forcing the casement open, I leaned out, peering at the street below. The morning breeze felt soft against my cheeks. Anything soothing about the sensation was dispelled by the sight of palace guards standing sentry below. From my vantage point, I could see at least four of them looking sharp in their crisp red and gold uniforms.

At the sound of the window opening, one of the younger scutcheons looked up at me. But a barked order from his sergeant caused the man to snap to attention. There had been more curiosity than menace in the young scutcheon's gaze. I should have been able to draw some comfort from that, but all I felt was despair.

I said hoarsely, "Then we didn't escape at all. We are still prisoners."

Horatio stepped behind me. Resting his hands on my shoulders, he turned me away from the window. "I was told that the guards have been placed there for our protection."

Told by whom? Protection from what?

Rubbing my temple, I said, "I don't understand. Why can't I remember how we ended up here?"

"I'll explain everything, but I think you need to sit down."

I didn't want to sit down. I needed answers, but my head still felt woozy. I allowed Horatio to guide me to the chair he had vacated. He eased me down onto the cushions that still bore the warm imprint of his body. I could easily have leaned back and drifted off to sleep, so I perched on the edge of the seat, anxiously awaiting more information from Horatio.

He retrieved a small bottle of ruby red liquid from the mantle. Horatio hesitated before offering it to me. "Miss Delray - er-Delphine said I was to give you this when you awoke. It is something called Rueful Morning After, a potion to dispel any lingering effects of the pixie dust. Delphine seemed sincere in her desire to be helpful, but I don't know if you should trust a potion brewed by a witch."

"I do," I interrupted, seizing the bottle from him. After the risks Delphine had taken to help me save Mal, I believed in her friendship and her magic.

Uncorking the bottle, I took a sip. The Rueful Morning After potion didn't taste half-bad, a bit like mulled wine laced with cinnamon. As I gulped down the rest of the liquid, it sent a rush of heat down my throat and through my veins, causing me to choke. Horatio watched me with alarm.

"I'm alright," I managed to gasp. I did feel revived, my mind clearer.

I handed the empty bottle back to Horatio. He returned it to the mantle and then lowered himself onto the ottoman opposite me.

"The potion helped?" he asked. "Do you feel better?"

I nodded. "But there are still fragments of my memory I cannot piece together."

"What is the last thing you do recall?"

I massaged my brow as though that would help. "I remember inhaling the pixie dust and Ryland started singing. The guards were all dancing and I think Florian fell and hit his head. And I was—"

I lowered my eyes, too embarrassed to meet Horatio's gaze as I recalled how I had been all over the man, kissing him. There was a button missing from his uniform. I must have yanked that off in my efforts to undress him.

Quelling a blush, I continued, "Then the king's majordomo appeared out of nowhere. He has an eerie habit of doing that." I frowned. "Or did I just imagine he was there?"

"No, he was there. He arranged for you and Hawkridge to be brought here in the royal carriage. While he assumed responsibility for the two princes, the majordomo allowed me to travel in the coach and look after you."

I rubbed my eyes. More vague memories returned of being lifted onto a velvet-cushioned seat, Mal sprawled opposite me. Being jostled along, Horatio's strong arms bracing me against the sway of the carriage.

"I remember some of that." I gave a hesitant laugh. "This is going to sound ridiculous and probably the result of being pixified. But I thought you told me that the majordomo is really Sidney Greenleaf."

"Yes, I did."

I gaped at him. "But that is impossible. He can't be the Great Mercato. That alarming old man with the wizard staff and the long white beard is—"

"Merely an actor that Greenleaf hired to play the part."

I pressed my hands to my brow, my head starting to reel again. How I wished I had more of Delphine's Rueful Morning After potion because none of this made sense. The majordomo was the real Great Mercato, the builder of the infamous aura chamber? How could he have perpetrated such a deception for so many years with no one the wiser?

And yet my mind traveled back to my last meeting with Withypole at the Winking Goblin. During his drunken ramblings, the fairy had tried to tell me something about the king's wizard.

"You must understand something about Mercato. He's a fake."

At the time, I had been more concerned with learning the history of the orb and the missing heir before Withypole passed out. Now I wish I had tried harder to get the fairy to focus, explain what he had meant about Mercato. Except it seemed rather obvious. Withypole must have been the only one in Arcady aware of the wizard's identity.

Well, no, not the only one.

I lowered my hands, regarding Horatio with a troubled frown.

"How did you discover the truth about the majordomo? And how long have you known?"

Horatio sighed. "About six months after I took up my post in Midtown, Withypole told me that the majordomo was really Sidney Greenleaf, and I should not trust him. At that point, I did not know how much I could trust Withypole either. Then one night I heard a noise coming from the Aura Chamber.

"It was dusk so the room should have been closed and locked. When I crept in to investigate, I surprised the majordomo collecting the memory shards. No one was ever supposed to do that except for the king's wizard. The majordomo tried to make some excuse. Resting his hand on my arm, he stared deep into my eyes. His gaze was strange."

"Almost hypnotic," I filled in, remembering how I had once experienced the same eerie sensation.

"If he was trying to mesmerize me, it didn't work," Horatio said. "When I accused him of being the real Mercato, he stopped denying it and admitted the truth."

"Then what? You allowed him to continue his deception, keeping his secret from everyone?"

I didn't mean to sound accusing. I had told Horatio so many lies, I had no right to feel disturbed that he had kept this secret. And yet I did, perhaps because I had always believed Horatio to be so honest, one of the traits I loved best about him.

Horatio sighed. "You have got to understand, Ella. I was new to my position as commander of the garrison, but I was already dismayed by the harshness of the laws I was expected to enforce. Greenleaf offered me a pact. If I kept his secret, we could work together to mitigate some of the king's cruel excesses. It has not been easy, but we have often succeeded."

"You were not able to save the Hanson and Bafton families from exile, even after the wizard promised they would be pardoned," I reminded Horatio.

"That was not Greenleaf's fault." Horatio insisted. "He obtained the pardon, but then the king fell deathly ill. While Sidney fought to save his majesty's life, Prince Florian gave the orders for Midtown families to be banished, even though he had no right to do so."

I slumped back in my chair, hardly knowing what to think. "You call him *Sidney?* Despite all this wizard's deception, you trust him. Do you consider him to be your friend?"

"If not for Greenleaf, we would have all ended up locked in King's Royal Prison. Instead, he sent us here."

"Surrounded by guards."

"Ones that Sidney knows and trusts. Only think, Ella. If Prince Florian was vengeful before, what he is going to be like when he recovers and remembers what happened last night?"

Horatio leaned forward and gathered my hands into his. "Sidney is our only hope of coming through all this unscathed."

Horatio looked so earnest, I nodded in reluctant agreement, but I was troubled by the memory of what Withypole had said to me.

"No matter what happens, Ella, you must never, ever trust Sidney Greenleaf. Even if he pretends to be your friend."

I had never had a chance to tell Horatio all that I had learned from Withypole Fugitate that afternoon in the Winking Goblin. But before I could do so, I heard a herald's trumpet blare in the street below.

When I stiffened in alarm, Horatio gave my hands a reassuring squeeze.

"That is probably Sidney. He promised he would come here this morning to advise us what we should do next."

Horatio rose from the ottoman and hurried to the window. I followed more slowly, still a little unsteady on my feet.

Crowding close to Horatio, we peered at the scene unfolding below us. There was no sign of Sidney Greenleaf. A royal herald dismounted from his horse and read a proclamation to the palace Scutcheons surrounding the Hawk's Nest. We could not hear a word, but whatever the herald said, it created consternation among the guards.

Horatio frowned. "I better go see what's going on."

"I am coming with you."

"No, you need to stay here until you are fully recovered. And you must be worried about Hawkridge and longing to see him." Horatio offered me a sad smile and caressed my cheek. "Go. Be with him."

I wanted to see how Mal was faring. But I could tell from the resigned expression on Horatio's face that he believed more than ever that I was in love with Mal. Why wouldn't he after the events of last night? He had witnessed me willing to sacrifice everything to save Mal, including any future that Horatio and I might have had together.

I might never be able to convince Horatio that he was the man I loved and perhaps I no longer had the right to try. Prince Florian was a notorious liar, but there was one thing he had said to me that rang true.

"Ah, Ella, what a devastating effect you have on the men in your life!"

I had brought Horatio nothing but disaster since the day I met him. If Sidney Greenleaf was able to help us and we survived this debacle, maybe Horatio would be better off without me.

I remained silent as Horatio strode from the room. When the door closed behind him, I shed a single quiet tear. Then I wiped my eyes and went to find Mal.

* * *

Propped up against his pillows, Mal sprawled atop the coverlet of his bed, a battered oak piece of furniture with newel posts shaped like cannon balls. Clad in his nightshirt, Mal's left foot was swathed in bandages. When I leaned down to hug him, he winced, but I was relieved to see he looked much better. The purple bruises on his face had faded to an ugly green and that spark had returned to his eyes as he teased me about being unable to handle my pixie dust.

"Be fair, darling. It was her first time." Delphine cooed.

"And my last," I muttered.

Delphine plumped up another pillow. As she eased it behind Mal's back, she giggled, "But it was all so amusing, especially the Chief Warder performing pirouettes."

"Wish I had been awake to see it." Mal grinned. "But after I blacked out, I wasn't aware of anything until I was rudely awakened this morning by Delphine licking me."

"A cat's tongue can be a bit rough," Delphine conceded.

"You weren't Ebony when you licked me. You were in your human form."

"It was a kiss, you ingrate." Delphine moistened her lips. "With perhaps just a wee bit of tongue."

Mal pulled a face and inched further away from where she had perched on the edge of his bed. But despite Mal's disgruntled expression, the two of them appeared to be on good terms again. That accounted for the current hue of Delphine's hair, a bright, sassy yellow.

"Anyhow I had no idea how I wound up back here in my own bed until Delphine explained everything."

"But how did you know what happened?" I asked Delphine. "The last I recall you and Waldo were waiting for me outside the breach in the wall."

"I got worried when it took you all so long to return and Waldo was getting fidgety. I decided to risk setting off any of Mercato's witch-warding alarms by transforming into Ebony. By the time I made to the top of the hill, I found Mal unconscious and that crazy Mimsey Peascod dousing everyone with her pixie dust.

"Then that odd little majordomo arrived and arranged for the commander to bring you and Mal to the Hawk's Nest. I raced back down the hill and transformed out of my cat shape. Waldo and I got back into the boat, well, after I smacked him around a bit for ogling me while I got dressed. We managed to return to Misty Bottoms just as the sun was coming up. I sent Waldo about his business, after another slap for trying to kiss me goodbye and then I gathered up a few potions and bandages from my house that I knew you and Mal would need. I whisked over to the Hawk's Nest in the nick of time before the royal carriage and the palace guards arrived."

Delphine concluded with a triumphant sweep of her hands. "Now, here we all are, together again."

"But why didn't the pixie dust affect you?" I asked.

"When I am Ebony, I am immune to magic dust, although never trust me near catnip." Delphine's brow puckered with a puzzled frown. "Strangely, Commander Crushington wasn't affected by the dust either."

Mal snorted. "Knowing Mr. Honorable, he was probably too noble to inhale."

I glared at him. "You owe Horatio your life. I could never have gotten you out of that dungeon without his help. So don't you dare sneer at him."

"I wasn't sneering, just stating a fact." Mal grimaced as he shifted on the bed, trying to ease his stiff body into a more comfortable position. "Much as I hate it, I am fully aware that I will be forever in Crushington's debt. Although considering my shop is surrounded by armed guards, forever might not be that long for any of us."

"Oh, pooh! Don't be so gloomy, Sir Sour Puss." Delphine gave his ear a playful tweak.

"Horatio believes that the majordomo will continue to help us." I paused as I said this, wondering how much I ought to reveal about the majordomo's real identity. Horatio had not given me permission to share the information, but he had not exactly forbidden me either.

The decision was taken out of my hands. Mal knew me far too well. His gaze sharpened as he studied my face.

"What is it, Ella?" he demanded. "What aren't you telling us?"

I hesitated a moment longer, but this was Mal. I had always had difficulty keeping secrets from him. In a few terse words, I explained what I had learned about Sidney Greenleaf's deception.

Mal looked stunned, but Delphine crowed, "Aha, I knew there was always something odd about that old goat with the beard, waving his staff around, muttering incantations. Entirely too bombastic to be a true wizard and what do you think you are doing!"

This last alarmed remark was directed at Mal. Recovering from his initial shock, Mal's face set in a look of grim determination as he struggled to rise from his bed.

"I need to get up and get dressed."

"No, you are in no condition to do that." Delphine clutched at the sleeve of his nightshirt, trying to pull him back down, but Mal succeeded in thrusting her away.

He managed to swing his legs over the side of the bed, but the effort cost him. The blood drained from his face.

"Delphine is right," I said. Stepping forward to help her, I placed my hands on Mal's shoulders. "You should rest. You are still in no state to go anywhere."

"I have to be." Mal gritted his teeth and looked up at me. "Don't you see, Ella? If the majordomo is really Mercato and he is coming here, we are all still in danger."

Mal tensed as a light knock sounded on his bedchamber door. "Don't answer that!"

For a moment, Mal's alarm caused my heart to stutter, but then I shook my head.

"Don't be silly. It must be Horatio."

Ignoring Mal's protests, I crossed the room. I was cautious enough to inch the door open a crack. But I flung it wide when I saw that it was indeed Horatio. Any relief I felt was dispelled by the sight of his face as he stepped across the threshold. I had never seen him look so grave.

"What is it?" I asked. "What did the royal herald want?"

"He came to announce that the king is dead." Horatio informed us grimly.

"Huzzah," Delphine cried, raising her fist in the air. When no one joined her cheer, she realized the full implications of these tidings.

"Oh, no" she said, lowering her hand. "Then that means... "

When she faltered, I finished the horrible thought. "Florian is now our king." A shudder coursed through me.

Horatio wrapped his arm about my shoulders. "Don't worry, Ella. I will find a way to protect you."

"How?" Mal snapped. "With the aid of your good friend *Sidney?*"

Horatio stiffened and then cast me a reproachful look.

"I am sorry, Horatio," I said. "But I felt they needed to know."

"This entire kingdom needs to know." Clutching at the newel post, Mal struggled to his feet. "But right now, we all need to get the frap out of here."

"What we need to do is not panic," Horatio said. "We should wait until Greenleaf arrives and hear what he has to say."

"You might be naïve enough to believe that man intends to help us, but there is only one reason he is coming here. He wants the orb or have you all forgotten that?"

With everything else that had happened, all thoughts of the orb had slipped my mind. Balancing on his good foot, Mal twisted one of the cannonball posts on his bed. It came away, revealing a hollow opening beneath. When Mal reached inside and produced the orb, Delphine clapped her hands.

"That is where you had the orb hidden all this time? Oh, you clever boy."

Although Mal panted from the effort it took to remain upright, he said, "We must get the orb far away from here before Greenleaf arrives. Unless Crushington can persuade those guards to stand down, we may have to fight our way out."

"There will be no fighting," Horatio said. "I have no intention of allowing you to start a war. You have caused enough trouble with that blasted orb. Now hand it over."

Horatio strode toward Mal and snatched the orb from his hand. Mal flushed red with anger. Despite hardly being able to stand, he appeared ready to launch himself at Horatio. I rushed forward, getting between the two men. As I stumbled into Horatio, I nearly knocked the orb out of his hand. Then an odd thing happened.

The glass orb began to pulse, emitting a soft glow. We all stared at it in stunned silence. Mal was the first to find his voice.

Gazing at Horatio with a mingling of awe and disbelief, Mal cried, "Frapping fairies. It's *you*. You are our long-lost prince."

Twenty-Three

"Don't be an idiot," Horatio snapped at Mal. He turned to me, as though I could provide him with a more reasonable explanation for the orb's behavior, one that Horatio's rational mind could accept. "What's wrong with this thing, Ella? Why is it doing that?"

I felt as shocked as Horatio. According to the ancient parchment I had found in Papa's library, the orb was not supposed to be activated until the time was right. Yet the glow from the small glass ball was getting stronger by the moment.

"The orb was designed by the fairies to reveal Arcady's true heir," I said. I gazed up at Horatio, expelling an awed breath. "*You.*"

"No," he said hoarsely.

"Oh, for frap's sake." Mal was beside himself with excitement. He forgot and put his weight down on his injured foot. Swearing with pain, he would have fallen if Delphine had not rushed to brace him.

"I performed every test and incantation I could think of on that orb," Mal said through gritted teeth. "Nothing ever happened, not until you touched it, Crushington." Mal hesitated. Leaning on

Delphine for support, he managed a stiff bow. The witch bobbed her head in a form of curtsy.

"Your Royal Highness," they murmured in unison.

"Stop that! Both of you!" Despite his fierce words, Horatio paled, looking as though he wanted to fling the glowing orb across the room. "Ella, surely you cannot believe this foolishness."

Another man would have rejoiced to discover that he might be of royal blood with a great destiny before him. But Horatio looked completely unnerved by the prospect.

"It may not be foolish," I said gently. "Withypole told me that the legend of the missing heir is real. He told me that our true prince would be revealed when the time was right."

"The time could not be any righter than it is now," Delphine piped up. "Not with that monster Florian about to ascend the throne."

"But I am no one," Horatio insisted. "A mere foundling."

"Exactly." Mal grimaced as he eased back down on the edge of the bed. "A *foundling*, a man with no idea who his ancestors were. But now the orb is showing you, Your Highness."

"Don't call me that!" Horatio growled. "I have no wish to be king."

I had never seen my stalwart commander look so shaken. I longed to assure him that everything would be all right, although I had no idea how. Discovering that Horatio was the lost prince was wonderful, but there were many obstacles to placing him on the throne, not the least of which was Horatio himself. He had expressed more than once his unwillingness to see Arcady plunged into civil war over what he believed to be a foolish legend.

"Take this cursed thing away from me," he said. Horatio tried to give me the orb, but the glass ball slipped from his grasp.

Delphine shrieked and Mal gasped. Miraculously, the orb didn't shatter when it struck the hardwood floor. But it stopped glowing as it bounced and rolled, stopping inches from Delphine's foot.

As she bent to retrieve it, I heard a creak coming from the stairs leading up to Mal's room. Someone called out, "Commander Crushington?"

My heart thudded as I recognized the familiar voice of the man I had once thought of as the majordomo.

Sidney Greenleaf! He sounded so close, his arrival imminent and the door to the bedchamber was ajar from when Horatio had entered. We all exchanged looks of sheer panic. Delphine reacted the quickest, transforming into Ebony far more swiftly than I had ever seen her move before.

Scrambling out from beneath her discarded clothes, the cat propelled the orb forward. She disappeared with it beneath the bed just as Greenleaf appeared in the door opening. As he pushed the door open wider, my pulse thundered in my ears.

How much had the wizard overheard as he was creeping up the stairs? Could he have seen the orb's glow through the crack in the door? Greenleaf's bland expression gave away nothing. The little man was already attired in the purple and black garb our kingdom decried suitable for mourning. He wore the traditional square shaped cap with black scarves trailing from it.

His gaze shifted about the room, thoughtfully studying each of us in turn. I feared that I must appear the very picture of guilt. As for Horatio, he stood frozen, having received his second shock, watching a woman turn into a cat before his very eyes.

Even Mal, who had a talent for looking innocent in the most appalling circumstances, was rattled. But he tried to brazen it out. Hefting himself onto the end of the bed, he dangled his feet over the side and leaned back on his elbows, doing his best to look nonchalant.

"Oh, do come right on in," he said. "Don't bother to knock, Mr. Green—"

Mal choked. He would have been far too smooth to ever make such a slip under ordinary circumstances. He bit down hard on his lip, but it was too late. He'd already betrayed the fact that Horatio had told us Greenleaf's secret.

If the little man was angry, he gave no sign of it. Even as he turned accusing eyes in Horatio's direction, his tone was mild. "It would appear that you have broken your promise, Commander Crushington."

Before Horatio could muster a response, Mal said quickly. "It wasn't Crushington who told me. It was someone else."

"And exactly who would that be, Mr. Hawkridge? Even the king didn't know. There is only one person besides myself and Crushington who knows my identity." Greenleaf paused and then rolled his eyes. "Of course. Withypole Fugitate. You should not believe everything he says. Fugitate is a liar and not at all to be trusted."

"Are you telling us that it is not true?" I challenged him. "You are not in fact Sidney Greenleaf, the real wizard Mercato?"

Greenleaf frowned for a moment, then he shrugged, "Yes, it is true, but it no longer matters who knows. The time has come for my charade to end. Bryce will be excessively disappointed."

"Bryce?" I echoed. "Who is Bryce?"

"Bryce Wetherbee. The actor I hired to portray Mercato."

"*Bryce Wetherbee?*" Despite his tension, Mal laughed. "That's as bad of a name for a wizard as Sidney Greenleaf."

"I entirely agree. Hence the Great Mercato." A fleeting smile touched Sidney's lips, but he immediately sobered. "However, this is no time for levity. I have some sad news to impart."

"We already know." Horatio recovered enough to speak. "The king is dead."

"Alas, our kingdom has suffered a double loss. Prince Florian has also perished."

"What!" Horatio exclaimed.

I could not understand why he looked disturbed by this news. My immediate reaction was one of overwhelming relief. Florian would not become our king. We need never fear being threatened by him again.

Mal made no effort to conceal his jubilation.

"Yes!" He pumped his fist into the air, grinning from ear to ear. Delphine so far forgot herself as to issue a happy mew from beneath the bed. Fortunately, Greenleaf did not appear to have heard her as Mal chortled with glee.

"That bastard of a prince has really snuffed it? That's the best thing I have heard in a twelve-month."

"Do try to show a modicum of respect for the dead, Mr. Hawkridge," Sidney reproved him.

"Excuse me for not weeping for that villain," Mal drawled. "I'm all out of clean handkerchiefs."

Horatio frowned. "But I don't understand. When I left you last night, you said that you would look after the two princes, and they would recover."

"Prince Ryland did. But after Florian was conveyed back to the palace, he succumbed to the blow Miss Upton dealt him during the skirmish at the prison."

"What blow?" I demanded. "I am sure I did nothing worse that whap him with a sunflower and... "

I trailed off as another memory from last night crystallized in my mind. Florian lurching toward me with that nasty leering expression on his face, me defending myself, smacking him with a sunflower. Except it hadn't been a flower at all. I'd bashed him over the head with a thick wooden cudgel.

"Oh!" Trembling, I sank down upon a wooden stool near the hearth as the realization sank in. I had killed a prince. There could be no worse crime in our kingdom. I would be charged and executed. My hand crept to my throat as though I could already feel the Royal Garroter's rope cutting off my air.

"I was only trying to defend myself from Florian. I never meant to—" I faltered.

Mal snapped, "Be quiet, Ella."

Clutching the bedpost, Mal struggled to his feet, defiantly declaring, "It was me. I crushed Florian's skull, and I am not the least bit sorry."

"Exactly how did you manage that, Mr. Hawkridge?" Greenleaf asked. "When I arrived on the scene, you were lying unconscious, halfway down the hill."

"Well, I-I hit him and then I staggered away before I collapsed."

"Don't talk nonsense," Horatio said. "I was the one who felled the prince."

"No, Horatio," I protested. "I remember you taking the cudgel away from me."

"Hush, Ella. Your memory is still confused from the pixie dust." Horatio moved closer, resting his hand protectively on my shoulder. "I killed the prince, and I am fully prepared to accept the consequences."

"No, you won't." Mal growled at him. "Because I did it."

"Stop it, both of you," I cried. "If you think I will allow either of you to take the blame—"

"Be quiet, Ella!" Mal and Horatio commanded in unison. They tried to talk over each other, both declaring they had killed Florian until Greenleaf flung up his hands.

"Enough! There is no need for these dramatic attempts at self-sacrifice because no one will ever know what happened last night. I have already begun preparing the official report. King August perished from a stomach ailment—"

"Because Florian poisoned him." Mal interrupted.

Ignoring him, Greenleaf went on, "As for the prince, I shall devise some suitable explanation for his death."

Greenleaf was willing to conceal the truth about Florian's death? I gaped at him, torn between hope and disbelief, but Mal seized eagerly upon the notion.

"We could tell everyone Florian tossed his hair and walked into a tree. Or he stopped to admire his reflection in a stream, fell in and drowned."

"Thank you, Mr. Hawkridge," Greenleaf said wryly. "I believe I can conjure a more noble end for our prince."

Although Horatio looked relieved, he protested, "What about the witnesses? The prison guards and Florian's own men."

"All too befuddled by pixie dust to have any good recollection and I can ensure that they remain so."

Horatio released a deep breath, looking grateful to Greenleaf for his intervention. Perhaps I should have felt the same. But I rose to my feet, regarding the wizard with suspicion.

"Why would you do that?" I demanded. "Protect me by covering up what really happened."

"Have I not made it clear, Miss Upton? I have a high regard for your late father and you as well, my dear." The smile that Greenleaf trained upon me was positively avuncular. Why did I not find it more reassuring?

He continued, "Could you imagine how devastating it would be for our kingdom if the truth got out? That the noble Florian poisoned his own father, and the prince was such a monster, that his betrothed was obliged to slay him. No, far better that the reputation of the Helavalerians remain untarnished as we embark on a new age of prosperity in Arcady. The kind and gentle Prince Kendrick will become our king."

"That simpleton?" Mal sneered. "He is more addicted to pixie dust than Florian ever was."

"A habit I shall help him to break. With my guidance, I am sure Prince Kendrick can become a wise and great ruler."

The wizard's guidance or his control? Kendrick was a weak man, far easier to manipulate than King August or Prince Florian would have been. I could not help wondering if Sidney Greenleaf had been quietly scheming for years, planning for the day when he would be king in all but name. What would his reaction be if he realized that the man who was our true king stood but a few feet away from him? Despite Sidney's seeming good will and affability,

I had little doubt what he would do to anyone who thwarted his ambitions. Horatio's life would be instantly forfeited.

Fortunately, Greenleaf appeared to be unaware of what had transpired just before his arrival. Greenleaf rubbed his hands together and said, "Now there is only one other small matter that needs settled, Mr. Hawkridge. The stolen orb. I want it back."

"Oh, I'll wager you do." Mal locked his arms across his chest. "And if I refuse? You'll have me arrested and tortured again?"

"I should be excessively loath to do so, but you must understand. The disposal of that orb is necessary for the safety and good of the kingdom."

"For the good of Arcady or your puppet prince?"

Horatio vented a wearied sigh. "For frap's sake, Hawkridge, just give him the blasted orb."

Mal cast Horatio a look filled with incredulity and reproach, dismayed that Horatio should be so willing to surrender the object that could prove his birthright. Perhaps Horatio believed we had no other choice, but he ought to have realized by now how stubborn Mal could be.

Mal affected a careless shrug. "I can't return the orb because I no longer have it. I have no idea where it is."

"Don't you?" Greenleaf asked softly. "Then perhaps we should ask your cat."

Mal stiffened, his face washing pale beneath his bruises. "What cat? I don't have a cat?"

"What about the one hiding under your bed?" Greenleaf smirked.

I had allowed myself the false hope that Greenleaf had not seen Delphine change to Ebony and hide the orb. But Sidney had just been biding his time.

My stomach knotted as the wizard ambled around to the side of Mal's bed and crouched down.

"Here, kitty, kitty," he crooned. "Come here. What is that you are hiding in your paws?"

Greenleaf flattened himself on the floor, stretching his arm beneath the bed. Ebony emitted a furious screech. Greenleaf swore and jerked his arm back, but during their struggle, Ebony lost control of the orb.

It came rolling out from beneath the bed. Mal attempted to grab it as Ebony erupted from beneath the bed. The cat tripped Mal and they both went down in a tangled heap of legs and paws.

The orb continued to roll straight toward Horatio as though the magical object was drawn to him. He froze, but he didn't dare touch the orb for fear of setting it aglow again.

Greenleaf could not fail to notice this as he clambered to his feet. Ebony had carved some deep claw marks on his hand. He dragged a handkerchief from his pocket to stem the trickles of blood. While he was distracted, I should have tried to grab the orb and hide it, but there was no time.

I can only describe what I did next as an impulse born of sheer panic. Seizing the fireplace shovel, I batted the orb away from Horatio as hard as I could. The orb flew and smacked against the wall. Dropping to the floor, it emitted a spark of light before cracking and splitting in two.

Ebony let out a frightful yowl and Mal gave an anguished cry. "Ella, what have you done!"

Still clutching the shovel, I stared down at the broken orb, feeling sick. My one terrified thought had been to protect Horatio but in doing so, I had ended any hope of proving he was the lost prince. I could not bring myself to meet his eyes.

But as he plucked the shovel from my trembling hands, Horatio whispered in my ear, "It's alright, Ella. Thank you."

He was not even upset with me. He sounded grateful and that made me feel even worse.

Mal was not taking the destruction of the orb nearly as well. He remained on his knees, his shoulders bowed in despair. Mal had risked everything in the quest for the missing heir, our friendship, his freedom, even his life. Discovering that Crushington was the lost prince had vindicated Mal's unshakeable faith in the legend. But I had shattered his triumph with a single blow. Never had I seen my friend so close to weeping. Ebony rubbed her head beneath his chin, trying to comfort him.

As for Sidney Greenleaf, he appeared as startled by my impulsive act as everyone else. His battle with Ebony had knocked his cap askew. Straightening it, he stepped closer to inspect the broken orb.

Greenleaf had clearly wanted to regain possession of the orb for whatever devious reasons of his own. Most likely to conduct his own search for the lost prince to destroy him. I braced myself for the wizard's anger, a flood of recriminations. But his reaction was the last thing I expected.

Sidney smiled. "Well, that ends that."

"I am sorry," I stammered. My apology was directed at Horatio and Mal, rather than Greenleaf. "I only thought—"

"No need for you to explain yourself, my dear," Greenleaf interrupted. "That orb threatened to become a source of trouble for this kingdom. It should have been disposed of years ago. You were wise to destroy it. Magnificently wise, one almost might say."

An odd amusement glimmered in Sidney's eyes, as though he was savoring some secret jest. He peered down at Mal who still had not found the energy to rise from his knees.

"Now that this foolishness of the orb has been settled, I am sure that Prince Kendrick will be disposed to grant mercy regarding any crimes committed by you, Mr. Hawkridge. But I would strongly suggest, for the sake of your health, that you take a long holiday far away from Arcady. Perhaps the Isle of Lothmara? I have heard that is a very popular spot with young men."

Dabbing at the scratches on his injured hand, Sidney's gaze lit resentfully on Ebony. "You had better take your cat with you."

Mal was too dispirited to offer one of his usual sharp retorts. But Ebony hissed and would have sprung at Sidney if Mal had not prevented her by gathering the cat into his arms.

"And now for our gallant Commander Crushington... " Greenleaf turned his attention to Horatio.

Horatio stiffened. "I expect no mercy from the king. I broke my oath as a Scutcheon commander to uphold the law. I am fully prepared to offer my resignation and accept the consequences."

"Oh, no, no, my dear boy!" Greenleaf wagged his finger at Horatio. "Despite your recent transgression, I am confident Prince Kendrick will pardon you because of your devoted service to Arcady. There can be a certain amount of unrest among the more lawless elements of a kingdom when a new heir assumes the throne."

Greenleaf stared pointedly at Mal as he said this before turning back to Horatio. "As Commander of the Midtown Garrison, you will be needed to keep order. Yes, all things considered, I think it advisable for the security of everyone, that you remain right where you are."

The way Greenleaf said this left me uneasy. Did the wizard *know*? Had he overheard what transpired in Mal's bedchamber after the orb revealed Horatio as the lost prince? For all his feigned affability, I detected a hidden threat behind Greenleaf's smiling words. Horatio would be safe if he remained a loyal Scutcheon commander. If he did not... I shuddered to think what Greenleaf might do.

"And lastly, but not least, our enchanting Miss Upton."

I flinched as Greenleaf trained his gaze on me. "I understand congratulations are in order. According to court gossip, Lord Redmond means to wed your step-mama. Your family will move to his estate in the Heights. What a splendid opportunity for you to abandon your more adventurous pastimes." Greenleaf's gaze skated disapprovingly over my masculine attire. "And become the respectable young lady you were meant to be. Prince Florian turned out to be a disappointment, but I am sure with your beauty, you will have no difficulty making an equally brilliant match."

Greenleaf sounded so sanctimonious and smug, I longed to smack him. I had to take a deep breath and remind myself, if not for the wizard's intervention, I could be facing execution for regicide.

Greenleaf beamed at each of us in turn. "Thus, my dears, happily ever after for everyone, eh?"

He bowed and exited the room, quietly closing the door behind him. But I thought I heard him chortling as he descended the stairs.

A heavy silence settled after Greenleaf's departure. Mal roused himself enough to set Ebony down. He crawled over to the broken orb. Picking up the two halves, he tried to fit them back together.

"Perhaps there is some way the orb can be mended," he muttered.

"Forget it, Hawkridge," Horatio said curtly.

"Or if the orb cannot be fixed, we'll find some other way to prove who you are."

"I *said* forget it! Can you not see how much your insane pursuit of this legend has nearly cost? We should consider ourselves fortunate to have escaped with our lives from this mad escapade. Greenleaf has been remarkably generous."

"Generous!" Mal croaked. "That evil conniving wizard is planning to steal your crown. You cannot just meekly step aside and allow him to do it."

"Sidney may be cunning and ambitious, but I don't think he is evil. Hopefully, he will help Prince Kendrick become a fair and just ruler."

"Do you really believe that? The kingdom does not belong to Kendrick. It's yours." Mal said. "You saw how the orb reacted to you. Surely deep down in your heart, you must—"

"No!" Horatio cut him off. "What my heart tells me is I am no legendary prince, and I am in no way suited to be king. As far as I am concerned, this madness is over. Now if you will excuse me, I must return to my duties."

As he reached for the doorknob, Mal pleaded with me. "Do something, Ella. Stop him."

I took a hesitant step in Horatio's direction, but he warned me away with a sad shake of his head. "I realize you and I have much to discuss, but not now, Ella. I am far too weary, and I need time to think."

Something in his tone filled me with foreboding about where his thoughts might lead him. But he looked so overwhelmed, I could not bring myself to press him, especially not with Mal and Ebony listening.

"All right," I conceded.

As soon as the door closed behind Horatio, Mal insisted, "You must go after him, Ella. Right now."

I turned back to Mal, feeling exhausted. "And do what?"

Clutching Ebony in his arms, Mal struggled to his feet. I was surprised that Delphine had not transformed by now. But since Mal was absently stroking her, I suspect she was enjoying his caresses far too much. She snuggled against his chest, softly purring.

"I will never accept that Crushington is the right man for you," Mal told me. "But he is right for Arcady. Brave, honest, fair, intelligent, and stuffed with honor. In short, our perfect king."

"But Horatio doesn't want to be king. He still doesn't believe the legend."

"Then you must convince him. Make him believe, Ella. You are the only one who can."

Twenty-Four

I stepped outside of the Hawk's Nest into an empty street. Horatio was already nowhere in sight. Despite Mal's urging, I decided not to immediately search for Horatio although I longed to do so.

I hardly knew what I would say to him. I agreed with Mal that Horatio would be the perfect king and Mal insisted that I was the only one who could convince him. But did I have the right to force upon Horatio something he believed was wrong?

My stalwart commander was overwhelmed by all that had happened at the Hawk's Nest. His entire orderly life had been upended. Small wonder Horatio insisted that he needed time to think, as hard as that was for Mal to understand. Horatio was not like Mal or me, impulsive, and quick to act. Somber and sensible, Horatio would mull everything over carefully before deciding what course his future would take. Whatever he decided, was it possible that his future could still include me? I had brought the man nothing but disaster. The unselfish thing to do would be to let him go.

But I was not that noble. I could not help hoping that somehow, someway, Horatio and I could be together and succeed in finding our happily ever after.

Meanwhile I had given little thought to the way I had left my family. I cringed with guilt, imagining the alarm of my stepmother and sisters when they arose to find me gone. If they read the letter I had left for Chuffy, it would seem as though something dire had happened to me and I would never return. My poor Em would succumb to hysterics.

I didn't know how late it was, but if there was still a chance I could prevent that, I needed to hurry home. Racing down the lane from Misty Bottoms, I winced when I trod upon a sharp pebble, but I did not allow that to slow me down.

As uncomfortable as my glass slippers had been, I wished I still had them to turn me invisible. On the way out of the Hawk's Nest, I grabbed a floppy brimmed hat from Mal's workroom. I hoped that would be enough to avoid being recognized in my masculine attire as I hastened through Midtown.

I was reassured to see that the morning was not as advanced as I had feared. The shops were just beginning to open, but an unusual number of people were already in the streets. The royal heralds must have been at work, blowing their trumpets and rousing everyone from their beds with the announcement of the death of the king and his eldest son. Midtown citizens clustered outside the shops, discussing the news in shocked, hushed tones.

A group of young ladies, a few of them still clad in their night-clothes, clutched each other sobbing loudly. I doubted any of those tears were being shed for the late king. I pulled my hat lower to shield my face as I passed. But I need not have worried. The girls were far too distraught over the death of Prince Florian to notice a strange looking boy slipping past them.

"He was so young, so handsome." one of them wailed, the ribbons of her nightcap fluttering in the morning breeze.

"And so noble," another wept. "Everyone is saying that the prince saw some hapless maiden fall into the mill pond. Prince

Florian dove in to rescue her. He managed to save the girl, but the prince became entangled in the reeds and drowned."

"Stupid wench!" The beribboned girl choked. "He should have let her die."

"No!" Another girl piped up through her tears. "I heard that it was a dear little child that the prince saved."

"No, I think it was a puppy," a third girl sniveled.

"An entire litter of puppies *and* a baby," someone else cried.

I had to bite my tongue to refrain from putting an end to these foolish rumors. This gossip had doubtless been generated by whatever tale Sidney Greenleaf had concocted to account for Florian's sudden demise. It vexed me that Greenleaf's fabrication would result in the villainous prince being forever enshrined as a hero.

But I could not expose the lie without revealing that I was responsible for Florian's death. If that was ever known, all the kingdom's besotted young maidens would fall upon me and tear my hair out by the roots until I ended up as bald as Mal.

Quickening my steps, I hurried onward until I was well out of earshot of all this annoying wailing and chatter. As I left the main part of town behind me, I was relieved to find the lane in front of my house empty and quiet. I had to pause to catch my breath, all the harrowing events of last night threatening to catch up with me. After my rush to get home, I felt ready to drop from exhaustion, but I braced myself to be confronted by a frantic Em and my two tearful sisters.

All was mercifully silent when I crept into the front hall. My family were notoriously late risers. Was it possible that by some miracle that the royal herald had not yet reached this part of town and my stepmother and sisters were still abed?

That hope swiftly died when I heard voices emanating from the kitchen. Sighing, I whipped off my hat, schooling my features into an expression that would be suitably contrite. As I approached the kitchen door, I caught the faint sound of Netta asking, "Shouldn't someone wake Ella? It is so unlike her to sleep this late. She is usually up well before any of us."

My heart fluttered with hope again as I pressed my ear to the kitchen door listening to Amy's reply. "I can't imagine how Ella could have slept through the herald trumpeting and banging at our door. I'll go wake her."

"No, dear," my stepmother said. "I will go up myself and rouse her, but I so dread telling her the horrible news."

"Ella will have to learn it sometime. I am sure the entire kingdom will be buzzing about it," Amy said.

"The poor girl will be devastated when she hears about Florian."

"But Mama, how can you have forgotten?" Netta protested. "Ella didn't even like him."

Indeed! How could Em have forgotten after the way we had quarreled over my refusal to marry Florian? But my stepmother had a remarkable gift for suppressing any memories she found unpleasant.

"Ella may have said she detested Prince Florian, but I never understood her," Em said. "Such a handsome, charming man and he so adored our Ella. I am sure that after the prince's tragic death, Ella will realize how much she loved him and be flooded with grief and remorse."

It was all I could do to smother a groan. But I was far too grateful to have avoided causing my family a great deal of alarm. I backed away from the kitchen door, then stole upstairs to my bedchamber as quietly as possible.

The first thing I did was snatch up the letters I had left on the mantel and tear them to pieces. I started to remove Mal's shirt when I caught the creak of footsteps as someone mounted the stairs. Shucking off the breeches, I shoved Mal's clothing under the bed.

A tentative knock sounded at my door. "Ella?" My stepmother called.

I scrambled into my nightgown, only to realize I had put it on backwards. But I had no time to correct my mistake.

Em knocked louder. "Ella, dear."

I leapt into bed, dragging the covers up to my chin as my bedchamber door inched open. Em paused on the threshold, peeking inside.

"Ella? Are you awake?"

"Yes," I mumbled in a sleepy voice. "Come in."

As my stepmother entered the room, I made a great show of stretching and yawning. "Goodness, Em! You are up already? How late is it? Why did no one wake me?"

"I thought it best you get as much rest as you can before I spoke to you." Em closed the door, leaning up against it. "My poor child. Brace yourself for some shocking news."

I shifted to a sitting position, plumping the pillow behind my back. "All right, consider me braced."

Em clutched her hands dramatically to her chest. "The king has died."

I started to shrug but stopped myself in time. "King August was quite old and very ill." I refrained from adding that poison was never good for one's constitution at any age.

"But there is worse news, my dear. Florian, our most beloved prince—" Em paused and then blurted out, "He is also dead."

I did my best to appear suitably shocked. I must have succeeded too well for Em descended upon me, ready to wave her vinaigrette beneath my nose.

I fended her off. "Em, please, I am fine. What happened to the bast— I mean the prince?"

"Apparently, Prince Florian rode out alone this morning to confront a dragon about to attack our kingdom. He managed to slay the beast but not before being fatally wounded." A tear trickled down Em's cheek. Wiping it away, she sniffed. "Such a heroic and noble young man."

I rolled my eyes at yet another version of Florian's death.

"What nonsense," I said. "There has not been a dragon sighting in Arcady for years. If there had been, I am sure Florian would have ridden in the opposite direction as fast as his horse could go."

"Ella!" My stepmother cried. "How can you say such a thing about your beloved, the man you were going to marry."

"He was not my love, and I had no intention of marrying him."

Em sat down on the edge of the bed and patted my hand. "There, there, dear. I am sure it is only your extreme grief causing you to speak so."

I tried to protest, but Em was not listening, her romantic imagination determined to transform me into a tragic heroine. I heaved a deep sigh causing Em to envelop me in a suffocating hug.

She only desisted when I gasped, "Em! You're suffocating me."

She drew back, looking mournful. "Of course, this tragedy will oblige me and Chuffy to postpone our wedding. It would be so insensitive of us to go ahead while you are suffering from a broken heart."

"No!" I cried. The sooner I had my family consigned to Lord Redmond's care the better.

When Em regarded me with surprise, I said in a milder tone, "You must marry as soon as possible. Such a joyous occasion will brighten all our spirits."

"Oh, my brave unselfish girl." Em patted my cheek. I tried not to cringe because my motives were far from being unselfish. Yes, I was delighted that Em would find such happiness, but with my family comfortably settled in the Heights, I would be free to pursue my own future.

Rising from the bed, Em continued, "I know you must be feeling that your life is over, but there will be many things for you to anticipate with pleasure. We will have a new king, which means a royal coronation and all the eligible lords in the kingdom shall be in attendance. I am sure you will find a new love."

I had already found my love, and I needed to see Horatio as soon as possible. But Em had never been enthusiastic about a suitor who was rumored to be a founding and a mere Scutcheon commander. She would be even less so with our fortunes about to change after she married the wealthy Lord Stanhope.

Flinging the covers aside, I prepared to bound out of bed when Em protested, "Ella, what are you doing?"

"Getting up to fix everyone breakfast and then I thought I would—"

"No, no, dear. Not in your delicate, distraught state. I am sure you have no appetite."

No appetite? I realized I was starving, hungry enough to eat a pound of porridge and a dozen eggs.

But Em insisted, "You just get back into bed and rest. Of course, you must try to eat so I shall send Netta up to bring you a cup of weak tea and a piece of toast."

"Em!"

Ignoring my protests, my stepmother thrust me back down on the bed. "I must go down and urge your sisters to get dressed. If we don't hurry into town, we shall not find a scrap of fabric left for our mourning gowns." Em paused, frowning as she tucked me in.

"Ella, why are you wearing your nightgown backward?"

"Well, um, er—"

"Never mind, dear." Em nodded sagely. "We all grieve in different ways."

Before I could even begin to make sense of this illogical statement, Em whisked herself out the bedroom door.

As soon as she was gone, I started to leap out of bed only to reconsider. It would be far easier to escape to go in search of Horatio if I waited until Em and my sisters left for town.

I flopped back against my pillow. After all the events of last night and this morning, I felt engulfed in a tide of exhaustion. I only meant to close my eyes for a few minutes, but I fell into a deep, dreamless sleep. When I awoke, I was alarmed to see the shadows lengthening across the room. It had to be late in the afternoon.

As I groggily knuckled the sleep from my eyes, I noticed that at some point one of my sisters had tiptoed into my room and left a tray on my nightstand. I regarded the dried-out toast and cold tea with little enthusiasm. But when my stomach growled, I wolfed both down. The meagre fare was enough to fortify me.

I got out of bed, washing, and dressing as quickly as I could. Donning one of my work-a-day gowns, sensible stockings, and shoes, I didn't have time to worry about beautifying myself. I winced as I brushed my hair, ruthlessly working out the knots.

I cringed as I regarded myself in the mirror. There was nothing to be done about the exhausted shadows beneath my eyes, but I managed to pinch some color into my cheeks. That would have to do.

When I crept downstairs, I was relieved to find the house empty. Em and my sisters must still be in town, busy soaking up all the gossip and shopping. I felt a pang of my old worry about how much Em might be spending. Then I reminded myself that would soon be Lord Redmond's problem, not mine.

As I hurried along the lane outside my house, I noticed that most of my neighbors had already hung the royal mourning wreaths on their front doors. Even Mrs. Biddlesworth had erected one, although hers was a trifle shabby from disuse. It had been a long time since Arcady had lost a king, longer than I could remember. I had not even been born when King August had ascended the throne.

When I reached Midtown proper, it was easier than ever to slip by unnoticed. The shopkeepers had chosen to remain open longer than usual to accommodate the rush of customers seeking the required purple and black fabric for mourning clothes. I dreaded encountering Em and my sisters, with the awkward explanations and prevarications that would entail. Fortunately, they were lost somewhere in throng of women shoppers, and I was able to work my way past the crowd and on to the relative quiet of the town square.

The plaza before Quad Hall was deserted which I would have expected, all government offices closed, owing to the death of the king. I was irritated to see the heap of floral offerings deposited at the feet of Florian's statue. But my indignation was somewhat assuaged when an obliging bird flew over and frapped on his head.

With all the offices closed, I was afraid that I might find the entrance to Quad Hall locked. But the massive doors were open as usual. As I crossed through the marble-tiled entryway, I found Major Frackles supervising two Scutcheons on ladders as they draped mourning swags between the hall pillars.

When he saw me, the major headed in my direction. I noticed that he and the other soldiers had added black armbands to their uniforms. Frackles greeted me with a sad smile.

"Good afternoon, Miss Upton. Although I should not say *good*. What astonishing and tragic news for our kingdom."

Astonishing perhaps, but I could not agree it was tragic. Still, I solemnly nodded my head.

"I was hoping to see Commander Crushington. Is he up in his office?"

"No, miss. The commander received an urgent note from that shopkeeper in Misty Bottoms demanding he come at once."

"Shopkeeper? You mean Malcolm Hawkridge?"

I tensed wondering what the blazes Mal was up to now. Had he decided that he could not depend upon me to persuade Horatio to fight for the throne? Perhaps Mal meant to take matters into his own hands, even if he had to hold Horatio captive until he convinced him he was the lost heir. Mal was so obsessed with the legend I would not put anything past him.

But Major Frackles brought an end to my worried thoughts when he corrected me. "No, it wasn't that scoundrel Hawkridge. It was that other odd hunched over fellow who sent the note. The one who runs that bric-à-brac shop." Frackles snapped his fingers as he struggled to recall the name. "You know the man I mean."

"Withypole Fugitate?" I murmured.

"That's the fellow."

I was more puzzled and alarmed than ever. Why would Withypole summon Horatio in such an abrupt fashion? It had to have something to do with Sidney Greenleaf about to seize control of the kingdom.

Dashing toward the exit, I left a startled Major Frackles gaping after me, my desire to find Horatio acquiring a new urgency.

* * *

A very different mood prevailed in Misty Bottoms than the rest of the kingdom. No one was hanging any mourning wreaths here. Despite the threat of any punishment, the Bottoms dwellers were making no effort to disguise their joy over the death of the king and his son. There was much hugging, laughing, and dancing in the street, the unrestrained glee encouraged by the landlord of the Winking Goblin lavishly providing everyone with free ale.

One raggedy fellow attempted to engage me in a wild jig while an old lady tried to shove a flask into my hand. I managed to avoid being swept up in the revelry, forcing my way to the end of Rock Gunnel Street until I reached Withypole's shop.

The sign posted in the grimy window announced that the shop was closed. But someone had added a hastily painted word.

Forever

What did that mean? The sign increased my mounting dread. I tested the doorknob, expecting to find it locked, but when it turned easily in my hand, I entered the shop.

The cramped room was so silent, I could hear the dust settling. The shelves were piled with an incongruous assortment of dishes, books, toys, porcelain figurines, vases, and paintings. I had always found this shop a sad testimonial to the desperate people who needed to part with their precious items for the sake of a few coins. On more than one occasion, I had been one of them.

Now that I knew Withypole's story, I realized the shop bore witness to the fairy's despair as well, the tragic loss of his love that had turned him into a gleaner with a gaping hole in his heart that could never be filled.

I threaded my way past wooden soldiers and tin trains, the painted eyes of dolls seeming to sadly follow my steps. As I made my way to the shop counter, I called out, "Withypole? Horatio?"

"Back here, Ella."

It was Horatio who answered me. His voice echoed from one of the rooms behind the counter. I headed in that direction, ignoring the KEEP OUT sign, just as I had done on that day when I had first discovered Withypole was a fairy. I had surprised him mournfully surveying his true reflection in a full-length mirror, his beautiful wings unfurled.

I hardly knew what to expect this time as I stepped across the threshold of the fairy's bedchamber where Horatio awaited me.

Horatio appeared so tired, a weary nod was his only acknowledgement of my unexpected arrival. I longed to wrap my arms around him, but I restrained myself as the realization sank in. Horatio was alone in the bedchamber, no sign of Withypole anywhere.

"Major Frackles told me that Withypole sent you an urgent summons, but where is he?" I asked anxiously. "What is wrong? Why isn't he here?"

"I don't know. The shop was deserted when I got here. Fugitate appears to have disappeared, but I found this."

Horatio gestured to a burlap sack resting at the bottom of Withypole's narrow bed. I crept closer to examine it and gasped. The sack was filled with glass shards.

"The stolen aura crystals!" I exclaimed, lifting one out to examine it, but I saw nothing except my own astonished eyes reflected back to me on the surface of the prism.

Horatio grimaced. "I owe Hawkridge an apology. It was Fugitate who broke into the aura chamber the night of the ball. He must have known I would discover evidence of his guilt when he sent for me. The sack was left out in plain view. I don't understand any of this, Ella. Why would Withypole have risked his life to steal aura crystals?"

"I can hazard a guess," I said, carefully placing the crystal back in the sack. "Didn't you tell me that you had recently complied with the law requiring you to have your aura collected?"

"I did."

"When exactly was that?"

Horatio's brow knit in an effort of memory. "I believe it was the day of the ball."

"Did you tell Withypole you had done this?"

"Yes, I mentioned it." Horatio frowned. "I recall being surprised by his reaction. He seemed agitated, though I had no idea why."

"Because Withypole knew your crystal would have revealed to Sidney Greenleaf what I suspect the wizard has been searching for ever since he built the aura collector. The identity of Arcady's lost prince."

Horatio groaned, "Ella, please. No more of that— "

I cut off his protest, saying, "Please hear me out."

Horatio sighed but gave a reluctant nod. I related as swiftly as I could all that I had learned from Withypole the afternoon I had found him drunk in the Winking Goblin tavern. The entire tragic story of his love for Marigold, how his jealousy caused him to betray her, how after her death he had tried to assume her task of guarding the orb and the identity of the lost heir.

"But he was so swallowed up by grief, he failed," I said. "Withypole wept when he told me he had broken his promise to protect the children. One of those was me because he owed a debt to my father. He passed out before he could tell me who the other child was. But I am now certain he was speaking of the lost prince. You, Horatio."

Horatio shook his head, but I insisted. "Don't you see how it all fits? Didn't you ever wonder why Withypole took such a risk by becoming your informant, trying to help you succeed in your role as commander?"

Horatio locked his arms behind his back and took to pacing as though he could avoid what I was telling him. But I blocked his way, bracing my hands against his chest.

"I believe Withypole was doing the best he could for you until the time was right for your identity to be revealed."

"I am sorry, Ella. I am still not convinced." Horatio's mouth tightened in a stubborn line. "But perhaps *this* will make everything clearer."

Horatio delved into the inner pocket of his vest and produced an envelope. "Along with the bag of aura crystals, Withypole left this letter. It is addressed to you. I was just getting ready to bring it to you when you arrived."

I took the letter from Horatio, both curious and anxious about what Withypole might have written.

The wax seal was unbroken, and I had to admire Horatio's restraint. If I had been in his place with so many unanswered questions, I doubt I would have refrained from tearing open the envelope, no matter to whom it was addressed.

Using my thumbnail, I pried open the seal and unfolded the letter. I was aware of Horatio watching me, maintaining a stoic silence. But I could sense his tension as I perused the brief message.

My dear Ella,
By now Commander Crushington will have told you that I was the one who stole the crystals. I don't know how to destroy the infernal things, but do not worry. I have taken Crushington's shard and yours away with me.
I pray you will not think too badly of me for deserting you. Now that

the weak Prince Kendrick will assume the throne, Sidney Greenleaf will achieve the full power he has long desired through his puppet king. He has tolerated my presence in Arcady thus far. But Greenleaf will be bound to perceive me as a threat to the fulfillment of his ambition, so it is no longer safe for me to remain. Fleeing Arcady is my only hope for keeping my promises to your father and my beloved Marigold.

According to the legends of my people, the time is drawing closer for the true heir to claim the crown. I have allowed myself to wallow in grief for far too long. Although it will not be easy, I must end my terrible gleaning addiction and head to the secret fairy realm along our northern border. I do not expect to be welcome there. I may even be put on trial for my many failures and transgressions, and it is no more than I deserve. But I need to be there to remind my brethren to keep the pledge the fairy world made so long ago to our good queen, Anthea.

But I repeat my warning to you. Never trust Sidney Greenleaf. He will pretend to be your friend as he once did with me and your father. But he will betray you. He will always put his own interests above those of our kingdom.

I know what a strong, brave young woman you are. It is up to you now to keep yourself and Horatio safe. You must look out for each other until that glorious day when all will be revealed.

I will leave you the contents of my shop to dispose of as you will. Until we meet again.

Your unfortunate, Withypole Fugitate.

The letter filled me with sadness for the fairy's tormented soul, but I was frustrated with Withypole for leaving Horatio and me without giving us a chance to say goodbye or question him. He had taken my shard away from me after my misadventure in the aura chamber. But out of all those prisms in that burlap bag, how had Withypole known which one was Horatio's?

The fairy must have some way of reading the crystals.

According to Withypole, the prisms held the very essence of a person, every memory one had from the moment of one's birth. If I had had a chance to speak to Withypole, I could have told him the orb had been destroyed. Could there still be a way of proving Horatio's identity by using his prism? I sensed that there was still so much more about the past— both mine and Horatio's —the fairy could have revealed if he had chosen to stay and do so.

With a disgruntled sigh, I handed the letter to Horatio, to see what he would make of it. He took it from me gingerly as though he feared the contents might explode whatever remained of his once well-ordered life. He read it swiftly.

"Blast Fugitate!" He swore and crushed the letter in his fist. Belatedly, he seemed to remember the letter was mine, not his.

"Sorry," he muttered, trying to smooth out the crumpled paper. "But this letter is a huge disappointment. I was hoping Withypole would provide some clarity."

Horatio folded the note and gave it back to me. As I tucked it in my pocket, Horatio admitted, "Frankly, I was hoping the letter might have contained information that would put an end to this notion of me being the lost prince. But I can see there is only one course left to me."

"What is that?" I asked anxiously.

"I told you how I grew up in the Foundling Asylum until I was fortunate enough to be adopted by the Crushingtons. I never wanted to know the circumstances of my birth, always afraid of what I might find. But I confess this strange business with the orb has left me unsettled. I need to discover the truth."

"How do you plan to do that?"

"I believe the Asylum kept records on every child, how and when they were abandoned, sometimes even clues about who the parents were. I intend to go to the Asylum and see if there is any information left about me."

"And if you find something that confirms that you are the lost prince? What will you do then?"

"I don't know. For most of my life, I have always been so certain of what was the right path to take." Horatio gathered my hands in his, his voice almost pleading. "What do you think, Ella? What would you have me do?"

I drew in a deep breath. This was the moment when Mal would have expected me to employ every persuasion I could muster to convince Horatio to accept his destiny and fight for the throne of Arcady. Mal insisted I was the only one who could make him believe. But even if I did have that power to influence Horatio, it felt wrong to use it.

Even though I knew how disappointed Mal would be with me, I shook my head. "This is not my choice to make. But whatever you decide, you will have all my love and support."

Horatio regarded me sadly. "But would you love me more if I was this lost prince?"

"No!" I cried. "Horatio Crushington, I hope you would know me better than that by now. If a prince is all I wanted, I could have married Florian, may the fairies help me!"

"I wasn't thinking of him." Horatio gave me a troubled look. "But I could not help noticing when we were in the dungeon, a certain tenderness between you and Prince Ryland."

"On his part, not mine. I was a young girl when I fancied myself desperately in love with him."

"Of course, you are so ancient now," Horatio said wryly.

I pulled a face at him. "Certainly, I am older and wiser. I admit that when I saw Ryland singing in the square that day, I fell for him at first sight."

"And when you first met me, you did your best to avoid me." Horatio winced.

"I am afraid that is true, but that was before I got to know you." I reached up to caress his cheek. "And that is the huge difference. What I felt for Ryland was a girlish infatuation. But my love for you has blossomed over time, growing stronger and deeper each day until I am certain you are the only man I will ever want. Not Ryland, not Mal. *You.*"

I draped my arms around his neck. "If you believe in nothing else, believe that."

I stood on tiptoe to brush a kiss against his lips. Horatio drew back, searching my eyes. He must have been convinced by what he saw because he clutched me in his arms and kissed the breath from me.

When he allowed me to come up for air, he groaned. "Oh, Ella, I have never wanted anything more in my life than to marry you."

"Then do it," I urged.

"But Greenleaf was right when he pointed out how your fortunes will change when your stepmother marries Lord Redmond. You could have so much more than I can offer you."

"As if I care about that! Even if you decided to pursue your boyhood dream of working in a stable, I will work right alongside you. Although I do admit I have never been quite comfortable around horses, but I am sure I could learn."

Horatio smiled but became serious again. "Very well, if you can wait for me until I travel to the Asylum—"

"Absolutely not. I am coming with you."

"Ella, I cannot allow you to do that. The trip that far north will be a long and dangerous one."

I fetched a long and gusty sigh. "You know, I so look forward to the day when you realize I am not some delicate damsel that needs to be coddled."

Horatio chuckled. "I realize that now, my dear. But there is your family to consider. Surely you don't want to leave before you see your stepmother wed and your sisters settled in their new home. And you must decide what you are going to do about Withypole's shop."

"Rot Withypole!" I grumbled, but I conceded Horatio was right. "When do you intend to set out on your journey?"

"I wish I could leave right now for my own peace of mind. The sooner I learn the truth about my lineage, the better. But I will need the new king's permission to absent myself from my duties."

"Do you think Sidney Greenleaf will allow that to happen?"

"He will have no choice. There is a tradition for a new king to grant favors to his subjects on his coronation day. I will explain that I need to attend to some problems that have arisen with the farm I inherited from my adoptive parents. Sidney could surely raise no objections to that."

I wished I could believe that. It was not in Horatio's nature to lie, and I wondered if he could be convincing enough to deceive the canny wizard about the true purpose of his journey. I had a feeling that Greenleaf wanted to keep Horatio under his watchful eye, one way or another.

"All right," I agreed reluctantly. "I will give you two weeks until you return for me."

"Two weeks! Ella, I could barely make it to the Asylum in that time. Give me two months."

"No. What about three weeks?"

"I will need at least thirty days."

Before I could argue further, my honorable commander employed a quite dishonorable method of persuading me. He smothered my protests with his lips, kissing me senseless.

When I finally emerged from his embrace, with my pulse racing and my head reeling, I would have agreed to almost anything.

"Very well. Thirty days," I said, kissing him quickly lest he divine what I was thinking. If he had not returned to me during that time, I vowed silently to go in search of him.

Many kisses later, we left the shop, locking the door behind us. Night had fallen but the revelry continued around lit bonfires and blazing torches. Horatio's arm looped around my waist as we paused to watch a bandy-legged man piping out a tune while couples danced, homespun skirts flying up and hob-nailed boots stomping in rhythm. It was wonderful to see the down-trodden bottom dwellers happy for once. Yet as I rested my head against Horatio's shoulder, I felt detached from all the merriment.

My feelings were such a tangle of contradictions. I felt sad about my impending separation from Horatio and worried for his safety on his arduous journey. We faced so many obstacles to our happiness. My stepmother would doubtless disapprove of my betrothal to Horatio to say nothing of how Mal would react. Whatever Horatio discovered at the asylum could have a huge impact on our future. And there was always the lingering threat posed by Sidney Greenleaf.

But for the moment, I managed to thrust my fears aside and think of nothing but my overwhelming love for this noble man. Horatio brushed a tender kiss across my cheek. As I nestled in his arms, my gaze was drawn skyward and I caught my breath at a streak of light breaking the darkness of the night, wondering if it was a good omen.

Perhaps it was merely a skyrocket someone had fired. Or maybe it was a shooting star.

Or maybe, just maybe it was the glimmering wings of a fairy heading North.

Also by Susan Carroll

The Valentine's Day Ball

About the Author

Author Susan Carroll began her career in 1986, writing historical romance and regencies, two of which were honored by Romance Writers of America with the RITA award. She has written twenty six novels to date. Her St. Leger series received much acclaim. The Bride Finder was honored with a RITA for Best Paranormal Romance in 1999 and also received the Reviewers Choice Award from Romantic Times magazine for Historical Romance of the year. Two sequels followed, The Night Drifter and Midnight Bride.

Ms. Carroll launched a new series with the publication of The Dark Queen set during the turbulent days of the French Renaissance. A blend of history, romance and intrigue, these six books relate the saga of the Cheney sisters, three women of extraordinary abilities who live in constant peril of being accused of witchcraft.

Her most recent title, Disenchanted is a humorous retelling of the Cinderella story.

Want updates when Susan has new books out, fun goodies to share, and other news? Click here. As a FREE BONUS for signing up, you will receive an Historical Romance Crossword puzzle.